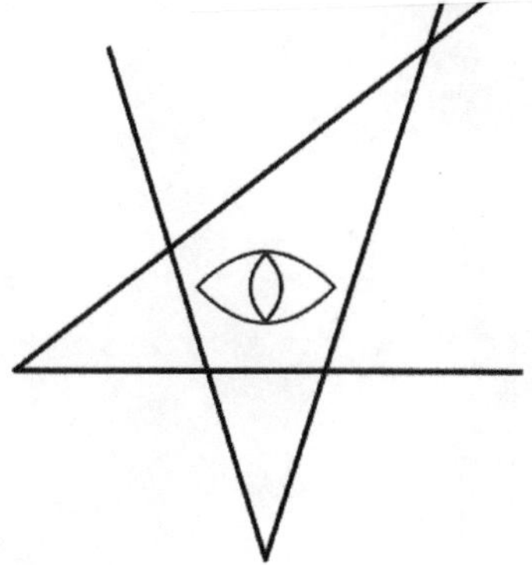

TENEBRIS

The Unholy Darkness

WRITTEN BY
J. A. BARRIOS

ISBN: 979-8-218-08832-3

Dedication

I dedicate this to those who did not think I would finish this book and to those who didn't support me. Your doubts are the fuel that charged my ambitions and I am now a stronger and more independent artist because of you. Thank you

More importantly, to the loved ones I had lost along the way. There are many, but three stand out as the motivation to complete this project and I want to honor them directly. Writing a more professional version of this story was the distraction that helped me along with my father's death. Luke Ellison, whose mortality reminded me that time is limited and working 70+ plus hours a week is nice on the wallet, but nothing compared to following true passions. And most recently Chris Fojt, whose love of art was surely an inspiration. Every time I saw him, he would eagerly say "You finished your book yet? I wanna read it!" I am sorry I took so long and that you had to go in the year that I was finalizing things and that you won't get to read this.

This one's for you.

Prologue
In the Beginning

A blanket of darkness. A vast empty void of nothingness. The abyss. These things were all of everything. Existence had no meaning at all. From the midst of this nothingness, deep within the center of the void, came the absolute start of existence.

Just as there was nothing, suddenly a jarring sound erupted and a light appeared. It was an enormous circular light of pure energy, conscious energy. This energy had a power, an ability to alter Its surroundings. With awareness of this power, the energy had a goal, a self-appointed destiny to expand existence; to become the *Creator*.

The Creator was given a canvas, which was this void, and Its power would be the paintbrush. The first mural was a realm to reside in. While holding Its position, two appendages grew from below the orb of light as legs, but the Creator wasn't just standing, the right leg made a stomping motion. With nothing but the void for the stomp to connect to, a monstrous mountain shot straight up from the nothingness in response and touched beneath the Creator's foot.

From the top of this mountain, the light stood high above the emptiness. A tendril of energy came off the orb forming an arm and the orb itself formed into a torso. The arm raised up above and from the bottom of the nothing sprung soil. This soil was so rich it sparkled from all the minerals and nutrients. Still with the arm high above, the Creator made a spreading motion with another tendril that slinked out of the torso forming another arm and dewy green grass grew on top of the soil.

In one quick motion the levitated arm dropped, and a baby blue sky appeared. The Creator grew a head from the torso and formed lips, then pressed them together, blowing energy toward the sky that formed clouds. It was a heavenly place, so much so that this domain was named, "Heaven."

The Creator constructed a fabric between Its fingers and wrapped it around its entire body of energy. From the chest, the Creator pulled the cloth off and thought of the term "perfection," then relieved the grip. The cloth began to dance as it dropped, twisting around into a ball and once it reached the bottom of the mountain there stood a hooded being in a white robe that was once the fabric, created just as its constructor, to be immortal. The Creator smiled down as the being gazed up to the light shining above, *my Morning Star,* the Creator thought in regard to the being below, who seemed just a few inches tall from the height of the mountain. Then the Creator snapped two gigantic fingers. Suddenly thousands stood at the bottom of the mountain, bowing down to their maker. They were loyal beings, loving and filled with innocence. The Creator named them "Angels".

Oh, how the creation of the angels produced immense joy and fulfillment to the Creator. Upon watching the angels as they knelt before the vast mountain, giving praise to the embodied light that stood above, the Creator felt troubled. This realm of theirs abounded with such wonders, but still the angels seemed to have no interest in anything but their maker. This domain was microscopic compared to the empty canvas that hung beyond the towering mountain; the Creator could not stop now, but what would come of the lovely angels that seemed to hang on every moment of the divine presence? To focus on the greater task at hand someone needed to be left in charge, to hold a sense of leadership.

The illuminated hand swooped down and held up the first angel at the head of the thousands, *the First Light,* the Creator thought and gently blew into the being's ear. The wind that passed through this angel's head formed the words, "Stand tall." Suddenly there were six other angels standing behind. The Creator continued to stare at the first angel and noticed their cloak had transformed into a tunic. The others also wore white tunics instead of robes, exposing their strong faces and short white hair. They each had the same face, and all held a similar expression - one of confusion with some specks of fear, for they did not know what their purpose was. All, that is, except for one. The first created. The Morning Star. *He* stood there, hands on *his* hips and confident of *his* creation.

While the Creator hoisted up these new angels in one hand, Its free hand wiped an enormous finger of light along the backs of the seven. Each face filled with enlightenment as two white feathery wings broke out from the angels' skin above each shoulder blade. Using the same finger, the Creator ever so gently tapped the left arm of the angel at the lead, the first one, and with a shimmer of light a golden band formed in place. The giant hand turned over, allowing these improved angels, these Archangels, to float down to the others.

There was something not yet complete with the archangels, however. The Creator thought long while watching them interact with the other angles until the epiphany revealed itself. The archangels needed to be personalized. The golden band on the lead archangel was just not enough. With that, the Creator gathered the seven archangels together once again and honored them with names: Michael, Azrael, Gabriel, Samael, Uriel, Raphael and Luzbel. As they received their names in turn, each archangel began to develop distinctive facial features and their own personalities to match. Luzbel was the only one who retained his features; being the first created, he kept the beautiful face that was given to him by the Creator originally.

The Creator wanted Its followers to live in luxury and comfort, so It provided them with the knowledge, tools, and materials to develop a kingdom. Hovering above the glorious mountain, the Creator watched curiously as the archangels used their artistic skills to design various architectures that would become the buildings in the domain. The archangels then took charge and directed all the angels to take part in construction, with a job available for everyone.

It was not long before a tragedy struck. Unstable foundation caused the bricks of one building to shift and topple over, crushing those that stood below it. The Creator arrived on the scene in a flash but had not made it in time. The unfortunate angels were only few, but the Creator was still distraught when they did not stir. The Creator had made the angels immortal; they never tired and if cut they healed but, regardless, their lives ended when their bodies were destroyed. That was when the Creator realized balance was essential. Perhaps that was how the Creator came to be in the first place. There was too much of nothing before and now there needed to be something.

Unsure of where to discard the bodies, the Creator thought of balance once again. This world so full of life, so pure and wholesome, there needed to be a counter. Back at the top of the mountain, the Creator stared into the black abyss and created another world far into the void. It was a desolate, acrid world, so hideous that the Creator refused to name it. The Creator took the bodies of the fallen beings and turned them into energy to incorporate into this other world.

Hastily, the Creator turned from the other world and focused again on Heaven and its occupants. The concept of balance was explained to the angels, how necessary it was. So necessary, in fact, that balance would seem to find its way whether the Creator anticipated it or not. So, a warning was established. All was so good and beautiful here that there must eventually come a time when a force would challenge this domain, something wicked. Thus, in addition to building a kingdom, the angels were also to prepare themselves for when a war would find its way to their doors.

In the center of the developing kingdom, the Creator constructed a circular structure with columns holding up an opened roof. The Colosseum. A place for the angels to train. Inside the battleground, at one end was a raised stage with a podium and at the other, a large armory filled with swords for them to defend with. The armory was locked shut, for weapons were poisonous and should not be easily obtained. The Creator fashioned a single key to open the armory and it was given to the Morning Star. Luzbel alone would be the main general in the holy war to defend against the Wicked, with his brothers at his side and the angels following behind.

Pleased with the development of this world and pleased with Its followers, the Creator decided to return to the canvas. However, It could not perform. The world It created had become too wonderful and the angels were far too distracting as they discovered knowledge, music, and expressed their love in many other ways. The time was just not right to leave the followers behind. With the wave of a left hand of light, It formed an empty pool in the center of the slowly developing kingdom. Water began to pour from Its right hand that hovered just above the pool. The archangels took notice first, then larger crowds awed at the rippling reflective liquid. Sensing their comfort, the time was now right.

The Creator shouted, “Solitude!” A chamber appeared on the mountaintop, enclosing the Creator inside. The doors to the chamber were locked shut, for the Creator needed complete isolation to generate perfection. This chamber was made of the same gray stone that formed the vast mountain. The Creator placed Its luminous hand on the floor and felt the rough texture transform into a smooth ivory material as It breathed the word “marble,” and the entire interior became as such. The floor glistened as the swirling white patterns glossed over the wall with the large wooden double doors, and across the walls to the Creator’s left and right. The marble material spread upwards and engulfed the ceiling so that all three sides connected.

In place of the fourth wall at the back of the chamber there was a deep void, the same void that had birthed the Creator. The head of the Light stared into the emptiness for a grand amount of time, until a muse ignited within the mind and the Creator simply said the word, “begin.” Energy shot from the Creator’s body of light into this black abyss, composing art. The energy caused a tremendous explosion, conducting wondrous ballets of miracles: Galaxies, solar systems, planets. *The Universe*. In time, the Universe became more complete, and it was filled with all sorts of interesting things.

The Creator took particular interest in a little planet called Earth. It vaguely resembled the world the Creator chose not to name. This planet housed nothing but oceans of magma and mountainous terrain. It was uninhabitable for any living organism. Earth, this hot dangerous place, was home to the first beings of this Universe. The Creator felt something special from this planet, unlike that horrendous other world, but had decided that this red planet would be the perfect place to start the newest project of mortal life.

“May this planet accept my gifts and construct occupants suitable for the world that births them,” the Creator stated, and sent down a bit of wisdom with self-awareness from the heavens, through the Universe, to planet Earth. Across a grand distance that meant absolutely nothing and within microseconds, the energy arrived. That is when *they* appeared.

They were the first creatures of Earth, the first of the Universe, to take a breath. It was a groundbreaking move forward for existence. They were perfect creations for an environment such as this. These inhabitants carried features that would later be found on creatures called "serpents." These inhabitants had two legs to hold up their bodies from the hot surface of the planet, a long thick tail to balance with, and two arms to aid their needs. Though this world lacked illumination, except for the fiery glow of magma, their lustrous yellow eyes saw everything. They roamed the planet aimlessly. Their tough scaly hide allowed them to climb the mountains and it protected them from the heat radiating through the surface.

There was, however, something missing. The Creator realized this once the earthlings, which It called *Serpenoids*, began to lose life almost as fast as they gained it. Rapidly, thousands became hundreds and slowly their numbers dwindled closer to the dozens. What could have been missing in this formula? Their exterior complimented the habitat as did their interior, assembled with many organs to operate the body. Their brains filled with consciousness which meant they knew they were alive, as well as the fact that they were dying.

In a panic, the Creator sent more heavenly gifts to salvage their lives; love, strength, weakness, hatred, and understanding. The gifts expanded the creatures' minds, but it didn't save them from death. Finally, frustrated, the Creator took a break from action and returned to Its original form, an illuminated sphere. Pondering possible equations that would result in sustainable life, the orb of light removed the lock and opened the chamber doors to view Its world.

A brilliant glow squeezed through the door as It revealed a peace no words could describe. Enchanting music filled the magnificent blue sky that hovered over an ivory kingdom. The Creator looked around for inspiration. What does Earth need? What elements make this realm exist? Love filled the land, the skies, and the immortal beings that lived in this society.

When the doors had opened all the way, all the angels stopped what they were doing. Their eyes gazed up to the glorious mountain where the Creator resided. Their eyes filled with awe as they stared at the marvelous pure light that occupied the doorway. Many ages had passed since they last saw their maker.

A gust of wind flowed from the Creator, past the doors and down the mountain. The wind reached the angels, it caressed their bodies and filled their minds with one single thought. *What does life need?* A symphony of muttering began between the angels. Their maker had blessed them with an opportunity to take part in perfecting the universe. The Creator looked upon them and waited for a response. Some time had passed before It heard the sweet words in the distance.

"I have the answer, my Lord!"

In a blink of an eye the Light in between the doors appeared at the location of the speaker. This Light hovered over the archangel with the most elegant physique. He stood proud with his left arm in the air. His chin rose up as high as his confidence and his elegant feathery wings fluttered behind. The Light above him reflected off the golden band around his arm.

"It is I, your Morning Star!" A warm thought filled this archangel's head in response to his statement. "Well, you see, my Lord, I know the answer. I understand what keeps our civilization going, other than Your grace, that is. What is this mysterious thing I speak of, You ask? I'll tell you, Father Almighty. Before you locked yourself away, you gave us something splendid, the pool of life. Do you recall this accordance, my Lord? You knew that your absence would tear us apart… despite my brothers' leadership and mine. Every day, each of us takes a drink from this pool and our bodies are reminded of our loving Master. It is quite possible that the Earth dwellers just need your love in this physical form as well."

All the angels in the kingdom applauded the archangel. A conceited smirk formed on his face as he basked in his glory. The orb rapidly zipped back up the mountain and into Its chambers. The doors slammed shut behind It. A few moments after they shut, a muffled voice seeped through the doors from the outside.

"Do not forget the aid I just presented you with. I can serve as a regular consultant in your project if you grant me that privilege, my Lord. After all, am I not your shining light?"

Back on Earth, everything was quiet and still. The living natives that remained lay on the ground, festering away with their pain. Those poor helpless creatures, from the moment they opened their eyes, knew nothing but pain. Dirt and thousands of decaying bodies surrounded them. All they could do was wait to meet the same fate as the others.

Suddenly, a strong wind began to pick up and blew in a heavy, musky air. The rolling sound of thunder filled the dying few with fear. From above fell sparkling droplets of water. An empty crater was filled to the top. The rain rejuvenated the sluggish creatures, they lugged themselves over to the pool of water that had been the empty crater and drank from it. In little time they had revitalized and gained strength once again.

Now that the conditions were right, the Creator sent more of Its heavenly gifts to multiply the remaining numbers into hundreds, then back into the thousands once again. The conditions were so perfect that a very select few of the Serpenoids altered in physique and in mind, gaining cognitive prowess, physical strength, agile speed, and keen sight. It was a miracle. Yet, there was still something missing. Someone for the creatures to stand behind and give them purpose. A leader.

A few bodies had not revived with the rain. The Creator gathered those bodies that laid in the dirt and brought them back to Its chambers, combining them together and coating them with a heavy layer of mud. The Creator placed two sticks on the top of this formation, then bent each backwards, forming two arches. After a kiss, the Creator threw this object back to Earth. The outer layer of the mud ball hardened into a thick plaster as it traveled through the Universe. The ball reached Earth and tore through the atmosphere. It began to crystallize as the flaming comet crashed down.

All the Serpenoids assembled, surrounding the crystal boulder that fell from the sky. It began to shake in its position and slowly crack. Two ivory horns pushed the sticks out and took their place. A head attached to the horns broke out of this divine egg. Underneath the head arose a body of incredible strength. The crystal shattered as the creature stretched out its two arms and pulled its two legs from the liquefied mud that filled the inside. The beast straightened out its body, towering over the other creatures. A pair of emerald eyes opened with a gasp as this being took its first breath.

At the head of the creatures, a single Serpenoid whose scales were a mixture of dark brown and beige, dropped to his knees. This Serpenoid was especially distinctive, the black scales on the back of the hood forming two diamond shapes. The rest of the Serpenoids followed suit and bowed down as well. They were amazed at the sight; standing before their very eyes and straight from the cosmos above was a colossus with smooth flesh redder than the magma that surrounded them. One thought was shared amongst them, and it was a word they didn't fully understand at first, but perhaps it explained this occurrence or the thing standing before them. Their mouths opened and spoke a single word in unison.

"Thandrua."

Section I
A Life on Earth

Chapter 1
A Life of Peril

Peering behind a boulder that stood at the mouth of a cave situated in a chain of mountains that consumed the desert world, two golden eyes stared out into the darkness of night. They gazed over the rocky terrain, scanning the night sky. Hundreds of glimmering specks of light flickered across the black canvas as the owner of the eyes cautiously stepped from around the stone. The being's black, clawed, four-fingered hand supported itself on the boulder, while its two feet stepped out from the cave. The thick black talons of its three toes tapped the ground nervously as its tail tapped the ground simultaneously. The luminescent semicircle in the sky shimmered light over the dark brown and beige scales of a long, slender, serpent-like body. Its head turned looking toward the view, the neck flaring out in a broad hood.

The being was named Sectoraus, the head of the Cobra Clan and wisest of the Serpenoids. Sectoraus continued looking out for a moment before signaling behind. With heavy steps caused by the heavy muscle from his two legs, out stomped a massive beast whose leathery skin was a radiant crimson. He towered over Sectoraus, the ivory horns that curved over the top of Thandrua's head made his tall stature all the more imposing. With his emerald eyes, he gazed out over the mountains down to the endless dry land. The beast licked the yellow fangs protruding from his mouth before speaking.

"A beautiful sight, is it not, Sectoraus?"

"Indeed, Lord Thandrua." Sectoraus responded, "and not a single speck of the *Fire*. Let me ask my brother to be certain. Solarious!"

A red and black striped Cobra stepped out from the cave, his hood expanding as he approached. He had a yellow oval shape in the center of his hood, resembling a single eye, which intercepted the vertical stripes of his colors. The Cobra known as Solarious stood alongside Sectoraus.

"Solarious, you have the keenest eyes of our Clan," Sectoraus said. "Tell us, is the horizon safe? Do you see the Fire?"

Solarious raised his right leg, placing his foot onto a rock. More comfortable in this stance, he leaned forward and squinted out to the world.

"No, Sectoraus, Lord Thandrua." Solarious scanned the land. "I do not see any sign of light."

"No," Thandrua looked up at the glowing semicircle solemnly, "still not total darkness though… Something is not right." Beneath their feet the ground rumbled, pebbles shifted along the rigid mountain. The two turned behind them, warily. "We must move on. The quakes are coming."

"We move!" Sectoraus' order echoed within the dark cave.

Thousands of glowing yellow serpent eyes looked out towards the commander. The first to step out was a third Cobra, Orpheus, with scales a collage of yellow and black, whose brute strength was evident in his thick, muscular frame. One more Serpenoid with a hooded head exited the cave, the last who completed the quartet of the Cobra Clan. Phineus, whose black scalp and hood at times blended into his reddish-brown body in the blur of his speed.

Immediately following them, thousands of light brown and greenish-brown Serpenoids scurried out of the shelter as the colony followed Lord Thandrua and the Cobra Clan down the mountain.

They clung alongside the rocky terrain, carefully finding their footing, grasping at any crevices and protrusions they could find. They could feel the rumbling vibrations quivering through the mountain, shifting their eyes more cautiously for pieces of rock tumbling down. The danger was near.

Sectoraus claimed the lead, searching for the most secure route personally, before allowing Thandrua to continue on. The Serpenoids worshipped Thandrua as their savior and praised him in godlike fashion. The only being of them all to not resemble a Serpenoid with thick skin instead of scales, the lack of a tail, and small lips that barely covered his fangs instead of the muzzle mouths that the Serpenoids had. His height and muscle mass struck fear in the Serpenoids, as well as a greater amount of respect and idolizing.

Thandrua was worshipped as a deity from the moment he fell from the sky after the first rains. Sectoraus could not allow anything to happen to his master.

Sectoraus gazed up at the Cobras that spread throughout the colony guiding the Serpenoids through their descent. To them, survival meant staying together, and they tried at all costs not to leave anyone behind. A philosophy more strictly adopted recently, with the recent changes in their world. Dangerous changes.

The mountain shook more ferociously still. Sectoraus thought of the previous cycle, how they fled up this mountain for refuge just before the coming of the great Fire. Now they raced down away from the approaching earthquake. He thought about how this was their life now, the fear of what could come next. There were what seemed like hundreds of cycles of contentment and peace after Thandrua's arrival. Now they were always running, always hiding. From the quakes, the sandstorms, the meteors, and most menacing, the Fire.

Progress came to a pause, the Serpenoids froze in fear when they heard the devastating sound of dense rock splitting apart. The mountain shook violently as a crack exploded from the ground and jagged its way into their foundation.

Not yet, Sectoraus thought to himself as he hovered not far from the safety of the ground. "Jump down!" He barked at Lord Thandrua. As long as Thandrua could get to the ground he could move away from the quaking mountain.

Thandrua hesitated a moment, looking at the ground for aim. The surface cracked. The zig zagging lines webbed throughout the rock and sent the Lord Thandrua down before he was ready. Already being so close to the ground, the drop wasn't far. Thandrua managed to land on his feet, but not without a hard thud.

Sectoraus scurried upward, clawing at the rock face, he had to get the rest down to safety. His arms made long strides as he hurled himself up, dodging a few Serpenoids that came tumbling down, along with clumps of the surface. Meeting with the red striped Solarious, the two guided the climbers around the side. Serpenoids continued making their way to the ground.

With more Serpenoids reaching free of the mountain, the Cobras found their way as well. Sectoraus remained alongside the mountain, now herding the colony from behind with Orpheus ahead helping to lower the Serpenoids to the ground.

Suddenly the cliff split between them, sending the Serpenoids at the center of the now gaping space flying into the air. They rushed through the air as they fell a great distance from the mountain. The Serpenoids crashed to the ground shattering their bones upon impact. Orpheus helped whatever Serpenoid he could, then peered over the expanding gap between him and Sectoraus.

Stifling air rushed out of the rapidly forming gorge. Sectoraus clung onto the edge of the precipice tightly, burrowing his black claws into the stone as rocks flew past him. He held tighter still when a gust of wind cut through the splitting mountain. The force of the air buffeted him, causing his tail to wave to the side.

"Sectoraus!" Orpheus shouted across the ever-growing canyon, "jump towards me before it takes you further! By Thandrua, I will catch you!"

They both closed their eyes and concentrated, using the unique mental unity only found between the Cobras. Sectoraus and Orpheus centered themselves in the midst of the chaos. Sectoraus felt his brother's fear, standing there, waiting to catch him. Orpheus could sense the tension in Sectoraus' knuckles as if he held a tight grip and the anxiety of a long and deadly drop.

They sensed one another and were connected. Sectoraus pushed off the ledge, using both his legs and thick tail, and leapt over the gaping space in the mountain. Orpheus held his position tight with his left hand and stretched out his right. Sectoraus came soaring through the air and gripped onto Orpheus' muscular arm.

Sectoraus dangled in the air, the Cobras still clutching onto each other's forearm. The part of the mountain Sectoraus had just jumped from snapped and cracked more as it collapsed on itself, crumbling deep within the earth. A dark gray cloud of rock debris and dust enveloped them as Orpheus pulled his companion up onto a ledge where they laid on their backs. Sectoraus worried, wondering how the others were. They panted, trying to catch their breath between coughing as the air cleared.

"I got you brother," Orpheus huffed out between breaths, "told you I would."

"Much obliged." Sectoraus rolled himself over with his tail and clawed to the edge, staring down at what once was the other half of the mountain. Past the dust he saw the crumbled remains. He saw what would have become of himself.

Then, he moved to the other side, looking down to see the colony with Thandrua at the head staring up towards them. A few casualties from the quake, but the colony was still plentiful and more importantly, Lord Thandrua had survived.

Sectoraus and Orpheus relaxed their hoods as they reached solid ground. The Serpenoids cheered them on, then rushed towards them. Everyone seemed to want to congratulate Sectoraus for risking his life to ensure their safety. With tears in their eyes, they hugged and patted him on the back. His head was spinning in a sea of gratitude. Sectoraus simply grinned and nodded in acceptance, but he was distracted.

Sectoraus moved his way through the suffocating crowd of Serpenoids; even though he was the tallest of his species he still had difficulty peering over all the serpents' heads. Their scales grazed past as he slinked by. Finally, he was through an opening and found what he was looking for. Off in the distance of the colony was Thandrua, back turned to them as he gazed out into the desolate world.

"I appreciate all your gratitude," Sectoraus said over his shoulder as he made his way out of the crowd, "now go, rejoice on another cycle survived," and waved his hand dismissively.

The Serpenoids gave a cheer and they frolicked away, chanting Sectoraus' name in a rhythmic fashion. Sectoraus was relieved to have a moment alone, he fixed his eyes on Thandrua and exposed his white fangs in a huge smile before walking over towards his master.

Sectoraus rushed over to Thandrua, the dry ground crunching with each step, and as he approached closer his smile wilted.

Everyone else was ecstatic and enjoying themselves, but Thandrua stood alone and away from the others, just staring off.

Sectoraus stopped at Thandrua's left side and followed his master's gaze. Sectoraus squinted his slitted eyes in an attempt to see what Thandrua was staring at. The silence hung thick; Sectoraus' tail twitched anxiously. The celebrations of the Serpenoids behind them had drowned into indistinct chatter. Sectoraus placed his clawed right hand onto Thandrua's shoulder.

"Thandrua," his voice was filled with concern, "what troubles you?"

There was a pause before Thandrua responded, "There are many more of the sparkles in the sky then there was the cycle before, and the one before that."

"Yes, it is very peculiar," Sectoraus now scanned the twinkling sky. "Very peculiar indeed."

They stood there in silence once again, the drifting wind carried the faint songs of the Serpenoids past the two leaders, watching the sky as if it were an entity of its own. The blue and white sparkles twinkled and glistened throughout the immense darkness. They were far between but still many, it seemed to them as if more sparkles would pop from the empty spaces and shine continuously after. Finally, the long silence was broken once again.

"What do you suppose they mean, Thandrua?"

Thandrua sighed in frustration, "That is just it," he turned to face Sectoraus, "I do not have the slightest idea. Something has changed after all these cycles. The quakes and the sandstorms have worsened, then there is the *Fire*. It seems to return in an almost rhythmic fashion, but there are few hints to anticipate its appearance, except…"

Lord Thandrua turned towards the mountain they had recently taken refuge in and looked up to the glowing semicircle in the sky. It shone a bright glow heavy on the land, cutting through the dark. The Serpenoids danced and laughed in its silver light.

"That," Thandrua pointed, "the shining *Great Rock* had not appeared in our sky until the cycle before the first light. As the cycle drags the Great Rock seems to fade into the sky, before the black transitions into blue and before the Fire appears, which seems to always rise from that horizon, I believe." His right index finger pointed to the right of the mountain.

"Ah yes, I see." Sectoraus squinted in the brightness of the Great Rock, "so there is something of a pattern."

"A pattern I am yet to understand!" Thandrua grew frustrated, "Look how it is now, remember how full and round it was at first? It is almost deceiving! There was a cycle when it was completely gone, remember?"

"That I do"

"That cycle, I thought we no longer had to worry about the terrible Fire, but then it came still. We lost so many that cycle. This has happened twice now! Something must be done, but what?"

They continued staring at the Great Rock quizzically, then gazed upon the Serpenoids. Their joyous cheer brought a smile to Sectoraus' face. He then turned to look at Lord Thandrua, who only had a quiver of a grin that wilted back down as he cast his eyes back to the Great Rock, thinking once again of the Fire, back to the cycle with the first light.

Chapter 2
The First Light

Lord Thandrua's remembrance took him back many cycles. Although to him it felt as if many more had passed, it was about sixty before the nomads altered their slumber cycles to coincide with the coming and going of the fearsome Fire and the glow of the Great Rock.

The rain had been thumping down hard, steady, pouring from the darkened clouds that hovered above the dry, rocky wastelands. Blue and purple veins of lightning pulsated throughout the dark ominous clouds. The thick humid wind carried the rain sideways as it fell. Awaiting its arrival stood thousands of Serpenoids, arms raised embracing the rapid pelts of the cool refreshing liquid.

Some hopped joyfully in place, some shouted with glee, and some simply stood there with their eyes closed and mouths open, taking in the full sensation of the water dripping onto their rough scaly body and rolling off of them onto the ground. Lord Thandrua cupped his hands and angled toward the sky with his mouth meeting the end of his palms, so the water could just slide right into his mouth. The Cobra Clan, however, used their claws to burrow into the brown dirt, creating ditches for the rain to collect.

In time, the heavy pouring rain fell more gently, the darkness of the clouds had lightened, and the droplets became few and far between, until finally it ceased. A few of the Serpenoids jumped in the puddles and small pools the Cobras had created. They happily splashed water against their own faces and splashed one another with their hands and tails playfully. Most of them held one another's hands and spun each other around in dance, their tails curving along the ground behind them. They had a song they chanted:

"O blessed Thandrua
Has graced us with rain.
We thank you kind savior
From the first time you came.

You dropped from the sky
When we were in pain.
We devote our lives to you
And worship your reign."

The rains were always a time for the simple wanderers to celebrate. Since Lord Thandrua's leadership, he and the Serpenoids roamed the lifeless land stopping to observe the sky and the landscapes, always enjoying themselves. There was no day or night, it was perpetually dark, but their eyes saw perfectly. When they tired, they slept curled on the ground, ending each cycle until Lord Thandrua would wake and declare the start of the next cycle. When it rained, it was always a celebration. Water was their only form of sustenance and the rain their only source of it.

Sectoraus stood, chuckling to himself as he watched the others enjoy their water. Within the grasp of his two clawed hands, he held a stone which had been hollowed into a receptacle for the water. He drank from his receptacle, until he noticed Thandrua approaching.

"Ah, my dear Thandrua!" Sectoraus greeted, "get enough to quench your thirst?"

"Yes, very much so," Thandrua nodded his head in response, his horns followed his movement back and forth. He placed his massive left palm on Sectoraus' right shoulder and faced his followers as Sectoraus did. "Seems as if we all have and by the looks of those pools, we will have enough for a few cycles more."

The winds slowly carried off the rain clouds, altering their shapes and patterns, and many of the yellow Serpenoids' eyes fixed themselves to the sky. It didn't take long for the rest that were still preoccupied to take the hint from the others and gaze upward as well.

"Sectoraus, do you see this?" Thandrua's mouth gaped open.

"Yes, I believe I do."

The black abyss sky they had always known now radiated with an enormous silver glow. A completely round luminescent rock peered beneath the clouds. Beyond that in the depths of the sky sparkled bitsy specks that spread scarcely throughout. The Cobras jogged toward their two leaders while Thandrua's emerald eyes scanned the sparkles and the glowing rock in disbelief.

"What, what could these be?" Lord Thandrua gasped.

"Straighten up Master, the Clan comes forth." Sectoraus gestured in a welcoming way as they came near, "My brothers."

"Sectoraus," responded the red and black striped Solarious, then gave a small bow while the other followed his lead.

"Lord Thandrua," The three spoke in unison and the crimson beast acknowledged their salutations.

"What is happening in the sky?" Questioned Solarious.

"Is this your doing, my lord?" Phineus asked.

More and more Serpenoids saw the Cobra Clan meeting with Thandrua and began to group around them as well. The Serpenoids closed in with their curiosity-filled faces as they all awaited the response from their almighty ruler.

"I…" Thandrua looked across the sea of glowing eyes, then over to Sectoraus who kept a solemn and very emotionless expression, then back to meet the eyes of his followers, "I do not know what this might be."

The crowd gasped, then broke into a series of chatter. The Cobras remained silent, staring at Thandrua in shock. Sectoraus' face now held an expression more of disappointment that Thandrua admitted to everyone how this was out of his power.

Although all the Serpenoids worshipped Thandrua as their deity, he held no cosmic power. Aside from his obvious physical appearance, his leadership skills and intuition are what separated him from the Serpenoids. Just as how the Serpenoids gave the name, Thandrua, to the bestial monstrosity like knowledge they had held beyond themselves, Thandrua too began to name things using his intuition. He gave the name, Sectoraus, to the Serpenoid that greeted him first. He was the tallest of the species and, in time, proved to be the most thought provoking as well. Lord Thandrua saw this and thought the name to be good.

Once noticing the hooded characteristic of Sectoraus that seemed to be unique from the rest of the Serpenoids and then later meeting three others with the same feature, Thandrua called them Cobras and further separated them from the population. In time, after witnessing that each other Cobra had their own personal abilities, Thandrua gave them names that he saw fit to their individuality; Solarious with the best sight, Orpheus the strongest, and Phineus with his agility.

Almost as if providing the names was some sort of ritual they were unaware of, it wasn't until after each held their own name that the Cobras became aware of the special mental bond they shared. The Cobra Clan was established from thereafter.

Not once did Thandrua refer to himself as all-supreme, at least not in the beginning. After waking from his birth out of the crystallized incubator, he became conscious with thousands of beings bowing down at his feet, claiming him to be their savior. At the beginning of his existence, Thandrua, like any creature, had a completely blank mind with no recollection of anything before. In a confused state he did not deny that he brought the rains nor deny that he was their deity. How could he, when his first perception was to be honored as such?

Sectoraus also believed Thandrua to be more than what he seemed and, pledging his allegiance, the two band together in leading the Serpenoids. Of course, with his intelligence, after some countless cycles of wandering the Earth awaiting nothing but rain, Sectoraus did realize the truth behind Thandrua and passed his gift to grant names. A truth Thandrua didn't seem to understand himself. The secret remained between the two of them alone, suggested by Sectoraus.

"Our lives are very drab and simple," Sectoraus said to Lord Thandrua once, "quite literally the only thing any of us have to look forward to is the rain, and nothing more. The illusion of superior guidance provides meaning to them, Thandrua. If they wish to worship you, then let them. It gives them purpose, makes them feel part of something beyond their physical world. Otherwise, what purpose do they have to live?"

With Sectoraus being his main advisor and friend, Thandrua did as he said. He did not like lying to the Serpenoids, but he did not want to take away their dreams. The Serpenoids were simple creatures, not only lacking much of a culture, but simple-minded as well. It was possible that they would still enjoy their meaningless lives without having something to place their faith into. Perhaps the deception was more meant for the Cobra Clan, they were far more cognitive than any of the other Serpenoids, or perhaps even for Sectoraus himself. Perhaps Sectoraus needed an idol to believe in or perhaps after all this time, in some way, he still believed there to be more in Thandrua. After all, Lord Thandrua was always thinking, always looking to understand the meaning of life, always gazing beyond the desolate land and believing there to be more than they knew. Perhaps that is the way of a deity.

Hysteria began to arise in the Serpenoids. They did not understand the large luminescent stone or the sparkling lights, the sheer mystery of them frightened them all. Not a single word could be understood out of the chaotic disarray of sounds

Lord Thandrua's nostrils flared with frustration, his left hand clenched into a fist, then released, and clenched again. His hand continued to do this almost in a rhythmic manner that synchronized with his heart pounding as his frustration boiled into anger. Thandrua narrowed his eyes as he looked upon the frantic Serpenoids.

Sectoraus gave the order for his clan to recollect everyone's composure, he took notice of what was overcoming Thandrua. Thandrua curled his upper lip as he began to snarl, exposing sharp yellow fangs. He had never expressed any emotions of anger to the Serpenoids, it was possible that he had never experienced those feelings himself, but his patience shrank, and his temper grew and just before he was on the peak of explosion, Sectoraus shouted, "enough!" Sectoraus screamed from the bottom of his gut as he stepped in front of Thandrua.

The word projected in the grand empty space of the land. Surprised, the Serpenoids settled down and looked toward Sectoraus for explanation. "What is the problem here, why panic? These lights in the sky are just that, they are up there, and we are here. I do not see them bringing harm to us, do you? Do *any* of you!?"

Sectoraus paused and waited for some rebuttal. He scanned his audiences' faces who were hanging onto his words, waiting for what he would say next. Sectoraus turned to meet Thandrua's eyes. It was not unlike Sectoraus to interject from time to time, but he needed to know how his master felt. The crimson beast, now composed, leveling out his breathing with an expression of relief and curiosity, gestured with his right hand to continue.

"Now, I understand this is quite peculiar, in fact it is very bizarre, but such is the nature of something new. New to you, to my brothers, myself, and new to the mighty Lord Thandrua as well. Thandrua is here with us, ruling over us all with his supreme grace, how could he know what is happening up there? Perhaps, this is something we get the chance to learn together."

The Serpenoids burst into applause as Sectoraus received gratitude from Thandrua for defusing the situation. Impressed, Solarious approached extending his hand to shake Sectoraus' arm for a speech well done. Orpheus followed the example, then Phineus after him. Finally, Thandrua stepped forward.

"Sectoraus is correct," Thandrua gave Sectoraus a reassuring pat on his back, "panic will not do us any good. It breaks down our structure, shaking the bond we hold with one another. The sparkles in the sky and the *Great Rock*, although mysterious in origin, are rather very pleasing to the eyes, beautiful even. Perhaps this is a rare and limited occurrence, we should settle down and enjoy its glory before this phenomenon passes."

Just like that, the Serpenoids were content again. They sat on top of the dirt, their tails in a coil on the ground, and gazed into the sky. Thandrua and the Cobra Clan joined them and the whole colony took in the wonders of the night sky. They found it calming, soothing almost.

The air was gentle and silent, save for the occasional gasps of amazement as the cycle continued on. Some Serpenoids had fallen asleep, their tails curled around them, while the rest continued their gaze. By now, Thandrua would have declared for the cycle to come to an end and for all to slumber, but the things in the sky were all too entrancing to sleep just then.

"Seems as if this is coming to an end," Sectoraus whispered to Thandrua after much time had gone on, "I count fewer sparkles."

Thandrua responded after a momentary pause, "No, something *else* is happening." Then he stood on his feet. Sectoraus stood with him as they witnessed the opaque sky transitioning into navy blue, perhaps violet even. The Serpenoids stood as well, waking the ones that slept ever so peacefully. The sparkles were all disappearing, and the glow of the Great Rock was fading.

"Look!" Solarious pointed to the horizon opposite of the mountains at the edge of what seemed like the land itself. Everyone turned to where he was pointing and gasped. The sky just above the horizon illuminated with an orange glow, as if a flare of fire erupted from a sea of magma, casting pink on the bottom of the clouds that floated in a now purple sky.

"What is happening?" Thandrua muttered, more to himself than anyone else.

The orange fire continued to flare, as if it were rising, its color deepening in the sky, hinting at a glint of gold beneath it. The purple eased as it dissolved into a celeste and the pink on the clouds shifted to orange.

Find shelter. A thought arose inside of Thandrua's horned head. A thought not of his own. The Serpenoids stood their ground, mesmerized by the wondrous display of color fading in and out. Colors they had never experienced before.

They all squinted, now that more of the orange became gold. It was becoming all too bright, some even had to turn away. The golden light seemed to concentrate together as what appeared to be an orb of fire slowly peered over the horizon.

Run. Another rogue thought exploded in Thandrua's mind and this time he listened. "Everyone, to the mountains, to the caves, now!"

They all scattered. Thandrua strode in full speed, not stopping to question the thoughts that seemed to come from outside of his own mind. A sound, grander than that of thunder, rumbled the ground as the stampede of Serpenoids ran for their lives. Unfortunately, not all turned to run, some were still watching, frozen in place. They were the first to understand what Thandrua's thoughts seemed to already know.

"My eyes!" They shrieked in agony as the bright light seared their retinas, rendering them completely blind.

Sectoraus could hear their cries as he cut through the frantic crowd, now running faster than ever. Rays of light beamed across the land and into the sky. Mercifully, the caves weren't too far off from their location. Most of the creatures of darkness found refuge deep within the cool, dark caves. The Serpenoids furthest behind in the stampede, however, weren't as lucky.

More screams of intense pain erupted, echoing into the caves as the rising light caught the unfortunate beings. The heat from the rays charred their scales as their bodies singed from the outside in. Some noble but foolish Serpenoids left the sanctuary of the caves, attempting to help the ones left outside, and they met the same smoldering fate.

Thandrua and Sectoraus hid deep within one cave as the Clan attempted to ease the remaining Serpenoids. Lord Thandrua covered his pointed ears while the cacophony of screams outside built to a crescendo. Cries of fear and sorrow echoed within the caves as well. All the darkness in the land outside was obliterated as the orb of yellow fire positioned itself high in an unsettling blue sky. Thandrua saw that this was not good, and that was the first day.

Chapter 3
The Vision

So many cycles had passed since that first light. Cycles of the Great Rock changing its face. Cycles of the Fire coming and going. Lord Thandrua believed it had been sixty cycles at the least. It was not common for the creatures of the dark to keep track of the cycles, but Thandrua began to after the cycle that the Fire came.

In the sanctuary of the dark night's sky, Lord Thandrua wandered alone in the desert. The rocky ground was dry and stiff; his heavy feet left only the slightest imprint of his four toes. Thandrua climbed over a hill, then another, as he proceeded to distance himself further and further from the cave in which he took refuge. Finally, he came to a stop with the cave completely out of his sight, let out a deep sigh of relaxation, and took in the night sky.

There was a yellow glow to the almost fully round Great Rock. The specs of light glimmered in the navy-blue atmosphere. A gentle breeze caressed Thandrua's leathery skin, comforting his heart and mind with its warmth. The claw-like nails of his right hand scratched at his forehead and absently he ran his hand over one of his horns. Thandrua was filled with nothing but awe as he gazed under the countless sparkles.

A moment of nostalgia fell across his angular face as he recalled a once lightless sky, until a few sparkles shot and skidded across the sky, and he was captivated once again. The beauty of the night was the only time he could have peace.

Slowly, the twinkling lights began to disappear, dissolving into the blanket of darkness, and the Great Rock faded away as well. The breeze ended abruptly, and the god-beast scanned the sky, watching it betray a hint of violet creeping over the edge of the horizon with a faint glow.

"No, do not go!" Thandrua panicked, "It cannot be coming already..."

The dim light became brighter as the Fire patiently rose. Thandrua stood frozen for a few seconds, mesmerized by the white light the Fire produced - it seemed to be even brighter than usual. Then he ran; the cave was far from his location and he didn't have much time. The pounding sound of Thandrua's heart filled his ears, it synchronized with each step he took. Rust-colored clouds of dust lifted into the air as each massive foot made contact with the barren ground.

As Thandrua ran, the dirt became less dry, the ground softened beneath his feet ever so slightly, giving way under his heavy steps, causing the yellow talon-like claws from his four toes to dig in. Now the ground was covered with silky sand, making it more difficult to run. The sand slowly transformed into a liquid clay-like texture. His running came to a stop as he struggled to pull his foot out of the sands. Thandrua used great force to pull his foot out of the sandy muck, causing a thick squelching sound. He was able to do this three times, but only moved himself a few inches forward. He sunk into the ground further and growled in frustration.

"The ground is taking me! The Fire will surely burn my flesh… I cannot let this be my fate." He thrashed violently in desperation, attempting to break free, but the ground only sucked him in faster. Thandrua and the sand continued to play the fatal game of tug-o-war until his torso was half submerged.

By now the Fire had reached the sky. A beam of light shone directly on Thandrua, hardening the liquefied sand to solid ground. A shadow cast behind him making his curved horns appear larger than they already were. He squirmed as he shouted, and then he heard a voice that was somehow both calm and brooding all at once.

"Relax and fear not."

"Who said that? Go now! Please go, the Fire will destroy you as well."

"No. I am the light, and I will not destroy you, Thandrua."

"You have vaporized so many of my followers and... h-how do you know my name?"

"Not I, the light you speak of is another, called the Sun. In time it will help create much life, becoming a fundamental source of energy and nutrients for life to prosper."

"Does that mean we just wait? Let this, *Sun*, come and go until more life is all around us?"

"Well, Thandrua, I'm afraid not. Unfortunately, I do have to admit I had not accounted for the effect the solar energy would have on beings such as you and the Serpenoids; beings that have thrived in total darkness for so long. With how well you and your followers took to the shine of the stars and the reflective glow of the Moon, I had underestimated the intensity of the Sun's direct light. No, the Sun will always be dangerous for you, and all of you will surely perish if you stay any longer. This planet is undergoing many changes. Very soon, rain will flood the land and the lava will overrun, destroying anything in its way. You must leave."

"How? There is no place to go."

"Wrong again, there is another. Another world like this one with no sun at all."

"*Another* world? How do I get there?"

"I will show you."

Thandrua now had the strength to break out of the hardened sand. Pulling himself up, he stood and stared into the light. At that moment everything started to move past him; it was as if he traveled forward without taking a single step, his surroundings whizzed by as he stood perfectly still.

Thandrua took careful note of the landscapes he passed through to memorize the direction he was being led towards. It was a straight trek, coming from the mouth of the cave his colony currently occupied. He saw a volcano spewing lava, a valley cratered by meteors, and a river of magma leading to an almost bottomless canyon. The distant depth was illuminated by a fiery glow from the magma of the Earth's core.

As the opening of the canyon reached Lord Thandrua, the movement stopped, leaving Thandrua hovering over the gap. His altitude gently decreased while he faced the wall in front of him. Light rays shone in the canyon revealing cracks in the rock forming a bizarre shape. A diagonal line slanted down from the top, drawing inward as it lowered on the wall forming a point connecting with a similar line that slanted diagonally outward. Overlapping the shape were two more diagonal lines but turned on its side, with the point facing to the left of the canyon wall and the opening facing the right.

Although difficult to comprehend, Thandrua awed at the massive shape's form nonetheless. Other than its size, the lines seemed to be unnaturally straight, not jagged or ridged and unlike any cracks he had seen before. What Lord Thandrua found most peculiar was the deep brooding hole within the center of the overlapping lines.

"The wall in front contains a marking, as you can see. In the center is your gateway to the new world."

Thandrua's body stopped descending as he came to the center of the marking. The dark circular hole was a few feet in front of him. There seemed to be no end to the tunnel. Thandrua inspected the wall, noticing grooves in the rock creating a simple path to the hole.

"Enter, Thandrua."

"I must get the others first; I cannot leave them behind."

"You may return to them later, but now you must enter."

Thandrua took a second to think, then pulled himself into the hole. In a flash he was on the other side. He stood in an empty desert with a gargantuan mountain far in the distance. Heat radiated from the ground, a raspy dry breeze blistered Thandrua's skin as he sniffed the comforting scent of brimstone. This world was fairly similar to Earth, except for the sky. A blood orange tone filled the atmosphere, not a solitary star or cloud was in sight.

The white orb peeked over the horizon and began to speak once again. "This is your new home. Here you'll make many discoveries, in the land and within yourself." Thandrua's surroundings faded, and he appeared in a sparkling cave, "When you return to this world with your followers, you'll arrive here. These walls are encrusted with particles of metal. There is a task that needs to be done in this cave; create tools."

Two metallic shapes, that later would be called a shovel and a pickaxe, appeared in front of Thandrua's eyes. He studied the designs to memorize the correct shapes.

"These tools will make your lives easier. Scrape off the particles from the wall and melt them together. In the back of this cave there is a wall with two holes. Place the particles in the larger hole on top and liquid metal will pour out from the smaller hole below. You must carve the shapes shown to you into stone and place them under the small hole. Let them cool. Once these molds have hardened into the tools, you may dig anywhere in this world, in the ground or in caves, and find more metal particles and various precious gifts.

You can insert whole clumps of rock containing the metal particles in the wall to receive more metal. Behind the wall is an eternal flame that will melt the rock and infuse the metal into liquid. You can establish a society with your new tools and discoveries. Do not get lost in your findings, but rather empowered by them. Here in this desert, you may live long and well, so long as you remain mindful of your home."

Thandrua stared at the two holes in the wall. He didn't quite understand the purpose of such a tedious task, but reviewed the information nonetheless. Rubbing his chiseled chin with his right hand, he thought of this task as a new purpose, something to separate the Serpenoids from aimless wanderers. Finally, Thandrua was ready to speak.

"I am most grateful for all the knowledge you have given me. Excitement fills my heart to start this new and wonderful life. However, I do believe I must leave now, I need to return to the others before they worry about my absence."

"Do not fret, you will be home soon. I must ask of you, be open and willing to compromise, even when times are most trying. Tolerance is most necessary. Always remember to practice tolerance and patience"

"I see," Thandrua didn't quite understand the meaning behind such wise advice. He thought quietly for a moment, "One more thing, you never explained how you knew my name."

"How could I not? I am *the* Creator."

Those final words, "I am the Creator," echoed throughout the cave and repeated inside Thandrua's head. The voice gradually grew louder causing Thandrua to become disoriented. He shut his eyes and grabbed his head just below his ivory horns in agony. Finally, the noise stopped and Thandrua opened his eyes. Surrounding him were all the sleeping Serpenoids inside their cave back on Earth.

Chapter 4
A Great Migration

The chiseling of stone, the clashing of metal upon metal, the exhausted grunts of endless labor echoed within the depths of a massive cave that contained a natural furnace. The metals in the walls shimmered behind the Cobra Clan as they supervised the Serpenoids in pushing their bodies to their limits, even if this was right after their long journey across the plains of their previous home, previous world.

Lord Thandrua walked amongst them, eyeing their labors, handling the new shovels and pickaxes they made. For the first time in many cycles, he felt joy as he held the still warm metal in his mitts. They had made it, stuck in the cave to create the metal tools for now, but away from the dangers of Earth. Without hesitation the Serpenoids had listened to Thandrua explain the vision he had of a new world, a safe haven. He was grateful of their faith, he hadn't any trouble with convincing, other than his own personal doubts. Now they were surely to thrive and prosper, and Thandrua thought of the sacrifices to get there.

Lord Thandrua awoke from his dream, his premonition, in a nervous sweat. He swore he had just journeyed to the other side of their land and into another world altogether. However, he had been laying on the warm ground encircled by the Cobra Clan that slept soundly. Phineus' tail flicked to one side, indicating he was in a deep rest. A sea of Serpenoids slept on the ground beyond them.

A dream? Thandrua thought to himself, disbelievingly. It had all felt so real; he was certain that this was no ordinary dream and he stood to wake the others.

"Awaken!" Lord Thandrua shouted and all the Serpenoids woke to the abrupt sound of their master's booming voice. The Cobras were the first to stand, the other Serpenoids followed their lead.

"I have an important message!" Thandrua announced, standing tall and mighty, "Wake, my followers!"

The air buzzed as the Serpenoids murmured amongst themselves. Thandrua scanned the sea of yellow lustrous eyes that hung onto his next word, but before he could say anything Sectoraus pulled the crimson beast to the side. The Cobra Clan pushed the crowd apart to give them a bit of space, though they were still completely surrounded by their followers.

"Thandrua, what is the meaning of this?" Sectoraus whispered into his master's ear as Thandrua bent his head down to keep the conversation between the two of them.

"I had a dream of a great light, not the one we fear, but another. It spoke to me and gave me knowledge." Thandrua whispered back.

"A great light?" Sectoraus was very confused, "Knowledge of what?"

"It called the Fire of the sky the Sun, said we were doomed if we stayed here… then showed me how to get to a new world."

"A *new* world?" *Thandrua has foreseen our salvation,* Sectoraus thought, then began whispering again, "This is miraculous." He looked over his shoulder, then behind Thandrua's to see the Serpenoids that stared at them, hanging onto the suspense of what Thandrua needed to say. "You *are* almighty. Tell them, just..."

"What is it?"

"This other light… do not mention it."

"It is what I saw."

"Yes, but what is it? It will create too much confusion. Just tell them how to be saved."

Lord Thandrua stood tall once again and the Serpenoids closed in, the Cobra Clan kept the admirers at arm's length while Sectoraus stood to Thandrua's right. The emerald eyes of the god-king took in all the Serpenoid faces that waited hungrily on his word. Finally, he spoke:

"I have had a vision." Silence encompassed them. "A vision of our world doomed to be terrorized by the devastating Fire, by the

Sun." The crowd murmured. "Yes, yes, I have given name to this threat, and I alone provide salvation."

The chatter broke out louder, Thandrua could see the panic rise. Sectoraus turned to his master and betrayed a slight smile and a short nod. He had done well. The Serpenoids were frightened, Sectoraus could even sense the uncertainty from his fellow clan members, although they maintained their composure.

"What do we do?" Called out one Serpenoid.

"Save us my Lord!" Cried another from the back.

"Almighty Thandrua! Thandrua! Thandrua!" The Serpenoids began to chant.

"Silence!" Lord Thandrua boomed over the chaos, "We must embark on a journey through our land to a vast canyon. Within this canyon we will find refuge, refuge from this world altogether." Now the silence fell heavy and their faces became confused. *A world apart from this one?* "I understand the ludicrousness of such a statement, but I can assure you this paradise is real and there are no options for us to stay." He was pleased to hear these reassuring words come from his own mouth, but deep in his heart he felt wrong for keeping the full story and wrong for putting so much faith in a dream.

Sectoraus stepped forward. "You have all heard the wonderful Lord Thandrua! How kind he is to warn us, how compassionate he is to provide us with knowledge of this salvation. Since the first light, since the coming of the *Sun*, you have all looked to Lord Thandrua for answers. Well, he has found the answer and we must honor his gift and follow." Now Sectoraus turned to face the towering leader before him, "We are eternally grateful."

The crowd exploded with applause and cheer, they would be ready and willing for whatever was to come next. Sectoraus leaned in close to his leader and Thandrua lowered his head to hear his companion. "And now, they will love you even more."

Sectoraus pulled away, he was thinking about what his master had said about the dream. *A Light told him…* Sectoraus didn't quite understand; the Cobra Clan shared a mental bond but not even they had ever communicated through their dreams. Surely the Light had to be a creation of Thandrua's dream, perhaps his own subconscious taking form to provide the premonition. Perhaps he had been right this whole time, perhaps there was much more to Thandrua than Sectoraus had realized.

Sectoraus watched the Serpenoids, pleased with his consulting and intrigued by the new journey ahead. He regrouped the Cobras and together they organized the Serpenoids, awaiting the distant traces of light to disperse and awaiting instructions from the deity that loved them so.

Lord Thandrua stood alone, thinking to himself. *More love?* He rested his eyes upon his followers. *Perhaps their belief is true, after all it was* my *dream. What of that light? Could it be my own subconscious giving me the knowledge I have forgotten? I am unsure about that, as I am unsure about how I could possibly handle* more *love.*

***

The pilgrimage proved to be much lengthier than Thandrua had imagined. The creatures of darkness were forced to scatter for shelter from two separate sunrises. Fooled by the speed he traveled in his dream, Thandrua thought they could leave and find the location within a cycle before dawn.

They had left just as the faintest signs of the shimmering deep orange light just beyond the horizon fell and indigo crept up into the safety of the night's sky. Lord Thandrua led the way from the cave with Sectoraus at his side, as usual. Behind them was a large group of Serpenoids that walked in lines side by side, led by the broad Orpheus. Followed behind them was Solarious, accompanied by his own group of Serpenoids, just as large as the first. Phineus moved about the two groups, monitoring them, making sure everyone kept pace and didn't stray behind.

The immense convoy of thousands of Serpenoids trekked forward from the cave that until recently had acted as a sanctuary from the Sun for over a dozen cycles. Thandrua's only direction, straight ahead, and maintained course as best he could. As much as he loathed the Sun, he was grateful to have it in his sight, when he noticed how the last remnants were directly away from the point they were trying to follow. He used it as a guide and motivation. *We are going to where there is no Sun!* Thandrua thought to himself, *I will watch the last bits of that dreadful light as I march on!*

In time, it was black as pitch. Only the yellow crescent moon and the billions of sparkling stars illuminated the otherwise lightless world. The nomads followed their leaders; practically all were silent, taking in the last thoughts of the world they now were emigrating from and anticipating what the next world would be like. Many felt fear; the unknown is a primordial source of fear, and they had no idea what to think of another world. Their Almighty Thandrua guaranteed them passage and assured them that there was not only a world aside from their own, but one made for their perfection, a paradise. However, even the mystery of paradise still aroused fear.

A long way they marched in the dry sandy ground, Thandrua leaving four-toed footprints and the Serpenoids leaving prints of their three-toed steps and tails. However, our scaled wanderers and their crimson lifegiver hadn't betrayed any signs of fatigue. By this point of their existence, they were all too familiar with the aimless journey about the lifeless land.

Shadows occasionally cast over their path as the dry winds shifted clouds across the moon's spotlight. Very dry the wind was indeed, and thirst slowly crept its way into Sectoraus' sharp mouth. He could sense his Cobra brothers, too, were beginning to crave the elixir of life and safely assumed his master as well as the rest of the Serpenoids would soon feel the same.

The sky had yet to rain during this cycle, nor the cycle before. To distract himself and not to disturb the silence that hung between the two shepherds, Sectoraus marveled the sky. How he enjoyed the stars shining their yellow, blue, and orange lights. As mysterious as they were, the stars still brought comfort to him.

Just beyond the horizon peeked a mountain range, with sulfuric smoke wafting out of what Sectoraus believed to be a small volcano. He thought he might have heard Thandrua say, *"the volcano,"* barely beneath his breath, but he did not question.

Instead, he casted his golden eyes skyward once again, not with comfort this time. He thought he might have noticed a hint of a purple hue blending into the black blanket, then stopped in his tracks and turned to look behind as he sensed something alarming from Solarious. Over the horizon from which they came, he saw it. The Sun casting its dreaded color transitions.

"Thandrua!" He warned and turned to face the ivory-horned beast.

"I see, my friend." Thandrua's voice was level and didn't betray the hint of fear that glowered in his eyes. "I did not think the destination would take this long. I presume the Cobra Clan is aware as well?"

"I'm sure of it. I believe I can see Phineus running to speak with Solarious." There was a pause as the two could see the large convoy come to a stop. "Thandrua, what do..."

"The mountain range up ahead." Thandrua faced forward once again, his stiff legs shifted into a jog. Now wasn't the time for questions, it was a time for action.

"It should be close enough to aid us in time; if we move, the others will follow. Hold that range in mind." Thandrua ordered.

Sectoraus gave a short nod and moved along with his hero. He envisioned the two of them below the volcano regrouping with the others. In the distance behind them, a cloud of dust from the dry land rose in the air as the entire colony of Serpenoids followed suit. The black sky became a royal purple, that into violet, as the thunderous sound of a frightened stampede came closer and closer to shelter.

Now the violet transitioned into indigo, and Sectoraus knew if he looked back, he would see a lighter shade of blue above the fatal yellow light. The ground beneath his feet radiated warmth more here than any other place and with the volcano well in sight, he knew Thandrua was right. They would make it just in time.

The Serpenoids rested inside a cave they found that dug into the mountains sloping down from the volcano. Some curled up hugging their knees as their tail circled around them and slept, others sat on large rock beds or laid on the ground to replenish their strength.

Thandrua insisted on staying awake to watch the day fade; he wanted to continue as soon as dusk hit. The Cobra Clan couldn't justify slumbering while their master remained alert and decided to wait with him.

"The canyon which holds our destination seemed to be much closer in my dream." Thandrua explained to them. "I had not considered that we would run into this problem at all."

"We will get there, my Lord." Solarious reassured.

"Yes, we will." Thandrua agreed, "I am just surprised this has turned out to be a full journey. Now, I am not so sure how long the journey will continue."

"You think we may face another sunrise, Thandrua?" Sectoraus asked.

"It may be possible, or what I fear most, more than one." Thandrua said.

Any further conversation, however, was kept to a minimum. Thandrua preferred the silence to keep the journey in mind. He looked out of the cave through squinted eyes, awaiting the signs of sundown. The Cobras faced each other, standing in a square, and sat on the ground. They crossed their legs as their tails curled on the ground around them. The Cobra Clan simultaneously closed their eyes and took this time to meditate amongst themselves. The meditation strengthened the mental connection that flowed between the four of them. Since the coming of the first dawn, they had found little time to do this as a collective and found their connection needed some fine-tuning.

A few tremors rumbled beneath their feet causing concern to slink its way throughout the shelter, especially for Thandrua. With the gusts of smoke pluming from the volcano, he knew this volcano was active. Recalling the tremors and the spewing lava he envisioned in his dream, he knew it could erupt any time.

Before long, the Sun had reached its highest point and moved across the sky to the other side of the mountains. The clouds became a blend of pink and orange while the darkened blues ambushed the golden light and the cool breeze marbled clouds in sight. It was time to move again.

"Awaken, my Serpenoids!" Lord Thandrua announced, "The next cycle begins anew! We shall leave this cave and climb the volcano to the other side." The ground shook slightly below them. The now fully awakened Serpenoids murmured amongst themselves.

"Please remain focused," Thandrua urged, "I have nothing but the greatest of faith in you all. These are but mere tremors, I have witnessed you all endure much more violent quakes whilst scaling along the mountains."

To this the Serpenoids agreed, then they swarmed out of the cave. The climb began fast, the sound of thousands of thick claws chipped at the rough of the volcano as the god-beast and reptilian beings climbed as fast as they possibly could.

The tremors shook more violently as the group neared the peak and scaled across to the opposite side. A silent fear shocked them all. The foundation shook more consistently; none knew what to expect, but the ground came nearer.

Sectoraus found himself first to touch the warm volcanic soil, and aided Lord Thandrua as he descended. The Cobras guided all the Serpenoids to the ground, with Orpheus and Phineus volunteering to stay back and ensure the slowest of the colony wouldn't be left behind. The wanderers stood, waiting as their group multiplied in size, and finally reformed into the travel groups they had during the cycle before. As Thandrua and Sectoraus lead away from the volcano, an earthquake shook the mountain range violently.

The vibrations rumbled up through the soles of their feet, reverberating throughout the bones in their bodies. The smoke coming from the volcano thickened into a black mass. An ear-deafening roar split through the air as the volcano erupted into the sky casting debris outward and fiery orange lava spewed from the volcano's orifice. The air grew dank with the sulfuric aroma as black ash fluttered about. All sides of the volcano became coated in the scorching lava and within seconds, it oozed down to the foundation of the rich black soil. Luckily, the wanderers traveled well away into the valley ahead before their first obstacle had become compromised.

Standing atop the hill that led into a vast valley, Thandrua gazed up at the stars. A few seemed much brighter than usual. Not waiting another second longer, he led the way down. The soft black soil gave way beneath his heavy-footed steps. Flaring his nostrils at the volcanic stench, Thandrua thought of the valley he saw in his dream, *hadn't it been a crash site?*

Now the Serpenoid colony crossed well into the valley. The earth was rocky but flat with no traces of any craters to be found. Sectoraus felt an invisible tug at the top of his head and looked up. His yellow eyes squinted then enlarged as he saw one, two, and now three stars rapidly growing in size. Or perhaps getting nearer?

"Run!" Sectoraus shouted as the three comets ripped through the atmosphere in a burning inferno.

They swarmed, charging in the only direction they had, forward. They just needed to get over the next hill and out of the valley, there they would be safe. At that moment, however, safety seemed but a fool's dream as the thunderous sound of the plummeting rock exploded into the ground up ahead at the right. The comet's impact sent dirt and rock raining all around, and a large crater was revealed as the dirt cloud cleared.

Before any of the Serpenoids could even react to the demolition, they saw the second comet blazing close behind and they continued to run forward. The ground shook violently as the comet behind drilled its own crater into the ground, polluting the air with more dust.

As the travelers made the climb out of the valley, the third and final comet struck close to where the last had crashed, destroying the space beneath its weight. The air cleared of ash and debris and the colony jumped and cheered with victory.

"We have all survived!" announced Sectoraus. Serpenoids all around congratulated themselves and sagged into each other's arms with relief; some held each other tightly at the thought of how narrowly they had escaped their end. Thandrua broke into a wide grin feeling pleased with the outcome of this obstacle, but while the other celebrated, he oversaw the land. Lava oozed from a fissure in the ground a distance ahead, flowing into a molten river that flowed towards and around another small cluster of mountainous terrain far ahead.

Lord Thandrua came down from the hill and pushed past the joyous Serpenoids, leading the way to the river of lava. Without a word, the colony followed.

The further from the valley they fled, the soft mineral-enriched soil hardened into the dry reddish-brown earth they were accustomed to. The ground seemed to harden the closer they moved toward the lava. Dark flaky dirt chipped under Thandrua's mass and the thick claws of the Serpenoids. They marched close enough for the fiery glow to illuminate the path ahead, but they were mindful to keep a distance from the heat as the river flowed parallel to them. The rhythm of their steps picked up the closer the next mountain range became.

The migrants continued on as the faint twinkle of dawn peeked from the land behind. The dark sky softened to purple while the clouds radiated with orange underneath and a pink hue along the tops. The deep orange from the horizon lightened into a golden glow. The wanderers moved even faster, almost breaking into a run.

They had followed the winding trail of the lava that happened to cut directly into the vast caverns. Hidden deep within the twisting caverns of this next range of mountains, the travelers rested. Some sat on rock, while others rested on the warm stony ground. The intimate proximity of the lava kept them from getting too comfortable. All the Serpenoids avoided the stalactites because of the quakes from their last cave of refuge, no one wanted to chance being impaled should a tremor come through.

Once again, Lord Thandrua insisted on staying alert. Stones of white quartz and mica embedded in the gargantuan stalagmites and stalactites shimmered in the red fiery radiance of the lava. Thandrua was transfixed, focusing his vision onto the countless sparkles that reminded him of the stars in the night's sky. It provided him with comfort, a distraction from the heat emitting within.

Even though Thandrua and the Serpenoids were more than accustomed to the heat of their desolate world, being inside such an enclosed space with a massive body of lava did not help with their ever-growing thirst. Yet, the shimmering sparkles of the stones gave Thandrua distraction from his parched mouth.

Lord Thandrua thought of the volcano and how lucky they were, and again felt pride to have escaped the comets falling from the sky. These things, as well as the river of lava, he had envisioned. However this cavern, and the mountain range as a whole, was not a part of his prophetic dream. The river had flowed directly to the canyon with their destination. Perhaps these mountains meant they were close, or perhaps it foreshadowed many more obstacles to turn up unannounced.

What Thandrua did know and what he had discussed with Sectoraus before his companion dropped into meditation with his brothers was the fact that they could not rest to begin a fully new cycle. The lava flowed on and on emitting a glow in the depths of the caverns. They must follow the river and the coverage provided them with a chance to travel during daylight but not suffer the fatal burn. It was clearly an opportunity that could not be missed.

Lord Thandrua then thought about the beautiful white light that had spoken to him in his dream. The memory of it seemed to be reassuring. The Light had mentioned of rains to come that would not end, filling canyons and entire parts of the land with water. *When would these rains come*, he thought as he smacked his sticky dry lips in an attempt to build saliva. Thandrua was suddenly very aware of his tongue, how difficult it was to roll around in his mouth, and how incredibly sharp his fangs now seemed to feel against it. Water was somewhere, but they wouldn't find it here.

Lord Thandrua gently placed his thickly muscled palm on the smooth scaly shoulder of Sectoraus, signaling his readiness. Sectoraus rose and the rest of the Cobras broke out of their meditative trances and began to regroup the rest of the travelers. There was but one direction and that was deeper into the cavern in the hopes that the lava would lead out in the direction of the canyon, and not into a molten pit of magma. The time had come to continue the quest for salvation from the Sun and the impending thirst.

Just shortly as they began to stir, something caught Thandrua's attention. *Drip-drip.* It was a faint sound, but it seduced the crimson beast's ears. *Drip-drip.* He looked about their space, craze in his eyes.

"My lord?" Phineus was concerned, as were the others except for Sectoraus who seemed more intrigued.

"Be silent!" Thandrua barked, the light from the lava cast a shadow over his face making the intensity of his look all the more grave.

"The master knows something." Sectoraus whispered to Phineus.

The god-king moved up to one of the stalactites hanging from the cavern ceiling and slid a finger on its tip. Staring at the tip of his finger, the glow of the lava reflected a shimmer of moisture. A wild smile grew on Thandrua's face just before another drip rolled off the stalactite. He quickly realized that the walls did not only shimmer with minerals, but from moisture as well.

"Water!" Thandrua announced before licking the tip of the cavern's structure.

The others quickly took his example and licked whatever stalactites they could reach. Some licked the side of the walls with gracious joy. Despite the heat of the flowing lava, the cave walls remained cool, as was the moisture. It was not nearly enough fluid to satisfy their prolonged thirst, but it was better than nothing at all. The brightness from the moisture was elating. None paid mind to the bitter taste from the minerals within the walls. Now they were ready to continue ahead.

One labyrinth of a journey it was for them, following the river of lava down the cavern through crevices and around bizarre structures made from the connecting stalagmites and the drops of time. Everyone remained silent; the anticipation to escape the tunnels was the only concern. All they could hear was the oozing sludge of the lava just continuing, on and on.

Over time the twists and turns became disorienting. The travelers had no idea which way was up or whether they were even moving in the right direction. They began to think the structures were all too recognizable. At one point, Sectoraus used his thick black claws to carve into a wall, hoping that if they had been lost, then the carving would show that they had passed there. He simply carved a circle, then scraped vertical lines at two points above the circle. Thandrua chuckled when he looked at the figure and recognized that it was to symbolize his horned head. Fortunately, they never saw the carving again.

After long exhausting twists and turns, the river plateaued to a straight path. A distant but recognizable sound echoed through the tunnel- a pattering wet drip. They were being led out. The oozing lava flowed directly toward a dim gray light that sluggishly came into view, the pattering sound becoming more distinctive. There was light coming from outside, but it was a dull grayish light, perhaps due to heavy clouds and rain.

They quickened their pace and the end of the tunnel expanded with view of the filtered light from outside of the cavern. Thandrua raised his left hand up behind him, telling his followers to stop. The angle of light in the sky put Thandrua in mind of the dreaded Sun rising, but the cover of clouds gave him hope, and the temptation of water to slake the thirst of his people was overwhelming. Impulsively, Lord Thandrua stepped out and the Serpenoids gasped with horror.

"Thandrua, no!" Sectoraus shouted as he turned to see the commotion and with horror found the crimson king standing out of the cave in the dim light of the early sun. However, to all the Serpenoids' relief, the great Lord Thandrua stood unscathed.

"Come on out." Lord Thandrua called as he turned his back to the rest of them, opened his arms and lifted his ivory horned head to the rain.

The Serpenoids rushed out. The Cobras tried to contain them and Sectoraus simply stood amazed. Thandrua stood there and none of the Serpenoids burned from the light. The clouds had shielded them and allowed the Serpenoids to replenish themselves. No one knew how long they were within the caverns. Sectoraus felt they had spent enough time in the caverns for the Sun to come and go for another two cycles, or perhaps it could have been the start of the very next cycle after they had entered the caverns.

The Cobra king didn't waste much thought on the length of their labyrinth, mostly he thought of Thandrua and now he projected the thought: *Lord Thandrua brought water from the very stone and shielded the burning light with rain!* Feeling the thought, Solarious looked over to his leader, then Phineus, and finally Orpheus and all four of the Cobra Clan nodded in agreement. *Lord Thandrua is the key to survival.*

The sky hummed with the distant sound of thunder, a cool wind pushed against their bodies and moved the dark gray nimbus clouds. *They have refreshed enough*, Thandrua thought and demanded to continue. Taking advantage of the clouds' protection, the Cobra Clan split the colony into three groups and led them, with Thandrua and Sectoraus at the front. The groups trekked in the direction of the lava, just as they had done in the caverns.

The rain continued, a thick veil of clouds mercifully filtering the light as it gradually grew brighter, but Thandrua remained aware that the Sun hung perilously above his followers' heads. They had wandered without any quench of thirst for several cycles; now they were soaked as they walked across a muddy terrain, leaving prints of their clawed feet.

The convoy of travelers had slowed their pace tremendously compared to how eager they were at the start of their journey. This was slightly due to fatigue, but mostly the abundance of rain. The winds made the rain come from several directions, even cutting into their eyes. A chill slinked its way beneath their scaly hides; the groups moved closer together, clutching themselves and holding onto each other with their tails wrapped around one another, anything to retain heat amongst their groups.

The heavy clouds grew darker as the day went on, even as the sun was surely climbing higher into the sky. There was no hint of the storm dying down at all, nor did Thandrua think it ever would. *Rain will flood the land*, he remembered from his dream, and with the sound of thousands of sniffles and the chattering of the Serpenoids' fangs, Thandrua was revitalized with new determination. They had made it this far; drowning could not be an option. With the Serpenoids' deity taking long strides ahead, Sectoraus found new admiration as well and trotted along, motivated by his master. Soon after, all the Serpenoids picked up speed and began their full march once again.

The boiling and oozing river of lava still acted as their navigator. Hope came to Thandrua's emerald eyes when he saw that the lava ahead disappeared in sight as if falling over a ledge. The crimson beast and the serpentine nomads found the prophesied canyon. They stood atop the cliff's edge, listening to the roar from the lava river pouring down into the great abyss and gazing out into the yawning chasm that stretched out before them. Far below, the cliff walls were illuminated with a faint glow of magma that flowed down the canyon, vanishing into the bottomless depths.

Wind howled louder out here on the precipice; all the Serpenoids looked out across the canyon that seemed to stretch onward forever, or down into the deep emptiness that seemed just as endless. Lord Thandrua, however, stared intensely at a section of the wall on the other side of the canyon, a little further along the cliff's edge from where the colony had gathered. There, it seemed to be clearer than when he had seen it in the dream, was the huge symbol he had seen cutting into the cliff face. Thandrua awed at the scale of the markings as he studied how the two pointed angles overlapped one another. One angle pointed directly downward with its opening above, V. The second angle intersected the first on its right side with the opening on its left, <. And just likc in the dream, a dark hole burrowed in the very center of the intersecting lines. Sectoraus watched as Thandrua crouched low at the edge, seeming to inspect the bottomless canyon. He approached when he saw his leader's shoulders slump as though in defeat.

"What is the matter?" Sectoraus asked. Thandrua's expression was troubled, and he did not turn or acknowledge the Cobra as he drew near.

"I fear we face an impassable obstacle now," Thandrua murmured, almost as though talking to himself, never taking his eyes off the symbol. Sectoraus followed his leader's gaze to the unnatural, perfectly circular cave on the far side of the canyon, then studied the strangely even cracks cleanly cutting across the canyon's wall.

He noted one line of the fissure stretched all the way up to the edge of the cliff, forming a slope that crossed near the hole at the center of the markings. He then traced a path from where that slope cut into the top of the cliff and followed the edge of the canyon back towards the Serpenoid colony, still huddling together for warmth, but stopped when his gaze reached the steaming river of magma that gushed into the canyon. Sectoraus nodded in understanding of Thandrua's fears; the lava's current rumbled over the ledge much too furiously to contemplate moving the Serpenoids across it.

"We have journeyed so far, and this trek has been so much longer than my dream had shown!" Thandrua cried out in frustration, "Why would it show me this passage and not the way to get there?" Sectoraus' head snapped behind them at Thandrua's outburst, but none of the Serpenoids seemed to have heard it; the winds were so strong here that his voice was whipped down the canyon nearly as soon as the words left his mouth.

"There must be a way, my Lord," Sectoraus laid a calming hand on Thandrua's massive forearm. "You are our life-giver, you brought us the rains, and even brought forth water from the stone inside the caverns..." Sectoraus' voice trailed off and his jaw hung slack as he turned back towards the mountain range still looming behind them, hiding the caverns they had exited from.

"The caverns!" Sectoraus repeated, his eyes widening. Thandrua's gaze finally broke from the symbol on the canyon, and he turned towards the Cobra, his head tilting in a wordless question at Sectoraus' excited tone.

"When we traveled through the caverns, there was a point where we could easily have crossed to the other side, the magma's flow was much narrower there," Sectoraus explained, "we must go back!"

Thandrua looked behind them at the mountains, considering Sectoraus' words, then lifted his head towards the skies at the ever-darkening storm clouds above them.

"I suppose there is no other choice." Thandrua said, "But if we are to retrace our steps we must move quickly. These rains are not like anything we have experienced before, I do not believe they will stop until water covers the land completely."

Sectoraus' face grew solemn, and his eyes narrowed in determination. "Then we will move at once, my Lord. I will have Phineus take the first group and help us set the pace, and Orpheus will follow the last group from the back to care for any stragglers."

Thandrua nodded his assent to Sectoraus' plan, and the two moved as one towards the shivering Serpenoids, their strides full of urgency.

The Cobras came forward to greet their brother and Sectoraus quickly explained the troubles and gave the three their marching orders, while Thandrua went ahead to his followers.

"We are nearly at the end of our journey! Our salvation from this world lies just on the other side of this canyon. I will lead you across the river of magma further upstream where it is safe, but we must make haste!"

The Cobras set about organizing their groups again; the leaders' hurried demeanor quickly influenced the rest of the Serpenoids and soon the whole colony moved with anxious purpose. Thandrua and Sectoraus set off together at a loping jog, and Phineus began following with his group. The effort of moving more quickly helped the Serpenoids warm slightly and took their minds off the cold rivulets of rain running over their scales. Orpheus' group dragged behind, clearly showing the wear of the long journey. As they all ran, Orpheus sometimes threw a thickly muscled arm around the shoulders of any Serpenoid who faltered, urging them onward.

Sectoraus could see the concern that lined Thandrua's face as they hurried back towards the mountain range. However, the sound of thousands of clawed feet pounding the earth in unison behind them gave him a sense of calm. He gazed up at Thandrua and the sight of his impressive stature renewed the feeling he and his brothers had shared as they left the caverns, *Thandrua is the key to our survival.* This thought resonated with him, and he could sense when the feeling spread to the other Cobras as well. They shared this trust and let it warm them, knowing in the end their life-giver would lead them to the paradise of his vision.

At their rapid pace, the Serpenoid colony returned to the base of the mountain much quicker than it had taken them to leave it. Sooner than he expected, Thandrua saw the dim opening of the caverns ahead, and slowed his pace. Sectoraus called for the groups to pause at the entrance, providing a moment of rest for the stragglers in the back group while those in front with Phineus began filing into the narrower caverns after Thandrua and Sectoraus. The heat from the magma inside the enclosed space of the cave was a welcome reprieve after the chill rain, and the Serpenoids, following their leaders back into the depths of the mountain, relaxed as their scaley hides warmed.

Thandrua was single-minded in his goal and strode ahead, still keeping a quick pace as he backtracked through the winding cavern. Sectoraus hurried behind his Lord, looking ahead for the point he had recalled where they would be able to reach the other side of the magma. The opposite side was narrower and, studying the walls as they continued into the cave, he could see that there were points where they would perhaps even have to cling to the wall to leave the caverns by that route. He flexed his clawed hands in anticipation and his tail twitched nervously, envisioning the many Serpenoids who would have to carefully cross over those choke points.

Finally, they reached the narrowed point of the magma flow, and Thandrua's powerful legs easily propelled him across it. Sectoraus followed suit, his thick tail swung behind him adding power to his leap. Phineus landed nimbly behind Sectoraus, and they stayed to help stabilize some of the smaller Serpenoids as they crossed over while Thandrua continued back down the narrower side of the cavern towards the exit. The magma's heat was almost overwhelming with how closely it flowed to the cavern wall, and Thandrua's crimson skin glistened in the sweltering heat.

The Serpenoids made their way across the river of lava and gingerly walked along the narrow path towards the cavern's exit, at times using their strong claws to brace themselves against the stone. Thandrua gazed up at the dark clouds when he exited the cave; the rain was coming down heavier than ever and the winds seemed to have reached new heights while they had been underground. As the Serpenoids began pouring out into the open, Sectoraus maneuvered his way back to his Lord's side. Thunder rumbled oppressively overhead, seeming to wordlessly convey all that the two might have said; they needed to hurry if they were to reach the other side of the canyon where the symbol was carved.

Without a word, Thandrua set off at an even faster pace than before, and after signaling to the other Cobras, Sectoraus followed suit. The oppressive heat of the enclosed caverns was all too soon a distant memory; sheets of rain sluiced over the backs of the Serpenoids as they ducked their heads against the wind. The taxing pace of their trek did serve to generate some body warmth, but many were soon shivering as they ran.

Before long, Thandrua could see the edge of the magma flow where it dropped off into the chasm and began jogging off to the left of it, following the canyon's edge. Through the downpour, Thandrua peered along the rim, searching for the gash that would mark the start of the fissure cutting into the canyon wall. Sectoraus spared a glance upward and thought it was likely the Sun was finally setting; a full cycle had passed as the Serpenoids had retraced their steps back towards the mountain and returned to the opposite side of the canyon.

Solarious called out and pointed up ahead as he spotted a break in the edge they walked along and Thandrua dashed forward. The red beast knelt down at the edge of the chasm, his horns pointing out over the abyss as he leaned forward to get a glimpse of the hole far below him down the sloping fissure. Without hesitation, he lowered himself to scale the canyon wall. Sectoraus watched as his Lord disappeared over the edge of the cliff. Glancing back, he saw that the rest of the Serpenoids were not far behind.

"We climb!" Sectoraus shouted his order over gale. With the aid of their thick claws, descent into the canyon didn't prove difficult, despite the buffeting winds and rain. Sectoraus, along with Solarious and Phineus, followed their horned leader's path as Orpheus guided the Serpenoids from behind the colony. They followed the fissure in the wall slanting diagonally downward.

The winds howled as though in mourning and Thandrua moved faster, hurtling his massive body at times, and his followers picked up their pace as well. Finally, there it was, following what he believed to be the indentations of the odd crack that carved along the canyon. Thandrua had at last reached the gateway at the centerpiece, just as he saw in his dream.

Thandrua halted there, on a narrow ledge just below the hole that would supposedly tunnel to this new and secure world. A hole that was barely wide enough to fit a single body at a time, so long as they crawled on their bellies. A hole so incredibly dark none could be certain how far it ran. Even Solarious with his keen sight couldn't see an end to the tunnel. Thandrua held no signs of skepticism and, as the ruler of the Serpenoids, declared himself first to enter.

Sectoraus felt uneasy of Thandrua's eagerness, now seeing the passageway with his own eyes, containing a darkness that not even their lustrous eyes could cut.

"Thandrua, you cannot enter such a place," Sectoraus warned. "We should send in one of the Serpenoids, shall he not return we take that as a sign of danger."

"No, my friend," Thandrua had a smile across his face, "it may not be possible to return, this portal may only work one way. If we wait for a sign only one of us may find salvation as the rest of us perish. No, we must all enter blindly, for we are sure to die if we stay. The rains will not end for many cycles, leaving deadly amounts of water, and when they do the Sun will be waiting for us. One by one we crawl to our fate, and it must be I who will lead the way."

So Thandrua progressed forward, reaching into the tunnel with his right arm, followed by his head, then the left arm. His body shimmied mostly in, then he was quickly absorbed in, like a vortex. Sectoraus panicked. "Thandrua!" he shouted his name into the hole, but the sound seemed to die as it entered the vacuum. Overcome with a sudden sense of courage, Sectoraus crawled in.

Once within the tunnel, Sectoraus was pulled in with a great force. He had no need to use his arms or legs to travel within. Even though his body moved at a vast speed, the tunnel was long, and he continued traveling within. From the emptiness of the black, spirals of green, blue, and red lights swirled in Sectoraus' vision. His body felt one with his mind, a single vessel connected along with his surroundings. Euphoria overcame him and the black returned within an instant, betraying an end to the tunnel where he met Thandrua's arms pulling him from a crevice inside of a sparkling cave.

Section II
Paradise

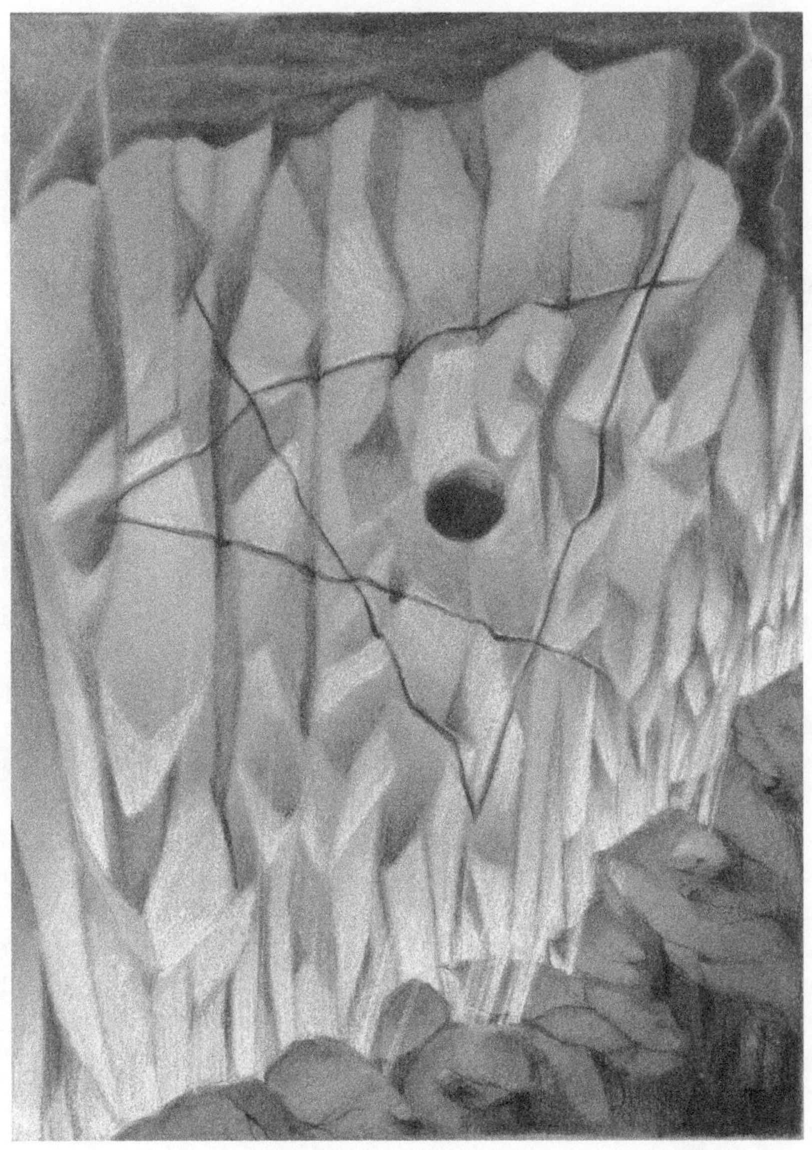

Chapter 5
A New Purpose

A cave that once gleamed with the dazzle of metallic particles, was now dull and barren. In place of the shimmering metal, the walls were covered in claw marks left by the Serpenoids. They spent such time on this new project, not stopping to rest nor sleep. None of the Serpenoids had any concept of how many cycles it would have been, especially after traveling such a trying journey. It was possible to say they spent what would have been three cycles, scraping the particles, melting them into the molds, and letting them harden into their new tools.

The Serpenoids were all eager to see this paradise that was prophesied to them. However, the cave that the cosmic tunnel led them to had no exit. The tunnel opposite of the portal stopped at a dead end. They needed those tools to escape. Their long and hard work was displayed in front of Thandrua as he inspected the sleek metal tools.

"There are about enough of these tools for all to go around." Thandrua observed the scarred cave walls, "We have used all the metal from these walls, and you have all done so well. This world is filled with various forms of metal, but we can only get to it if we use the tools that lay before us. All the other metal lies within the dirt and stone. A lot of very hard work is ahead of us, but before we continue mining, we may go outside, see our new world."

The Serpenoids applauded Thandrua, the sounds echoing off the walls making their thousands of claps sound like millions. Each Serpenoid grabbed one tool and began marching to the other end of the cave. The Serpenoids may have been exhausted, but none showed any outward signs. Ecstasy was in their hearts as they anticipated the prospect of their new paradise. The Serpenoids were also satisfied with their new calling to mine and create. They had never seen metal before and very much enjoyed how the tools shined. They walked through the cave, whispering amongst themselves about what they were to find. Before long they reached the other end of the cave.

The exit was blocked, just as it had been when they first arrived, a single wall that seemed to have been spared the twinkle of metal. Aside from that, it could have been just like any of the other walls within the cave, except they *knew*. They could feel the exit just behind its stone. Now with the tools and thousands of eager hands, the Serpenoids chipped at the wall creating an entrance into their new home. With their speed and ambition, it took no time at all.

Before any stepped a scaly, clawed foot out, Lord Thandrua stood ahead with the debris at the mouth of the cave. Joy filled his angular face as he stepped out looking across the land; it was exactly like in his dream. Outside of the cave was a vast empty desert with a blood orange sky hovering above. Hilly sand dunes loomed off to his right and the glow of the magma created a soft warmth in the far distance to his left. Thandrua sniffed the air, inhaling the scent of dry sulfur brushing against the hair in his nostrils.

Thandrua turned to face his followers and spread his arms out wide, as if offering the world to them and said, “Welcome home!”

The Serpenoids ran out of the cave from behind Thandrua and once they were out from the cave, their faces were captivated with awe. The heat blanketed around their scaly bodies as the soft warm breeze caressed them. In their eyes this place was beautiful. The orange sand beneath their black clawed feet radiated warmth and comfort. They scanned the skies and although they had very much enjoyed the beautiful displays of the stars and moon, they smiled at their absence here. They truly were home. In unison the Serpenoids chanted melodically, “Hail Lord Thandrua, savior of our race! Hail Lord Thandrua, who blessed us with his grace!” and ran about the land. Cheering with joy and celebration, they had reached salvation.

The Cobra Clan questioned that the sky didn’t hang black with darkness but illuminated completely with a red-orange hue. Thandrua, however, assured them it wasn’t from the presence of any sun. Not only was it a different color than they were used to seeing, but it was empty of anything. Not a cloud in sight, except a thick smog coming above from the cave they had just exited and realized it must be a part of a volcano.

Lord Thandrua, along with the Cobra Clan, casually walked from the cave. They stepped in what were their comfortable positions, Thandrua and Sectoraus side by side at the lead with the rest of the Cobras walking in a diamond cluster; Solarious to the right, Orpheus to the left, and Phineus at the back.

The Serpenoids didn't explore very far but chose to see what was on the other side of the dunes to the right of the cave. To their surprise they saw the dunes dip down into a valley that opened up to a grand crystal-clear lake that reflected the color of the sky above. Their excitement could not be contained. Never had they seen such a vast accumulation of water. The Serpenoids ran down into the valley, stopping at the lake's shore. They drank away the long thirst that their labors created. Some jumped into the waist deep lake and splashed around, taking in deep breaths of their new home.

Looming opposite the lake, seeming to rise straight from the water, towered an immense mountain. They could just see its peak, high in the sky, but its mass was vast. It had a grayish brown exterior, covered mostly in jagged rocks. The Serpenoids thought one could see the whole world from there.

Before following the Serpenoids, the Cobra Clan observed the volcano they had exited. Spouting out of the ground from behind the volcano oozed lava that flowed into a long river of magma. It rushed a distance off to the horizon and continued on into the land opposite from the cave. They couldn't make out where it ended, not even Solarious, who could only see its distant illuminating glow beyond the horizon. They soon joined Thandrua who stood atop the dunes.

Lord Thandrua took in the desolate scenery and the joyous faces of his pleased followers. He had led them to paradise, the promised land, for this world was indeed perfect. A place that not only seemed to fit what might be their ideal home, but a place that gave them a new niche; no longer nomads roaming aimlessly, but miners to discover what lay beneath their feet. And most importantly, a place where they could live in peace.

Their celebrations lasted two full cycles, playing in and around the lake, making songs of their travels and almighty leader. Even Lord Thandrua gave them extra time to relax before calling in the new cycle, allowing them to stay curled up absorbing the heat from the ground just a while longer before going back to the festivities.

After two cycles of party came and two cycles went, they wasted no more time and dove quickly into their new routine. Thandrua would wake and declare the new cycle, the Cobra Clan would distribute the tools amongst the Serpenoids, then lead them away from the lake in the direction opposite of the mountain. Sectoraus suggested that they dig out of sight from the valley they rested in.

The Serpenoids dug a hole throughout most of the cycle, first digging wide around to make a large circle, then focusing on depth in creating a pit until the Cobras would lead them back to the camp to replenish their thirst. If they had found anything they would travel to the cave that contained the oven within the volcano, which Sectoraus and Thandrua dubbed the Kiln. After melting down the metal they would return to camp to slumber. They dug a ditch into a full mine over the span of five cycles before finding anything worth a trip to the Kiln.

The Serpenoids would do this and build more tools to aid their task: wheelbarrows, chains, and hammers. Designs provided by Sectoraus, which seemed to come to him naturally as though he had been the director of such a job his entire life.

Within the rock, at times, they found beautiful precious gems. Whenever the opportunity arose, they would present Thandrua with breathtaking gems. The gems Thandrua fell in love with instantly, giving each of them different names to describe them. Oh, how they sparkled with his reflection, the emeralds mimicking his eyes, the rubies akin to his red leathery hide.

Lord Thandrua grew tired of standing and sitting on top of the boulders that his followers had rolled into their valley. Once enough of the metal Thandrua had called "gold" had been obtained, he had the Serpenoids fashion an elegant throne for him to sit on with his mighty grace. This throne sparkled with emeralds, sapphires, rubies, and any gems they could find. Thandrua would sit on his lavish royal seat by the shore of the clear lake until the end of each cycle.

In time, Thandrua gave the order to stop production of tools, which had become more than plentiful. Now he demanded the search to procure more gold and gems. With Sectoraus' intuitive wisdom, the Cobra designed a tunnel system for the Serpenoids to better excavate in the hole, and called it "a mine."

They did their routines every cycle, collecting whatever metals and gems they could find, until their dig site became too deep, too wide and didn't show any signs of significant treasures. After they rendered one mine barren, they would walk further from that site, going further out from the Kiln, and begin another mine. The gargantuan mountain, which Thandrua named the "World's Mountain," shrank from sight out by these mines.

While the Serpenoids were out mining, Thandrua and Sectoraus would stay behind sharing their thoughts with one another. Together the two would brainstorm on their new society while observing the serene view of the lake. After some cycles, they reconfigured the Serpenoids' system. Seeing how large and deep a mine may go and how much material they may find, the leaders decided to split the workers into two groups. Orpheus and Solarious led a team to the dig site while Phineus monitored a team in the Kiln. This was especially effective once they obtained enough metals to keep the Serpenoids busy with the furnace throughout a cycle.

That's how it was and that's how the Serpenoids were separated into their jobs. A new level in their colony's small caste system, one made of miners and one of forgers and welders. With all the progress and especially all the beautiful jewelry the Serpenoids' Lord decorated himself with, Thandrua saw this to be good. The two teams would have the chance to reconnect with one another during their "recreation" time after working, when all would congregate at the lake for a little while before going to sleep in the valley on a nearby plateau. However, even in their sleep, in time did they seem to separate into their working groups.

Because the two teams were filled with thousands of eager workers toiling at the same time, they were at times permitted to have whole cycles off duty. There was a wealth of land in their new world and there was no haste in digging it all up at once.

Sectoraus noticed that the sand and gravel would harden after being mixed with water and left to dry. He suggested to Thandrua to use this method and create slumber chambers on the plateau over the hill that led toward the lake, one for the miners, one for the welders, and one for himself to share with the Cobra Clan. These shelters were built just tall enough for Thandrua to stand inside of and large enough for all the Serpenoids to curl up on the floor peacefully to sleep. There was enough space for some to walk about if they had to step out, but mostly they were nestled snugly together to save space.

The Lord's chamber, though only occupied by Thandrua and the Cobra Clan, was twice as spacious as the others. While standing, there was plenty of room between the tips of Thandrua's horns and the ceiling of the chamber. It was spacious enough to fit most of the colony if needed. Before the Serpenoids would turn in for slumber, Thandrua would arrange for a few to carry his throne into his slumber chamber, where he would sleep encircled by the Cobra Clan who curled up on the ground before him.

At the end of every cycle, Thandrua would walk about and observe the camp. He would see their hard work in the exhaustion of the Serpenoids returning from their job sites and watch their satisfaction as they enjoyed some time at the lake before slumber. Thandrua saw this and said it was good. The Serpenoids enjoyed their work and he loved that they were fulfilled. He found the gems they presented to him to be marvelous, all the different colors he had never experienced before, glimmering in his eyes. In some way they reminded him of the billions of stars filling up the sky of their last world.

As more gems were presented to Thandrua he would ask them to be inlaid on his throne. In time his throne became busy with gems, and he no longer wanted his seat to be encrusted with precious stones. Thandrua still wanted some of the gold to be visible for his pleasure. When the Serpenoids discovered the volcano's obsidian material could be polished into crystal, Thandrua ordered for a staff to be made. An elegant accessory that he requested to be a mix of the obsidian and onyx gemstones. The top of his staff held dark purple amethyst crystals for contrast. The more gems they found, the more interested he became in them. Especially the rubies, he always found them most pleasant for they resembled his complexion. Thandrua kept his collection of jewels piled in his chamber.

The time Sectoraus and Thandrua had spent together just gazing out at the horizon or occasionally sharing ideas dwindled as their lust to ogle and hoard the gemstones increased. Thandrua ordered the welders to create a golden scepter for Sectoraus to show his rank. In the reddish orange desolate world, Lord Thandrua and the Clan sparkled as they decorated themselves with jewels. A greedy monarch he and Sectoraus became, while the hard-working Serpenoids never rejected a single order.

Chapter 6
A Change in the Balance

On one cycle, like any other, the miners dug thoroughly in the ground while some smashed chunks of rock with large hammers. Other than some small chatter here and there, they mostly remained silent save for the grunts and groans of their exhaustion. Even the two Cobras, Orpheus and Solarious, stood in silence as they monitored the Serpenoids, hoods relaxed. There was a time when the Cobras would meditate during the labor, but as the cycles went on, they meditated less and just blankly watched the miners hard at work. In the distance there was a sound carried through the air interrupting the silence with a start. A sound familiar long ago in their old world, but now so many cycles had come to pass since that life that it was a sound forgotten. It was the sound of thunder.

The miners stopped digging and listened, dropping their tools on the tough terrain. The rumble of thunder was a sound heard often on the former lands; it usually came with a storm. Since they arrived in this new world, however, they have yet to hear thunder. It never rained in the new world and there weren't any clouds to produce rain for that matter.

The thunder quieted after an intense crackle and there was no change in the weather. Cautiously looking about, the miners continued their digging. Orpheus and Solarious continued to scan the skies for any sign of clouds or precipitation, anything. With his keen sight, Solarious stared out in the desert, noticing a figure barely visible in the distance. He nudged his clan brother and pointed towards the figure.

"Orpheus, do you see that?"

"What do you speak of?" Orpheus squinted his yellow eyes in the direction Solarious' claw pointed, "I think, perhaps…" The figure came into his sight better and he could see it, whatever it was, moving closer. "Hardly can tell, but I believe I see it now," The indistinct figure came closer into view, and they could make out that it walked on two legs, "Not something but perhaps, some*one!*" He stood to look over the Serpenoids. "Have any of the miners strayed and gotten lost? Or could that perhaps be one of our scouts searching for a new location?"

"We have yet to send anyone, this mine still holds more stones." Solarious focused all his vision onto the figure, "I do not think that is a Serpenoid."

The figure was walking in their direction, becoming easier to see the closer it moved. The creature walked poorly on its two feet stumbling onto its sides with every other step. It held itself with its two arms wrapped around its chest, then fell to the ground after a few more steps.

"It fell, you see?" Solarious pointed again.

"Whatever that was, it does not seem to move anymore." Orpheus said, glaring as hard as he could, "We should go over, it may need help. Perhaps it *is* a Serpenoid lost and wandering about? I do not see any missing in the numbers, but perhaps we have overlooked one. Oh, by Thandrua, perhaps from another cycle!"

With the tension of this unexpected occurrence the two Cobras flattened their neck muscles, opening up their broad hoods. They both left the Serpenoids attending to their task and ran over to the figure they had seen. A few Serpenoids saw their supervisors leave in a hurry and began telling the others that something was happening.

There was still no movement from the fallen wanderer as Solarious and his brother approached. Standing over it and staring at it blankly, the thing was revealed to be a creature unlike any of them. Two arms and two legs seemed to be all the likeness they shared. It had a single head, but with short white hair on its scalp and its hide was a soft fair skin in place of scales. Its tail was missing. Its feet contained five toes with no talons, its hands with five fingers but no claws.

The creature laid crookedly on the ground and bled from two small stumps behind its shoulder blades. It quivered slightly as the Cobras watched. It was clothed with nothing but the sand that stuck to its bloodied body.

"You believe this… *creature*... is alive?" Orpheus knelt to the ground, observing.

"It no longer seems to breathe." Solarious placed two fingers under the creature's small angular nose, then lowered his head to listen by the creature's mouth, "although I think I hear something."

The sound was very tiny, very faint, barely even a sound at all, but it came from the creature's mouth. It was speaking unconscious mutterings, completely indistinct, but words they were. The two silenced and did their best to concentrate on what was being said. They couldn't make out a single word.

"Can you hear what is said?" Orpheus asked Solarious.

"Nonsense, but it sounds almost as if it were pleading." Solarious said.

"What-- what do we do?" Orpheus looked to his brother.

Solarious thought for a moment before answering, "We should take this creature back to Lord Thandrua."

With his massive strength, Orpheus carried the creature in his arms while Solarious gathered the miners to return to camp. As they approached nearer to the lake, all the curious miners crowded behind. Thandrua sat in his bejeweled throne by the lake, staring at the gold and rubies reflecting off the water. Sectoraus stood on Thandrua's right hand side, holding his newly constructed scepter as he gazed at it admiringly.

"Looks like the miners have returned early today, Thandrua." Sectoraus pointed out.

"I think they are carrying a body; someone must have gotten hurt." Lord Thandrua stood from his throne and Sectoraus displayed his hood while his tail curled slightly as the two hurried to meet with the crowd.

"What has happened?" The crimson king asked.

The Serpenoids, as curious as they were, stopped several feet away from Lord Thandrua. Orpheus placed the body on the floor, "We found this creature roaming alone past the mine. It was weak and fell. We thought you could help this creature, my Lord."

"Sectoraus, bring it to the water and clean it up." Thandrua ordered.

Sectoraus pulled it by the arms to the lake and washed the blood from its skin. He poured water into the creature's mouth (in which Sectoraus was surprised to see small flat teeth instead of the thin sharp fangs like his own) and the being's eyelids began to quiver and open slowly. The Creature's blurred vision focused on the yellow slits staring down at him. "It can't be!" It gasped and then fainted into unconsciousness again. Thandrua pushed the creature's body with his foot and turned to Sectoraus who had relaxed his hood.

"Leave it lying there, I suppose it will wake when it's ready." Thandrua scanned what the miners had brought with them from the cycle's labor, "Send the miners back to their duties."

"Alright miners, return to your site!"

Although disappointed, thinking they had done enough for the cycle, the Serpenoids returned to their work as ordered. Sectoraus studied the creature while he tossed and turned in the dirt. He was mumbling under his breath. The only words Sectoraus was able to understand was "Please" and more peculiar, "Father."

"Hmm. Thandrua, what do you suppose it meant when it said, 'It can't be'? And what do you know of 'father'? That word is strange to me."

"I only know of the Serpenoids. I suppose we just have to wait for it to awaken."

Sectoraus thought a great deal to himself. There had only ever been the Serpenoids. It was majestic when Thandrua first arrived in their lives, but now there is another being. *What did it mean, could there be more?*

The cycle passed on and the miners returned with their work completed. The forgers, who typically worked longer, were still absent from the rest of the colony. Thandrua met with the miners to inspect the load of stones they brought back with them. This time he was more satisfied.

The creature began to stir and pull himself to the water. Sectoraus helped him drink before he sat up. The Cobra leader ran to Thandrua to inform him the creature was now awake. The two returned with a rush of Serpenoids that followed to cure their curiosity. The creature rubbed his eyes and looked up at the ivory horns that came out above Thandrua's brow and curved over his head, then down to his green eyes.

"My body is in pain," he moaned

"Drink more water, Creature, it will help." Lord Thandrua spoke directly to him before Sectoraus could interject, "We have not lived here terribly long, but I have not seen any others before. Are you from here?"

"No, but I suppose this is my new home."

"Very well then, welcome to our sanctuary." Sectoraus greeted, "I am Sectoraus, king of the Cobras. This here is the Almighty Lord Thandrua, lifegiver of the Serpenoids and ruler of the land." He stood proud when he introduced himself, as did Thandrua.

Still very weak, the creature managed to squeeze a raspy chuckle before saying, "*Lifegiver!* HAHA! Is that what you believe?" He began to lift himself from the ground before Sectoraus pushed him back to the ground with his left foot, then cracked the creature across the side of his face with his golden scepter.

"You will not speak so condescendingly of Lord Thandrua!" Hissed Sectoraus, hood unfolding open in his anger.

"Oh, how foolish, how ignorant you are, *all* of you!" The creature held himself up with his hands, then beneath his voice, "Most of all *you.* If you are unknown to these monsters, those *other ones* will never have a chance." He seemed to be staring beyond the towering hulk and the snarling Cobras, as if speaking to an invisible force. A stir of confusion broke throughout the onlookers, the pale grey eyes of the beaten creature shifted back onto Thandrua. "Lift me. I am more of a god than this beast. Make me your deity now."

In a growling rage, Thandrua started forward, he had taken all the blasphemy a god-king could take and felt the throbbing urge in his beefy palms to wring them around the foul-mouthed creature's slender neck. Snarling through the sharp yellow teeth he clenched together, his aggression became futile as Sectoraus stepped between the enraged beast and the mysterious visitor, slamming the bottom of his scepter onto the creature's head once again and rendering him unconscious as a cut split open above his left eyebrow.

"That should teach it a lesson," Sectoraus snorted then scanned the spectators, "Orpheus! Use the chains from the Kiln to subdue the Creature. Ensure that it does not escape."

"As you wish." Orpheus gave a curt nod then turned and jogged toward the trail of volcanic smoke.

"See to it that Phineus and the forgers return as well!" Thandrua hollered after, then turned to his still curious followers. "This cycle has been long enough; I will have to dismiss recreation and declare for this cycle to come to an end." Some unenthused chatter sprung up amongst the Serpenoids, but Thandrua spoke over them. "Recreation will be extended for tomorrow's cycle, but for now let us slumber and move away from this cycle. That is all."

"You heard your Lord!" Sectoraus shot an intimidating glower to the unhappy Serpenoids. They took the hint and did as they were ordered, retreating into their mud-made hut.

The Serpenoids laid on the ground but could not yet end their cycle. Filled with unanswered questions, they spoke of what they had just witnessed. They were curious and scared. Scared of what the creature had said. Scared of what the introduction of this creature could mean. But most of all, they were scared from the reactions of their leaders. Never once had they witnessed such displays of violence. They spoke of how Sectoraus forced them to their chamber with his vicious glare. It was frightening to think of Sectoraus behaving that way toward them.

Some time later, Phineus returned with his welders, along with Orpheus that held several thick chains, and sent the welders to their chamber once learning that the end of the cycle had been declared. Solarious greeted his reddish-brown brother and gestured for the two to join their leaders by the lake.

"Yes, Orpheus briefly mentioned that you two have found a… *creature* of some sorts." Phineus said while they descended the hill that led to the lake.

"I told him little." Orpheus panted, as Phineus gave him a hand with the chains. "I figured it best not to arouse much commotion with the rest of the Serpenoids and better to see for himself."

"Very wise indeed," is all Solarious said, but by then they had reached their horned master and tall brother that stood above a motionless body on the shore of the lake.

Orpheus wrapped the chains tight around the creature's arms and legs, still out cold, but if he were to wake, he would not be able to move a muscle. Solarious explained to Phineus how they found the creature and Sectoraus filled him in on the rest while the brute twisted the chains, then they moved to their respective slumber chamber as well. Solarious aided Orpheus with carrying their prisoner.

They all slept soundly and peacefully, the miners had drifted well away by the time the rest arrived and the forgers, although filled with mystery as to what had happened and what was being kept quiet, found sleep with ease knowing they would be informed by the following cycle. There was one of the blacksmiths that lingered by the royal chamber, attempting to settle his curiosity by peering into the entryway. However, Orpheus came out and blocked the entrance, crossed his arms, and stared down the Serpenoid until he too retreated for slumber.

The Cobras slept in their usual circle on the ground, but instead of Thandrua in the center they kept the creature closed in. Yes, they too flowed with the peaceful ocean of slumber, all did, except for Thandrua. He slept sitting on his throne and grunted occasionally in distress. He was having a bad dream. The word "tolerance" repeated in his head as he tossed his body left to right on his seat. Thandrua saw the creature, enlarged, hovering above and cackling as he pointed a wicked finger mockingly down at Thandrua. He felt a terrible pain throughout his body. Finally, Thandrua awoke, frustrated with his lack of sleep and insecure pride. He directed his attention to the still unconscious creature.

Lord Thandrua snatched his staff as he stomped over in a rush, stepping over Solarious, and cracked the creature in the ribs with his staff. He woke with a yelp, causing the Serpenoids to rush out from both huts, still bleary eyed. Thandrua began to kick him.

"How dare you come onto my land and insult my authority! Miners, you are relieved from your work this cycle," He pointed to the group that crowded the entryway, "this creature will take over for you. Sectoraus, take him to the mines."

"As you wish, my Lord." A sinister grin formed onto the cobra king's face. *The Creature will learn respect down there.* "Clan, take him to the mines, we have a new recruit."

Orpheus pulled the creature by the dangling chains as his body dragged on his back, headfirst, and the rest of the Cobra Clan followed. The active mine was a decent hike away. The short white hair of the prisoner became stained with orange from the sand, the flesh on his back burned from the friction and his two stumps flared with pain. However, the slit above his eye seemed to have healed over in his sleep.

They had passed three of the former mines that were left barren before reaching the current one. The chains were untangled before being shoved into the mine and the weakened visitor slowly raised to his feet before a shovel was tossed at him. The prisoner stood there defiantly until the hissing Cobras began to pelt him with rocks, forcing him to dig. Time dragged as the prisoner made excruciatingly slow progress digging the hole deeper and wider. The supervisors watched their slave, their broad hoods making them look menacing as he unearthed some chunks of quartz, but nothing truly interesting and they therefore continued to push him further.

In time, the Cobras grew tired; judging by their weariness they agreed it must have been near the end of the cycle. Orpheus and Solarious hopped down into the mine. The prisoner turned at the sound of their drop and thrust his hand out, but Solarious had leapt forward and secured the shovel before the creature could resist. A moment later Orpheus threw his weight into a punch straight at the creature's face. His nose cracked and he fell backward unconscious, they doubted he was dead. Phineus tossed down the chains from above when he saw the creature had been incapacitated. They dragged him all the way back.

The Serpenoids had a long leisurely day, it had completely made up for the recreation they had missed on the previous cycle.

Thandrua sat on his throne at the edge of the lake, gazing into the ripples of the reflected jewels. He made a gesture with his right hand at Sectoraus, who stood silently at his right, then slowly stood from his seat.

"Your Lord request this cycle to come to its closure!" Sectoraus announced slowly turning in place to see all the Serpenoids around, "Return to your chambers and rest well, until Lord Thandrua may bless us with the next cycle!"

"Hail Lord Thandrua!" The Serpenoids chanted all around the valley, the hillside and lake, then proceeded toward the two chambers over the hill. Sectoraus pulled three Serpenoids to the side to carry Thandrua's throne into his chamber. Some of the Serpenoids swam from the lake, most were already on the land by the hills, but they managed to separate themselves into miners and welders again and one by one entered the two large mud-huts. The trio of Cobras came marching in with their beaten prisoner as they saw the Serpenoids filing into their huts. A small smirk flicked Solarious' face as he understood why he felt so sure the cycle was coming to an end. They snaked their way around the Serpenoids heading for slumber and retreated into the spacious hut they shared with Thandrua.

While everyone slept, Thandrua had another dream. He was completely alone, surrounded by a blanket of darkness so thick he could barely even see his body before him. Thandrua panicked; where could he have been in such darkness? He tried running, perhaps he was inside of a cave and if he moved, he might be able to find the reassuring orange glow of the sky. There was no glow, and he hadn't left the spot he had been in. Thandrua clutched at himself, grabbing for his gold necklaces that hung around his neck -- they weren't there. He didn't know what to do, he called for Sectoraus in desperation. No response. At last, a light broke from the darkness and before his eyes was a giant ball of light, the same light from his premonition. It spoke in its frightful and calming voice:

"You have done wrong, Thandrua."

"How do you mean? I led the Serpenoids to the paradise, I made the tools just as instructed."

"Your prisoner is what I refer to, the one you call Creature."

"What am I to do? It threatened my superiority and in front of my followers!"

"He gave you words and in return you gave him pain. Besides, a true leader mustn't feel threatened surrounded by one's followers. Superiority is held in the faith of one's followers, not in the praise one demands. A wise leader should understand their place, confident yes, but never with arrogance."

"Easy for a hallucination to say."

"Release your prisoner. He serves a penance to be removed from his home, not enslavement. To learn humility and rise from it. Remember to be patient and tolerant, in time he will be integrated into your colony and may prove to be a valuable asset."

"What if I continue to use his labor?"

"I hope that you too would not need to learn humility, but perhaps that is the only route laid out before you."

"Oh, is that so? I cannot be removed from this land. My followers will not let it happen."

"If your followers follow you too blindly then they too would have to experience humility. I warn you, a plague could be unleashed here."

"What do you mean, *plague?*"

"A plague. Something unfortunate to upset the very paradise I have given you. Something that would hopefully restore balance."

Thandrua thought for a moment before responding. The matter-of-fact way the light had spoken angered Thandrua more than frightened. "You are just a dream, my subconscious guilting me, since I have never brought harm to anyone. How will you curse my home if you do not even exist?"

"You do not know it yet, but I am as real as you, and I hold more authority than you may realize. Just listen. When a foreigner resides among you in your land, do not--"

"You can tell me things that I do not know, somehow, that is all! I do not need you and that *creature* is my servant indefinitely."

"I hoped it would not have come to this, Thandrua."

The figure of a hand stretched out from the light towards Thandrua. The index finger touched him over his left eye. Thandrua woke in pain, screaming and covered his left eye. The Cobras woke with a jolt, all four displayed their hoods as they sprung from the ground. Even the Serpenoids awoke startled from both huts, and all rushed out to Thandrua's shelter once again. They tried pouring into the chamber, but the Cobra Clan guarded the entryway, holding back the pushing bodies. A searing burning sensation penetrated Thandrua's left eye. He removed his hand, revealing a fresh scar.

"Thandrua, what has happened to your eye?" Sectoraus knelt before him, gazing up with concern. The scar was formed in the same shape as the symbol that held the portal to this world. The Cobras turned their heads in response to Sectoraus' question, a few of the Serpenoids pushed passed before Orpheus directed his force back to guarding, the other two Cobras pulled out the few Serpenoids that made it inside. At the doorway, all the Serpenoids craned their necks attempting to see their lifegiver. The Serpenoids were scared, they panicked from hearing the sound of their leader in agony as Thandrua began to grope his eye again. A soft chuckle was released from the worn-out prisoner that sat in the middle of the commotion.

"You did this!" Sectoraus pointed towards him, "Orpheus, punish him."

Orpheus charged towards the creature, snarling with anger. He was stopped by Thandrua's voice.

"Leave him be!" Thandrua was off his throne, he stood tall. He walked to the creature, stared him down, and cleared his throat before speaking.

"I apologize for the previous cycle."

"Maybe if you asked more questions, you would have understood that I was only joking." The prisoner lifted himself from the ground and sneered at his would-be punisher. "I suppose you don't even understand what jokes are anyway, all the apologies are mine."

"I find the tone in your voice questionable, but I will not think too much about it. Let me restart. I am Thandrua, I rule the Serpenoids as well as this land. Who may you be, Creature?"

"I am a castaway, abandoned by the ones that once loved me."

"How tragic," Thandrua narrowed his eyes as he towered over the newcomer. "Do you not possess a name?"

"I hold my name in mourning, Thandrua."

"You refer to him as *Lord* Thandrua." Sectoraus snapped before pulling his right hand back to smack across the prisoner's already broken face, but Lord Thandrua caught his arm before he could get the satisfaction.

"No, Sectoraus, let me speak with him more. He is new and it is obvious he does not understand our culture."

"Your servants should learn to keep to themselves." Said the creature and didn't flinch when Sectoraus hissed at him before storming out of the chamber, clearly offended. Thandrua had never restrained him before.

"That is Sectoraus, my loyal companion, he is no servant of mine. Only he calls me Thandrua. The others refer to me as 'Master' or 'Lord'. If you are to be in my kingdom you must understand this. We have never met any other beings. We are not used to such informality or lack of respect, but you are new and do not yet understand who or what I am. It was I that brought life to the Serpenoids." Thandrua held his head high, "They recognize me as their lifegiver. They have known of my true nature for countless cycles; they worship me, and you will learn to do so as well."

"Ha! You wish you were *the God*."

All the Serpenoids gasped and gulped nervously. They whispered amongst themselves, "How could he say such a thing?" The Cobra Clan stood together glaring at the slanderer from a distance. Thandrua slanted his hairless brow, flared his nostrils then forced a smile upon his face.

"What is *that* supposed to mean?"

"What happened to your eye?" The creature had a smirk across his face, an awkward silence fell on the group. Thandrua gently touched the scar over his left eye, the stinging sensation lingered still.

"You insult my status, my honor! I gave you a chance to redeem yourself and you disrespect me! You disrespect the intelligence of my followers. I am done with you, *Creature*. Orpheus, escort the Creature to the deepest barren mine. Drop him in and stand guard. You will remain in that hole until you learn to respect me as the Almighty that I am."

"Then it will be a long time until we see each other again... *Oh Great Lord Thandrua*."

The black and yellow spotted brute yanked a dangling chain from the prisoner's bonds, leading him away from the resting area until they reached a hole deep enough to hold their prisoner. Sectoraus ordered Phineus to take the miners to the working spot. He had also sent Solarious with the blacksmiths to the Kiln. There was one of the smiths that had to be called after, who stood gazing out to where the creature was being dragged. Once they had all departed, finally Thandrua and Sectoraus were alone.

"That creature is insatiable!" Sectoraus gestured outward, "It was very difficult for me to allow it to speak to you in such a way."

"You did your best, my friend. My being has never been questioned by any. Myself from time to time, but mostly to keep myself in check."

Sectoraus nodded to himself thoughtfully before speaking again. "Thandrua, may I ask you?" He let the words hang, as if uncertain to even continue. The Cobra turned around, took a couple steps away while his hood relaxed, then turned back to his master, "What *has* happened to your eye?"

Thandrua traced two fingers along the still stinging mark. He passed Sectoraus, stepping out of the hut, and stared toward the World's Mountain in the distance beyond the vast shimmering lake. The mountain was broad, strong, it embodied the way Thandrua perceived himself to be. At this moment, the awesome structure only reminded the god-king of how he was beginning to feel, vulnerable and weak.

"Only you can I tell this to." Finally, Thandrua broke the silence, "I was dreaming, dreaming about the Sun and it burned me. I awoke with my eye aching and this scar to bear."

"The dream hurt you? That is *quite* bizarre."

Thandrua turned around to face his most loyal follower. Sectoraus seemed perplexed, so Thandrua explained further. "This is not the same Sun from our past home, but the light in my premonition."

"Another light? Oh! Forgive me, I almost forgot. The one that told you how to get to the canyon leading us to this world?"

"The same."

"I do not understand, Thandrua."

"Neither do I. It claims to be its own entity, to be real outside of my dreams. It did not elaborate much, but stated it can do things and then did this to me to prove its point. This… *light*, referred to itself as the *Creator* in the premonition."

An uncomfortable silence followed. With the Serpenoids away working, there was nothing to cut the silence. Only the sound of the air between them. The god-king stared at his loyal companion, unsure what to say next, if anything at all. Thandrua shifted his stare to the amethyst of the staff in his hand. He rotated the staff, watching his distorted reflection in its facets.

Sectoraus himself felt overwhelmed with the news. First, the arrival of an insubordinate being unlike any of them, then the revelation that the precognition of their pilgrimage was truly outside of his lord's doing, coming from some other mysterious being. And how did he allow himself to forget about the Light all this time until now? Was Sectoraus so far in denial that Thandrua's power might have limitations that he suppressed the very thought that would challenge his beliefs? Finally, after a great deal of silence Thandrua spoke again:

"I am disfigured now," he hung his head low, "I am not the untouchable I perceived myself to be."

"No," Sectoraus said flatly, Thandrua lifted his horned head to look at him. "You are Thandrua, everything that makes what you are is spectacular. Whether you are Almighty or not, you are still my master and ruler of the Serpenoids." The long black claws from his right hand scratched thoughtfully under his neck, "I shall return, I need to wander." Sectoraus left Thandrua's side before his companion could make any inquiries.

Sectoraus went out of the valley. The sand gave way as the distressed Cobra stomped up the dunes. Sectoraus had no destination in mind, just heavy with thought. The Cobra thought of the conversation he had just had with Thandrua before walking off.

The Creator... creator of what? Where are its creations? This despicable creature may be Its creation. Yes, it would have to be. That would explain why that thing is so dishonorable! Thandrua said It called the Fire, the Sun. It must be the creator of that ghastly thing as well! How else could it know? Yes, if this really is some Creator, *it is the creator of abominations! It created that scar on Thandrua's face... the scar! It is the same as the marking in the canyon, the symbol that led us here. Did it create this place? This is no abomination, this is a true home.*

Sectoraus looked to the opening of the Kiln on his left, then back to where he had left Thandrua behind. *That marking means something. It is our salvation. Thandrua bears the marking now. Perhaps this Creator is trying to tell us that Thandrua* is *our salvation. He has only ever done what is best.* With a spark in his yellow eyes, Sectoraus was struck with an idea, *The marking is a symbol,* and went towards the volcano.

At the cave, Sectoraus informed Solarious of his idea, then the two directed the blacksmiths to design a new mold for the molten metal. All standard production was placed on hold, though the forgers didn't mind much. These orders came directly from Sectoraus, and they followed every word he said as if it came from the Lord Thandrua himself. The process wasn't overly difficult. A group of four carved the design into stone slabs until one created something that satisfied Sectoraus' vision. Once there was a final design all blacksmiths wanted to volunteer to work on the mold, creating duplicates and filling the molten metal into the grooves creating an emblem.

Sectoraus remained silent and kept to himself while the iron cooled. He thought of their prisoner. He still could not understand how the Creature was so different from them. Its soft smooth flesh, its hair! What perplexed him most of all was the audacity of the being, completely alone and who knew how far it was from its home, yet it felt confident enough to act as it did. *No, that is not a good creation. It is like the Sun, sinister! If there are more creatures like that one, they cannot be benevolent. Not for us.*

Sectoraus pounded a fist against the side of the cave. *Look at me now! I am thinking as though I believe in this light of Thandrua's dreams! This so-called* Creator *may have done some good, but it cannot be entirely benevolent. Not with things like the Sun taking away our last home and not with this Creature interfering with our paradise. If this Creator is some kind of entity outside of Thandrua's dreams, then it must be a malignant force slandering our faith in our Lord Thandrua. This emblem, however, should guide the Serpenoids in the right direction.*

"What troubles you, brother?" Solarious approached with care.

"Nothing." Sectoraus straightened himself up, "I am fine, there is no trouble."

"Well, it is just that," Solarious seemed to be looking for the correct words, "you seem to be deep in thought and it concerned me, for I cannot feel any thoughts coming from you. You have closed yourself to me - why is that, Sectoraus?"

The Cobra king moved away, "I just do not understand what is happening."

"If you are frightened, brother," Solarious placed his hand onto his brother's shoulder, "do not be ashamed. I, too, am frightened. How could our Lord be hurt in such a mysterious way? And that Creature… I just have no idea what to think."

"Do not think. We still have each other, and nothing will take that."

"Come then, it is almost done cooling. Do not be alone."

***

Lord Thandrua sat in his throne along the lake watching the miners enjoy their recreation and playing happily in the crisp water. The Serpenoids laughed as they splashed each other, picking up and throwing one another into the cool liquid. Some swam about while others floated restfully on by. All, however, kept relatively close by. The water stretched far out to the grand towering mountain and all the Serpenoids felt more comfortable near one another.

Lord Thandrua chuckled to himself, overcome with the joy around him. His pleasures were interrupted after a while when he reached for the scar over his eye. *Shall this pain recede?* Thandrua thought as he edged forward on his seat, staring down at the water that crept along the shoreline by his feet. He gazed at his wavering reflection, traced a finger over the marking. The beastly deity winced with pain and knelt at the edge of the water. He cupped the liquid in his hands and splashed it against his irritated face. Thandrua looked at the reflection again as his eyes were caught by the large ruby that dangled from a golden chain around his neck. He put the ruby to his eye and the cold that emanated from the stone soothed the burn.

Standing up from the water, Thandrua saw a group hiking down the dunes toward the valley. He could make out the figures of Sectoraus and Solarious leading the blacksmiths from the Kiln. He rubbed his wet eyes when he saw that Orpheus and Phineus marched with their brothers as well and went to meet them.

"Sectoraus, who is in watch of the Creature?"

"Not to worry, Thandrua. Four miners are standing guard while Orpheus and Phineus are here. They will return to their post shortly. As a group we must show you our love and appreciation for you."

"Oh, Sectoraus, if this is in regard to what we spoke of earlier... I am highly aware of the love from your clan and my lovely followers."

"This is more than that, my Lord." Sectoraus stood at the lead as the rest of the Cobra Clan separated themselves from the Serpenoids. "This is about our devoutness, Lord Thandrua."

All four Cobras turned their left arms, showing off their bicep. A fresh seared wound occupied the center. The scent of charred scales and flesh still lingered from the moist blistered scars. It was in the form of the mysterious symbol on Thandrua's face, containing an almond shaped eye with a vertical slit pupil representing Thandrua's very own.

"You are not alone Thandrua. We, too, are now scarred."

Thandrua approached his advisor and took hold of his arm. A tear came to his eyes as he observed the markings on the other three arms. "That marking is haunting, as well as a blessing. However, your gesture brings me joy and it changes my opinion. This is no scar; this is a symbol. It is our symbol, representing how we have overcome death and continue to reign supreme!"

"Precisely!" Sectoraus turned to face the crowd, "Serpenoids, pause with your leisure and listen to me! This cycle, Lord Thandrua awoke in pain, bearing this marking. The same marking that brought us to this sanctuary, the marking that powers our society!" Sectoraus paused and scanned across the sea of yellow eyes, all rapturously fixed on his every movement. "The marking is completed as a symbol with Thandrua's eye in the center. Thandrua is almighty and wise. Our Lord is always watching and will always be on our side. The Eye of Thandrua is the insignia that symbolizes our order and keeps our faith strong!"

The Serpenoids applauded Sectoraus' speech and bowed their heads in Thandrua's direction, then rushed forward crowding the Cobra Clan. Everyone wanted to see the symbol up close. They awed as they viewed the seared flesh. They all recognized the marking from the canyon. Earlier that cycle, the Serpenoids were confused when it appeared on their deity's face, confused and frightened. Seeing it on the Cobra's arms, however, filled them with longing. They all clamored to have one of their own.

Chapter 7
The Birth of the Oracle

Three cycles passed with the prisoner remaining in the barren mine unchained; the depth of the hole made it impossible for him to crawl out. Everything within the Serpenoids' way of life returned to normal. Thandrua sat on his throne by the lake with the Cobra sporting the dark brown and beige look standing at his side. They spent one cycle comparing jewels, another thinking of new ways to use metal. It was Sectoraus who presented the idea to create cuffs and locks to better restrain the lonesome prisoner.

Quite a distance away, the majority of the Serpenoids dug in the ground searching for metals and gemstones while Orpheus and Phineus patrolled around the mines. Not far off from the other side of their camp, in the Kiln, the rest of the Serpenoids melted and molded the metal from the previous day under the guide of Solarious.

Time came and fled as the cycle gradually ended. All the Serpenoids regrouped by the lake, the Cobras sat on the ground in a line facing Thandrua's throne, their hoods down, and the rest sat behind them. Thandrua stood from his golden seat, turning to face his assembly, and raised his staff up high:

"You all have done well, there has been a great amount of work done and for this we are all grateful. Now, it is time for this cycle to come to an end; we shall rest our eyes and bodies until the cycle is ready to begin anew."

The Serpenoids were disappointed. They had worked harder than usual and were called to slumber before they had time for recreation. The Serpenoids had yet to even clean themselves from their work. But Thandrua was tired and ready to end the cycle, so Sectoraus ordered three Serpenoids to move Thandrua's throne back into his shelter. After the beastly god-king stepped into his home and returned to his seat, the Serpenoids bowed their heads before moving to their respective slumber chambers. The miners went off to the one on the right of Thandrua's, the forgers to the one on the left. They curled up their bodies on the ground close by one another, and soon after they were all fast asleep. The peaceful sounds from the Serpenoids' breathing filled the silence around them.

One slender Serpenoid within the forgers' shelter, however, wasn't sleeping at all and cautiously stood from the ground. The Serpenoid scanned the sea of sleeping soot-covered bodies to make sure everyone was asleep. Being extra cautious, he stepped over one body, then another, and exited the round hole to the outside. Glancing to the large domed shelter that housed his leaders, he crept to the entrance and peered in, confirming the Cobra Clan peacefully sleeping curled around the throne, in which slumped a very unconscious Lord Thandrua. He inched his way to the crystal-clear lake and picked up a stone bowl left on the shoreline. The Serpenoid drank from the lake, washed the black from his scaly greenish brown face, then refilled the bowl. He walked away from the group, a long way, out of the valley and past the Kiln, constantly glancing over his shoulder to ensure nobody took notice of his absence. The sight of the camp faded away. Finally, he seemed to have reached his destination, stopping just before the ground dropped into the barren mine which held the Creature.

The Serpenoid lowered to the ground and crawled to the edge of the hole. He peeked down. The prisoner held himself in a ball, legs curled to his chest and his arms wrapped around them. The Serpenoid studied the creature; he had only seen him from a distance crowded around the other Serpenoids before. The prisoner's pale skin was stained with mud and dried blood; however, he didn't seem to be physically scarred. The being had endured many blows to the abdomen and the head. The Serpenoid even recalled when Sectoraus drew blood from him, but his skin held no evidence. Even the two bloody stumps he had behind his shoulder blades had healed and shrank to look more like welts. The Serpenoid was startled when he heard a voice coming from inside the hole:

"I know you are watching me." The weak prisoner said, "What do you want?"

The Serpenoid remained silent. He tried to keep out of sight, but his curiosity caused him to continue peeking. The Creature looked up at him after several seconds of silence.

"Will you just stare? I know you are there. I can see your yellow eyes; they glow in this darkness."

Finally, after much reluctance, the curious Serpenoid responded, "Do… do you want some water, Creature?"

"I would appreciate that," with his mouth completely dry, the prisoner smacked his lips, anticipating the thirst quencher.

The Serpenoid held the bowl of water in his small hand and slowly attempted to lower it. The creature stood up and reached out his arms.

"I can't reach it, you are too high up. Just drop it straight down, I can catch it."

The Serpenoid did exactly as the prisoner said and dropped the bowl straight down into his hands. The prisoner quickly drank from the bowl, not making a sound nor spilling any. Leaving just enough water to pour it onto his head and wash the reddish tint from his white hair.

"Thank you." He sighed deeply with relief; some strength had already returned to his voice. "I haven't had water in a long time." Hands still wet, he rubbed his face, then smacked his lips some more, enjoying the remnants of moisture lingering within his mouth. "Who are you?"

"Wh--me?" The Serpenoid was confused.

"It is just you and I here. What is your name?"

"Name? You asked for my name?"

"Yes, I want to remember who you are. What do they call you?"

"Serpenoid."

"No, I mean to distinguish you from the other Serpenoids."

"Sometimes they call me blacksmith, welder, or forger."

"No, you misunderstand me. What do they call you when speaking directly to you?"

The welder thought about this for some time, scratching his scaly head, "They have no word for it, I am a blacksmith. Lord Thandrua speaks to the Cobra Clan with names, not to the rest of us Serpenoids."

"That won't do. You obviously think differently from the others, you deserve to be recognized differently."

"This is just our way, we are for the most part one and the same, so we do not get individuality, just the Cobras."

"But you are an individual. Since I am not of your society, I will give you a name."

"My *own* name? Perhaps I should have not come here."

"You did, though, and now you are here connecting with me. Nothing simply happens, there is always a reason. *Remember* that." He thought for a moment before addressing the Serpenoid again, "Vander, I shall name you Vander."

"Vander," the Serpenoid nodded his head thoughtfully before betraying a grin.

"Well, Vander, you did a very good deed. I am not the only one that would recognize that either, this I can guarantee."

Vander stood abruptly and looked all about. "Lord Thandrua will not be pleased with me here."

"Not who I meant, but never mind that now. You are correct though. Your *Lord* would not be pleased if he were to catch you aiding his enemy."

"What does *enemy* mean?"

"Oh, sweet innocent Vander… you will learn that in time. Now go."

"Yes, I must return now before someone notices my absence. Thank you."

Vander returned to the camp, cutting by the three domed shelters and quietly making his way down the hill of orange sand approaching the lake. Laying down to drink from the lake before returning to his hut, Vander's eyes began to hang heavy. It was a tiring walk from the camp to the pit which held the prisoner and before he knew it, he drifted into slumber.

His nostrils sniffed a foul stench in the air. His eyes fluttered from the sting of the charred scent, and he thought to himself, *something's wrong*. Vander flicked his eyelids open, sat up and looked around. He was still by the lake. Surely much time had passed, Vander thought it strange none of the others had found him there; surely they would have hydrated before setting out to the mines.

Where is everyone? Vander's mind in somewhat of a daze, the Serpenoid looked around him to find Thandrua's throne, which had toppled over into the lake. The back support was submerged in the water, legs up in the air. Gold and the various gems from the throne sparkled off the water's surface. That was when Vander noticed smoke in the water's reflection, coming from behind him. Vander spun around, his tail swishing on the ground behind him. He spotted the smoke over the sand dune leading to the camp, floating up into a thick black cloud.

He ran up the hill, the foul aroma strengthened. His heartbeat raced. He knew the smoke wasn't coming from the volcano of the Kiln, it was definitely the camp. *What is happening at the camp?* Once Vander reached the top he dropped to his knees. He couldn't believe his eyes.

Thousands of Serpenoids laid lifeless on the ground before him. Many bodies were mutilated, blood stained the sand. Most of the bodies were charred black, some still burned. Tears ran down his scaly face and dripped onto the sand. Vander wiped his eyes and observed the massacre. Once he was able to pry his eyes from what used to be Serpenoids, he fixed his attention on the shelters.

Smoke poured out of their openings. Behind their hand-built huts was an enormous fallen golden figure which seemed to resemble Thandrua. He glanced at the statue once; he couldn't remember building that but for some reason its presence didn't seem out of the ordinary. Vander swallowed hard and cautiously made his way toward the homes, stepping over the Serpenoids.

Vander stopped at the first structure, this would have been the chamber for the welders, the one *he* would have been in. With great caution, Vander nervously peered inside. His senses were assaulted by a pile of smoldering Serpenoids. He crumpled to the ground and gagged from the sight and smell. After his coughing attack, Vander's eyes shifted to the right. His attention had been captured by the Lord's chamber which remained smokeless, unlike the miners' home on the other side of that. He went to investigate, but found himself standing outside the opening, staring in disbelief, in fear. Time went by as he debated on entering.

"Help…" A feeble voice said within the dark. Vander took a step back as he heard a heavy dragging sound from inside. The sound drew nearer. Two scaly dark beige Serpenoid arms jutted out of the opening. The coarse black claws from the hands dug into the sand as the Serpenoid pulled itself forward. The Serpenoid stopped at the entrance with half his body still inside. A hood with the black markings of Sectoraus flopped opened from his head as he looked up.

"Sectoraus?" Vander said, almost to himself.

"Help-- help me." The king of the Cobras begged.

Vander began to pull Sectoraus out of the chamber before releasing his grip, screaming. Sectoraus was missing the lower half of his body. His spine dragged along the sand. Blood gushed from the waist.

"Please… help." Sectoraus' voice was weak and shaking.

"I will help you, Sectoraus." Vander slowly nodded his head, realizing what had to be done. "Forgive me, Lord Thandrua."

Vander stood above Sectoraus and gave one powerful stomp onto the Cobra's neck. A crunch of bones and a deep sigh of relief were the last sounds heard from Sectoraus before he too joined the fate of the Serpenoids. The vibrations of the neck's snap found its way into Vander's heart, causing him to collapse, wailing on the soft sand. He yelled and repeatedly slammed his fist into the ground with anger, deepening his fist's imprint. A faint glow lit the horizon in the distance. Vander cleared the tears in his eyes and was stunned by what he saw. It was a sunrise painting the horizon.

"It is not possible!" Was all he could say when he was stricken with his own fear. His throat tightened and he gasped for air. The rising light blurred as complete darkness blanketed Vander's sight. He might have felt his back hit the warmth of the sand behind him. *Might have,* had he not been suffocating and using all his remaining consciousness to hold on. His chest was tight, he was terrified but felt like he needed to just calm down and all the pain would stop. If he could regulate his sharp gasps into steady breaths it would soothe him, but he was too afraid. Afraid of not breathing, even though he wasn't breathing because he was afraid. It didn't matter though, the Sun was here; whether he could breathe or not, his time had come.

Lord Thandrua, the Cobra Clan, all the other Serpenoids were all gone. He hadn't the slightest idea what had happened while he dozed off. Sectoraus maimed, many were burnt to a crisp, *it couldn't have been all of them, could it?* He only knew that he was the last remaining and now he too would no longer be. Vander's serpent-like body convulsed as a piercing pain tore through his chest. He no longer strained for air, didn't seem interested in it anymore. The darkness hung thicker still and there was no longer the sensation of his body, then no more thoughts. Everything that had existed melted away. There was only one lingering thing left behind. The void.

To Vander, a clear moment felt like such a void, as if his consciousness and time itself stopped completely. An eternity might have passed before thought came flooding back in. *What has happened, where am I!?* Vander attempted to rise, but there was nothing to rise from or even perhaps nothing to rise with. He remained blind without any sensation of his physical self. *What is this? How do I get back to before?* Vander felt completely helpless. *What* is *before?*

Suddenly vision flashed back before his eyes. However, his physical self was still detached. He saw Serpenoids all around him, he could *see*, but he still couldn't seem to move. Then it hit him, he was seeing, but just that, watching from his eyes as opposed to looking through them. As if he were a bodiless consciousness gazing through the viewport of what was once his vessel. He saw the cracked dried terrain from the world they left behind. Fear flooded him once again when he saw his kin drop one after the other around him. They seemed weak and needed… water!

Thunder exploded above the morbid scene, a cool crisp droplet of water pelted on the scaled head of Vander (He was aware of it but couldn't *feel* it) then another and a couple more. The drops multiplied and picked up speed as rain tumbled from the heavens and seemed to revive the fallen Serpenoids. More thunder roared and a flaming comet tumbled through the clouds, crashing into the softening dirt. The comet looked more like a divine egg than cosmic stone. The sky pulsed blue as a flash of lightning revealed a silhouette of a tall Serpenoid, a Serpenoid that unfolded a hood around his head. It was Sectoraus, Vander was sure of it, as sure as he was that the egg would… *Crack*!

Its shattering sound mocked the thunder as the two ivory horns of the red hulking beast that is Thandrua stood majestically from the shattered remains of his vessel. Awe swept Vander as he gazed up into Thandrua's green eyes and he knew, he felt it, this being standing before him had saved his life and everyone else's. Just as suddenly as that image came it faded, and a new scene took over Vander's vision.

The god-king Thandrua stood proud with an assembly of Serpenoids listening eagerly to his wisdom. The star-stricken sky sparkled behind the two curved horns, emphasizing the grace of his majesty. The royal blue slowly lightened to a softer shade and Vander knew the Sun would come soon. There was no fear, he watched as Thandrua led the colony into the dark safety of a mountain's cave. As they entered, however, it was no longer a cave but the edge of a gargantuan canyon at which Vander stood.

The winds pulled and howled, and the rain sprinkled down from the grey clouds covering the sky, blotting the deadly rays of the Sun. Vander peeked down into the abyss of the canyon and saw the slightest hint of the glow of magma. Fear, fear rose up inside of him once again. He could fall down what looked as if it would feel like an endless drop. Almost endless, until the eventual burn of the scorching molten rock. Vander's yellow slitted eyes lifted from the depths and fixed on the thousands of Serpenoids who appeared tiny from his view on the peak, clawing and scaling their way down the rockface. That was when Vander saw what they were headed to. A large crack on the side of the canyon wall formed the shape of what he now recognized as "the Eye of Thandrua", but its center was occupied with something other than the pitch-black hole that worked as a gateway from this world to the next. Its center held Thandrua's enormous unblinking eye, staring deep into his very soul.

Vander was lifted off his feet and pulled toward the black pupil of the eye, although he struggled to cling onto the cliff's edge. No, he didn't want to move from that spot, he didn't want to risk the drop. His wants were in vain though, as an invisible force seemed to drag Vander's resisting body to the center of the eye. And the scene changed once again.

The laboring sounds of the Serpenoids echoed throughout a cave that radiated heat far hotter than the perpetual heat of the land outside of the cave. A furnace flared as clumps of rock and stone were dumped into a crevice in the back of the wall. Flame jutted out of a second hole as silvery liquid metal seeped out from it. Vander bashed a small hammer onto a shovel, flattening the back side then indenting the scoop. The clink and clang of metal thumping against metal rang on like the bells of an ancient church with the occasional spark of contact flashing in the otherwise complete darkness. For a moment, Vander felt at peace. After all that happened, after all he witnessed, he was back in the Kiln doing what he knew how to do best. The tranquility only lasted for a moment because that thought first came into his head naturally, then he realized what he had thought. *After all that has happened?* What *has happened!?*

Looking down at his hammering clawed hand, he was perplexed, the shovel was no longer there. Vander continued clanking onto a metallic tool, but one he did not recognize. Its sleek metal body was flat and long; the two edges seemed sharp, and it formed a piercing point. Even though he did not know the device, for some reason looking at it stirred his fear. There was something sinister about the curved edges that formed together into the piercing tip. However, too mesmerized to step away from the tool, Vander lifted it from a bronze hilt that held this... *blade* as his eyes widened. He gawked at the prisoner who stood in a barren mine staring straight back into Vander's eyes. The Creature's pale grey eyes gave a comforting but also lifeless feeling that froze Vander with fear. A fear of what the Creature has seen or done to have such lifeless eyes.

He radiated raw power as his beaten body stood there, almost defiantly, and smiled sinisterly at Vander. More creatures with similar soft-skinned bodies seemed to be standing behind the prisoner. They were other prisoners, and there were many. That was when Vander realized that the prisoners were not in an old mine and not shackled as prisoners. No, the Creature with the pale grey eyes and white hair stood strong with a large army of what possibly could be this Creature's species, except with different colors of hair, eyes, and complexion.

Vander found that scene, too, had faded and he once again dropped to his knees at the revelation of the mysterious slaughter of his colony. Smoke rose from the slumber chambers planted on top of the hill that overlooked the crystal-clear lake with Thandrua's elegant throne still toppled over onto the shore. From the horizon a light peered, glinting off the debris of the enormous golden statue which seemed to represent his Lord. Vander remained in his place on the ground. At first, he groveled out of his continuous fear, but finally after feeling completely lost, Vander gave into the urge to look toward the sunrise. After all, he had never completely *seen* the Sun and has always had that slight curiosity to witness it for himself.

I am alone, he felt utterly broken, *I am the last and I am ready.* The Sun was in plain view now, its light bled the orange sky to a fearful red. The lonesome Serpenoid continued to watch as the deadly orb of light rose higher and higher. He was ready to be blinded, ready for the searing pain to combust his scales into flame, as he had seen so many others in the past. *Please, I am ready,* he pleaded as the sun reached the sky and the solar rays beamed toward the ground. Vander flung up an arm to shield himself. The golden sunlight transformed into a shimmering white light as it touched Vander's scales, he felt warmth spread within his body and his sight collapsed into the void once again. The darkness only lasted for a fraction of a second before the white light tore through the void, through Vander's cover, and engulfed all sight. Vander uncovered his face and all he could see was an enormous circular light of pure white in place of the sun.

As a matter of fact, it was not only that the Sun radiated with pure energy but nothing else in the world seemed to exist any longer, just the light and the light alone. There was no red from the sky, the stench of charred Serpenoid flesh evaporated, Vander even had lost touch with himself. There was nothing but his consciousness and the light.

"Take me now!"

"Do not fret, Vander." a voice said within his consciousness, its voice was calm and soothing, as well as harsh and deep. It sounded like that of Thandrua, as well as that of the prisoner; it sounded not unlike his own, and at the same time sounded so completely alien he wasn't sure how he was understanding it. But he understood.

"How did…"

"The life that you know is only one aspect of so many other perspectives, other worlds and understandings. Vander, you have been led down a path that does not require thought, but solely action. The Universe is composed more of thought than action."

"I do not understand. Why do you call me Vander, how do you know that name?"

"There is little I do not know. As for understanding, you are not meant to understand, not yet at least."

"But you should not have known! For I only *just* received the name, myself... What are you?"

"I am the beginning. I am the hand that paved the ground you walk on, the paint in the colors of your sight. I am the water that dripped from the sky in your last home and the water that fills the lake in this current one. I have orchestrated all, the Father and the Mother I am. I am the Creator."

"*You!*" Complete realization exploded within his consciousness. It had been as if his entire existence was led to this very moment, when the very last piece of the puzzle would sink perfectly into its empty socket. "I understand now, it was *you* that saved the Serpenoids from dying of thirst, not Lord Thandrua. This whole time, it was all a deception. You are the true lifegiver."

"I am, if that is what you wish to call me. But do not misjudge Thandrua, he only claims to be an almighty deity because you and your Serpenoids convinced him so. He was placed there to lead your kind, nothing more, but through your hope you made him into more."

Vander became aware that he was looking through his eyes, using his sight once again. The white light that had occupied his entire vision, and his body as well, receded to an orb in the familiar orange sky of home. The Serpenoid's knees sank into the dry sand that baked below, reminding Vander of his body. The comforting scent of brimstone wafted through his nostril, reminding him of his sense of smell. Reminding him of another smell, the strong odor of burnt-to-a-crisp flesh that now overpowered the previous volcanic scent. Vander picked himself up from the ground. He looked about at his surroundings, then faced the Creator again.

"Please tell me, Creator, what happened here?"

"Nothing, yet. This is a vision. This is the only way I can speak to you, through your dreams, your subconscious. I used to visit Thandrua's dreams. I am here to grant you the responsibility to save your race. The one with wisdom beyond your world to provide knowledge for those who seek it."

"Why me? If you visit Thandrua's dreams, why can you not ask him? Or Sectoraus, why not him? Or someone else with authority?"

"Thandrua refuses to take my warnings. As for Sectoraus, I have no use for any of your so-called superiors. You are good at heart, I could sense this with the way you would watch your Lord's prisoner, the curiosity that seemed to separate you from the rest. That is why I decided to choose you. You can speak my words, make Thandrua understand, it will save all of you."

"What do you mean?"

"The prisoner you refer to as *Creature*. He was to live amongst your kind. Banishment from my care was his punishment, not to be tortured as he has been. I had warned Thandrua your world will become plagued. There must always be repercussions to one's actions. You must weld what you mine." There was a pause, the phrase lingered within Vander's mind, "must weld what you mine."

Vander's head filled with the warm thoughts that began to speak to him in the voice that was his own as well as of a stranger's once again. "Please, speak with your prisoner. When a foreigner resides among you in your land, do not mistreat them. The foreigner residing among you must be treated as your native-born. Love them as yourself. For only through the expansion of knowledge and love may one truly grow. He has knowledge that may advance your colony."

"And we are foreigners ourselves. We left our native land long ago. I would not have wanted such treatment upon arriving at a new home. Yes, I understand. Anything to save my brethren. I thank you for this, I am grateful you chose me."

"You chose, Vander. Your compassion is truly remarkable. Until we meet again."

The images around Vander faded into emptiness and his vision turned to black before opening his eyes in wake. The crystal-clear lake was laid out before his yellow eyes. It was the slight wet dab of the water's edge against his muzzle that made him realize he had slumped over and fell asleep on the shoreline. His hands sunk into the wet sand, which clumped under his claws, as he lifted himself to his knees. After brushing off the clinging sand, Vander frantically turned his head. Thandrua's throne wasn't sunken into the water, it wasn't anywhere in sight and Vander guessed it must be in the Lord's chamber for it was still the slumbering portion of their cycle and all were peacefully asleep.

Vander sat on the dry part of the sand, digging his feet into the wet part of the shoreline, and pondered in silence. He dropped his face into his hands, readjusting to the reality that surrounded him. Or was it reality? The heat of the air, the wet of the ground had not felt even the slightest different from his dream. The dream-this vision-he'd just had was so vivid, so solid. He knew this was no ordinary dream, although he did not recall ever even having had dreams during his sleep before.

The voice he had heard in his mind, so soothing and so beyond his physical understanding, brought warmth into his heart with the simple memory. This was not some hallucination, there was meaning in the vision, a warning. He had to confront Lord Thandrua. He stood up abruptly and jogged up the hill straight toward Thandrua's chamber. Vander glanced at either side of the hand-built cave, checking his and the miners' chambers. No smoke, no destruction, all was safe again. *Safe in a memory*, he thought, for Vander understood that their entire colony was as safe as a shelter built on a fault line.

Vander stood at the entryway to the Lord's chamber, peering within and scanning the hand-built walls and the sand-covered ground. Upon peeking further in, he saw the four Cobra brothers slept soundly in their coiled balls encircling the jewel-encrusted golden throne. There, the large red king laid back with legs sprawled, left arm dangling over the armrest while his right hand clutched the obsidian staff and his horned head slumped to the side. Vander stepped in with care, leaving all urgency of his stride outside of the shelter. He was entering his masters' chamber, uninvited whilst they slept, and even with such an important message he knew he was crossing his boundaries as a welder. *I was given this message.* He thought to himself, giving him the bravery that shrank with each step just as his feet sunk into the sand.

The heavy breathing rumbled over the light steady breaths from the sleeping Cobras. Slowly he moved in closer still, watching the Clan. A thought suddenly occurred to him, *I wonder if the Cobras dream?* This idea had never come across his mind before, since he had never before experienced a dream himself. Now there he stood, just an arm's length away, unsure whether to step over or around the Cobras to Thandrua or to speak from there, waking them all at once. He glanced at Orpheus who laid closest to his feet, then Solarious, Phineus, and finally Sectoraus who slept with his scepter clutched in his hand. Finally, taking in one deep breath of courage, he stepped forward and decided to creep over the bulking Orpheus. As Vander's foot touched the sand inside the circle, the yellow and black spotted Cobra's eye twitched awake. In a swift, slithering manner Orpheus rose onto his two legs and clamped a hefty, clawed hand onto Vander's right shoulder.

"Do not move." Orpheus spoke with such force, his voice alone would have stopped Vander even without the muscled Cobra's clawed hand digging into his shoulder. Now all six of the other Cobra's yellow eyes glared at them and when Vander looked to

Thandrua again, his gaze met the emerald eyes of his no longer sleeping Lord.

Thandrua's head snapped up as he straightened in the chair. The rest all stood, flaring their distinctive hoods, making them all the more intimidating while closing in on Vander, making any movement impossible. Sectoraus grabbed him by the throat and pulled him out of the pack. The pressure wasn't tight enough to choke Vander completely, but his firm grip pressed the tips of Sectoraus' nails into the scales along the neck. Vander squirmed as he was hoisted in the air.

"Serpenoid, the cycle has yet to be announced, why do you sneak into our chamber whilst the Lord slumbers?" Sectoraus spat, gazing up at the frighten Vander that clutched at the grip around his neck

Thandrua stood and reached out a hand toward Vander, "You may put him down. I am awake now, tell me what brings you here that could not wait until the next cycle?"

"My Lord, my deepest apologies." Vander coughed, rubbing his throat where the mark of Sectoraus' nails lingered, then lowered into a kneeling bow getting as close to the ground as he could. "I just had a dream. A dream of extinction and warning! I had to tell you now, sire."

The Cobras looked perplexed, wondering what he could be talking about. Thandrua stood abruptly, his face betraying shock as though he knew exactly what Vander had meant. Remaining silent, Thandrua slowly returned to his seat with his eyes fixed on the messenger. Thandrua studied him for a moment before gesturing with his right pointer finger to come closer. The tension was thick as the Cobras hissed intimidatingly, carefully watching Vander.

"Tell me." The god-king demanded, finally breaking the silence. "This dream, what did it warn you about?"

Vander glanced behind his shoulder at the Cobra Clan, then looked past them out the chamber into the desert world. "Death, my Lord! The genocide of our kind and much horror to come."

The Cobras began to whisper amongst themselves. Thandrua leaned in closely and pulled Vander toward him, then spoke under his breath. "Did you… speak with someone in your vision?"

"Yes, my Lord." Vander whispered in return. "It was energy, as bright as the deadly light, but this one was as comforting as the other was fatal. It called itself *the Creator*."

Thandrua sat back, green eyes widening in disbelief. "No, it is not possible." Thandrua muttered to himself, then reached for his still-burning scar with his left hand. His middle finger tapped twice on a corner of the irritating burn mark. "Leave us!" he waved off the Clan.

"But Master…" Sectoraus protested before Thandrua snapped, "I said leave us! Wake the others, begin your cycle duties, and leave us be!"

Sectoraus refrained for a moment before taking his order, he didn't hide his contempt. It was a troublesome dream to have of the Serpenoids' extinction. Thandrua had said a light scarred him within his dream, now this welder claims to have had a precognitive dream of his own. There was definitely a connection and perhaps Thandrua was right about this light existing beyond his dream. The last thing Sectoraus wanted was to leave Thandrua alone in such a stressed state, but he was loyal and always did as his friend wished.

Thandrua sat in bewilderment, holding Vander's gaze with his own as the Cobras ushered the Serpenoids away. Away from their sight and out of earshot, they continued their silent staring contest well after the others left, then Thandrua stood and paced, circling around his throne and visitor.

"So." Thandrua finally broke the thick silence, "You saw it…" He took a deep and slow breath before finishing his question. He closed his eyes and furrowed his brow as if he had come to a puzzling predicament, for saying what he was about to say out loud meant everything about his own dreams were truly real, "the Creator?"

"Yes, sire." Vander inclined his head, then stood, "That is what it called itself. Said it was *The* Creator, of everything as we know it, even you."

"So, it is true, then." Thandrua said this more to himself as he touched his scar once more. "It gave me this as a warning. It still lingers, the burn. Did it tell you why our destruction is coming or how?"

"The *Creature*."

"I am to release him, I assume?" He continued his pacing, "It all comes back to that last dream."

"You have had many before?"

"A few, yes. It was how I learned of the Sun, of this paradise. Now you know the truth, I suppose. I am no god."

"Why did you keep this from us? You said it told you about the Sun, how long have you known of this *Creator*? Were you trying to trick us, keep us blind?"

"You have every right to be upset. A bit of it was just that, trickery, but mostly I did not want to admit it to myself. Something greater and beyond myself? Even after this scar I still could not believe, did not want to."

"You are still my king, Lord Thandrua, but I do believe. I felt it and that was no dream. You must free the Creature! More will come, I am sure of it!" Although he kept his composure, there was much panic in his voice. "The Creator spoke of a plague; these creatures might be just that. We are all alone and have been since the beginning. This one creature has completely altered our lives, what are we to do with more!?"

Thandrua took in Vander's fearful gaze, frozen in place as he considered the information in his head. He placed both arms behind his back before breaking eye contact and continuing his pace. "I am afraid it is too late; I cannot free him."

"No, Lord Thandrua, you still do not understand. You must release him! I saw them, the *creatures*, and there were so many! Hundreds!" Vander pressed. Force was behind his words, but nothing seemed to penetrate Thandrua's horned head.

"Do not speak to me in such a way." Thandrua stood at the entrance of his abode, his green eyes glaring. "I do thank you for your warning. This destruction you speak of cannot come to completion now that I can anticipate such an event. When and *if* more of these soft-fleshed creatures arrive, we will be ready. I will once again be a hero and you along with me."

Lord Thandrua motioned for Vander to come towards him. When he did, the crimson god-king placed his right hand on Vander's shoulder, guiding him down to kneel before him. Vander didn't resist in the slightest, even lowered his gaze to the ground. "You are hereby promoted," Thandrua announced, "no longer will you have to work in the Kiln, or the mines for that matter. You have a connection with this Creator, you were gifted with a vision, and I am sure this will not be the last. As of this moment you are my... *Oracle*, with a place in my order."

"The honor is mine," Vander rose from the ground once the heavy hand lifted from his shoulder, knowing the conversation of releasing the prisoner was long over.

"Take water to this creature, clean him up. I want you to find out who he is and why is he here."

"Yes, my Lord." Vander turned to leave before Lord Thandrua stopped him for one more word.

"Listen, I understand your concerns, but please keep what we spoke about between us. It is not time for the others to know."

Almost reluctant to answer but finally Vander did, "I will... My Lord."

Chapter 8
The Oracle's Plight

Vander was no longer an ordinary Serpenoid, skilled with the insight of premonition. Only Lord Thandrua truly understood what this meant; Sectoraus found it peculiar that he dismissed Vander from the Kiln altogether. Although he would never verbally question Thandrua's word, Sectoraus did not agree with the promotion. Vander was given the highest of privileges in the eyes of the Serpenoids, to be counted within the hierarchy, alongside Lord Thandrua and the Cobra Clan. Thandrua anointed him *The Oracle* and ordered for the Cobra Clan to be converted into the Lord's Brotherhood. Vander was given a spot for slumber within the Lord's spacious chamber.

Free from the labor of the Kiln, Vander stood next to Thandrua just like Sectoraus, taking leisure by the lake as the Cobra Clan escorted the forgers and miners to their work sites. Sectoraus, as always, stood to the right of Thandrua's throne and now the Oracle stood on his left. The three took ease in their workless cycles but with much discussion, debating on the fate of their new visitor and discussing the visions of what was to come.

Sectoraus, jealous of his companionship with Thandrua, didn't seem to fully accept Vander's new role. The Cobra king was generally short with the Oracle; he simply could not understand how a Serpenoid could be so different. During the first cycle, Sectoraus kept any feelings of disdain to himself. However, after Thandrua had urged Sectoraus to include the Oracle in the Cobra Clan's meditation sessions, Sectoraus became bitter quickly.

"Meditation is sacred between us Cobras," Sectoraus had argued, "There are no others that possess the ability. Is it not enough that he spends the cycle within our discussions?"

"Sectoraus my friend, there is no need to feel threatened." Thandrua soothed, "the Oracle's premonitions may be very significant. If he learned how to meditate, perhaps it could aid him to foresee any dangers at will."

"I do not understand, you cannot truly believe in this dream he has claimed to have. The destruction of our colony? It is preposterous! It is just a dream, it cannot be the same level as the dreams you have had in the past, can it?"

Lord Thandrua took a moment to think before answering Sectoraus. He had told his companion about the light in his dreams, the supposed Creator, and Sectoraus had urged him to keep that information from the colony to protect his reign. Sectoraus knew of the devastation Vander saw within his dream, but he didn't know that Vander, too, was approached by this Creator. Thandrua felt as if he could always tell Sectoraus anything, but if he told the Cobra that the Creator was in Vander's dreams as well, then what would that make of himself? Sectoraus had stood firm in his belief that Thandrua was the lifegiver when they weren't completely sure themselves. Telling Sectoraus everything now would admit that he wasn't. Was Thandrua ready to admit it to himself?

"So, Thandrua?" Sectoraus asked again when the silence held too long, "Is Vander's dream the same level as yours? Has he seen the light of the Sun that speaks as well?"

"I have learned from you, Sectoraus, that some things are best kept to oneself." Lord Thandrua straightened, towering over his friend, "Teach the Oracle to meditate. That is an order from your Almighty ruler."

"I see," Sectoraus lowered his eyes. He was hurt, but by Thandrua's refusal he felt he got the answer he sought. He decided not to pry any longer.

From that conversation forward, Sectoraus had the Cobra Clan meditate more regularly and the Oracle would sit alongside them. After the forgers and miners returned from their work, Sectoraus would group his brothers together and sit inside of their chamber. Sectoraus told the Oracle the key to meditation was focus and a mind of clear thought. The first few times Vander sat in the circle they formed, occasionally peeking through squinted eyes to see the others. They all sat crossed-legged and perfectly still. It was astounding to

Vander how not one would stir, not even a quiver of muscle. *Clear your mind, clear your mind!* The Oracle continued to remind himself. His mind was too busy trying to clear itself. He just didn't know if he was doing it the right way.

"Sectoraus, I am not certain--" Vander was cut off.

"Clear your mind, Serpenoid!" Sectoraus hissed, "Perhaps you are not fit to meditate amongst us." He refused to explain any further.

Solarious stood from his spot next to Sectoraus and cleared his throat, "Allow me." He stepped past Orpheus and stood behind Vander. Solarious moved the Serpenoid's shoulders back, "You want your head to align with your spine and stomach." When Vander held his position, Solarious returned to Sectoraus' side. "Close your eyes," the Cobra Clan gently closed their eyes and Vander followed, "now simply breathe."

The Cobras inhaled in unison with Vander shortly behind. The sounds of the Serpenoids were outside of the chamber, but within was a silence only interrupted by the rhythmic breathing of the group. After some time Solarious spoke again, but almost in a whisper, "Vander, think of a container, the container is black. Focus on it." Solarious paused for a moment and watched the concentrated look on Vander's face. "Now lift its lid and stare into the darkness within. It is black, focus on it." Solarious paused again allowing Vander to visualize the imagery. "Allow the darkness to engulf your mind... let loose of my words… let your mind become the darkness."

The Oracle felt his thoughts halt, his mind had shut off. Or was it wide open? He could feel the energy radiating within the circle. Vander wondered if this was what it was like for all of them. He could feel them seated around him as four warm spots in his thoughts. However, there was one energy that stood out the most. It was the heat of burning magma and Vander could feel it across himself. *Sectoraus. Was it his animosity that made him burn this way, or was it the strength of his mind?*

***

Even though Thandrua believed Vander was experiencing similar dreams as he had before, he still would not let go of his pride. Their prisoner remained captive, occasionally released into the mines to labor with the Serpenoids. Vander was allowed to take water to him and learn all of what he knew. The Creature, as they continued to refer to him, might as well have lived with them their entire lives. He knew of the Sun and the dangers it posed for the dwellers of darkness. He knew all about their lives within their previous home, which the Creature called "Earth," even the time of the great thirst, when the Serpenoids were dying of dehydration before the coming of the first rain and the arrival of Lord Thandrua.

Thandrua felt very insecure and threatened that this newcomer knew more than even he, the Almighty Thandrua, knew. He masked these feelings through hatred and mistreatment of the prisoner. The Serpenoids mistook this for strength, for they only knew what they were told and did not think to question it further. They hadn't the slightest idea that something terrible was on the horizon. The Serpenoids didn't even know the full extent of Vander's acceptance into the Lord's brotherhood. Vander urged Thandrua to spread his vision of the destruction of the Serpenoids, but his master refused to let the information leak.

"It would create too much panic," Thandrua reasoned. "The Serpenoids would not be able to continue in the peace of their cycle. There would be so much panic that it could break down the very fundamentals of our society. There would be tremendous disorder… and that very well could be the destruction you have foreseen."

"If that is your wisdom, my Lord." Vander accepted.

"It is for the greater good of the Serpenoids." Thandrua stated with finality.

The Serpenoids never questioned any decisions from their Lord Thandrua. The god-king called an assembly after anointing the Oracle and simply announced that the Serpenoid, Vander, was to join their ranks after being gifted with visions to protect their livelihood. They never made the connection that these visions were of fear and paranoia.

But was it truly acceptance? Perhaps Thandrua didn't trust that after all these cycles, one of his followers not only suddenly developed independent will, but also had received a premonition through a dream. What was to stop him from speaking with the other Serpenoids, to influence them away from Thandrua? Paranoia is all it was. The mysteries of something new. They have lived for countless cycles, Thandrua as their god and everyone at his will. They had never encountered any other living beings until the creature that they now kept captive. Thandrua had never once had this new feeling of fear, fear of losing his reign and respect. Now everything had changed. His place had been challenged and his face had been scarred. The Serpenoids now saw that even their great Lord Thandrua was at the mercy of pain.

It all came down to the prisoner, who not only seemed to have more insight than Thandrua, but after all the harsh beatings and all the blood loss, didn't even seem to keep a scratch aside from the two scars behind his shoulder blades. Who was this creature and where did he come from? It perplexed them all, so Thandrua sent the Oracle on a cyclical basis to converse with him alone, until the Creature would release his own personal information.

***

Vander did as he had always done every other cycle. He practiced his meditation in the royal chamber. He had complete solitude, the Serpenoids toiling far away at their work sites and the Cobra Clan supervising them. Lord Thandrua and Sectoraus enjoyed their freedoms by the lake and since Thandrua sat along the water in his throne, the chamber was completely empty. The Oracle took advantage of this time; practicing with the Cobras was one thing, although he always felt that he wasn't fully part of the circle, still not grasping what the others seemed to. Besides, Vander wanted, no, *needed* to master the skill. He needed that confidence in the meditative group. The Oracle had also experienced something more than any of the others ever had. The conversation he had with the

Creator, or vision, whatever it was, Vander knew he needed to keep that channel open. So, Vander meditated in the closed silence of his new large sleeping chamber before going out to fulfill his task.

Once Vander could hear (or possibly feel?) the far-off sounds of the Serpenoids returning, He ended his meditation and left the hut, enjoying that he didn't need to duck his head like he had to when he used to sleep in the welders' chamber. The Serpenoid stepped out, breathing in the brimstone, scanning their still camp with the smaller, vacant chambers. Vander stretched his arms out, then picked up two stone-carved bowls from a pile outside the chambers and briskly walked around the royal chamber, pausing for a moment to observe the pristine lake. His yellow eyes scanned up and back down the goliath of a mountain in the far distance, admired the lake once more, glancing briefly at Sectoraus and Lord Thandrua in their repose by the shore. Vander descended the small hill. His two masters overlooked the lake and faced in the direction of the mountain as Vander approached the back of the throne.

"My lords." The Oracle greeted as he neared, clearing his throat first.

"On your way to the Creature?" Lord Thandrua asked the rhetorical question- which he did every time Vander would go to visit the prisoner. The two companions turned their sights on Vander as he passed them. Sectoraus didn't say a word.

"Yes, Lord Thandrua. Just getting some water first." Vander lowered to the water, filling his bowls.

"Very good. Perhaps this cycle It will tell you something useful." Thandrua also said this each time.

"Why, yes, this is my goal, my Lord." Vander left them; the Cobra and beast craned their heads to watch Vander off before continuing their palaver.

Vander walked out toward the wasteland to the pit where the prisoner resided. He had the two bowls secured safely in his clawed hands. Vander always carried two bowls of water: One to quench the Creature's thirst, after a long and hard cycle of working in the mines, and one to wash off the dried sand from his matted hair and face. Most cycles they met were shared in silence as Vander would watch the Creature enjoy the splendors of the lifegiving liquid. Others, they would speak for some time, the prisoner telling what he knew of the Serpenoids and Vander retelling the trials they had overcome until they reached their sanctuary, although the prisoner always seemed to have already known these things.

That was Vander's cycle task as the new Oracle. The same routine, not welding or mining but storytelling until Vander tired. Each time they would end with Vander asking for a name and the prisoner would always respond, "I will not speak my name", until the captive was finally ready to tell his tale.

On the eleventh cycle of this new routine, the Creature drank from the bowl in the depths of his living tomb while Vander stood at the top of the hold, waiting for something, anything. The prisoner gazed up at him and his colorless eyes locked onto the yellow serpent slits. "You will come, each time, and ask me the same question? Tell the same tales?"

"Yes," Vander responded, "it is what my Master asks of me."

"Then, I suppose the time has come," the Creature finished the water and tossed the bowl up, Vander catching it in his claws. "That light you speak of in your dreams, the Creator, that is my... father, and he once called me Luzbel, his Morning Star."

Chapter 9
The Creature's Tale

The Father created us, has created all indefinitely. It began with our home, a place of magnificent beauty beyond any description with trivial words. Everything that this dry torrid world is not. Such rich soil covered the ground which grew the softest green grass, so gentle to our delicate bare feet. Parallel hovered a crystal-clear blue sky with a wondrous cool breeze. The Creator worked on the universe while we created an entire city, a kingdom, built from the smoothest white marble and filled with instruments of music, the greatest conversations of philosophy, and all the joys the rest of the Universe has yet to experience.

I was the first created, then He created legions of disciples, whom He called angels. They worshipped the Creator in appreciation and took pleasure in all that was good in our domain. I was chosen to be separate from all others, making me beautiful and perfect in every way possible, then my brothers to follow. There were seven of us, the archangels, to keep order and oversee all the angels. Unlike the others, we bore wings on our backs, we had the gift of flight. In a way we were not unlike the Cobra Clan and, like Sectoraus, I was the favorite. All others were more formal with the Creator and only I personalized our connection by calling the formless being "Father."

In time, the Father brought word of a prophecy that one day (days are what we called our cycles) something wicked would interfere with the Grand Plan and I, along with the archangels, were to lead the angels in battle against it. I was taken aside and told that I alone would be the first to identify the *Wicked.* The Creator instructed me on characteristics which could be used to identify the Wicked, which He called the

Seven Deadly Sins: greed, lust, sloth, gluttony, envy, pride, and wrath. We seven archangels were to challenge and defend our paradise from the Wicked and must always be on guard for any one of these sins which might herald the Wicked's coming.

The Creator blessed me with preexisting knowledge of war tactics and the skills to create and wield any weapon, but the art of the sword was my specialty. We did not have to mine like you Serpenoids and were blessed with the supplies of raw material to create the metals we needed. I alone, as head general of the holy army and sword master, had access to our weaponry and trained angels and archangels alike in combat. We trained and practiced. Masters all my students became, not only in war, but in art and philosophy as well. Even though I strongly urged everyone to prepare for the inevitable war, we had nothing but time and the Wicked showed no signs of drawing nigh.

With the luxury of time, the angels developed various skills. Sculpting from the stones, decorating our buildings with figures, totems, anything their creative minds desired. They created oils to paint wonderous things on canvases, murals in tribute to the Father, and even to capture our beautiful world in still form. They invented and constructed instruments with which to develop such pleasant music.

I found it funny how the angels enjoyed discussing their ideas of what the rest of the universe would become like. Why did it matter to them? They were the common folk, all they needed to do was enjoy what was created for us and be vigilant for signs of evil.

We archangels, however, were in charge, we were the ones who should be discussing such philosophies. Which we did. I loved sharing beliefs on the great Universe outside of our domain with my brothers. The others of course had their thoughts as well, they were nice, but I especially loved talking about *my* thoughts. I also loved to spar with my brothers; as head general and sword master, I had to keep my swordplay at peak form, of course. My brothers each had their own favorite thing to do, but so often it was outside of what I had in mind. Michael was always willing to discuss philosophy with me, however he favored music more, along with Uriel. Gabriel kept his hands busy with painting and Raphael invested in sculpting. At least Azrael and Samael were fun enough to always be open to spar with me. Oh, how time passed us, and with it we developed our little cliques.

Time was in our favor in our realm. The length of time between each rising Sun in your former Earth is considered to be *one day.* A single day on Earth would be about the equivalent of forty days in paradise, perhaps more. Here, however, I cannot estimate what the time would be. Such an incredibly slow crawl that time is practically nonexistent.

The Father left us to ourselves most of the time, the privilege of life and independence wrapped into one. Because of this distortion of time between realms, each moment He spent in His workshop felt like ages to us. When my Lord first came to a crossroads (that was when your Serpenoids died in drought) it was *I* that suggested the rain. Had it not been for me, you all would be extinct. This He appreciated, and on occasion took me as the personal assistant on the creation of the Universe.

Now, it was forbidden for any to step foot inside the master workshop, so I made my contributions from outside the workshop doors. I became well acquainted with the marvelous view atop the summit of our Mountain of Knowledge where the workshop stood. How I enjoyed looking down upon my family as I leaned firmly on the doors, just waiting for the thoughts of the Father to erupt within my mind for my assistance. Many of my suggestions were used and I continued to be the favorite. From time to time, He would remind me so with divine gifts.

Once I began guiding the Creator with the cosmic projects, I was blessed with a gift that enhanced my leadership. It was the ability to use my mind to move objects at my will. Doors opened before me, cups for water became unnecessary, and my sword flew to my hand as a magnet!

However, my favorite gift was always my first. From the moment He individualized me, I wore a gold band around my right arm, it signified my superiority. I would go around and flaunt it - oh, how it shone in the marvelous light. None seemed to pay any mind, except for *him*! *Michael*! Michael was forever trying to lower my pride, saying how humility was what the Father truly wanted of us. That the true reasoning behind the Father's encouragement of my pride was to test my lust for more. That was Michael, always *so* jealous that he had to constantly contradict me!

"Ring the bells of the colosseum," I would direct the archangel Azrael, and my closest brother, every several days to continue training and battle tactics with the angels.

"Brother Luzbel, may this wait another day?" Michael interjected on occasion, "Many of the angels are in the theater practicing a symphony and many others are enjoying their music."

"There is a war coming, Michael," was always my rebuttal. "I enjoy the arts as much as any, but we must keep fresh on our form. The Wicked will not be kept at bay with music."

"I understand, brother, but do not distract the angels from their joy. It is what is truly important. If anything, how about waiting until the musicians have had their fill. I will go to see if the painters or sculptors are busy with projects of their own."

"I suppose we will tell the citizens that a practice will be held at a future date, that way it doesn't interfere with *their* plans."

"Each time we have this conversation, Luzbel, I tell you exactly that."

"Yes, yes, Michael. That you do, but am I not the general of the holy army?"

I always thought it would be best to have our practice at random times. For when the day the Wicked comes it would come unannounced. Unfortunately, I would always give into Michael's nagging and eventually our practicing became exclusively arranged. However, I did not give Michael the satisfaction of winning everything over me. Something he would constantly criticize was my choice of words to refer to the Creator, my Father.

"Luzbel, why must you use those pronouns when speaking of the Creator?"

"The Creator is *my* Father! I have the freedom to call Him whatever I choose!"

"That's just it, your *Father.* The Creator is all-divine, not a male, the Creator is Its own entity. Not even an angel. Don't you find this disrespectful?"

"Will we always have this ridiculous conversation? Do you not think it more respectful to see the Father as one of us? Not alienated as some formless thing?"

"Do not twist my words, Brother Luzbel. You know I respect the Creator with all my love."

"Well then, *Brother Michael,* you love how you see fit and I will love my own way."

The sibling rivalry was strong, there was a rift. Michael and I spent very little time with one another. He spent most of his time with Raphael, Gabriel, and Uriel, studying the Father's philosophy instead of listening to what some of us other intellectuals had to offer. I mean, *I* was the one that personally worked alongside the Father. Compassion and the art of the selfless, Michael always went raving on.

A paranoid one he was to boot! Michael spread fear that the Wicked could grow in strength from our differences, and that the seven of us should always compromise and tighten our bond to defend against the Wicked. The audacity of the fool! No challenger could defy the army I built and trained! And with the seven of us too? I knew when the Wicked came, differences aside, we would band together and triumph! Anyway, with my skills and abilities alone, what being could stand a chance?

I kept my distance. I spent my time working on plans for the Universe, creating my own philosophies. The Father, after all, encouraged independence and it seemed rightfully so. No, I had no need for Michael's counterproductive ways and because of this my brothers, Azrael and Samael, remained at my side. They seemed to understand what I wanted to propose. That for the living, the best philosophy would be to aspire to be as great as one can be in the short time they would be given. That self-interest would be of critical importance for mortals' limited lifespan, so long as your intentions were pure, aimed towards a greater good.

You see, by then the Father had been working on a new living race of beings called *humans*. Unlike my kind who were blessed with immortality or you Earth dwellers that are practically immortal (aside from your need for water), these humans were to be truly mortal. Short lifespans and constant aging throughout their short lifespan. It was the perfect study in balance, to create a being that would understand suffering and continue to thrive beyond such obstacles.

I remember when the Creator spoke to me as I waited outside of His chamber doors. Through His thoughts, I was told that the cosmic design had reached its fill for the time being. Observing us angels gave the Creator a longing to understand life. I was asked to help design various creatures that were simple in mind, but together they would sustain a balance in the natural world.

We filled the Universe with so many breeds and species. Many were my designs. I was encouraged to imagine what a creature would look like and hold the image in my thoughts, and He would conjure it from my thoughts within the closed chambers. Then came a time when I was asked to further advance the living creatures as the Creator's designs evolved them to be more like us, walking on two legs with sentience in their minds. The reasoning was that the more intellectual their minds became, the better understanding they may have for their lives. That was how the idea of humans first came to be.

I remember the time, I was in the colosseum practicing my footwork, when the workshop doors suddenly screeched opened and the divine light burst forth. The Father called the archangels forward. We seven abandoned our individual practices without a second thought and took flight into the sky. We gently descended to the threshold of the doorway (myself landing first of course) and bathed in the glory of the Creator's pureness.

We were overcome by a shared thought, to imagine how the humans should live. He told us to ponder our philosophies until the Creator was ready to execute His plan. The chamber doors of the creation workshop closed then, leaving us to our independence once again.

Michael and I fought constantly. He was too focused on how supreme beings like us should live while I just wanted for the humans to enjoy their pathetically short lives with ease. I will never forget, it felt like decades from the moment He locked the workshop to begin working on human life until the doors opened once again. I can't explain how wonderful it was each time those doors on top of the Mountain of Knowledge would open and His light would pour onto us. Like usual when the doors opened, it would signify that the Creator needed my assistance.

I glided up to Him in such a graceful manner, only to be turned away, for he wanted the aid of Michael and Gabriel! My spirit was crushed. *I* was the favorite, I was *The* consultant, not them! That is how it became from that moment forward. Michael and Gabriel spent extensive amounts of time within the workshop with the Creator, with my Father. *Inside of the workshop*! Redesigning all the original plans for Earth.

Indeed, I was jealous, but how could I not be? Even Azrael pointed out once, "Are you not supposed to be the Creator's favorite? Were you not the original aid for creation?"

I would always reassure him, "Yes, yes, my brother. I'm sure He just wants another set of eyes to be certain of the plans, and to keep some sort of balance." The Father was keen on balance in the order. This was something I had to keep reminding myself though, for I truly was furious. Whenever I had assisted in creation, I would spend short amounts of time outside of the workshop. Only once was I allowed to enter the holy domain and set my eyes on the breathtaking window to the Universe, the black void of nothingness that allowed one to see all things at will. Most of the time, I would be called to share my thoughts and then He would send me on my way, and I would go back and forth, *back and forth*. This did get tiresome, but I didn't mind, I was creating the Universe! The Father had chosen me and me alone...

What they were doing now was very different. Gabriel and Michael went in once and remained there, with the doors locked shut. I, Luzbel, head of the archangels, the most beautiful, the most perfect being, only received His love in incremental doses. But they were there. Right there, within the enclosed doors, having extended private moments together, *conspiring*. And there they still were when the rumors leaked out that changed everything.

Word spread that they were at completion for the humans and had been for some time. How did this knowledge come about when they never left the workshop? I haven't a clue, perhaps Uriel went to speak with them through the doors. Anyway, it did not matter how the word leaked, but that was when I learned that the humans were no longer to be mortal, but were granted the privilege of everlasting life, courtesy of that pathetic Gabriel. Michael had influenced the great Creator to apply this throughout Earth and have all the beings live side by side in complete harmony.

Of course you might think this sounds splendid, absolutely wonderful! Why would one not want immortality for all creations? Balance was the answer. For balance! Balance is the essential key to the Universe. How many times had the Creator lectured me on the meaning of balance? I understood all too well. That was why immortality would have been only for us in Heaven, for you and your kind here, and the Earth creatures must age and die! My plans for all future beings hinged on mortality; the surety of the end of their existence was what gave it meaning and this would lead to enlightenment.

That was all gone, revised by those two meddling brothers of mine. However, the Creator is wise. Azrael told me more leaked information, how my good Father seemed to anticipate a disturbance and created a failsafe. These humans would taste everlasting life on the sole condition of leaving one simple tree unscathed. You see, the Creator likes His tricks, His experiments within experiments. These tests of will were at times placed in a project; they showed the magnificent Orchestrator what alterations an experiment needed. All for the sake of maintaining the balance! However, the humans obeyed.

Why allow Michael and Gabriel to alter the humans' fate but still create a test that would erase all of that? That was when my eyes were finally opened. That's when I saw the Wicked thing, and it was disguised within my brothers. After all the years, centuries, millennia! I was so blind, but how could I have known? I had always anticipated the Wicked would invade our world, possibly coming forth through the window within the workshop, a being completely and utterly hideous, the embodiment of the deadly sins. Now I saw and I understood, wickedness lived in the core of perspective and that perspective was Michael's and Gabriel's.

"The time has come!" I told Samael. I was overjoyed and when Azrael flew to us to see what I was going on about, I shouted once again, "The time has come!" Only they understood my anticipation of this holy war against the Wicked, so I ordered them to rally the angels at the armory. I had awakened and it was finally time to fulfill my destiny, to become the general of the holy army and protect our way of life. Confused the angels were, as they gathered at the colosseum where we kept our weapons locked away tightly behind a door to which only I held the key. The colosseum was not far from the music hall and some angels still held onto their instruments. They were all clad in white robes, with their cowls over their heads, and they murmured amongst themselves quizzically for impromptu gatherings were abolished long ago.

I could hear their concern and questioning, "Where is Michael? Where is Gabriel?" and of course, "Shouldn't the Creator be here?" I stood on the balcony of the Colosseum at the head of the arched entrance. Flanking me on each side, its gleaming white marble pillars towered above. I looked down, the angels all looking so beautiful in the bright background, and finally they all quieted and turned their attention to me as I raised my right hand high, calling my sword from its hilt. My golden band glinted and my blade shone, drawing the attention of any others that remained in confusion. A cool breeze tickled across my fair skin as I inhaled its sweet crispness and spoke:

"The time has come, my angels! The Wicked thing that He foretold has arrived. It has been created by the Father, by Michael, and by Gabriel! It is Mankind! Can any of you recall when we last saw the Almighty's grace? This has been by far the longest absence we have ever endured. They have spent much time working on Earth and Man, which were supposed to be mortal and contain such free will that they would have to struggle to make the right choices, rendering them perfectly balanced beings. We all understand the importance of balance, do we not? It has been brought to my attention that the humans now contain everlasting life and are in a world filled with beasts and animals of all nature but living in complete harmony. Now I know this sounds wonderful to us, but where is the balance? Michael has had such an interest in these humans and wants them to be so much like us that I can make only one conclusion. They are making us obsolete and will replace us with them! Don't you understand now!? Can't you see with clear eyes, like I do? Michael is the Wicked and has upset the balance of the Universe and worse, has corrupted the mind of The Creator!"

An outburst of debate broke the moment my final words left my lips. I saw the division spread amongst them. I saw how one side understood my concern and defended me while the other side spoke of me as a blasphemer. I saw Uriel and Raphael make their way to the front of the assembly, their white feathery wings guiding the angels to the side. That was when I levitated the key and sent it flying into the lock of the arsenal, then signaled for Azrael and Samael to distribute the weapons to the army.

Uriel stepped forward and curiously gazed up to me in the balcony. I continued, "If the Creator is perverted, what else has been infected? I have long been chosen to protect our livelihood from the Wicked; see that all who oppose me must be compromised as well!"

"Brother Luzbel!" Uriel called out, "I believe you have gone too far, Luzbel. Do you not see how you have disturbed the peace we strive to maintain?"

"I have awakened, Brother Uriel!" I responded, pointing my blade down at him. "The disturbing thing is this new love for humans and how we have been cast aside."

"What do you propose we do?" asked Raphael finally, after a long uncomfortable pause where he and Uriel shared a questionable look.

I turned my gaze away from them and pointed my sword at the Mountain of Knowledge, for the workshop at its summit could be seen in the distance just over the columns of the colosseum. "We storm the workshop! I can kill the humans!"

Frantic, Uriel flew to stop the distribution, but I was faster. I shot my free hand out and clenched my fist. The rest of the weaponry sprang out of the armory. Chaos broke. The angels were quick to arm themselves. The opposing sides commenced battle. Uriel was bashed about, caught in the frenzy. Raphael sprinted up the stone steps in my direction but was stopped by a kick to the face from Azrael. He then turned to me and said, "We must go now!"

I leapt into the air and flapped my elegant wings out of the Colosseum, Samael and Azrael followed. Behind us a roaring mass of angels charged out from the pillars and began to make their way toward the mountain, still fighting off the angels that didn't want to believe my accusations. I could hear the onslaught; instruments breaking, glass shattering, statues toppling over. I dared not to look back, my home was being destroyed in the wreckage, my people were killing each other in the riot.

That's when he hit me from the right; Gabriel flew into me at full force. We spiraled through the air. He was on top of me and I flew with my back towards the ground, defending myself. I looked swiftly to the workshop and saw the doors were opened; Michael stood at the entrance. Gabriel unleashed a barrage of hacking blows with his sword, and I parried each one. I spun, knocking my brother off me temporarily and gazed back at the workshop. Michael had vanished, then I heard the air cut swiftly as I saw his wings soar over my head. Michael turned and charged at me; however, Samael intercepted his attack. They locked arms and tumbled to the ground, breaking off right before they crashed into the reflecting pool and soaring back into the air.

I continued toward the mountain; the workshop doors remained open, and it was dark inside. The Father wasn't there. Then from below, Uriel flew up towards me. I readied myself for the attack, but it did not come for Azrael tackled into his midsection and they flew off into the blue sky. The air was filled with the clashing of metal upon metal, the cries of the wounded, and the rumble of the archangels. I had reached the mountain and flapped my wings heavily to carry me up the immense rocky structure, hovering above the steps that climbed to the summit. I was almost at the door when Gabriel returned and intercepted my path. We both landed on our feet right outside of the workshop, interlocking our blades.

No words were said, we locked eyes as we fought. One attack. One parry. Gabriel ran at me, spinning his sword overhead and aimed the slash straight for my neck. In an upward motion, I blocked his blade with my own gleaming sword and shoved him forward. I leapt over his head and landed behind him. Right as I was about to impale his spine, he spun and parried. We locked blades, the workshop at my back and his to the spiraling steps leading down the mountain. I kicked him in the chest and Gabriel staggered back. I flicked my hand and the air caused Gabrielle to tumble head over feet down the mile-long staircase.

Alone now, I ran into the workshop. As I crossed the threshold, my weapon disintegrated into dust. I had no use for it any longer, anyway; I needed only to make my way to the opposite side of the room. By slamming the large doors behind me I was secured, none could open it from the outside. I turned in awe as I stared across at the emptiness in place of a wall. It was void of space from a distance, but as I approached, I saw the Universe appear. It was as if I could see everything at once. All the planets and galaxies in the Universe, the Serpenoids mining for metal, even the battle just outside the door, and then I saw it. *Eden* was what they called it; I saw all of it. The vast green grass, the thick jungles, the sparkling oceans, the elk and monkeys and lions together in harmony. I thought of the Serpenoids and how this world had become completely unsuitable for your needs. Then, I saw them! The *humans.* There were only two, one man and one woman. The man was off in one area observing the animals, and the woman sat under the supposedly forbidden tree, stroking her hair.

I stepped closer, inches away from the window and concentrated until only the image of the woman filled the view. I took in a deep breath, directing my thoughts at the window for Earth to hide my true presence, then leaned my head into the portal. I couldn't touch her but I spoke with the woman, in a different form, but I spoke with her nonetheless. And I did it, I convinced her to break the one simple rule those pathetic humans had. Before I could rejoice, before I could watch her make the man do it, I was blinded. My vision was taken over by a pure white light. It was the Creator, my father.

I felt warm, at peace, but only for a fraction of a second before the energy shot me back into my realm, sending me through the double doors of the workshop and tumbling down the mountain. I slammed onto the ground with enough force to leave cracks within the marbled floor. Aching, I turned over to see that the battle had stopped, and for quite some time it seemed. Much of the destruction from the battle had been mended, only betraying minute signs of distress. It was as if my brothers and the angels had been awaiting my return. My consciousness was only on Earth for a moment, but in my home it seemed I had been gone for several days. I looked over at Azrael and he turned away, then to Samael and he wore an expression of embarrassment and guilt.

I lifted myself to my knees and held onto the ground for support. The tile beneath my palms rumbled as if an earthquake was afoot, but instead of a tremor, my surroundings began to change and shift. The ground around me began towering up, creating a circular pit. Platforms jutted from the towering walls on the right where the angels stood and looked down upon me. In the center morphed a balcony where Michael and Gabriel each stood behind their own podium. Azrael and Samael were on their knees, encaged and facing towards Michael on a platform to my left. Everything seemed so dark, the risers casting heavy shadows, and all the solemn angelic faces gazing down.

There were no whispers or murmuring, no gossip of any kind. Silence was the only musician performing. I cast my right hand in front of my face, as I was blinded by the Father's light once again. His energy had never seemed blinding to me, but now it was almost unbearable. The orb of energy that is the Creator hung over us, casting ominous shadows over Michael's and Gabriel's faces. The father spoke to us through thought and said the word "Commence".

Michael nodded in response and hammered three times on his podium with a gavel. From behind him, Uriel and Raphael came floating by in a circular motion on separate platforms and levitated in the space between myself and the others.

"Explain to us why we are gathered here." Michael ordered.

The two glanced at each other before Uriel took the lead to speak. "We gather here today as Luzbel stands trial for his actions of heresy."

The angels that acted as the audience broke into an uproar, Samael and Azrael remained on one knee with their heads hanging low. Michael banged his gavel three times more.

Uriel waited for silence before continuing, "Luzbel arranged an unorganized assembly at the Colosseum and spoke against you, Brother Michael. He spread the slander that you and Brother Gabriel were the Wicked that we have all been trained to fight against."

Michael and Gabriel looked toward each other before they, as well as everyone else, shot their piercing gaze down at me.

"He tried to claim the Father's mantle for himself, he tried to change the plans of Creation that you have worked so hard on!" Raphael accused.

"That is a lie…" I tried to stand but an invisible force pushed me back to my hands and knees, then I heard within my head, *You will have your chance to speak.*

"Continue." Michael gestured with his hand, taking no notice of my struggle.

"He spoke of how you were misleading the Creator from our way of life, focusing more on the humans being divine rather than balanced through mortality." Raphael explained. "That's when he distributed the weapons, with the aid of brothers Azrael and Samael."

Raphael gestured over to the left at my groveling brothers in their pedestalled cell. "Uriel and I attempted to put a stop to the madness, but the others attacked us in retaliation. The citizens attacked one another, some in the defense of their lives and in loyalty to the Creator, and some under the influence of the blasphemer. That is all I have to say."

"Thank you." Michael hammered away, the witnesses were transported back behind Michael and the platform holding Azrael and Samael then floated toward the center. "You are accused of treason for following the deception of Luzbel. Explain yourself; only one shall speak."

The two accused faced each other and made an agreement in silence before Azrael stood. He glanced down at me; he was too high for me to make out his eyes, but I could tell there was a glint of cunning behind his shame. He cleared his throat then spoke, "I acted solely on my duty as a loyal soldier."

Again, an uproar exploded in the audience and Azrael raised his voice, "Is Brother Luzbel not head archangel and general of the army against the Wicked!?"

I couldn't help but form a grin, I was very intrigued on where my most trusted companion would take this argument. Michael requested silence, for the angels still had yet to simmer down. It wasn't until the Creator flooded our hearts with a warm sensation that they quieted, then Michael addressed the question.

"Yes, Brother Azrael, the title of general was appointed to Luzbel by the Creator on the chance that the Wicked came to threaten our way of life. If this had been the case, I would reward you for being so obedient." Michael let his words linger before continuing. "*However*, Luzbel led the army to fight against one another, to fight against yourselves, resulting in many casualties and leaving our beautiful home in destruction and misery. This appalling behavior created a mass division and, in doing so, led Luzbel to taint the sanctity of the Creator's project. How do you explain that?"

The silence was thick, Azrael contemplated heavily before responding. "A tragic and unfortunate set back. You see, there was a dispute on what we were fighting against."

"You were fighting against each other."

"No, our intent was to stop the Wicked. It was for the greater good!"

"Ah yes, the greater good. Something tells me the greater good will, in time, become the center of most pointless wars. So, what *was* the Wicked?"

Again, Azrael thought long and hard before looking down at me, then up towards the light. "My Lord, I wish to speak directly to you." The answer, *Go on,* whispered within our heads.

"The humans, Luzbel claimed the humans to be the Wicked, as was the way Michael intended them to live. Michael's philosophy for man obstructed balance, which is wicked and would destroy our way of life, thus rendering Michael the Wicked."

A gasp of surprise came from the audience. Michael stared at Azrael, though if he was in disbelief of the accusation of being the Wicked, it didn't show on his face. The Father answered through thought, *You believe the project I have worked so endlessly on to be wicked?*

"No, Creator." Azrael's voice became small. "Not originally."

Then you believe that I chose Michael as my aid, when he is the Wicked? You claim that this choice on my part was wicked in nature?

There was no response.

You accuse me of not knowing what the Wicked is, then? That I am blind to my own creations?

"Well, I don't know. Couldn't the Wicked have clouded your judgement?"

"My judgement? My *judgment was clouded? Azrael, tell me what are the things that are wicked in nature?*

"Greed, envy, pride, wrath..." Azrael's hand began to tremble, he glanced down at me one last time before he broke into tears and collapsed onto his knees, "Creator, forgive me!" He wept, "It was I whose mind was clouded! I was following orders, just doing what I thought you would want. I killed my brothers, I k-killed ssso muh-many!" He was getting choked up in his despicable sobbing. Those emotions were so unnatural to us, his sobs hideously contorted his angelic face. Azrael took a moment, wiped the tears from his eyes. He was more composed and cleared his throat before speaking once more, "I see now. It is Luzbel who is the Wicked!"

My heart sank; I was betrayed. Betrayed by my brother, the one I trusted most. The anger, the hurt, it flooded me, enraged me! I fought against the invisible barrier and stood straight up. "You coward! All of you!" My voice roared with disdain. It was hoarse, bellowing, in a way I had never heard myself to be. "You all were so quick to follow me when I enlightened you, and this is how you repay me!? Azrael, you pathetic whelp. You grovel on your knees when you stood right by my side. I saw your face! You took pleasure in your slaughter. Samael, why do you not say something?" But Samael kept his head down in silence.

Michael slammed away on his gavel to retain order, but that didn't stop me. "No, now it is my turn to speak. I am innocent, the only innocent! The humans were originally to be mortal, and I made it so; now they will depend on you more. Can you not see that I did it for you, for balance! And now you all accuse me? *Me!?* I am Luzbel, perfect in every way, the general against the Wicked. I am not wicked, it is all of you!"

"Silence!" The Father's voice boomed and this time it wasn't in thought but at a piercing frequency. I had to cover my ears from the intense white noise that filled the air. Suddenly I was levitated in the air for all to see. Then He spoke again, but this time through thought. *Luzbel, you are tried for slander, deception, and heresy. Your accusations include me as the Wicked, but I am the Creator. You led your own people to fight and kill one another. You sabotaged my creation. You claim to fight for balance, but it is out of sheer jealousy and nothing else. Now you will become the balance you long for. I hereby find you guilty of all charges and sentence you to banishment."*

The skies darkened and thunder shook the world, shook the Universe. The golden band around my arm exploded into dust. Whatever had held me, lowered me to the ground, surrounded by the other six archangels. They clawed and ripped at me, tearing away my tunic and garb. I was left naked, as I am now. Then Gabriel stepped behind me. He gripped tightly onto my left wing and tore it off with his bare hands. I screamed with an agony that echoed throughout our domain as the muscles ripped and the cartilage snapped. I huffed and attempted to hold back that unnatural emotion from my eyes. *Tears.*

I had never once felt pain in my existence. It was an excruciating searing sensation. Gabriel then took hold of my other wing and pulled it apart as well. Blood splattered over his face and torso; I fell to the ground. Blood gushing from the stumps where my beautiful wings once flapped. Stinging. Burning.

Thousands of eyes stared at me, whispering amongst themselves, gasping in terror of the gore. I continued screaming with my face pressed to the cold marble floor as my blood stained the tile red. When I finally lifted my head, I scanned the sea of faces, vision blurred by tears. Many of the angels held their hands to their mouths at the grotesque sight. Azrael had vanished, Samael kept his back turned, Michael just shook his head in pity.

"Father," I whispered.

I heard the Father's thought, *Exiled for eternity.* Gabriel gripped me firmly by the back of my neck, and we floated towards the workshop

"Please, Father! I am your shining light. I am the Morning Star!"

Banished into darkness, where your light will shine unnoticed.

We approached the workshop, but the Father's warm light stayed behind. Gabriel stopped at the window to the Universe. And for the last time, I heard one more thought from my Father. *Banished forever, from my love.* Then Gabriel collected his strength and hurled me into the abyss.

Luzbel pounded his fist against the ground as Vander stared down the hole, seeing the prisoner in a new light. He felt pity for him; no, it was more than that, he felt *sympathy* for him. To have his entire family turn their backs on him and send him to serve a penance here, to a place where the Serpenoids called sanctuary. A part of him felt a bit insulted, but most of his thoughts were preoccupied with the agony of what this fallen angel had endured, whether he had committed treason or not, only to be beaten and forced into slavery. Vander had a small tear in his eye, which he cast away with the wipe of a clawed finger.

"Luzbel, I am so sorry, for all of this."

"No, do not use that name. I am no longer Luzbel. That name died along with the archangel that held that name. No, that is no longer who I am. I have been reborn now; I am Lucifer!"

***

Vander ran all the way from the prisoner's pit straight to Lord Thandrua with the new information. He had never heard of such tales, of anything like the life of Luzbel. *Lucifer,* Vander corrected himself. Once he made it to the royal chamber he waited outside, catching his breath for a moment. The area was silent, the Serpenoids were still out working away at their cycle tasks. Vander entered the shelter and saw it empty. Quickly he went for the lake, certain his Lord would be seated by the shore.

Coming down from the valley, the Serpenoid could see Lord Thandrua in his throne with Sectoraus on his side. Moving closer, Vander saw the two were admiring the gemstones they received from the cycle before. He cleared his throat, but his two leaders were entranced.

"My lords!" Vander raised his voice.

"Ah, Oracle," Thandrua closed his fist around the gem in his palm, "what is your urgency?"

"The prisoner finally opened up." He shifted his gaze between the two, "Opened up about his origin."

Thandrua stood abruptly, "Let us go into my chamber." The three began walking uphill before the red beast turned to his companion, "Sectoraus, I must hear this alone."

"But Thandrua…" Sectoraus was cut off by Thandrua.

"Leave us be and I will inform you later."

"I see." The Cobra did not dispute the privacy his master needed with the Oracle any further, though he sneered at Vander before walking off. Sectoraus was beginning to see that his place with Thandrua was no longer as sacred as it once was. The Serpenoid was now more important.

Lord Thandrua stood on the hillside and watched as the Cobra king stormed off. He did not mean to offend his friend, and he felt his heart sink. However, the information from a being that knew more than himself was sensitive information. Sensitive to Thandrua's reputation. After Sectoraus was a distance away, Thandrua and Vander continued toward the royal chamber.

Once inside, Thandrua began pacing. He seemed to do that more these cycles than ever before. Vander waited for his master to be ready and watched the crimson god-king move back and forth. Thandrua huffed to himself, anticipating what knowledge he might receive. Finally, he stopped and after taking a deep breath, "So, Oracle, what did he have to say?"

Vander retold his master the tale of the former archangel Luzbel and the life of those who worshipped the Creator in the realm of Heaven. He told him of their cosmic creation, the workshop on top of the massive mountain, and the society the angels built in their master's absence. Vander told Thandrua of the rebellion that took many lives and left their kingdom in misery. Finally, he spoke of the judgment that cast the archangel into their realm, where he donned the new name, Lucifer.

"Lucifer believes he has lost his telekinetic ability during his banishment… I know this is a lot to take in." Vander concluded.

Thandrua returned to his pacing, "This is… this…"

"It is the truth." Vander completed the open sentence, "The truth that the Creator is real. That we are not alone and there is more to this than we have perceived."

"This is something we cannot release to the others."

"My Lord, you cannot..."

"I can do as I please! You will not tell the full story to anyone else! At the end of this cycle, I will gather the Cobra Clan and tell them a version of this tale. A version without the Creator."

"The Creator is the key!"

"Lucifer is the key. It will be a story of how Lucifer betrayed his brothers, caused a schism within their society, and attempted to kill his equals. The Cobra Clan will understand it better this way. And after Lucifer was captured and held accountable for his treason… his brothers forced him into a hole like the one in the canyon that brought us here."

The Oracle's head sank with defeat. He shut his eyes tight and sighed, "If that is what you wish, Master."

Section III
The Plague

Chapter 10
Up From the Abyss

Lord Thandrua paced within his chamber alone. Sectoraus spent less time with his royal companion after the revelations of their prisoner. Thandrua felt lost, understanding more and more that this entity, the Creator, was a true force. However, it still was not enough to humble him. His fractured ego needed the worship and the fabrication of his power more now than ever.

The twinkle of the deity's pile of gemstones called to the beast. Thandrua began admiring his collection of jewels, and a sense of bliss began to envelope him. Suddenly, Thandrua's thoughts were interrupted by a small tremor beneath the very rust-colored ground he stood upon. His emerald eyes enlarged. It was a sensation he hadn't felt since their lives in the old world. Without another thought, he strode toward the mine site; it was quite a distance from the camp, but Thandrua's long strides covered much ground.

The tremors grew ferocious as he passed the old barren mines, further over the horizon and closer to where the Serpenoids labored in their current mine. Just beyond, he could make out various figures hurrying in his direction as well. It was the mining crew with Orpheus and Phineus, who exposed their hoods. Thandrua ran to meet them.

"My Lord," Orpheus said with such gravity in his voice, "what is happening? The mine began to jolt, we had to evacuate. It feels like," he paused and shook his scaly hooded head in disbelief. "I haven't felt anything like this since…"

"Since our previous home." Thandrua's mind had been in the same place, "It feels like a quake, but this land has not done this before."

"There is more," Phineus pointed back toward where they had run from. "Just over the horizon, we were scared of the tremors, but what we saw in the sky… we had to find you."

Without another word, Thandrua pushed past them, Phineus signaled for the miners to come along. Although all were frightened at what might be happening, they returned to the direction they had just fled from. In all their memories of the quakes, danger could be anywhere. So long as they stuck together, with Thandrua at their lead, they trusted they were safe.

Nearing the mine, Thandrua and the Serpenoids halted as they gazed into the sky just over the horizon.

"You see, my Lord!?" Orpheus pointed, "The mine shook and we knew something terrible must be happening once we saw that brewing."

Lord Thandrua said nothing, merely stared at the sky where dark, sinister clouds formed. They were a deep purple within the frightening red sky. Some distance behind them came another group; they had to be from the Kiln, with Sectoraus far ahead hurrying to get to his awestruck master's side. The Cobra king's hood flared open once he caught sight of the dark clouds.

"Sectoraus and Solarious approach with the forgers, Sire," said Phineus. Although their crimson skinned god-king heard him, Thandrua continued to gape at the storm brewing.

The curse, Thandrua's thoughts raced, all the Serpenoids' chatter sounding like indistinct muffles to him. *The land will become plagued. It warned me and yet I did not release Lucifer. Is it too late? What is to come? Is our paradise to become the equal of our last home? Is this world now to become riddled with dangerous storms and disasters as well? How long until the forsaken Sun appears here as well?*

The storm ahead grew thick and nasty as Sectoraus reached his master, "Thandrua, what is…" But before he could finish his question the clouds exploded with the roar of thunder and the ground rumbled. With a bright flash, a single purple beam of lightning erupted, illuminating the lightless atmosphere. Peculiar it was, the lightning seemed to burst up from the horizon and connect to the clouds, not the other way around. This happened within a faction of a second and most of the watching eyes did not catch the phenomenon.

The onlookers swept back as one final quake shook the world and a gust of orange debris puffed from the ground where the lighting struck (or shot out from), as if the quake tore open the very ground itself. The storm seemed to immediately calm after the lightning strike, however.

Thandrua stared at the horizon, his eyes transfixed by the receding storm clouds, and then at long last, he spoke, "Sectoraus! Orpheus! Let us investigate." He turned and motioned to four Serpenoids holding digging tools. "Join us, the rest of you stay here with Phineus and Solarious."

They all began to move forward, the remaining Cobras nodded in agreement, but before they ventured, Lord Thandrua turned to Phineus.

"What of Lucifer?"

"We left him at the mines, Sire. Orpheus and I thought to get the Serpenoids away first, and what should we care if that ugly creature was engulfed by the rubble from a cave in?"

Lord Thandrua stood there, taking in the information. He wasn't sure whether they made the right decision or not, but merely grunted in response and strode toward where the ground had erupted, toward the mine.

The howling winds dropped to a whisper and the darkened clouds had all but evaporated within the heavy orange sky as the group reached the abandoned mine. They passed the surface of the pit leading to the Serpenoids' recent site and Thandrua shot his emerald eyes down the shaft, meeting a pair of grey eyes as Lucifer calmly sat cross-legged, returning the look.

"You're doomed, Almighty Infallible Lord Thandrua." Lucifer sneered, "You and all your slippery snakes!"

The Cobras hissed ferociously through their gritted fangs at the mocking fallen angel.

"Pay no mind to him," Thandrua said as he continued walking past the mine and through an almost fog-like air created from the debris of the ruptured ground. Just ahead, they could see a crevice in the ground from shifting tectonic plates, or was it truly from the lightning bolt that impaled the ground? Still just a short distance away, but clearly visible, the crack wasn't very lengthy; rather, the lighting revealed a deep abyss, wide enough to cause concern of falling in.

The group moved closer to the crevice, Lord Thandrua at the lead and Sectoraus and Orpheus close behind, with the four Serpenoids approaching with a bit more fear in their step than their guide. The abyss yawned, just a few more steps ahead, when they all froze in place; shock jolted the investigators to the ground - something was coming out of the hole. As a matter of fact, several somethings were coming out, or rather, reaching out from the depths. Still very confused as to what they were, no, these did not appear to be claws like those of Thandrua or any of his Serpenoid followers, but resembled hands and arms like that of Lucifer.

"Orpheus!" Thandrua turned quickly, "Bring the rest of the company!"

With not a single word to waste, the brutish Cobra turned and doubled back to where they left the others, watching from a long distance away. With that, the two royal companions approached the crevice as the four Serpenoids waited behind.

"More creatures?" Sectoraus peered down with disgust.

Many more, the beast lord thought, "Grab the arms and pull them out. We will put them with *Him*."

Sectoraus snatched a soft fleshy arm whose hand was feeling around for grip against the coarse rust-colored soil. He yanked at it, barring his black claws into this tender skin; a scream followed. A creature was pulled from the darkness, confused and disoriented. Sectoraus did not find it strange that this creature had different hair and eye color than their prisoner but was curious at a strange appendage that dangled between this creature's legs. Sectoraus also noted that the creature's back was smooth and didn't show signs of stumps like Lucifer's had when he arrived. All this was quickly dismissed as Sectoraus dragged the creature across the rocky sand before hurling it into the mine.

Lord Thandrua cuffed his meaty red palm around a pair of thin arms attempting to pull themselves from the hole. Unlike his devoted disciple, Thandrua was delicate, pulling the body out and carrying the being in both his arms. This one also had the appendage between the legs, as did the next creatures the Serpenoids removed from the crevice.

Thandrua was taken aback at the sight of the next one he carried in his arms. This creature had quite a different figure from that of Lucifer and the other creatures they recovered. This one had long black hair with a swollen chest and a more rounded lower half, whereas the others had shorter hair and a less curved figure. The strange one Thandrua carried didn't seem to have the dangling appendage as the others did. He didn't think too much more into this creature's appearance before lowering it into the mine with the rest.

The Cobra Clan arrived with many Serpenoids, although they had sent many back to their camp. The Serpenoids required no directions, the new arrivals understood what they had to do. A short while was all it took before the combined efforts of the party had removed over thirty of the new arrivals and threw them in the mine with Lucifer. Many moans of pain and panicked screams of fear lifted from the mine. Thandrua led his group to relieve themselves back home. Lucifer continued to sit cross-legged with an expression that was nothing short of unphased.

All the people roamed this way or that around the mine, completely oblivious to the fallen angel in the center. They would stagger around him, sometimes into him, and into each other as well. They were deeply absorbed within their own minds. They had no awareness of who was around them, where they were, and even more frightening, *who* they were.

The shrill screams of hysteria dragged on and on, people clawed at the walls, yanked their hair, frantic and dazed. After a great deal of time, however, one seemed to notice Lucifer beneath this mad scene and pushed passed the crowd to confront him.

Her long black hair flowed behind her as her slender body squeezed past the insane toward the white-haired man. "What is happening?" She asked.

He looked up at her but didn't move his head immediately and stared past her eyes, almost as if he was seeing into this being. *A woman!* The fallen archangel observed.

"You seem to be the only calm one in this madness," the woman said, "you must know something."

There was still no response.

"I think… I think I remember."

"I do know what is happening, but we shall get into that in a moment," the tranquil Lucifer finally said, "First, what is it that you remember?"

"My home… my *city!* It was destroyed, I think."

"Ah, I see," Lucifer gave a slight smirk, "and you are?"

She broke eye contact and thought for a moment, "I don't remember."

"I see..." Lucifer stood and took hold of her left hand. "Well, then come with me... Lilith. Yes, Lilith will do. Perhaps it will come back to you in time, but for now let us seek any others that might have *awakened*."

He let her hand drop and moved past her, and Lilith followed. He moved with such speed that she fell behind and had to push through the flailing bodies darting past her. Lucifer, on the other hand, stepped past them with grace, as if he were casually taking a stroll all on his lonesome. Lilith looked about her and could see more people were beginning to regain awareness, seeming more composed. The confused still moved frantically as if blind, yelling incoherently; some of the men were fighting each other.

Lucifer would walk past those that stood calmly, seeming to be emerging into consciousness, and tap them on their shoulders as an invitation to join the small group that collected behind him with Lilith. In time, there were more that gained curiosity and joined his group than those who still seemed lost within themselves or caught up in a scuffle. Lucifer ended his rounds by returning to the center and holding his spot, turning slowly to catch the eyes that stared at him, murmuring amongst themselves, longing for answers.

"This," Lucifer began, spreading his arms as most of the chatter died, "this will not be easy. You have all been taken from what you know and brought here to begin anew. Some of you might remember where you came from or what you were doing last; dismiss any such memories. You will never find a way back to where those memories are from." There were screams of disbelief and the chatter broke out again. Now the fighters had stopped their brawl and tuned in, the dazed now very much aware and frightened.

"Settle yourselves! Fear will not aid you here!" Lucifer shouted over the hysteria, "You have begun a journey called *eternity*. Unfortunately, it seems this eternity will be rather dreadful. Our captors, you might have seen, hold no notion of what is *humane*. However, there is a way."

The fallen angel paused for effect, letting his words settle and sink in. At this point, every person had stopped their inner turmoil, all eyes were on him. Lucifer turned on the spot, meeting their gaze with his. He could sense their hungry minds. Lucifer smirked wildly, for he always enjoyed the effect his speeches had brought in his former life. Finally, after relishing in the silence long enough, he spoke again, "My name is Lucifer! I urge you to listen to me now. I may not have the answers to your personal reasons for being here, but I do have knowledge of this world and of many marvelous things. Freedom is a certainty, but only if you do as I say and keep great patience. With your aid and devotion, together we can take down the false *Lord!"*

***

The miners and welders crowded in the camp. None swam in the lake down in the valley, nor took rest in their respective huts, or even enjoyed quality time with one another. No, instead, the Serpenoids gossiped among themselves, clustering just outside of the royal slumber chamber where their leaders were consulting with each other on the arrival of the unwelcome guests.

"I plead, this is only the beginning," Vander the Oracle urged. The Cobras glared at him with their hoods still open as Lord Thandrua paced back and forth. They had yet to place his throne within the hut; since returning from the phenomenon, the brotherhood stowed themselves away before the Serpenoids bombarded them with their curiosity. "It is now too late to avoid the plague."

"A *plague,* you call this?" Sectoraus did not hide the smugness in his voice, "With only thirty of them it is but a mere inconvenience."

"It is very spacious in that old pit," said Solarious. "Easy to leave and forget about them altogether." The other Cobras nodded their heads in agreement, their hoods relaxing as they spoke.

"No, you do not understand!" The Oracle shook with frustration, "We will be flooded! I have seen it. They are not the last, but the first of many."

The Cobra brothers traded silent glances with one another. Vander crossed his arms and glared. It was moments like these that he suspected the Clan used their special mental bond to shut him out, reminding Vander that he may be a part of their ranks but was still not included within their inner circle. It angered him. They were now on the path to his vision of destruction, and they needed to work together in unity, all of them.

"Will no one say anything else!?"

The crimson god-king stopped his pacing behind Vander and turned to see the Cobra Clan standing side by side together, blankly staring at the Oracle that stood in front of them. "They will not harm us," said Thandrua, stepping next to Vander. "We can create more chains. We have enough metal at the ready, do we not, Solarious?"

"Why yes, my Lord." The striped Cobra responded.

"Very well then." Thandrua looked over toward the entryway, seeing the eager Serpenoids crowded about, their concerns and inquiries amplified by the empty space of the chamber. He rubbed the stinging mark over his left eye before looking directly at Sectoraus, "What do you suppose we tell them?"

"Tell them not to worry. The creatures will be incapacitated and out of sight so we can all go about our regular cycle." No one said anything else. The Cobras, the Oracle, and the deity all continued to stare at Sectoraus expectantly, hoping he would say more. The head Cobra shifted his yellow eyes to the marvelous scepter held in Thandrua's hand, then to the golden chains that hung around his clan brothers' necks. "Better yet, we tell them to enjoy the remainder of this cycle and when we ready for the next cycle's tasks, the miners will be accompanied with the aid of our guests."

"No, no, you cannot!" Vander protested before anyone else could speak, "That is not the right way, that is not how anyone should be treated!"

"Watch your tone-" warned Solarious, but before he could say anything more the Oracle snapped back.

"No! My head may not be misshapen like the four of you, but are we not supposed to be equals within this covenant?"

Orpheus chuckled under his breath, Sectoraus scowled at the Oracle while Phineus drove his attention to Solarious.

"I was going to say, watch your tone, for the Serpenoids are listening outside." Solarious' voice was calm and his eyes held no expression, "They are curious and startled enough as it is. They do not need to hear a quarrel amongst their leaders."

"...Understood." Vander's voice dropped just as his eyes did.

"Get this straight," Sectoraus crossed his arms as his hood began to unfold, his glare piercing. "Yes, you are given the privilege to lead with us. Yes, I may favor my brothers." Sectoraus stepped toward the Oracle and jabbed a finger into his chest, "But do understand that even my brothers stand separate from Lord Thandrua and myself. We are *not* equals."

"Enough!" Thandrua was done listening to their feud. "Vander is correct, putting the creatures to work in the mines and having them work alongside our own would not be compassionate, and may not be safe.

"Thank you, Sire." The Oracle bowed his head.

"However," Thandrua's green eyes looked gravely into Vander's and Vander's alone. "The time has passed to prevent this plague; it is here now. Whether more may arrive or not, my priorities are for the safety of the Serpenoids. My compassion is to them and you five alone. No, these creatures will not labor with our miners and welders. They will work alone."

Vander stared at him in shock; Sectoraus smirked, looking pleased, and the others remained silent. Vander hoped they could all coexist together in peace. Perhaps in time the creatures would even volunteer themselves to aid in the Serpenoids' production, but not like this. He wanted to say something, wanted to do something, but he couldn't. There was nothing that would change his master's mind anyhow. They all lacked foresight, something only Vander himself could understand. No matter how much he debated, he could never get them to see past the here and now. How could they, when it was all they ever knew?

Looking at Sectoraus, Lord Thandrua nodded his horned head towards the entryway, signaling his companion to address the colony. Sectoraus moved to exit, and the rest of the clan followed. Before Thandrua left with them, he held Vander's stare. Thandrua's look was almost apologetic, even though he felt that this was the only solution for the best interest of the colony. Or was it his own best interest? Thandrua was big and strong, perhaps showing a less aggressive action would let down his followers. It was what they expected from him. The Oracle lingered in the chamber alone once his master left; he stood frozen with anger, with fear.

"Calling an assembly!" Sectoraus hollered as Orpheus pushed back the crowd. The Serpenoids separated, opening a path from the royal chamber to the center of the grounds where a large boulder sat. The Cobra Clan stood around it as Lord Thandrua lifted himself onto the rock to stand high above his followers.

"Silence for your Lord!" Sectoraus ordered one more time and the crowd obeyed.

"Thank you," Thandrua spoke softly to his companion, then projected his voice, "Thank you all!" He scanned the sea of yellow serpent eyes. "I understand this has not been easy. The phenomenon earlier this cycle has shaken us all. These past several cycles as a whole have been trying. First with the arrival of Lucifer and now the coming of these other creatures. No, I do not know from where they have come, nor do I know why."

The crowd moved uneasily and began to babble once again, but quickly quieted when Thandrua spoke up again. "Do not fear, my loyal Serpenoids. This will not hinder our lives, but rather aid us for a new future. The Clan and I have decided these intruders will be put to your cycle duties. As you all have done so well, it is now time for you to enjoy the shine of your labors as we have. In short, you are all free of your duties. We will keep the intruders bound and those of you who are the most skilled in your tasks will show them exactly how to work your art."

Lord Thandrua paused allowing the information to sink in. He watched as the Serpenoids understood and their fearful faces sparked with pleasant smiles. Looking over to his chamber, Thandrua watched Vander exit and step toward the lake by himself.

"Recreation is indefinite!" Thandrua declared, "You are all secure in my rule and I am utterly grateful that such beings would turn up, granting you all the luxury of enjoying life leisurely. That is my gift to you!"

The Serpenoids applauded the news, but the applause was weak. Many cheered with excitement, but the colony as a whole seemed unsatisfied. They spoke amongst themselves as they clapped unenthusiastically. Their questions had not been answered. What were these creatures? Had they been fallen angels like Lucifer? And where did they come from, was it from within the depths of their world, or another, like how the Serpenoids travelled through a crevice from their former world?

They had always been grateful with what their Lord Thandrua gave them, always had accepted everything without protest. Now these newcomers were to replace the Serpenoids in the mines and the Kiln. Some of the Serpenoids felt joy in the idea of perpetual recreation, but others did not. They enjoyed their labors, it had given them skills, given them purpose. Now their talents were to be passed down to another. Perhaps it was an honor, which is what those who cheered and applauded gleefully thought.

"Assembly is over!" Shouted Sectoraus. "You heard the Lord Thandrua, that is all! Enjoy the remainder of the cycle, for tomorrow we begin a new way of life!" Sectoraus looked up at Thandrua; he felt uneasy at the lack of enthusiasm of the crowd. Making eye contact with Thandrua told Sectoraus that his master felt the same.

With a rumbling thud, Thandrua dropped down from the boulder.

"Nicely done, my Lord," Phineus said as Thandrua and the clan huddled together.

"That was rather unusual," said Thandrua.

"Yes, they did not react as I thought they might," agreed Sectoraus.

"That had never been the case before," Thandrua said, taking another look around at the Serpenoids. "What do you suppose..." he trailed off in thought.

"This situation is quite different from anything we have experienced before." Solarious chimed in, then gazed over to the lake where he saw Vander meditating by the shore line. "Perhaps they are awakening as the Oracle has."

"Yes, yes," Sectoraus thought about that for a moment, "Perhaps not in the sense as Oracle who believes to be connected to whatever it is he thinks he is, but perhaps developing more of a self. Minds expanding."

"It is not belief, my friend, it is knowledge," Thandrua responded, then looked over to Vander as well. "He is not satisfied with our decision."

"He is afraid," Sectoraus said. "We are in control here and we are making the right steps to ensure security for our colony. Besides, the creatures are on our land. They must do whatever it is we wish of them."

The group remained silent for a while, pondering. The dry hot air breezed by them, wafting brimstone through their nostrils. Heavy indistinct conversation from the Serpenoids filled their ears. It was a peaceful moment, but only a moment. Thunder cracked in the sky a distance away, in the direction from where the crevice had opened up.

"Perhaps," Lord Thandrua spoke solemnly, "the Oracle is rightful in his fear."

Chapter 11
Plans Set into Motion

Chains shifted and rattled, the grunts and groans of exhaustion rose with the chiseling of stone in a vast quarry. Its width engulfed three of the old mines and it descended to such a depth that a long ladder had been placed by one end, leading down to a ledge wide enough for several bodies to move about with carts and tools, then another ladder below that one. On the precipice where the ladder hung stood a hulking figure, arms crossed, yellow and black spotted hood expanded around the Cobra's head while his tail draped on the ground idly. Orpheus acted as a guard as he watched the hundreds of miners push the limits of their bodies down below.

These miners, however, were not clad in smooth scales, nor did they have luminous yellow eyes suited for their dark environment. They did not work as the Serpenoids did, with ferocious speed that hinted at enjoyment and skill. No, these miners were covered in a hide of soft fleshy skin, ranging across many different shades and colors. Skin that blistered and cracked due to their labors and the radiating heat of the stifling air. They were sluggish with fatigue, moving as one does when forced to work beyond their own will. It had been long since the last break they were given and just as long since they were gifted with water to quench their thirst.

These miners were not the Serpenoids Orpheus devotedly served to protect, but slaves. “Slaves" was what Orpheus called them, as did his brothers and most of the Serpenoids. Lord Thandrua referred to them as “intruders,” usually. "Human" was the name Vander the Oracle used to refer to them. He said during meditation he had communed with the mysterious Creator who told him about the permanent guests.

Human was what they were, coming from the old world of the Serpenoids, Earth. A world completely altered from the one they had fled. It was covered in water, mostly, and land that gave life to many things beyond the Serpenoid’s comprehension, such as plant life, living organisms that covered the lands throughout the world.

It wasn't explained how they arrived, just that they were damned in the sense that Lucifer was damned. When life ended for them on Earth, new life brought them into the Serpenoids' world. In some way it was both a punishment for the humans to live in this world, as well as a punishment for the Serpenoids to have these humans occupying their home. This punishment seemed to have become ineffective, however, as it allowed open freedom for the Serpenoids who formerly worked hard in the mines and the Kiln. At first, the Serpenoid miners worked alongside the damned, showing them how the work was done. Every other cycle the slaves were herded to the Kiln to learn the art of forging.

Their numbers kept growing, and at volumes that alarmed Lord Thandrua at first. However, in time, seeing how well the intruders picked up the skills of the labor, the fact that more continued to arrive seemed promising. The mines were expanded, not only to provide the miners with more room to work but to provide larger areas for them to work on. The Kiln was constantly busy, thick smoke pluming regularly from the volcano that housed the oven. The original Serpenoid welders were the first to retire indefinitely, transitioning the slaves to become the sole forgers in the Kiln that was supervised by Phineus.

More new ideas for the metal came to Sectoraus and Thandrua as they collected the gold and lavish jewels they decorated themselves with, wearing wrist cuffs, necklaces and especially the golden crown that now sat between Lord Thandrua's ivory horns. Piecing together metal, a fence had been built around the crevice from which the intruders crawled out. The fence led into a pit that expanded into the quarry, denying the new arrivals any chance to go anywhere but to their imprisonment. There by the crevice stood a group of Serpenoids who rotated shifts, keeping watch, ensuring the humans couldn't go beyond the fence, and occasionally the guards would enter to cuff and chain the new arrivals.

As the slaves' numbers grew and grew, fewer Serpenoids worked in the mines until they too had retired completely or took up positions as guards. From this prejudice was birthed a new dawn for the Serpenoids. Their minds expanded. They lusted for names of their own and privacy of their own. Thus, Lord Thandrua allowed them to abandon the two slumber chambers and the colony began building smaller, individual homes.

"Give me a hand here." Lord Thandrua watched one day as one yellowish Serpenoid built his own small chamber and struggled to place the stones that would be the roof on top. The Serpenoid asked a green Serpenoid that was walking by with a ladder.

"I had the same problem," the darker Serpenoid said as he placed the ladder down, "Lend me some of your mud sealant when we are done here. My stones need to be secured."

Thandrua walked by, observing more of his followers busy with their projects. He noticed that not all the shelters were domed. Some of the Serpenoids placed their stones together in a square shape, making those homes more box-like. The beastly ruler passed by a Serpenoid that sat on a stone-made bench, gazing to the horizon.

"Do you have any problems, Serpenoid?" asked Thandrua.

"No, Sire," the Serpenoid turned to meet Thandrua's green eyes before looking off to the horizon again, "just thinking."

During this new dawn, Vander kept mostly to himself. He spent his cycles watching the people slave over the stones and gems and meditating off on his own in a chamber the Serpenoids built for his solitude. He had begun etching various symbols and shapes along the walls of his home but kept quiet on what they were. He didn't commune with the Creator much at all, in fact it was rare when the unseen voice would greet him, but there was always a connection that held strong. This connection gave Vander hope that one cycle, in time, harmony could be shared between the captives and the Serpenoids.

Vander was gifted with something of a throne of his own, not nearly as elegant as Lord Thandrua's, but a seat for him to sit and ponder on within his home. Some Serpenoids would line up at the Oracle's home requesting a name for themselves, for his insight provided him with a wide range of names to appoint. Sectoraus became jealous. He felt it was not right to allow Vander such power even though Sectoraus had been Thandrua's second for countless cycles. The Cobra's dislike for Vander grew even greater. He approached Thandrua and mentioned how he saw Vander appointing names as taking power from Thandrua, and Lord Thandrua agreed.

"If any were to name the Serpenoids, it should be their Lord." Sectoraus told Thandrua. In a short time, the nameless Serpenoids began to meet with their almighty royal figure, who had the Oracle provide him with names to give.

The Oracle made a few attempts to continue palaver with Lucifer and receive his insight on the people, as he had been instructed by the Creator. However, his efforts were useless, for Lucifer now refused to speak to the Serpenoids and simply did as he was ordered.

Unlike the slaves, who increasingly lost the softness of their skin and the sparkle in their eyes, Lucifer's body continued to hide any indication of wounds; however, his white hair had grown, falling just to the top of his shoulders. None of the Serpenoids knew Lucifer's opinions on how the damned were treated. The guards that watched saw very little of Lucifer but when they did, he was always found deep in the crowds of the workers. The guards told Lord Thandrua how dedicated Lucifer had become to his job. So dedicated that the other slaves worked twice as hard when around the fallen archangel. This was only how it appeared.

Lucifer actually did very little work. In fact, the more slaves that crowded him, the less work he did himself - manual work that is. Lucifer was hard at work, but in a very different sense. The slaves looked toward Lucifer as their leader; he was the first enslaved and had knowledge from the cosmos. He was a motivating presence and gave the slaves hope. Hope that didn't seem to have a specific form, until the building of the shrine.

Lord Thandrua had become pompous with vanity, eyeing himself in the lake's reflection, and commanded that a replication of himself be built so that he could gaze upon it, one large enough for all to see his glory. It would be built just outside the grounds of the Serpenoid colony. A select group of slaves was escorted from the quarry to the camp on a cycle basis and collected pure gold to slowly build the Thandrua monstrosity. It took them twelve cycles to build the legs alone, and that was when Lucifer began to have secret meetings.

"Thank you all for meeting," Lucifer kept his voice low, but all was quiet within the quarry at the end of a cycle. Faint chiseling clinked and clanked in the distance from the slaves that continued to work near where Orpheus stood guard. Some slowly rolled boulders and large chunks of stone from one end to the other; it gave the illusion that they were preparing these to be taken to the Kiln, but actually it was a way to obstruct the gathering from sight. The handful of slaves that knelt around Lucifer, with Lilith to his left and a stocky-framed man to his right, listened intensely.

"We will be sure to pass the message on to those that continue the endless work." Lucifer rotated his shaggy-haired head to see his audience. "Since each one of you have arrived here, I have spoken to you all about the importance of unity and the eventual rise of my reign. I assure you freedom is within reach, and with the building of this shrine, now is the time to begin our gradual rise to rebellion."

Lucifer paused here to let his words take effect as he eyed the nodding heads of the prisoners, "I must warn you, however, this will take much time and cunning. We must cover our tracks well and prepare until the moment is right. Not a moment before, or all my plans for an uprising will surely fail. Patience is key here, as well as trust in my judgement."

"We are undoubtedly devoted to you, Lucifer," Lilith inclined her head to her leader.

"Thank you." Lucifer squatted down and began to draw in the dirt with his finger. "I have a design here that will need molding from those of you that work in the Kiln. Some of you may recognize it from your past lives, if you remember, and if you come from a time with such development of iron. It is a form of tool, but unlike the ones which we are forced to use within our enslavement. A tool new to this world and more importantly, to our captors."

He continued tracing, not looking up to catch the curious eyes that watched him. The figure's length was not unlike a shovel or pickaxe, but its shape differed. Crossed at one end with a small and rounded part which could work as a handle. “This next part will be forged very differently. The mold is only one phase, then we would need to keep the metal hot as it is hammered into a thin steel.” The other end Lucifer sketched stretched to an arm's length, forming a sharp point at the very tip. Lucifer stood straight now, "This tool is called a sword."

***

Back at the slumber grounds of the Serpenoids, Lord Thandrua and his loyal companion Sectoraus stood dwarfed by the massive unfinished golden structure. They walked around it, gaping at the awe of its majestic glow, looking past the scaffolds and ladders the slaves had set around it. Their eyes rolled from the two feet that stood before them up to the torso-less waist.

"Magnificent, is it not?" Thandrua whispered in amazement.

"Almost as much as its model." Sectoraus glanced down at his leader's legs then back to the statue. "They need to finish, I want to see how your face glows with the gold."

"They are making fine progress, my friend." Thandrua smiled at his eagerness then continued to stare at the pair of legs, "Yes, just the torso and head left. I have decided once the sculptors get past the chest to command them to build another in bronze, but of your likeness."

Sectoraus inclined his head, "The honor is my own."

Lord Thandrua glanced over his shoulder to the metallic Eye of Thandrua that stood next to his chamber, as large as the entryway. "Once my statue is complete, the whole world will have knowledge that I oversee all."

"Yes, the world," Sectoraus thought for a moment, "Thandrua I have been thinking..."

"Yes, my friend?"

"We roamed our past world endlessly, it proved to be extremely massive. I think it is safe to say we never discovered all parts of the past land. We have been here for all too many cycles now, camped here in this same spot just a short distance from where we had arrived. Our mines go further out, but we still have yet to see more of this land."

"I suppose we have kept the colony sheltered and comfortable, staying by the lake. What do you propose?"

"I do not imply that this is not a wonderful area to thrive in, nor do I mean for us to relocate. Just that, what else *is* out there? Our quarry has expanded tremendously and, like the mines before, in time the quarry, too, will become barren." Sectoraus allowed silence to build for a moment to let that fact sink into Thandrua's horned head, who nodded with understanding, "I propose that we have an exploration of our world."

The crimson god-king gazed outward across the lake, where Serpenoids enjoyed their leisure, to the World's Mountain in the distance that seemed to block the end of the world. He shifted his horned head to the right; from behind the World's Mountain, just above the horizon, stretched a mountain range that followed the seemingly endless expanse of sand. Thandrua turned, eyeing the volcano of the Kiln, and his eyes followed the stream of lava that flowed behind the structure and rushed its way far down more endless sand in the other direction. The deity knew that way led to the quarry as well as to the crevice for the damned, but beyond that? He fixed his eyes back onto the mountain.

"I have admired the World's Mountain since our arrival." Thandrua spoke at last, "Its wide structure and towering height, dwarfing any of the mountains we had seen in our former land, always captivated me. One cycle, I will manage to reach its summit. As far as exploration, Sectoraus..." Now his emerald eyes met the Cobra king's yellow slits, "it would be rather useful to know what lies beyond the quarry, where the river might lead. Perhaps the land to the other side of the mountain as well; surely something more ought to be out there."

"Excellent, I will inform my brethren. We will decide on who shall leave and which would stay. We will see to the completion of your golden likeness before any expedition is acted upon."

Lord Thandrua extended his right hand, Sectoraus took hold of Thandrua's forearm and shook. They parted ways after giving a short curt nod of the head, Sectoraus in the direction of the Kiln, Thandrua to a small hut that stood off from the circling huts of the colony. The chamber also bore an Eye of Thandrua as well as a line of a dozen Serpenoids, patiently waiting. When Lord Thandrua approached, the Serpenoids bowed in respect as he let himself into the chamber.

"Sectoraus just spoke to me about exploration of the land; what say you of such an adventure, Oracle?"

Vander sat cross-legged on a bronze seat, eyes closed. When Thandrua spoke, his face twitched as if losing concentration, then he opened his yellowed eyes. "The Serpenoids have been waiting long." Disregarding what had just been said, "Perhaps you can allow me to present names without your supervision as I had before?"

"You know how this society works, Oracle," Thandrua crossed his arms and glared, "but before we proceed..."

"Yes, Sectoraus." Vander thought for a moment, "He wants us to journey away from your slavery and shrine?"

"A selected group." If Thandrua caught the disdain in Vander's voice, he did not show it, "He proposes to explore beyond the horizons, see what more is out there. Perhaps we will find more raw material."

"Perhaps we will find danger." Vander closed his eyes and thought for a moment, "This is not an immediate adventure, I hope?"

"No, Sectoraus wants to see my statue completed and needs time to organize a group."

"Good. It will also give me time to take a further look into this, see if any insight is provided. Now, may we go on about our cycle task?"

"Yes, yes. Give me your seat and bring in the first guest."

"As you wish, my lord." Vander stood to the side as the massive beast sat in his place. He walked to the entryway and escorted a single Serpenoid to kneel before their god. The Oracle stood by Thandrua's left and whispered into his ear, "This one will be named Nimod."

***

The cycles came and the cycles went; construction of the golden Thandrua statue progressed. The waist developed a muscular stomach, and the stomach a chest. The Serpenoids, on occasion, would group together and marvel at the slowly growing figure. They loved the idea of having their beloved lord towering high above them, but not as much as they adored their names.

They would introduce themselves to each other as if just meeting one another for the first time. At times, one could hear a Serpenoid shouting their names against the wind, announcing their individuality. "Warrell! My name is Warrell!" There would even be times when Serpenoids would shout their names in the echo of the Kiln or the vast quarry. The slaves did not fancy this, however.

The slaves worked hard and endlessly, especially now that they began building the bronze Serpenoid feet and tail to stand along the golden Thandrua. Lord Thandrua and Sectoraus had made an announcement to both the colony and the slaves of the upcoming journey. Since then, the labor force had increased. The few water breaks the prisoners were given became sparser, about once a cycle. Even cycles lost meaning within the quarry and Kiln. Sectoraus ordered Orpheus and Phineus to keep watch during the slumber of a cycle. He suggested to his brothers to meditate when they were tired. Every couple of cycles Solarious would trade positions with one of his clan brothers to allow them some time to actually sleep.

When he wasn't standing guard, Solarious gave Sectoraus a helping hand on preparation for the journey to come. The Cobra king had decided that he and Solarious would lead the journey while Orpheus and Phineus maintained the order in their absence. They had also come to the decision that the two traveling Cobras would each take their own team in opposite directions to cover more ground and spend less time away from their colony. Sectoraus would lead to the left of the World's Mountain and Solarious to the right.

The two spent their cycles watching the slaves in the quarry, observing which ones were the strongest and least fatigued while the golden Thandrua's chest developed broad shoulders and arms outreached as though offering the world. They had agreed that each would build a team of a handful of Serpenoids and a few select slaves. They hollowed rocks to fill with water, used pebble-sized chunks to plug the water in, and attached chains to them to carry along. Sectoraus still mulled over the idea of having the slaves push a wheelbarrow filled with the water in addition to the chained ones; he hadn't the slightest idea of how far they would travel and whether they might run out of water.

The Serpenoids weren't the only ones busying themselves with preparation. Lucifer managed to find blind spots in the constant guard of the Cobras. He had his secluded areas in the tunnels of the quarry to arrange meetings, which he did in small groups. He could only keep so many people from working without notice, even though there were many in the quarry. Lucifer always arranged his gatherings during peak working times and ensured they were covered by groups of miners.

Occasionally, Lucifer would volunteer to move to the Kiln when Orpheus would bring his forgers and swap workers with Phineus. The Cobra Clan believed rotating the workers would keep them sharp in their duties. They figured doing the same task over and over would become very mundane, for many miners and blacksmiths would ask to move to another work site every few cycles past. Because of this, the Cobra brothers didn't find anything odd in Lucifer requesting a transfer.

Of course, Lucifer wasn't interested in the art of metal forgery, nor was he trying to keep himself from the insanity of repetition. The Kiln had become rather large; the Cobras had their slaves demolish walls within the cave, creating more rooms and enlarging the space to fit more workers with enough room to mold and shape their tools. Orpheus was the single guard for the large cave and would occasionally walk around observing the slaves' handiwork, but for the most part he stood guard at the mouth to ensure no runaways. With this freedom, Lucifer explored the tunnels of the Kiln, finding secret nooks where excess bronze and iron could be stashed for later use.

At the end of a cycle at the quarry, when Phineus allowed some slaves to rest before he would sit and meditate himself, Lucifer got to work. Waiting for the guard to give the order of which slaves could rest and which must continue on, then watching as the black hood was well out of sight, Lucifer would collect the slaves that were sent to rest. At the far side of the quarry, Lucifer had begun combat training with these slaves. He taught them how to fight hand to hand. Previously, he had the shovel head and picks removed from a handful of tools, rendering them simple staffs. It was at these secluded times that he would use those staffs to demonstrate how to wield a sword.

***

Lord Thandrua was ecstatic watching the slaves climb the ladders and platforms that were built around his growing statue as they carried a large hunk of gold and attached it to the golden neck. His idol was nearly complete, the slaves simply had to carve a face from the hunk and attach the horns. In time, he would be staring at himself in the glint of gold as his trusted friend would set out to explore their world.

Thandrua turned to move toward the hillside that led to the lake. As his stomping feet passed each small slumber chamber, any Serpenoid that was inside came out of their entryway and acknowledged the crimson deity in a bow. He held a small smile on his face but, without even a mere glance towards his worshippers, Thandrua continued forward waving a dismissive hand.

When the creature, Lucifer, appeared, Thandrua had feared the loss of the Serpenoids' worship. Now, however, their devotion was stronger than ever. Lord Thandrua gave them names, Lord Thandrua gave them freedom of expression, and Lord Thandrua gave them life, true life. The Serpenoids had enjoyed their craftsmanship within the Kiln and the exciting search for stone and metal, but they enjoyed the leisurely freedom even more.

Thandrua listened to the laughter and joyous conversations as he overlooked the shimmering water. Songs filled his pointed ears, for the Serpenoids with their new leisure spent much of their time developing songs in honor of their Lord Thandrua. *They are mine eternally*, he thought to himself, and yet he was not satisfied. The massive leader stepped down the hill, using his scepter to steady himself, and paused at the lake's shoreline. His four toes wetted slightly as the gentle caress of the water ebbed back and forth, sinking ever so slightly into the wet sand. His reflection wavered while his crown glinted and the jewels around his neck sparkled.

The deity felt hollow as he grasped at his many necklaces, a longing he couldn't understand. *I have everything.* He thought again and turned his head side to side watching the rubies from his crown bounce back to him from the reflection, *I do not believe I need any more gems on my crown.* Thandrua turned around and caught sight of his developing statue over the hump of the hill before him. *Perhaps when my shrine is complete. That is it; it is not whole, so neither am I.* It was almost as if he had to convince himself, but the longing held on still.

Now he gazed to the distant horizon in the direction toward which Sectoraus would journey. Lord Thandrua thought to himself that perhaps he should be the one to lead the expedition. It had been so long ago when he led the colony to their sanctuary. Back then he was needed, not as an idol for worship but needed for survival.

Turning to his right, his eyes were captivated by the immense World's Mountain beyond the stretch of the lake. Thandrua could not understand it, but something about that mountain called to him, something more than its impressive size. Perhaps that was what he needed, solitude, like the mountain before him. Time to keep to himself, away from the Serpenoids, the slaves, and even his trusted Sectoraus.

The Lord Thandrua continued longing after the mountain, well into the end of the cycle. Well after the Serpenoids tired from their easy, privileged lives. After Solarious and Sectoraus had finished their preparations for the cycle. Lord Thandrua continued to stare off toward the mountain until Sectoraus had reached his side and told him how everyone was eager to sleep. Thandrua, at long last, declared the cycle's end.

Chapter 12
Completed Projects

"Hold steady, steady!"

"We got it!"

"All clear! pour it down!"

The shouting came from a group of the five male slaves that huddled around the large golden head of Thandrua. They were separated by two platforms that hung from the scaffolding above and just below the left side of the statue's head. On the bottom shelf, two strong-armed slaves held up a long golden horn that curved back and over the head, pressing the horn's end tightly against the scalp. A third stood with an ironing plate away from the horn-handlers. The remaining two slaves stood on the platform above, holding a large hollowed-out rock between them filled with magma; a chain was attached to it, running through a pulley which was held tight by a female slave at the foot of the statue. Their veins bulged in their thick arms, hands scarred black, as they readied themselves to pour the molten liquid onto the seam between the horn and head.

"Go!"

The two above tipped the container slightly as the searing ooze dripped around the horn's base. The third immediately stepped forward and smoothed out the now pliable gold material. The slaves on top secured the container upright, then signaled below to lower it to the ground. About half a dozen other slaves, men and women, stood around the figure securing the ladders and scaffolds. Now that the magma-filled stone reached the ground, they applauded the success.

A short and safe distance away, Lord Thandrua along with the Oracle and the Cobra Clan stood side by side. The colony of Serpenoids gathered all around in a large circle, watching. After many long cycles, the finishing touches were being made to Thandrua's shrine. Just the previous cycle, the right horn was welded on, but only after the magma container (which had not been secured by a chain) slipped from the handler's grip and melted the flesh of three slaves that stood below. Only one survived, who rested in the quarry now, disfigured.

Most of the slaves remained at the quarry as well, working as they did every other cycle. This was a monumental moment for the followers of Thandrua, and an unfortunate few Serpenoids remained guard while all Cobras attended the event. The red lord practically held his breath with anticipation, taking in short, halting gasps as the slaves climbed down his model. There he stood, the golden Almighty Thandrua. Firm stance, outstretched arms, angular face gazing emptily beyond the horizon. One final addition remained before the masterpiece would be complete - a set of eyes.

One single slave scurried up a ladder, over a platform, then up and over a couple more before he stood in front of the chiseled face with two hollowed sockets where the eyes would be. Now Sectoraus bowed onto a single knee and his brothers followed almost in unison. The watching Serpenoids mimicked them in turn. Even the slaves knelt after seeing their captors do so; they did not want to disrupt what appeared to be a ceremony. The only ones who continued to stand were Thandrua, mouth agape, and the single slave high above who inserted a polished emerald stone into the left eye socket, then another into the right.

Lord Thandrua's mouth closed and formed into a genuine smile. The moment he had been waiting for was now complete as he stared into the deep green of the statue's eyes. Sectoraus stood first, clapping his black-clawed hands, and the rest of the Serpenoids burst into cheers and celebration. The Cobra Clan shook each other's forearms with congratulations, as if they had personally created the masterpiece. Even the slaves were content, no injuries this cycle and now they only had half of the Sectoraus statue to worry about.

The only to remain reserved was the Oracle. Vander hadn't cared much for the building of such a shrine. He thought Lord Thandrua and the Clan had more than enough gold and gems on their persons, creating a sky-high statue was over the top. He had tried to convince Thandrua that the statue could possibly distract the

Serpenoids, causing them to idolize the shrine more than Thandrua himself.

"That is absolutely preposterous!" Lord Thandrua had dismissed. "If anything at all, it should make the Serpenoids more awestruck when they rest their eyes upon their lord in the flesh. Besides, if they were to spend excess time in worship before the statue, then I should have more time to focus on the greater good of the colony."

It was obvious to the Oracle that his Lord had his mind set on the golden shrine, nothing could alter that. As the cycles went on while the humans shaped and molded the monument, Vander had noticed the lust in Thandrua's eyes. Overall, there was something different about him. From the way Thandrua would gaze at the constructing figure, it seemed that he had needed this more for himself than for his followers.

Vander was especially uncomfortable leaving the slaves in the Kiln unsupervised. He was most eager for things to return to their usual order. He kept glancing over his shoulder in the direction of the Kiln while the left horn and the eyes of the shrine were installed. Sectoraus was confident that the Kiln was close enough to the colony that if any slaves should decide to escape, they would see. Besides, Thandrua wanted all present for the completion. But even now, while all others celebrated, Vander couldn't help but look toward the fuming volcanic structure.

***

A thick and heavy cloud plumed out of the volcano as the slaves used the kiln to melt the excess material that Lucifer had stowed away. Deep within the gaping mouth of the steaming cave echoed the shuffling sounds of chains and the loud banging of the forgers hammering away on metal, accompanied by grunts of exhaustion. They moved with ferocious speed, filling the cross-shaped molds with bronze for the handles and iron into the mold for the sharp lengthy blades. The swords that had already taken shape were laid onto a flat surface, glowing red from the heat and sparking as the hammers secured its form.

"Make haste!" Lucifer urged. He stood by the cave's exit, observing the dozen slaves working harder and faster than they had ever done for their captors. His shaggy white hair brushed down onto his shoulders, he kept his arms placed behind his back and his grey eyes darted between the blacksmiths.

"It is not often they leave us to ourselves like this." The slave leader reminded them, "They will be distracted with their ceremonies for now, but will not be absent forever. Our time to create the swords is now!"

The slaves acknowledged his words with a short quiet cheer. More material was melted, more blades and handles were fused together. Two women flipped the swords over and over upon the flat surface as two muscular men slammed their mallets. Lucifer strode over and lifted one that he thought looked acceptable and dunked it into a vat of water (which had been left there for drinking) creating steam and a loud hiss.

“This is the tool that will ensure our liberation!" The fallen angel held the hilt tightly in his right hand as he pointed the glistening blade above his head. "I- we have endured many hardships in this world, meeting the exhausting demands of these monsters' greed. There is no quenching their thirst. As we gave the intensive labor for *Lord* Thandrua's golden idol, our tormentors requested the construction for a bronze idol of Sectoraus. Will there be no end? As we focus solely on Sectoraus’ idol, will they order one for the Oracle as well? How about Solarious? This tool will bring that end!"

Lucifer pointed the sword toward his captivated audience. The look of recognition showed in a few of the slaves, as if they might have remembered such a device from their past lives. Whether they did or not, all the slaves within the cave marveled at its shine. Hope was the longing that twinkled in their eyes, well after Lucifer lowered the blade to his side.

"Now, continue on. We are making great progress, but time is scarce. I want to see dozens, no hundreds before the serpent oppressors return." The blacksmiths took not a second longer to return to their pressing task. Lucifer stepped towards the mouth of the cave. He felt confident; he had loved being the leader of an army and, finally, he once again had his army to lead. Lucifer held the sword flat across his open palms, stared at it longingly. Though his body was still bare, he no longer felt naked. He had missed being a leader, but he longed even more to lead with a sword in his hand.

It has felt like an eternity, he thought to himself as he recalled the last time he wielded a sword. He had trained for so long and trained hundreds of others alongside him for an epic war that had never come. When he finally led his army to battle, it had been against his own kin. These were different times. Now he had a foreign enemy to slay, an enemy that lusted over the greedy materials from their land. An enemy that was almost gluttonous with how much of the jewelry they decorated themselves with. An enemy that made a mockery of the great Creator in their blasphemous belief system.

The Wicked, he thought suddenly, and realized his crusade had not ended when he was cast out of his first home. *They are the Wicked, not I! No, it was never me. Never.*

The fallen angel slowly moved toward the exit to the opening of the valley that stretched to the Serpenoid camp. Lucifer gazed up to the cloudless, blood-orange sky and felt a deeper longing. *It was all for you,* and he held back a tear that almost escaped his eyes.

Lucifer was struck with a longing to feel the wordless speech of his former master once again. The Creator had visited Thandrua, and on some more recent occasions the Almighty Light had conversed with the Oracle. Lucifer would have been lying if he said he didn't feel jealous, betrayed even. However, if his face revealed a sense of sorrow, it was gone in the blink of an eye as a bitter expression engulfed his features. Lucifer stretched a hand out at a rock that laid in the sand by his feet and when the stone did not stir, he clenched his hand in anger. *The Wicked began there,* he reminded himself then flashed his sword up to the sky. "I will return!" he vowed, then turned back to the depths of the Kiln.

***

The cheer and worship carried on throughout the valley and the lake. Many Serpenoids remained by Thandrua's golden likeness, bowing down around its massive feet. Lord Thandrua was pleased with how the statue had turned out, but most pleased with the reactions of his followers. The Cobra Clan gazed with wonderment as its golden shine glowed within their yellow eyes. Sectoraus had stepped forward, moving past the worshiping Serpenoids and slowly extending his right hand, and gently placed it against the cool gold surface.

Sectoraus had taken a special fancy to gold above all other precious materials the slaves scoured the depths for. Unlike Thandrua, whose possessions became more and more encrusted with rubies and other stones, Sectoraus kept his mostly pure. The golden bands cuffed around his wrists, his necklaces and neck brace, even his scepter and later the staff he had were pure gold. The exception was a pedant he wore on a golden chain around his neck. It was the Eye of Thandrua symbol which held an emerald in the center for Thandrua's eye.

"Amazing," Sectoraus finally spoke in a light voice, almost a whisper, "just marvelous."

"It is, is it not?" Thandrua had stepped beside him and the two craned their necks to glimpse the top. "Your likeness has been coming along smoothly as well."

"An honor it will be to stand along your side both in our flesh forms as well as our idol forms, but this is an honor I must practice patience on."

"How do you mean?" Thandrua now looked into Sectoraus' eyes searching for a response.

"I will not get the chance to watch mine completed as we have done cycle over cycle with yours. I will leave for the journey at the start of the next cycle."

"Ah yes, so the time has come?"

"I did say once your shrine was complete," Sectoraus gestured at the statue before them as further explanation.

"Then so be it. You have everything set then, correct? I believe your canteens were all filled last cycle."

"That they were, and they sit in the carts awaiting our steps."

"I care little of the slaves, but you have yet to share with me which of the Serpenoids you and Solarious will take."

"We will each take two Serpenoids, there were many volunteers but I have chosen Playtoug and Nimod. Oolag and Fitfs will accompany Solarious. As far as the slaves, it took much time to decide but we have chosen about three or four each, they rest now in the quarry."

"Very well." Thandrua stroked his chin thinking approvingly, "Any more necessary preparations?"

"Yes, I would like to hold a meditative ritual, involving all of us."

"Not just you and your brothers then?"

"I believe it can strengthen us all together. It may be a great amount of time before either of us returns so I believe it will serve as a wonderful farewell... especially should anything happen to either of us."

Lord Thandrua turned away and looked at all the Serpenoids around. Sectoraus guessed his master hadn't thought of such a possibility. Of course, Sectoraus thought of it each cycle, himself, leading to this moment.

"My Lord," Sectoraus said. Thandrua was taken back, they were always too close for such formalities. "We do not know what is out there. This was to be our sanctuary, but that seems to have altered now. Perhaps out there it is like our last home, with dangerous storms or erupting volcanoes. And I do not plan to return until I have found something to report, or once our supplies begin to perish."

There was a long pause, the thin air breathed its warmth between the two leaders. The sounds of the Serpenoids seemed distant, almost nonexistent. Finally, Thandrua placed one ring-covered hand on Sectoraus' left shoulder and simply said, "I understand," then turned to walk away. Before stepping any further, he looked over his shoulder and told Sectoraus, "I will tell the Oracle of your ritual. We will round up the colony. You see to your Clan."

Chapter 13
The Opportunity of Union

The sea of Serpenoids sat upon their knees on the orange sand. Lord Thandrua's golden idol stood behind them facing the opposite direction. Across from them was the royal chamber with the large metallic Eye of Thandrua. Alongside stood the Oracle, Phineus, Orpheus, Solarious, and Thandrua adjusting the crown upon his head. In the large space between the relic and the followers, Sectoraus dragged his staff in the sand, drawing the configuration of crossing lines that formed the symbol of their faith.

The Cobra king drew the oval shape last in the center, then finalized it with a single vertical dash for the pupil. He looked over to Vander and nodded his head once. The Oracle returned the gesture then led Thandrua by the arm to where Sectoraus stood.

"You sit here." Sectoraus instructed his red friend.

Vander moved to the point at the bottom, then the Cobra Clan moved forward, exposing their hoods. Orpheus stood at the angle that pointed to the left, Phineus to the opening on the right. Solarious and Sectoraus stood side by side in the gap at the top of the symbol, across from their deity. Simultaneously they all sat as Thandrua did on the sand. Then the Oracle spoke:

"All should close their eyes and ease the thoughts from your minds." The Serpenoids did so, but not until after they had seen the Cobras do it first. "Meditation is an unusual practice at first, but I have become a master ever since the Cobra Clan taught me. Now just listen to my words and no other sound. Your thoughts are silent, your breath is silent, the air is silent.

"Sectoraus has requested that we all connect indefinitely before his and Solarious' departure. Now as my words fade out, think of the comforting darkness behind your eyes and think of the bond we share as kin, who are sitting all around you beyond your closed eyes."

Not a movement was made, not a sound was spoken. Even the slaves that watched, bound in their chains, remain silent. Within just a moment, all who meditated began to breathe in synchronicity. Sectoraus felt the reassuring company of his brothers' mental connection, it comforted him so. He then began to feel the energy he received when in company of his master, Lord Thandrua, it pleased him so. Finally, he felt a surge that forced him (as well as all the others) to inhale a deep sharp breath as he became greeted by the Serpenoid colony, it fueled him so. They remained silent, connected, for a great length of time.

***

Hidden from sight within the dark cave of the Kiln, Lucifer watched the Serpenoids worship their new shining idol. The mallets that banged on the swords echoed throughout as the slaves kept pushing themselves to construct as many of the sharp tools as possible. Lucifer continued to spy on the Serpenoid colony even after he watched Thandrua and Vander gather the celebrating Serpenoids. He noticed that Sectoraus gave orders to two of his clan brothers. The big yellow spotted one and the slender red one with the black head went in the direction of the quarry.

Lucifer kept his eyes on the striped Cobra, expecting him to come to the Kiln. Instead, that one went out of sight down the valley and later returned with Serpenoids that Lucifer guessed were in the lake. Some time after that, the other two brothers returned with the Serpenoid guards that had been supervising the quarry. They were gathering for something and it seemed the Serpenoids trusted that their fences were sufficient to contain the slaves working in the mines. He also guessed that meant that they still felt confident he and the blacksmiths would remain in the Kiln.

This is looking very promising, he thought to himself and continued to watch. The hammering, the sizzle of heated metal cooling in water, and the grunts of labor continued to fill Lucifer's ears. Every now and then a slave would shout out to their supervisor, "Forty-seven! Fifty-three! Sixty-sixty!" giving Lucifer the count on completed swords.

He lost interest in the sword count and focused mainly on what his enemies were doing. Now there was a division; the Serpenoids knelt in a group facing towards their leaders leaving a large space between themselves and the others. *Something important is happening,* Lucifer figured. *A ceremony? A prayer?*

"Eighty-one!" The slave shouted out.

Lucifer watched now as Sectoraus used his staff to draw something in the sand. Finally, once Thandrua, the Oracle, and the Cobra Clan had seated in their spots where Sectoraus had been marking, Lucifer began to smile. *They're meditating!*

Quickly, the fallen angel returned deep into the Kiln and looked around. The slaves were certainly tired, but still they pushed themselves without break. By the flat surface was piled a display of shiny sharp swords, "We have a chance!" He announced and production came to a halt. All the slaves' eyes were upon their leader.

"The Serpenoids are in a group meditation, we may not have long but this is an opportunity." The slaves waited for instruction as their leader had stepped in closer and pointed a finger, "Zaktarr, Solomon, Reivaj. Gather as many swords as you can, take the carts, but take them to the quarry. Shout for Lilith and drop them over the fence, she will stash them in a safe place."

"Lucifer, what of the guards?" Zaktarr, the stout one of the three asked.

"They have returned with the rest of their kind. Now act fast and then return here. I will begin to stash the rest into some of the secret spots I've found here."

"Yes, master!" The three agreed and quickly began to fill a cart.

***

After their meditative ritual, thousands of yellow eyes opened simultaneously as Sectoraus opened his, then Lord Thandrua's eyes opened immediately after. The Serpenoids looked upon one another in wonder, embracing their neighbors, feeling more connected with each other than they had ever felt before. The Oracle and Cobra Clan continued sitting, posture perfectly straight, seemingly unphased by the development. Thandrua however, gazed down at his hands, eyes wide and transfixed as if he had awakened for the first time in his life. He nodded his horned head to himself. An understanding formed about the Cobra Clan that he had never thought of before. Finally, Lord Thandrua lifted his gaze forward to Sectoraus, who now stood along with the Cobra Clan and Vander, and met Sectoraus' patient eyes that rested upon his own.

"Is this what it is like for you?" Thandrua spoke softly, still in wonder.

"It is different for us." Sectoraus said dismissively but with a grin on his face.

"How so?" Thandrua slowly stood.

"The abilities of the mind are difficult to explain through words. However, the Clan and I are already connected, even without meditation. I cannot begin to pretend I understand what you or the Serpenoids experienced, not even Vander, but perhaps as your first experience…" Sectoraus pondered for a moment, "it might be as if jumping into the cool lake after a long exhausting cycle."

The Serpenoids murmured in agreement while they continued to be grounded even now after their leaders stood tall. Thandrua turned, gazing upon his followers as he considered this and smiled. He felt warm inside to the idea that his Serpenoids may have shared the same experience as he. Then he turned to Sectoraus again, "So how would you say it was like for you?"

The Cobra king raised his head looking to the blood-orange sky thinking heavily, weighing his words before speaking. "What we experience might have been stronger. As I had said, we are already connected and a surge of energy from the collective seemed to empower me." He looked at his brothers who nodded silently in response. "My goal here was to fuel our connection and hopefully expand it so we may stay bonded with each other despite what distances our travels take us... and I hoped it would connect me to you indefinitely."

Thandrua smiled and patted Sectoraus' shoulder reassuringly, "It may not be in the same capacity as you are accustomed to with you and your Clan, but you and I are always and *will* always be connected."

Chapter 14
Departure

The cycle had been called to an end. One last slumber for the colony as a whole, before the two Cobras with their crews parted ways to expand their knowledge of the land. The four Cobra brothers slept curled up on the ground within the royal chamber, they laid more closely together than they usually slept, with Thandrua slouched in his throne just past them.

The crimson god-king had not fallen to sleep just yet. He was on the verge, but could not keep his eyes from his Cobra Clan, from Sectoraus. He would miss him greatly. Thandrua knew he would return one cycle though. He had to. Now, breathing deep and slowly as his horns bobbed slightly along with his head, the master was sound asleep.

Throughout the slumber grounds the sound of restful sleep seeped from the small huts that were scattered about on the hill overlooking the lake. The lake, silent and still, reflected the deep orange of the sky and almost looked as if it were a solid surface. Supplies were grouped together and awaited the journey as two four-handle crates held various containers of water with a couple of shovels and pickaxes laying nearby. Just over the hill was the golden statue of Lord Thandrua generously offering the world with its arms spread wide to those who gazed upon its glory. Welcoming to all but the humans of course.

Far from the colony rested the quarry, which remained unsupervised while the colony slumbered together one more time. The slaves from the Kiln had been returned within its fencing well after the ritual. When the Cobra Clan went to escort Lucifer and the blacksmiths, they had seen the workers were still hard at work forging the metal needed for the quarry and a small pile of precious stones. They were upset to find that despite having the whole cycle to work the results were minimal. The slaves received some light beating before being shepherded back to the quarry. Little did their serpent oppressors know, the slaves had made tenfold the product than what was displayed.

"Lucifer, they are magnificent!" Lilith awed at the shine of the swords' blades in the darkness. She and Lucifer stood in front of a hole that had been burrowed into one of the many nooks within the quarry. A handful of men and women peeked over their shoulders, attempting to catch a glimpse of the metallic weapons.

"True tools of magic, they are." Lucifer grinned with his arms crossed.

"When will we use them?" Lilith reached her right hand out to grab one of the swords before Lucifer snatched her hand away.

"Do not touch!" The fallen angel snarled with disdain. The other slaves stepped back startled. "You shouldn't give into temptation, instead, you should inspire it."

"My apologies, wise one." Lilith clasped her wrist to her chest. "I was only curious when..."

"At the start of the next cycle, half of the Cobra Clan will leave, their leader included. With Sectoraus gone, it will only be a matter of time for the other two Cobras to again leave us unattended."

"We are unsupervised now."

"Yes, but in short time they will become less organized and much easier to attack with surprise. I give them just a few cycles more."

The small crowd behind them began to stir. They were restless, exhausted. They had been made to push their physical limits, cycle in and cycle out, since they arrived. They knew it had been a long time but weren't sure how long. They understood time differently than the Serpenoids and where they came from, they measured cycles by the rising and falling of the Sun. They called them "days." It was difficult for them to tell how a cycle correlated to a day. There was no day or night here and most of them only remember the idea of the passing of a day, but some seemed to think a single cycle might have been what they would consider two "days." Others, however, thought the opposite, that there were twice as many cycles within a day. All understanding of time as they knew it, lost.

"Will we not practice with the swords?" A man in the crowd had asked, and Lucifer turned to address those behind him.

"We have practiced enough with the practice tools." He answered dismissively. "We are to only take the swords out when the time comes to rebel, before then we risk the exposure of our grand plan. Not until I have gained control over their society will we have the freedom to practice with the actual weapons. Luckily, they do not have weapons or even understand the concept, so the little training you all have will suffice to slay our enemy."

***

The next cycle held the gray melancholy of farewells. The cycle began with the Oracle gathering the Serpenoids for a proper sendoff. While Vander did so, Thandrua organized the two teams that Sectoraus and Solarious would take with them. Before grouping with their teams at the assembly, the two expedition leaders prepared their farewells to their clan brothers.

Their goodbyes were simple. Lord Thandrua stepped out of their shelter leaving the four Cobras to slowly wake. They all stood up from the ground stretching their arms, tails, and hoods in a yawn. Their hoods relaxed, their tails slackened, and they all stood there. No words were spoken. The departure was close at hand. Sectoraus looked over his three brothers as they gazed back at him solemnly. Sectoraus gently nodded his head as they came in close. Sectoraus opened up his arms, embracing them in a huddle, still without speaking a word.

After their moment of silence Sectoraus broke off, lifted his golden staff and went outside; Solarious followed, then Orpheus and finally Phineus. The Cobra Clan walked down the hill to the assembly held by the lake. The two teams were already there, loaded and ready for the move. Vander stood between both teams watching as the Cobras descended the hill. Sectoraus and Solarious broke away from the other two clan members and linked up with their company, Sectoraus to his left and Solarious to the right. They awaited as Thandrua geared up for the formal farewell.

The Serpenoids all gathered along the hillside watching Lord Thandrua and the Oracle who stood facing them with the large crystal lake to their backs and the towering mountain beyond the water. On Thandrua's left was Sectoraus, gripping tightly onto his staff accompanied by two Serpenoids, a greenish Serpenoid with black stripes and the other with yellow spots, two male slaves that held the crate of water containers between them and a third female slave. All three of the slaves were connected by slack chains cuffed around their ankles and collars. To Vander's right stood Solarious who had the slightly larger company of two Serpenoids and four slaves.

"Bittersweet looms throughout this cycle." Thandrua raised his voice toward the stare of all the yellow eyes. "This cycle begins with a journey to explore our land in the hopes for more resources and expansion. For the time being I lose my best friend, but not forever, they will return once their supply of water diminishes. Perhaps they will find other creatures out there. I am confident to say that I doubt anything may harm these teams led by the finest Cobras and Serpenoids!" Thandrua turned, gesturing to the two teams as the crowd applauded.

"The World's Mountain will serve as a beacon to our travelers. Even though they will mark their trail, if needed they shall follow in the direction of the mountain. From there they may find their way back here to the lake and home. In honor of these two brave explorers, I will give name to their direction. To the left of the World's Mountain where Sectoraus travels shall be known as Sectorway. And to the right where Solarious embarks on his, Solariside. Now, their journeys begin!"

As thunderous applause erupted, Orpheus stepped forward to holler toward the teams. "May the Eye of Thandrua guide you, brothers!" Sectoraus and Solarious inclined their heads to their brother's farewell and to the gratitude of the colony. Solarious had moved in to say his farewells to Vander as Sectoraus did to Thandrua.

"Until we meet again, my Lord." Sectoraus whispered into Thandrua's ear as they embraced each other. The warm sulfuric air breezed around them.

“Be careful, my friend.” Thandrua pulled back and held his companion’s gaze with solemn eyes before he turned to the approaching Solarious.

"May hardships journey away from your path." Vander said to Sectoraus.

"Much obliged." Sectoraus stared at him for a moment, "Please, take care of everyone for me."

"You need not worry about us." And the two inclined their heads.

All that remained were the two Cobra leaders who grasped onto each other's forearm, "Farewell brother," Solarious said, "May the Eye of Thandrua watch over you."

"And you, Solarious. Until we meet again."

The two teams began their march away from the lake in their respective directions. Both team leaders at the head, with the Serpenoids behind, and their slaves shuffling along in their chains carrying the supplies. The colony moved their gaze from Sectoraus' team to Solarious' as they moved further apart and increasingly distant from the lake. Lord Thandrua glanced to where Solarious had gone, but diverted most of his attention to his companion, Sectoraus.

Instead of watching the teams off with the rest of the colony, Vander retreated to his chamber to meditate. He held the teams close in his thoughts, especially the two leaders. He was still new to meditation and unsure of how it worked exactly, but he had a heart filled with positivity for them and they needed all the good fortune they could get. The Oracle’s mind was even more heavy with Sectoraus. The two never had seen eye to eye. Of course, one couldn’t blame Vander for lack of trying. He had only wanted them all to get along. Any animosity was strictly from the Cobra king. Sectoraus had a temper, but it was because he had great passion for his role. Vander understood this. He meditated on the hope that his pride would not harm the expedition.

Eventually the two teams disappeared over the sand-covered horizon. The Serpenoids dispersed to enjoy the lake, or worship the idol, or simply to relax in their huts. It was a great cycle after all. The air was warm, the sky was a beautiful red and something new to come. Soon, at least.

Lord Thandrua lingered longer, all alone, watching the empty desert to where the little figure of Sectoraus had diminished into the distance.

Section IV
Sectoraus' Journey

Chapter 15

New Discoveries

Sectoraus stepped with his golden staff at a casual pace, his hood remained relaxed while his tail dragged in the sand behind him. The journey would be long, he figured, and there was no rush for any particular destination. Perhaps finding a new water source would be a suitable goal and in time would become necessary. They wouldn't run out of water for quite some time, Sectoraus reassured himself after glancing over his shoulder to the crate carried between two of the slaves. They would have to ration as best they could, although the slaves seemed to thirst for water more often than the Serpenoids needed.

The soft sand was pleasant to step in, as it always was, but Sectoraus knew the further they would travel, the more strenuous the formless ground would make their journey. Long had it been since the sky held any traces of volcanic smog from the Kiln. The further back they left the grayish clouds, the more vibrant the blood orange sky became. It was truly breathtaking.

Looking behind them, Sectoraus could vaguely see what he guessed was the summit of the World's Mountain peeking beyond the horizon. He thought of what Lord Thandrua had said about the mountain, then his thoughts strayed back to his master himself. It felt strange to Sectoraus to leave Thandrua and everyone behind, but the journey itself felt oddly reminiscent of their past lives as aimless nomads. Seeking through rocky terrains and crossing mountains to find some kind of refuge from the burning sunlight. The fear of the sunlight he did not miss, but the sentiment was still nostalgic nonetheless. The beauty of this journey was that they were free to travel without fear.

Sectoraus continued to lead in silence, trying to maintain focus on the stronger connection he'd made with his brothers. He felt that Solarious, too, had hiked far from sight of their home, walking along a stretch of mountains they had never seen before. Looking over his shoulder again, even the last remnants of the World's Mountain had retreated completely out of sight.

This is where the journey truly begins, Sectoraus thought and continued to dip into his mind. Something troubled him, but he couldn't figure out what it could be. Sectoraus had trust in the Cobras he left in charge, and it seemed the slaves had become more complacent over the past few cycles. There was no reason to worry, but something tugged at his mind still. He could sense that Orpheus took his position supervising the quarry and Phineus guarding the Kiln. He knew the Oracle went to meditate as the two teams left and when Sectoraus tried to think of Vander, he could only sense an immense emptiness. *Must be submerged in a deep trance,* was Sectoraus' conclusion.

Perhaps it was merely the realization that he had never left Thandrua's side, until now. Occasionally Sectoraus would check up on the mines and the Kiln while his deity remained in their settlement. However, though some of the old mines were rather far off from the colony, he had never considered that to be a separation. Especially now the slaves were recruited and the mines had become the vast quarry, Sectoraus and Thandrua were hardly ever apart.

Sectoraus thought about his past, before he bore the name "Sectoraus." The Cobra hadn't been much different from any other Serpenoid. In fact, he had yet to develop his signature hood. He was simply a greenish-brown Serpenoid who marveled at his surrounding world; the hard cracking terrain, the large spiraling rock formations, the vast mountain ranges and smoking volcanoes. The Serpenoids were only just beginning to understand their environment let alone understanding themselves, then death came. Sectoraus remembered the confusion when other Serpenoids began to choke and fall.

He remembered running to catch one of his brethren who had collapsed onto the ground, holding the convulsing body as air escaped it. He remembered most when the dying Serpenoid's eyes rolled upward, black forked tongue lolling to the side. The young Serpenoid who would become Sectoraus urged the fallen Serpenoid to rise, even attempted to lift it onto its feet; there was no success. More and more around him followed suit. Some ceased to move all together, some groaned in pain and crawled on the ground. Sectoraus recalled in the crowd of Serpenoids there had been others who had yet to fall and the four had grouped together. They held tightly onto each other. They spoke to one another about fear, questions. There had been so many questions even before the others fell and suffocated, but in that moment all they could think of was, *What is happening? When will we fall too?*

Their final question was answered as they weakened, slowly giving into the gravity that weighed them down into the dirt. The four clutched onto each other tightly still, when a breeze chilled their scales. The fluffy white clouds overhead darkened and grew thick. There was a rumble in the sky. The clouds grew angrier, then something began to fall from the sky. They were tiny pellets that soothed the flesh of the Serpenoids and made them slick with moisture. More rumbles cracked behind the clouds as a heavier downpour opened upon the land. "*Water*," was the word the young Serpenoid who would become Sectoraus said.

A ditch nearby collected water as a puddle began to form. The Serpenoid pulled himself into the water as the other three followed. Submerged into the crisp, sweet lifegiver, the Serpenoids that had held onto each other felt a deep connection explode between one another. Their scaley bodies tingled and when they stood, they stood anew.

Each of them had transitioned in color as distinctive patterns grew on their bodies. They stretched for the skies as their necks flattened and a large hood encircled each one of their heads. They noticed the other Serpenoids around them stirred back into motion and rose as well. The four guided the struggling weak ones to sip from puddles on the ground.

The Serpenoids had rejoiced in the pouring rain. The four Cobras were happy, but their happiness faltered when they were bombarded with more questions. They had no understanding of what had happened or even who they were. Young, yet-unnamed Sectoraus only could guess the rain was what fueled them, but still felt lost.

The feeling was ripped away when the clouds crashed with thunder and violent lightning flickered. All eyes raised to the dark empty sky at a light streaking their way. The bright object descended from the cosmos, engulfed in flames. The Serpenoids gawked with wonderment until the thing crashed into the ground. They jumped away with fear, but one approached the object, the beige Cobra with the two black diamonds on the back of his head.

He studied the crystalized stone as it began to quiver and when two ivory horns burst through, he stepped back cautiously. The crimson flesh of the creature arose from inside and the Cobra could think of nothing else but to bow down to it and call it "Thandrua."

The towering beast, this Thandrua, stared with vibrant green eyes wide at the sea of Serpenoids bowed before him. They gave him the name of their hearts, the name of the one who came from the sky, the name of the bringer of rain, the lifegiver.

From that moment on, they had traveled together, exploring the land, and the whole time the tall beige Cobra never left his side. It was when Thandrua saw how thoughtful this particular Cobra was that he named him "Sectoraus." Sectoraus gave Thandrua the title of "lord," and the two would shape their society together.

Together until now, that is. Sectoraus tried to call the beastly deity to his mind, but this didn't work as it did with his clan brothers. He had hoped he could tether a similar connection with Thandrua after the ritual but, seeing as Thandrua had never meditated before, it did not surprise Sectoraus that they couldn't touch minds. However, when Sectoraus thought of Thandrua, a warmness expanded within his chest. He held onto the pendant that dangled around his neck, bobbing against his scaled chest with each step. Sectoraus considered it to be a good sign.

After the leader realized the World's Mountain had faded from view, great length of time passed as the group journeyed onward. The sands were far and endless. The only differences in their surroundings were the various dunes they crossed, trekking up and down just to go back up and back down again, then continue into the stretch of sand.

Their footprints trailed far behind, giving guidance to any that would come after them. Far off to the travelers' left they could make out the faint glow of magma. There was a river of lava that flowed from the Kiln and off around the far side of the quarry, and it seemed to extend for a great length past the horizon. It wouldn't have surprised Sectoraus if this were from the same source, thus he believed it was so.

"Water," was all Sectoraus had to say for the female slave to grab a rock from the crate and pass it to Playtoug, who passed it to Sectoraus. They did not stop their march. Sectoraus popped open the stopper and took a deep gulp. He then passed it behind him to Nimod and said, "Take a sip, no more, and pass it behind."

"Very appreciated, master." Nimod thanked Sectoraus and did as instructed. Playtoug took a sip next and passed it to the female. She drank and aided both men to drink from the rock so they wouldn't have to stop and let go of the crate.

"There was barely any left in that," said the last man to sip. He was older than the other and had a burly beard.

"Hush!" The woman whispered, "Do not let the Cobra hear your complaints. We will have more."

"As if these things have compassion." Whispered the younger, thin man, "I am just disappointed I am here and don't get to help Lucifer with the *plan.*"

"I said hush," the woman repeated.

"Yeah, we wouldn't want them to hear anything about that," said the bearded man.

"Exactly! We could always turn back any moment," the woman said.

"And who knows what they would do to us then," the bearded one added.

"Alright, you two made your point," replied the young one. "I was just looking forward to it, is all."

"Hey, less chatter, more walking!" Playtoug tugged on the leash.

More dunes came, long, high, and sometimes small. Some dunes seemed so vast the travelers veered around them. After a great distance more, the soft sand became firmer. The ground was flat to walk on with ease; it reminded Sectoraus of Earth. On their path they occasionally passed by small pebbles and rocks, and eventually Sectoraus raised his staff at one such spot. "Stop and rest here," he ordered.

His company stopped as instructed. It was clear everyone had become exhausted, though nobody spoke up about it. The slaves were most exhausted, the two men especially. This was evident by the way they dropped the crate onto the ground with a loud thud as the halt was called. Sectoraus and the Serpenoids turned at the sound as dust lifted off the ground, engulfing the crate.

"Be mindful you do not break that, *slave*." Sectoraus hissed.

"My lord, we have just been walking so long," the slave with a beard said. "It's really heavy, too."

"That is why we stopped to rest." Sectoraus sneered at him, but looking at the exhaustion in their faces he then understood. These humans were nothing like the Serpenoids. They were not accustomed to travel like this. Sectoraus then looked at Playtoug and Nimod; they weren't looking as miserable as the slaves, but thirst was hidden in their eyes.

"Pass out the water." Sectoraus paused, waiting for his canteen, then added, "Give Nimod and Playtoug each their own. You three may share one."

The two men handed over a water-filled rock to each Serpenoid while the female popped the plug out of one for themselves. They all waited, watching Sectoraus open his with a satisfying pop. He placed the hole towards his mouth as the clear fluid poured out, falling into and around his mouth. Neither the Serpenoids nor humans drank until Sectoraus was done quenching his own thirst first.

After relieving themselves of the dry desert thirst, they all laid on the hot sandy surface. The Serpenoids rested with ease, comforted by the heat against their backs after a gratifying hike. It had been ages since they traveled to anywhere further than the mines.

"This reminds me of home. Our old home, I mean," said Nimod to Playtoug.

"Oh yes." Playtoug agreed, "I miss the journeys. Had no idea that I did, but now? This is the life we were meant for."

"Are you not happy with your lives?" Sectoraus seemed perplexed. "You have so many freedoms."

"Oh, forgive me, sire!" Nimod sat up urgently. "Please, do not mistake that for ungratefulness. I do love this new life you and the great Lord Thandrua have gifted us. It is easy and secure. It is just different."

"I agree," Playtoug sat up as well. "It is a good life. I just miss the wondering. Exploring new areas, seeing the different shapes of the land."

Sectoraus contemplated this for a moment before speaking, "No, I understand. I do miss climbing the mountains. Just not while they were falling apart." He laughed a little. "If you excuse me, I am going to meditate over there"

As the Serpenoids reminisced, the slaves rubbed their feet, avoiding the patches of dying skin on their heels. Unlike their slavers, the humans were utterly exhausted. They too spoke amongst themselves, but in quiet whispers.

"This is horrendous," complained the frail-looking, pale-skinned man.

"I'm beat, but I can only imagine how you two must feel," chimed in the lady.

"This break was exactly what I needed. My arms more than anything," the man with the beard said as he stretched out his arms. "Shoot, if I weren't tired, since we have this moment, I would say let's fool around some."

"Ha! Keep dreaming." The woman playfully pushed him away.

"No, I wasn't talking about you." The bearded man said, then they all laughed. They turned to look at the Serpenoids quickly. They didn't seem to pay the outburst any mind.

"I'm sure these monsters wouldn't allow any funny business anyway," the woman said.

Sectoraus sat cross-legged away from the group and sunk into meditation. Silence. Blackness. Emptiness. The Cobra's eyes opened when his energy had replenished itself.

"Alright, that was enough," Sectoraus stated as he stood up turning to look at his team. "We continue on."

Begrudgingly the men lifted the crate again.

"Did you want me to carry it this time?" The woman offered to the frail-looking man.

"No, no it's okay," he declined.

The woman looked over to the bearded man.

"We got this," he said, despite the strain in his face.

The group began their travels once again. This new terrain stretched far, almost to the same length as the sandy dunes they had been traversing. It became tiresome, more so than it already was. The hard dry flaky ground was not as forgiving as the sand. The three slaves slackened their pace and Nimod, who held the reins of their chain, had to tug harder and harder. The humans' flesh was soft and weak compared to the reptilian scales of the Serpenoids. They moaned and complained about the aches of their feet.

Sectoraus ignored these pleas. He would not stop until he was tired. However, he did slow his pace, a little. Nimod and Playtoug switched control over the slaves, the chain they pulled grew heavier as time crawled by.

As the wanderers continued on, Sectoraus noticed the river of lava curving closer toward them and in time it no longer ran parallel to their left but became an obstruction in their path ahead. Its glow became more radiant as the sound of the flowing sludge roared louder. The endless horizon that had laid out before them now blurred with the distorting vapors of heat and gases rising into the air, and gradually all they could see ahead of them was the bubbling magma.

Sectoraus lifted his staff, and his followers came to a halt. He slowly approached the deadly edges of the molten river. The two Serpenoids remained silent with anticipation while the slaves began to whisper between themselves.

"Oh yes, we're stopping," said the bearded man. "Thomas, let's put this down."

"I don't think we're resting," said the male slave known as Thomas.

"Look at all that lava," the lady was entranced by the glowing orange and yellow sludge.

Nimod and Playtoug looked over at their slaves. The humans quieted down. They weren't as disciplined with the mastery of silence as the Serpenoids were.

"It seems to go on quite far." Sectoraus finally said after looking up and down the river a few times, "I do not think we can walk around it."

"What shall we do, oh wonderful leader?" asked Playtoug.

Squinting across, Sectoraus responded, "I say we cross it." He turned to see the frightened faces of his team. "There are obstructions on the other side stopping me from seeing very far, which could only mean there is land not far across. Seems crowded with boulders."

Sectoraus returned to study the river a little more. "Also, this lava carries rocks and there are plenty that are not moving, like those over there." He pointed to a collection of stones motionless in the moving fluid. "We could step over those."

The slaves stayed close together while the Serpenoids considered this. The more slender slave pulled out a water-rock and handed it to the woman. With his eyes he signaled to give it to their master. She quietly offered it to Sectoraus.

"Ah, thank you." Sectoraus scratched out the stopper before taking a drink and passing it over, "We should rehydrate before we cross. Perhaps rest as well. I believe we are well past the cycle's end anyhow."

"Oh yes, thank you!" said Thomas.

More than relieved, the three humans slumped down on the ground after snagging their own water from the crate. Sectoraus was just about to whack the rocks out of their hands and tell them to ration by sharing one but, looking to the overflowing crate of water-rocks and seeing how exhausted and tired their faces were, he kept the lesson to himself. He took another swig of water.

"Nimod, Playtoug, you two could each have one to yourselves as well." After all, they all had been good about not touching the water since their last stop.

Nimod and Playtoug curled onto the warm sand, their tails encircled around their bodies. Soon after, they drifted to sleep. Two of the slaves fell to sleep first, one propped his back against the crate while the other laid on the ground, placing an arm under his head and tucking his knees close to his chest. The third stared into the beyond that they had traveled from and washed her face with the remains of water from her container. Then she too rested her head against the crate and slept. Sectoraus did not slumber, but instead waited for the last of the slaves to drift off before submerging himself into meditation.

The rattling sound of chains caused Sectoraus to open his yellow eyes. The slave that had laid on the ground rubbed the collar around his neck as he inched closer to the other two that his chain connected with. Sectoraus guessed that the slave had just been waking up or turned in his sleep, causing the chain to tug taut. The Cobra king had been meditating for a while and figured that his companions had rested enough and woke the others.

Sectoraus stared at the chains connecting the slaves to their necks, then down at the dangling shackles around their feet.

"Nimod," he addressed the Serpenoid, then pointed to the pickaxe that laid in the sand. "Break the chains on their feet and collars."

"Sire?" Nimod wasn't sure if he had heard his master correctly.

"You heard the order." Sectoraus did not see a reason to repeat himself.

"What if they try to run?" Nimod turned to look at Playtoug for support.

"They cannot make it across the river in those shackles," Sectoraus said. "Besides, where will they go?"

The slaves did not protest when asked to get down to their knees and lowered their heads onto the sand. The connecting chain was to the ground, and with one big overhead swing, the chain cracked with a puff of sand from the impact. The older bearded one was free from the leaner pale slave and the woman. With another crack of the pick against the chain, all three were now free to move independently. The broken chain dangling from their collars still reached their feet. Sectoraus tugged on the chain attached to the bearded one, pulling him close.

"Now, slave, spread your legs for Nimod to separate your shackles," Sectoraus ordered and the Serpenoid approached with the pick. The bearded one did as he was told and closed his eyes tight when the tool raised into the air. The same was repeated for the remaining two and the slaves now had complete mobility.

"Thank you so much!" the pale one groveled.

"Very good." Sectoraus eyed the freed slaves, then pointed toward them, "Now, send one of them over the river."

With the pickaxe, the spotted Serpenoid pushed the older one forward. Without protest, although reluctant with fear, he approached the river. He looked down at the smoking magma, then up at Sectoraus.

"Go on," Sectoraus ordered, nodding his head forward.

The man looked at the river once more, the sluggish orange goo bubbling heat into his face. There were rocks floating along with the lava, but he saw that some rocks stayed in place. Wincing, he gingerly stepped forward, looked around for a moment, then took another step. Sectoraus edged Nimod on to follow the slave after he was a few stones forward, then told the other two slaves to pick up the crate and proceed across as well. By now, the first slave had gotten a little more than halfway across and seemed to be moving more quickly. Sectoraus started to cross the river with the last Serpenoid following behind.

As Sectoraus approached the first stone, he could feel the lava's fuming heat on his leg as he raised it to step onto the rock. The rock itself was even hotter to the touch despite the protective hardened scales on his feet. As he continued on the heat lingered, slowly becoming less tolerable. The ooze surrounding him bubbled and popped, dispensing the volcanic gas. Sectoraus looked up and noticed the younger slave close to him dripping with sweat and fighting on the surface of the rocks to maintain his grip on the handle of his side of the water crate.

To Sectoraus the heat of the rocks was becoming more noticeably hot, but then looking at the slave he thought of something. Because of the difference between their skin, the heated stones they crossed on must be scorching to them if Sectoraus could feel this amount of heat. Even the golden cuffs around his wrists and his broad collar and golden chains began to feel uncomfortably warm on his hide.

Despite the heat from the magma, they made it across one by one. The Serpenoid behind Sectoraus seemed to straggle behind some, but he continued crossing. Sectoraus marked deep into the ground with his staff while the others waited for Playtoug. He took a look around and saw they had crossed into a small valley, with the ground covered mostly in brown and tan gravel. There were boulders and rocks everywhere and even strange piles of rocks that seemed to be spread about and spaced evenly. He also noticed that the rocks were grey, not like the orange he was used to.

His thoughts were suddenly interrupted with some commotion behind him, then a scream followed by a splash. Playtoug had lost his footing on the last two stones and fell into the lava. Screaming in agony, the Serpenoid was still able to grab onto a stone to keep from being dragged away by the current. His screams droned on as the smell of burning flesh wafted through the air and his body slowly melted from the waist down. The bearded slave tried to reach out with the pickaxe, but Sectoraus snatched it out from his grip.

"Do not be foolish!" snapped Sectoraus. "He's doomed! His legs must be mostly disintegrated by now anyway, and you could have fallen in with him. And worse, we would've lost the pickaxe!"

The group turned away, averting their eyes from the gore, and Sectoraus watched as the poor whelp grew weaker from pain and released his hold. Still screaming, he was swept away by the current, and not long after, sunk into the lava. Little time was given to mourn the fallen Serpenoid, however, for they all heard a deep bellowing.

Looking into the valley they heard it again, but it grew louder as one of the strange-looking rock piles shifted.

They stared, speechless, as the rocks pulled together and a figure stood before them. It stood towering on two legs, taller than Thandrua. The sound of stones grinding against each other filled the air as the creature stretched its four massive arms about.

They stood there, frozen in shock as the thing fixed its eyes upon them. The eyes, appearing as two hollow points in the rock of its head, were illuminated with the same fiery glow as the magma. It stared back for a moment, cocking its head to the side as though trying to figure out the creatures that stood before it. Then it opened its mouth, which contained a fiery glow similar to its eyes, and made a few short shouts in the air. They heard the low bellowing again, this time it was everywhere. The adventurers began to look all about them as more of the rock piles revealed themselves to be these four-armed hulks.

They slowly stepped back before realizing they had no more space to back up, aside from crossing the river again. Then they heard a rapid bubbling coming from the lava. Slowly more of the rock creatures emerged from the depths of the magma and made their way to shore.

Time was running out; the wayward explorers were now surrounded. Sectoraus scanned the area, looking for possible escape routes. They were completely cut off from the sides. If they could just push forward and run fast enough up the hill, they could get out of the valley. Perhaps there they could find safety. The creatures moved slowly, so outrunning them seemed plausible enough, they were just outnumbered. They were only five and Sectoraus counted more than a dozen of the rock creatures. Sectoraus gripped his staff tightly between his two hands, Nimod readied the pickaxe as Sectoraus came to a decision while his hood unfurled around his head.

"Run forward and up the hill! Leave the water!"

They sprang, darting past the closest creatures which, at the sudden movement, leapt to grab their prey. The other monstrosities rushed in. Sectoraus swung his staff about as his companions tried to run by. Nimod stood by his side, doing the same with the pick. The metal made loud clanks and bangs as it ricocheted off the living boulders. Sparks of friction exploded with each hit but it didn't seem to hurt the monsters at all, seeming only to keep them at a distance.

The female slave held back. She had taken a shovel from the crate and tried to fight off their attackers with Sectoraus. She was able to hold one rock creature at bay, but her efforts were futile. Another monstrosity came up on her side. It raised its two left arms and struck her. She was thrown onto the ground.

Dazed and with the wind knocked out of her, she moaned on the ground. Hearing the thuds and feeling the ground vibrate, the woman looked up at a fast-approaching monster. She screamed as it stomped a toeless foot onto her right knee, shattering it instantly.

Sectoraus tried to make his way over to help but was too busy protecting himself from the living boulders. The creature lifted the slave halfway off the ground, pulling on her arms with its top set of limbs. The slave squirmed and groaned as the creature secured her by the waist with its bottom set of arms then slowly opened its mouth, expelling lava onto the slave's face.

Nimod running forward and slammed the pike on top of the monster's head, splitting it apart. The creature collapsed onto the gravel, lava oozing out from it. Unfortunately, Nimod was too late. The slave shivered as her skin melted away from her face in a white and red liquid, revealing the skull beneath. Sectoraus fought his way to Nimod's side and took a moment to shake his head in pity as he heard the slave wheezing, then he stomped on her neck to end the suffering.

The monsters were on them again. The two slaves started making their way up the hill when the younger one stumbled. He tumbled back, his momentum carrying him the rest of the way down. Two monsters closed in on him.

The bearded slave continued running up the hill as the two creatures grunted at each other and fought over the whimpering young man. Sectoraus looked away as the slave's body was torn apart in the struggle.

"Nimod, up the hill with the slave!" Sectoraus ordered, turning his staff horizontally and pushed hard against the onslaught. He managed to shove one rock creature back and it fell into the rest of the mob, giving the Cobra his chance to run for the hill. Sectoraus ran and ran, the bearded slave almost fell backwards but Sectoraus caught him in time as he made it back to the remainder of the group.

Finally, they reached the top of the hill and Sectoraus looked down into the valley. Three of the stone creatures stood at the bottom of the hill staring up at them, groaning. The rest seemed to lose interest, resting back down on the gravel seemingly like a pile of rocks.

We made it. Sectoraus thought to himself trying to catch his breath, *we are safe.* He swung the golden staff onto his shoulder and turned around to see just a few feet away from them something neither he, nor any Serpenoid, had ever seen before. A wide-spread area crowded with thick, enormously tall structures with many twisting arms that stretched off from their tops at odd angles.

"What are these?" Sectoraus gaped in awe.

Silence hung for a moment before the remaining slave stepped forward, "Trees, this looks like a forest. Usually they have green leaves on the branches." He gestured to the wood, "You have never seen them?"

"Never." Sectoraus didn't take his eyes from the trees, "Only mountains and rocks and gems do we Serpenoids know of. We have never been out this way. How do you know of them?"

"I remember from my past life; I was a woodsman." With the expression on the Serpenoids' faces he explained further, "Many lands where I'm from were covered in forests, I used to cut them down. Humans use wood for many things"

Although the trees in this forest were dead and dry, they towered into the sky and spread for a wide distance creating a dense forest. The trees were so plentiful the adventurers could barely see past the first few rows. They approached slowly and cautiously, still checking behind them in case the rock monsters came up from the valley.

With Sectoraus still in the lead, they came to a stop just before the forest began. Sectoraus looked up and down, amazed at the majestic structures, and placed a hand onto the trunk of a tree, rubbing his hand over it. Through his scaly palm, Sectoraus could feel the coarse, rough exterior of the brown bark. He nodded his head at the new information.

Sectoraus thought for a moment, tried to peer through the wood, then said, "In that case you lead," and pushed the slave forward.

The trio moved through the forest slowly, not only because the trees were so crowded, but also because it was dark, almost pitch black. The Serpenoids saw fairly well; they were creatures of the dark, but they were more used to darkness in the open. Especially after the time they had spent in this world, their eyes had become accustomed to the red sky giving its slight illumination. Their eyes needed a moment to readjust to the total darkness. The mountainous trees that blocked the sky gave Sectoraus and Nimod a bit of nostalgia for the true darkness they had once called home. Their navigator, however, didn't see very well at all; his human eyes needed light.

Just as the Serpenoids adapted to the subtle light here, the humans had adapted to the near darkness. In the desert land, the glow coming off from the magma and the sky's hue became essential light sources for the humans. Within the wood, however, the nearest source of magma was the river down in the valley, and the sky was completely obscured by the twisted branches as they gradually went further and further into the thick.

Their soft steps crunched and snapped twigs that lay scattered about. The ground was cluttered with them. Sectoraus took a deep breath. Even the air was different here. It was cooler, softer. The beautiful aroma of brimstone that gave Sectoraus the comfort of home was faint. The scent he noticed more prominently was something he did not know how to describe. He could only assume that was the scent of the trees.

Suddenly startled, they came to a stop at the sounds of a deep rumbling off in the distance. The dangerous realization was clear; they weren't the only ones that lived in this world. They would advance, then pause each time they heard a rustle in the wood or the sound of a crying howl, which the slave said reminded him of wolves.

What could be waiting for them in these trees, Sectoraus wondered. What might find them or what if something already had. He could see enough now, his eyes slowly adjusting to the dark, but wished he could see more. Remembering how the rock creatures came from the magma unscathed, if something else lived here then it must also be suited to this environment.

He also thought of Thandrua, how he wished to tell him about the creatures in the valley and these trees. All kinds of new tools they could make with the wood. He also thought of Solarious, curious what his brother's journey held. Whether they had also discovered other creatures or whether they lost any of their group, as Sectoraus had.

They heard movement again, louder than before. They all stopped and formed a triangle, looking in each direction. The movement fell silent, but then they heard the breathing. It wasn't a breathing anything like either of the Serpenoids or humans. This was heavy, like a snorting exhalation, coming from something of great size. They looked about and heard the soft careful footsteps before the snap of a stick betrayed the location of the movement. They all turned to the same direction and saw two glowing red eyes advance at them. The trio scattered out of the way as a colossal black and brown, fur-covered quadruped tore through the trees.

The explorers readied themselves, the slave armed himself with a thick branch as he muttered, "This is like no bear I've ever seen."

With a growl, the bear opened up two ivory mandibles from both sides of its muzzled mouth, swinging at them with large thick claws as they dodged its attacks. They tried to stay light on their feet, constantly moving about. The bear was much too quick for any of them to attack the beast. Nimod was barely quick enough to jump to the ground as the bear bit a chunk of bark off the tree where he had just been.

Sectoraus ran up and jabbed the end of his staff into the thick thigh of the monster, but he couldn't pull it back in time and a powerful kick in the abdomen sent him tumbling back. The bear spat out the bark in anger and roared as it stood on its hind legs, revealing its gargantuan fangs as well as its full, monstrous height as well.

The beast swiped a claw at the man. The slave was exhausted and could not dodge in time. The heavy black paw connected with the slave's face. His neck twisted around as his formerly attached jaw went spinning further into the wood. They heard the howling coming from various sources behind the bear, causing it to stop its onslaught for a moment, turning towards the fast-approaching footsteps. Several furry figures leapt onto the beast. Sectoraus and Nimod ran.

They wasted no time, speeding through the forest as they jumped over fallen trees and overgrown roots. In the distance behind they heard the sound of a few yelps from the other creatures, then a final roar of the bear. A roar of defeat.

Sectoraus suddenly choked as one of his necklaces caught on a branch. Nimod had continued ahead before he heard the struggling gasps and turned back. The Serpenoid tugged at his leader's necklace, breaking the chain. The two left the gold abandoned in the dirt as they continued their escape. They jumped down and hid underneath a small nook, catching their breath for a moment. Then, like music to their ears, they heard the flowing sounds of water. It was coming from a creek just up ahead. The frightened explorers scampered to the water and began to drink, scooping the water up with their hands.

The cool crisp water was a celebration for them. It provided comfort as well as quenching their thirst from all the running. All the fear. The delicious liquid dripped from their mouths as they caught their breaths. However, they soon found their celebration might have been premature.

Reality struck them with the howling sound of the creatures that the slave had referred to as "wolves." They looked up towards the hill they had jumped down from and saw seven silhouettes. Their yellow eyes glowed in the darkness as they stared at the Serpenoids. Their pointed ears stuck in the air listening. The largest of the pack stood slightly, not fully erect like the Serpenoids and humans, but hunched over with knees bent. Its two front limbs were more like arms than legs, hands with claw-like nails. The others stood as well.

Sectoraus tightened his grip on his staff that he was quickly growing a deeper respect for, and stood as straight as he could, broadening his shoulders. The alpha wolf snarled, showing its sharp white fangs before howling in the air. The pack charged at the Serpenoids, running fast on all fours. Sectoraus and Nimod sprang to their feet and ran as fast as they could, following the creek.

Just ahead the trees began to spread out. They were nearing the end of the forest as the creek expanded in size. These wolf creatures were gaining on them. Sectoraus and Nimod could hear the panting of their pursuers closing in. They picked up their pace.

Almost out now as they splashed about with every step. The ground beneath them had become slightly overrun with water. Sectoraus felt relieved but also scared. The creatures behind seemed as if they would continue pursuing, even if they were out of the forest. And what was next, what would be waiting for them on the other side? Sectoraus thought he could see the orange flicker of flame just beyond the trees.

They had just made it out into a clearing of marsh when they heard a growl coming from one of the wolves. It leapt for them, pinning Sectoraus to the ground. The rest came out of the wood. Sectoraus held onto the wolf's neck, pushing it away from biting his face. It snarled as saliva dripped onto the Cobra and scratched at him with its claws. Had it not been for the broad gold collar Sectoraus wore, the beast would have torn out his throat. Suddenly it yelped as blood sprayed in the Cobra's eyes. The wolf's detached head fell forward.

The rest of the pack ran back into the forest and Sectoraus could hear multiple footsteps going after them. He pushed off the wolf's heavy body and a clawed, scaly hand reached down to pull him up. Sectoraus thought it was Nimod who had saved his life and now hoisted him from the ground. He was surprised, however, after his slitted eyes followed the hand up the scaly green arm to see the face of his rescuer.

Although similar in many ways, this was no Serpenoid. The figure was stocky and stood slightly shorter than the average Serpenoid, perhaps about the height of the humans. He grasped its hand and pulled himself up. Its hide was much thicker and coarser than the typically smooth Serpenoid skin. Sectoraus could tell just by the feel of its hand. In its other hand it held a long sharp tool made of bone that dripped with blood. Its two orange eyes met Sectoraus' and opened its elongated mouth, revealing teeth that were long and dull, and it let out a sour smelling breath before speaking.

"Ya barely made it out," its expression was stern, but then it seemed to brighten after sizing up Sectoraus. "Welcome to our swamp!"

Chapter 16
The Rebellion

It was the end of a cycle, all the Serpenoids were peacefully sleeping. Lord Thandrua slumped in his throne, letting out a growling snore with every breath. Phineus and Orpheus accompanied their master, curled on the ground, sound asleep. It had been the third cycle since Sectoraus and Solarious set out on their separate journeys. Since their absence, the two other Cobras had only monitored the slaves at the beginning of their cycle. Come slumber time, Orpheus and Phineus would leave one or two Serpenoids standing guard at the quarry in their place. They would also send other Serpenoids to escort the forgers in the Kiln to the confines of the quarry.

Lord Thandrua agreed with the two Cobra brothers when they explained that the slaves had proved to know their place and did not require such strict supervision. They were surrounded by a fence anyhow. The Oracle had been unsettled that the remaining Cobra Clan altered Sectoraus' routine so soon after he left. Vander didn't voice his concern; he knew they wouldn't heed any of his warnings. It had become apparent to him that his role didn't include giving his opinion often.

However, in this case Vander didn't feel the need to try to push his insight as he had when the enslavement began. He understood all things found their way to come together and that at times one could simply watch where they would go as opposed to intervening. The Oracle meditated by the lake whilst the others slumbered, like he had done the previous two cycles.

Vander wasn't the only resident within the desert abstaining from slumber. The quarry was very much awake, other than the two Serpenoids who now slept seated on the ground with their backs to the entrance of the fence, leaning against one another. During the end of cycles past, the Cobras had always managed to raise the ladders that connected the bottom level to the midsection and the mid to the entrance at the upper level. It had seemed the two Cobras had failed to mention this to the Serpenoids they had appointed to supervise, for this was the second cycle in a row that they had left the ladders fully extended.

Down at the bottom of the pit all the slaves congregated around Lucifer, who stood in the center with Lilith and Solomon alongside him. They stared at Lucifer eagerly. Many of the slaves bore lacerations and blisters on different parts of their bodies from their hard labor and from the heat of the desert life.

The slaves closest to the inside of the gathering held the smooth shiny swords that had been stashed within the quarry. The slaves spoke amongst themselves. Those that held the weapons turned them in their hands, admiring the cool metal blades, adjusting to the deadly heft in their hands.

“All the swords have been distributed,” Solomon whispered in Lucifer’s ear.

Lucifer cleared his throat, ending all other conversation.

"The time has come." The fallen angel announced, raising his sword while turning on the spot to catch all the eager eyes, "We have been oppressed for far too long. After all the suffering I-- *we* have endured, now is our time to fight back. It is time to show them what happens when you force conscious beings to do the greedy bidding of others. You have all shown impeccable patience; this I am most grateful for. The plan could not have succeeded if we had chosen to rush. We are organized, we have our weaponry, and the incompetent Serpenoids have even unknowingly aided us by leaving the ladders to the entrance.

“So I urge you on now, follow me up the ladders; I can guarantee our sorry excuse for guards are deep in sleep. Those of you with swords follow me and the rest behind them. After we are free of this prison, we will embark toward the Kiln and collect the swords I have hidden there to arm the rest of you."

Mindful to not wake the guards, the slaves acknowledged the speech with nods and soft grunts. Lucifer bowed his head to collect his praise, then the slaves parted to form a path for their leader. Each rebel fell in line behind him as he passed, heading to the first ladder. The metal creaked and echoed in the silence of the cavernous quarry with the weight pressing upon each step. Lucifer made a gesture with his hand to his followers below as he slowed his pace, and the ladder quieted.

Lucifer had reached the walkway of the quarry's midsection. Before moving toward the next ladder, he peeked over the ledge to observe the line of bodies that followed his ascension, watching their awkward one-handed climb as they clutched their swords like lifelines. With just one more ladder to ascend, Lucifer took each step slowly, causing even less sound to be heard. Although if they had woken the guards, they could easily rush at them and slaughter them. There were only two weaponless guards, far too distant from the colony's slumber grounds to reach anyone else or sound an alarm. Nothing would stand in the way of Lucifer's plan.

He reached the top and gestured with his palm out at the slaves below him, signaling them to stop. The rebel leader peaked over the surface to locate the guards who sat across from the ladder, backs against the gate. Lucifer could only see the back of the Serpenoids' heads but judging by how their heads hung he knew they were sleeping and pulled himself onto the dusty orange ground.

Lucifer's pale feet silently stepped and slowly crept over to the gate. His army waited close behind. The fallen angel pushed his shaggy white hair aside, gently placed his left hand through a part in the fence and readied himself to lift the latch. With the sword in his other hand, he aimed at the back of one guard in a spot between the shoulders. The silence was thick as the anticipation grew. The slaves shifted on their feet, eager to break free, yearning to use the weapons they had labored so heavily on. All excitement to the side, they waited silently still.

The motion was lightning quick; Lucifer thrust the sword forward between the gate and through the Serpenoid. Blood squirted from the blade's exit wound. The victim made a strangled yelp before gagging on his own blood. The guard that slept beside him woke with a start and gaped at the sharp metal that impaled his companion through the chest.

Before he had time to even comprehend what had happened, much less react, Lucifer extracted his weapon with a wet, fleshy sound and threw the gate open, knocking both guards to the side. The living Serpenoid screamed as he pushed off the bloodied body of his companion, attempting to get up. Lucifer kicked the Serpenoid over and kicked again into the guard's ribs. Slowly the Serpenoid attempted to push himself off the ground with his hands, but the weight of the fallen angel's foot placed onto the guard's lower back kept him in place. Lucifer lifted his sword with both hands above his head and chopped down at the Serpenoid's neck with one swift, practiced motion. Blood spattered onto the rebel leader's pale bare skin.

The slaves watched in awe as the head tumbled to the ground, then a grin fell upon their faces as blood gushed out of the Serpenoid's neck, staining the already orange ground a deep, rusty red. The slaves' cheers roared as Lucifer hoisted the decapitated head in his palm, turning on spot for all to see while the horde poured through the gates.

"Our first steps to freedom!" The blood-covered slave king announced, "Now, let us make our way to retrieve the rest of the weapons!"

The men and women shouted in agreement, raising their swords and fists in the air as they marched to the Kiln. Unbeknownst to themselves, there was something primal radiating from their hearts that shone within their eyes; Lucifer alone saw this and in accordance to his cause he knew it was good. Vengeance was soon to be on the horizon and the fallen angel would have not liked it any other way.

The pace of their march was quick. Lucifer sneered at the sight of the golden Thandrua idol as it grew nearer. It wasn't long before they reached the tunnel within the smoking volcano of the Kiln. Many waited outside and watched in the near distance, but the clay-built homes of the Serpenoids held no signs of activity. Their new cycle had yet to begin and all were still sound asleep. Lucifer escorted a group of his avengers into the Kiln, showing the various places he hid the swords as the slaves collected their own. Before long, all blades were out and the slaves swung them in the air, testing their purpose. There were enough for most, but some still waited empty-handed.

Now, all awaited Lucifer's direction. "Beautiful, you are all beautiful! Your swords accentuate your beauty that has been repressed by the wicked Serpenoids. Retribution is within sight. You may kill any Serpenoid that stands in your path, but one thing I ask of you. Do *not* kill any members of Thandrua's covenant. They may be the worst of the oppressors, but they will serve a great purpose under my regime."

The final step was nearing execution. Before they stormed the slumber grounds, Lucifer directed the few weaponless slaves to carry chains and to take some of the empty containers from the Kiln and fill them with the hot lava that flowed nearby. They carried at least four vats with two slaves holding onto each, marching in the front with their leader as the rest followed a distance behind.

All of their excitement quieted as they approached the first of the homes. With a silent nod, Lucifer directed the people carrying the hot lava toward the first four homes. Each readied their position by the entryway of these homes. They looked toward their rebellious leader. They waited.

Lucifer gazed about shelters, listening to the faint breaths of peaceful innocent slumber. He gazed up to the blood-orange sky, watching its perfect emptiness. His white shaggy hair brushed against his face in the calm breeze. He took in a deep breath of the brimstone in the air. It was sour and made his nostrils flare, reminding him of his hatred of the place.

"Now!" Lucifer shouted and the slaves poured the lava into the shelters. Piercing shrieks of agony exploded from within the homes as the stench of seared flesh wafted out and with that, the rebellious leader gave the direction they had all been waiting on for relentless cycles, "Attack!"

Lucifer put a hand on Lilith's shoulder to keep her at his side. He watched gleefully as his minions swarmed around them, scanning through the masses. "Solomon!" He hailed the dark-haired man as he passed by, "The two of you stand with me. We watch, savor the moment."

"I want to slaughter those monsters." Solomon snapped.

"Watch, and enjoy." The fallen archangel's grey eyes pierced deep into Solomon's brown eyes, "You may have your fun soon. And in just a moment I want you two to fetch me the Oracle from his shelter. Before then, we will admire my masterpiece."

Solomon held his tongue and lowered his sword. He and Lilith stood on either side of their leader. The rest of the slaves stormed the grounds, either running into the huts or greeting those curious enough to wander out investigating the mayhem. The Serpenoid blood was spilt everywhere. Their scaled limbs were severed and heads decapitated, eerily the yellow eyes still glowed open even once the heads had been removed.

Lord Thandrua, Orpheus, and Phineus rushed out of their chamber to witness the chaotic massacre. Thandrua's staff slipped from his hand as he dropped to his knees in disbelief. He watched as his faithful followers were slain before him, his captives spreading throughout the grounds and the valley toward the lake.

Orpheus was the first of the three to step forward, rushing into the mayhem as his hood unfolded. A male slave, face scaled with dehydrated skin, charged at the brutish Cobra, swinging his sword carelessly. Orpheus remained composed and simply stepped to the side. The sharp blade hissed past him, cutting the air instead of his face. The Cobra snatched the man by the scruff of his neck. Orpheus slammed the slave's face into his knee, crushing the human's nose in, causing teeth to explode.

Now he wielded the fallen's sword. Someone ran up behind him. Before she could strike, Orpheus slashed at her legs with his heavy tail and caused her to trip. He turned to her and drove the blade straight down into her gut. She screamed in pain, holding onto the wound after the Cobra pulled back the sword. His victim's screams became a gag as blood spewed out of her mouth. Orpheus stared at her, then his sword. The weapon felt foreign in his hand, but intuitively he saw its purpose and charged forward.

Phineus stepped in front of Thandrua and rubbed his eyes to see the horror displayed. His mouth dropped open, seeing the bloodshed and the helpless Serpenoids succumbing to their doom.

Then his eyes fixed onto his brother, Orpheus, who did his best to fight against the rebels.

Orpheus held the sword in his right hand and used it to parry the attacks that fell upon him. Turning in circles, for he was surrounded, he used his free hand to punch and shove while he blocked slashes with the blade. He bashed in skulls and faces with the hilt of the sword, incapacitating his foes in that fashion before he finally understood to drive the blade into the enemy. Frozen for a moment, he stared at the blood-covered tool in his hand after pulling it out of an enemy. He looked from the dripping blade to the slave on the ground, gagging on his own blood. Suddenly, Orpheus gave out a battle cry and submerged himself into the fray.

"Beautiful, is it not?" Lucifer turned to Lilith.

"I don't know, Lucifer. It is quite gruesome." Lilith felt sick to her stomach. Her palm grew clammy as her grip on her sword loosened.

"No! This is everything we have been waiting for." Lucifer's smile faltered. He turned to Solomon. "And you?"

"It is marvelous." The ferociousness was ablaze within Solomon's eyes.

"Yes, thank you! That was the answer I was looking for." Lucifer closed his eyes. "Listen to the screams. It is like a symphony pouring out from the amphitheater."

"I want to contribute," Solomon grunted.

"Yes, yes go ahead." Lucifer shooed him away with his hands. "You and Lilith. Go collect the Oracle from his chambers. Remember, I need him alive, but kill whatever you may along the way."

A distance away, a man and woman stuck together as they gutted the nearby Serpenoids. They both held expressions of disgust. Disgust for the Serpenoids? No, it was the bloodshed. They wanted freedom from slavery just as everyone else, but not like this. They both turned, searching for who would be their next victim. The woman stopped and turned to look toward one of the Serpenoid homes. She heard a laughing and tapped her companion. They went to investigate.

"Owen, is that you laughing?" said the woman as she stepped into the dome. A man with long curly hair stood before a Serpenoid who appeared to be kneeling.

"Wha- oh, Sara!" The man called Owen glanced over his shoulder, addressing the woman. "Check this out. Look how it cries!" He laughed sadistically as he stepped to the side.

Sara and her friend gasped. Rivers of tears pouring out from the Serpenoid's eyes. Its legs were severed at the knees. Its arms were raised in defense, revealing bloodied stubs in place of its hands. Sara felt ill, then gagged at the sight of the Serpenoid's discarded legs next to her by the entrance.

"Isn't this sweet?" Owen smiled deviously, then returned his attention to his victim. He snatched the Serpenoid's left arm and hacked at the elbow. Once, then twice, before wrenching it off, as its crying became ear-piercing shrieks of agony.

"Just kill it, you monster!" Sara yelled.

"And deny myself all this fun?" Owen turned to her, "What are you, some Serpenoid lover? What about you, Alexander? You want to show this creature mercy too?"

The man with Sara, Alexander, turned around and walked away. Sara, however, went into the shelter, holding her sword out. She moved around Owen quickly and drove her blade into the suffering Serpenoid's chest. It gasped, yellow eyes widened, then it was dead.

"You bitch!" Owen pushed her to the side, knocking her down. "It was mine! Mine!" Before she could even register what was happening, he raised his blade and sunk it down between her breasts. Owen pulled out his bloodied sword and stormed out of the shelter.

"You better run away, Alexander!" He hollered to the man who left his friend to die. Owen turned around and in the next moment his anger subsided when he saw a wounded Serpenoid struggling to stand nearby. He rushed at it, sword raised in the air, a wide grin contorting his face. He was nearly upon the Serpenoid, then stopped in his tracks and gasped in surprise. He felt a sharp pain in his ribs and when he looked to his left, he saw the muscular build of Orpheus. The Cobra stared into his eyes as the man slid off the sword, crumbling to the ground.

As Orpheus did his best to protect some Serpenoids, Phineus ran with speed to join him, hood and fangs exposed as he hissed furiously. The slender Cobra used his agility to dodge and duck all attacks directed at him. A small group of Serpenoids moved in close to their protectors.

"Phineus, take this!" Orpheus tossed one of the fallen swords to his clan brother who deftly caught it.

Now Phineus not only dodged the slaves' attacks with quick and easy side steps but used his blade to counter the hacks as he had seen his brother do.

More Serpenoids ran to join the growing group, running past the slaves' savage roars and slashing swords. Not many were fortunate enough to make it through unscathed.

"Look, they're grouping together!" One woman shouted to her slave companions as she noticed the small resistance to their rebellion. They made their way to the Cobras that fought gallantly.

Finally, a shadow fell upon Phineus as he glanced beside him to see his Lord joining the fight. The red beast swung his obsidian staff around, cracking the jaws and bones of his attackers. A woman ran over. Thandrua whacked at her legs, causing her right knee to bend at an unnatural angle. He turned to a man creeping up from behind and drove the jewel-encrusted end of his staff into the man's throat. Blood sprayed back in return, blending into Thandrua's ruddy complexion.

A shouting rebel ran toward them, both hands raised above his head with a sword. Phineus swiftly ran to meet him. The Cobra slid on the ground and sliced off the slave's left leg. Phineus jumped back up, drove the blade into the man's side as he fell over, and tossed the legless slave's sword to his master.

Lord Thandrua caught the sword by the hilt, then pivoted and slashed a slave approaching from behind. Quickly turning again, he raised his hefty foot as another slave's face smashed directly onto it. Thandrua shouted his pride, a sword in one hand and his staff in the other. He ran further into the chaos, bent forward and thrusted his head to the side. His long horns knocked two foes to the side. Quickly, Thandrua cracked open the skull of one with his staff before driving the blade into the other. He turned, swinging the sword horizontally to decapitate another slave that tried to run up behind him.

Phineus fought three or more at a time, moving as fast as he could between opponents. He impaled one slave, twisting out of the way of another oncoming attacker to stab a third, then turned around and engaged with the second even as he used his tail to push back yet another assailant. Phineus' tail whipped into this slave with all the force of a solid kick to the gut; the slave fell back, winded. At times the dexterous Cobra abandoned his duel to save a Serpenoid from the blow of a slave's sword, then quickly returned to his brutish brother's side.

Orpheus held his ground. All slaves came from the front as Serpenoids retreated behind him. The broad Cobra hissed intimidatingly as he locked swords. His strength gained way always, pushing whoever parried him off balance and providing the perfect opening for a killing blow. Phineus rejoined his side as Lord Thandrua returned to them as well.

The trio surrounded the group of Serpenoids that took refuge in their care. Most were too terrified and helpless to fend for themselves; they cried and quivered as more rebels approached. However, there were a few Serpenoids that now gained the courage to defend themselves after seeing their Lord fight off the approaching slaves.

These Serpenoids followed their leaders' example and picked up the discarded swords from dead slaves. The triangular perimeter their leaders formed developed into a circle as the armed Serpenoids bravely stood alongside their leaders. They taunted and encouraged the slaves to approach.

"Do not engage!" Lucifer ordered as he emerged from the crowd. "Remember, I do not want the Lord and his Clan slain."

"Lucifer," Thandrua pleaded, scanning the scene of disembodied Serpenoids and charred shelters, "what have you done here? So many of my followers... lifeless."

"Exactly, heathen!" The former archangel pointed his sword to the red beast, "Now lower your swords if you do not wish for all to be rendered lifeless. Take a good look, you are outnumbered, and it is just a matter of time before you three are incapacitated."

A thought dawned on Lucifer then as he looked around, *if the Oracle isn't with them, then...* He turned to look to the shelter the Oracle would normally reside in. Lilith stood at the entryway empty-handed.

"The Oracle isn't in here!" Lilith called out to her leader.

Lucifer looked around to the Serpenoids that were scattered about the camp. He heard the hoots and shouting of joy coming from the lake and caught sight of a couple of slaves that ran down the valley.

"Chain the survivors," he ordered and ran toward the lake himself.

As he descended into the valley, he saw a group of his minions surrounding the Oracle. They had not yet used their weapons on him, but instead pushed and kicked him about. Lucifer stopped for a moment then hurried over.

Before he shouted at them to stop, he flung his sword forward. The weapon flipped, blade over hilt and struck one of the slaves in the back. The group jumped and turned around, weapons at the ready, before they realized the sword had been thrown by their own leader.

"Halt!" Lucifer stormed up to the group and pulled his sword from the body that spasmed on the ground, "This one is not to be harmed."

"You killed Figgens." One man stepped forward as the rest drastically stepped back, alienating the accuser, "We were just having fun with this disgusting Serpenoid."

"This is no ordinary Serpenoid! This is the Oracle!" Lucifer now held his blade at arm's length just below the slave's neck, "And if you favor your head where it is, you would be wise not to question my judgment."

The fallen archangel looked down at the beaten Vander and thought back to when the Serpenoid first visited him and brought him water many cycles ago. Lucifer held out a hand and after Vander reluctantly took his grasp, the rebel leader hauled him up, "This one is the most useful of them all."

"Lucifer, what have you done?" Vander stood, brushing the sand from his body, but he asked his question with little surprise in his voice. He had seen this event coming and knew deep down that it couldn't be prevented.

"I am simply doing unto others as they have done unto me." He flashed a smirk before turning to move out of the valley, "Come, follow me. All of you, come!"

The freed slaves did as commanded. Vander lingered thoughtfully for a moment, gazing out to the lake one more time. Turning, the Oracle picked up his pace to catch up with Lucifer.

"Are these the swords you had spoken of before?" Vander asked.

"Why yes, they are." Lucifer turned his side to side. “Magnificent, aren't they?"

"How did you acquire them? I had seen them in a vision, and you spoke of them during battle with your kind. Are these from your former world?"

"Ha! *Heavens* no! We created them ourselves. You provided us with the material and tools, we simply bided our time and took full advantage of your offerings."

Vander stayed quiet as they reached the slumber grounds. He thought about the irony in the situation; had Lord Thandrua not enslaved Lucifer and the humans, they would not have had the need for revenge. If they were not enslaved and forced to mine and forge, they would have not had the easy access and bountiful material to make devices to rebel with, like the ones they held now.

The Oracle gasped at the scene as they passed a couple of huts and made their way to the army of humans that waited by the monuments. He felt queasy from the burnt smell that hung in the air and used all his strength to keep his eyes up, averting his gaze from the bloodbath. Through his feet he could feel the mushy texture of moist sand squelching between his toes. Had he been walking by the lake he would have found the sensation pleasing. However, knowing the slaughter that just took place, the Oracle had no desire to see the origin of the moisture.

The former slaves detained their new prisoners, forcing them onto their knees after lining up the survivors between the golden Thandrua statue and the unfinished waist and legs of the bronze Sectoraus statue. Each captive was bound by chains; further down the line a couple of the former slaves bound the last remaining captives. Vander didn't take the time to count, but at a glance he could see there were maybe a hundred or so Serpenoids displayed in front of him. *Or perhaps more like two hundred,* Vander thought, trying to fool himself. Their colony had been a legion before. The rebels were the legion now.

At the head of the crowd of prisoners, Lord Thandrua, Phineus, and Orpheus were forced to their knees. Their hands were chained behind their backs, the Cobras' cowls withdrawn. All three looked up with relief to see Vander remained alive. Thandrua bore a smile; something good in the middle of such a tragedy. However, their expressions of relief faltered upon realizing how freely he seemed to walk amongst the rebels. Now, they were just confused.

Lucifer stood in front of the crimson prisoner and his stern face broke into a genuine smile when Thandrua gazed up to him.

"Ah, now it is you who looks up to a superior!" The fallen angel smirked.

"What happens now, Creature?" Thandrua spoke through gritted teeth.

Lucifer gave a curt nod to one of the men that stood behind the three leaders. Thandrua gasped in pain and stumbled forward as the hilt of a sword delivered a swift blow to the back of his head with. His crown slipped off and rolled away from him. Orpheus slammed his tail into the back of Thandrua's assailant.

"Chain his tail up!" Lucifer ordered, "Restrain the tails of all of these serpents. Hurry up!"

The rebels moved quickly, grabbing extra chains and making quick work to attend to the Serpenoids' fifth appendage.

"Oh my, how the tables have turned!" Lucifer clasped his hands together and held them to his chest with joy as his army behind him laughed cruelly. The Cobras snarled in defense while the Serpenoids hollered behind, out of protest, out of fear.

"Oracle, your hands are free and you allow your Lord to be treated as such!?" Orpheus snarled.

Vander did not respond, not with his words anyhow. He remained completely silent and shifted his gaze elsewhere in shame. It broke his heart to see everyone in chains. He wished he could do something, but he was not a fighter. Violence was not something he thought he could cause, not even in self-defense. He also understood too well that he was outnumbered. Lucifer had spared his life once; he may not the next time.

Two rebels grabbed Thandrua by the shoulders and lifted him back to his knees. Blood began to trickle down the side of his head from where he was hit. Lucifer spat on the ground in front of the beast. He shifted his gaze to the golden, bejeweled crown that lay discarded in the sand and snatched it up, slowly placing the crown on his own head.

"Now, listen here!" Lucifer announced, then readjusted the crown, "Thandrua, do not forget your manners. What happens now is, *I* am the ruler. You may all refer to me as Lord Lucifer and nothing less. I will also accept: Master, Your Excellency, Morning St-- no, no not that, but how about *Dark* Lord? Yes, I do like that one!"

The former slaves cheered and applauded their leader as the fallen angel bowed to their praise. "This is my kingdom, as I had claimed upon my arrival, and rightfully so. I helped create this world, as I did many others. Just like this lovely crown upon my head. I helped create this and it is mine now too. And it was because of me that you, Thandrua, and your Serpenoids thrived for so long on Earth."

"The Almighty Thandrua gave us life when he brought the rains with him!" A brave Serpenoid shouted from the back.

"Aw, you see that, Thandrua? Still loyal even in shackles." Lucifer's whimsical expression darkened as he looked to one of his men and ordered, "Kill him!" At his word, the defiant Serpenoid's head tumbled forward from its body. The Serpenoids around screamed and tried to shift away from the growing puddle of blood.

"Listen and listen well, Serpenoids! This monster is no god, he had no stake in your creation. A valiant leader he may have been to you, yes, but a great deceiver he has been as well. For there is another, a true almighty entity. *My* former master. The *Creator.* Creator of the very Universe itself. Gave you rain, gave you life. The Creator told Thandrua of the Sun and of this sanctuary. The Creator gave Thandrua insight and the power to keep this world as a sanctuary for you all, but pride stood in the way. He feared me and put me away and damned you all to your fate."

The Serpenoids were shocked. They murmured with those closest to each other. Some protested in denial until the blades were brandished at them, then silence fell among them all. Both Phineus and Orpheus stared at Thandrua, wide-eyed and conflicted. It could not be true, not after all these cycles.

"Master, is it so?" Phineus said almost in a whimper.

"...It is." Thandrua let his horned head hang low as a few tears dripped from his eyes, soothing the scar over his left eye slightly. Shame enveloped him. Oh, how many times had he wished to be truthful to his followers, to lower the pedestal they had placed him upon, before had he become all too comfortable with his worship. He knew deep inside he would tell them in time, at least the Cobra Clan, but he had never imagined it like this.

“Strip this monstrosity of his jewelry!” With the Dark Lord’s command, the rebels surrounded Thandrua, yanking and tearing away at his layered necklaces. Gems, bits of gold and pieces of silver scattered around him as his royal chains were broken. The men and women snatched at the precious pieces. They had slaved over those for so long and now the humans could not be denied what was rightfully theirs.

Lucifer gestured for his followers to move aside. "You see, he is a false idol. You call him lifegiver, but his face remains scarred and watch as he bleeds before you now. I do not claim myself to be the Almighty, but I am more godly than this beast. You have all witnessed the abuse I had endured in your imprisonment and see now how I do not hold any scars from *any* injury."

"Hail Lord Lucifer!" Cheered the men and women who now tasted freedom.

"Yes, yes, praise me!" Lucifer closed his eyes for a moment, savoring his glory, "I have released you from that imprisonment as promised. I have reshaped you from the madness of entering this world. I gave you all new names and now I shall give your new identities, reshaping what you are as you pledge your allegiance to me."

Lucifer paused as his audience dropped down to a single knee nearly in unison, almost as though they were directed. The new king smiled at the obedience displayed.

"To be completely honest, I was angered when the first of you arrived and were thrown into the pit with me." Lucifer said, "I had contempt for humans; being in this world was punishment enough, but to share it with humans? I was outraged! I used that to fuel my vengeance towards Thandrua, but through these many cycles of training, you have proven to be beyond human. I do understand some of you hold onto whatever remnants of your past memories you have, and some are newer to this domain than others. However, through the strength of trials we endured while enslaved together, the skill of deception you have developed to keep our coming rebellion hidden, and the malintent you have learned in this hardening life has made me reconsider.

"It is downright disrespectful to consider yourselves human when you are blossoming into something so much more beautiful. Those of you who have been here the longest even begun to show a physical transformation from your pathetic human qualities. No, *human* will not do, and *human* will not be my army; I think *daemon* is better suited for your beauty. Prosper, my daemon army, and live free!"

"Hail Lord Lucifer!" The newly dubbed daemons stood, pumping their fists and swords up toward the blood-orange sky. Lucifer could not hide the smile that spread across his face. He felt whole, complete.

"Now, the first duties of our new order," the daemon king gestured to the towering idols. "Bring these eyesores down and throw our prisoners into the quarry! We have much construction to begin!"

Chapter 17
The Swamplands and New Friendships

Sectoraus stared at the sight of his savior as the brute sized him up with his own gaze. Sectoraus had never seen anything like this being before him. After seeing Lucifer and the humans, Sectoraus had thought that other beings might also look like themselves. However, Sectoraus had encountered three different types of beings within this cycle leading up to this moment.

Now he saw that there was at least another kind that more closely resembled the Serpenoids, only more ruggedly built. More savage. Even the being's long thick tail looked ferocious, with rough scales protruding outward almost like spikes.

Sectoraus had found it odd that the being had some type of covering wrapped around its waist. It reminded Sectoraus of the dryness of some of the slaves' skin, the ones that have been within this world the longest. Their savior had a necklace and some bracelets, but these materials were not made of the gems or gold like those that Sectoraus wore; they seemed to be sharp teeth.

"What are you doing here!? Who are you?" It asked impatiently, breaking the silence Sectoraus was suddenly aware of.

"I am Sectoraus, head of the Cobra Clan, leader of the Serpenoids." He straightened up.

"Serpenoids, eh?" The being thought about that for a moment before pointing out with the sharp bone-made tool, "And your friend there?"

Straggling behind Sectoraus stood Nimod, who stared at one of the two tree-made poles that flickered with a fist-sized flame. Sectoraus caught his attention, and he came forward. Captivated by his savior, Sectoraus hadn't given the flames a second thought until now, seeing his companion's reaction. He did find the small structures peculiar. Flame without a source of magma, that also didn't spread about. Before he could become completely mesmerized, Nimod spoke, rousing Sectoraus from his musings.

“My name is Nimod,” he began distantly, still entranced by the flames, “I am one of the Serpenoids that follow the Cobra Clan and Lord Thandrua.”

“Lord Thandrua? What does that mean to you, leader of Serpenoids?" The brute steered its attention to Sectoraus, "This Lord Thandrua follow you as well?”

“Thandrua is the Almighty that allowed the Serpenoids to live. He does not follow any. He is the Lifegiver.”

“I see,” the being thought for a moment; Sectoraus didn't think the being quite understood Thandrua’s importance. Abruptly, it held out its right hand in greeting, a thin webbing of skin stretching as its four fingers extended, “I am Draquan, head warrior of the Krocdylius. Come follow me”

Sectoraus and Nimod shook their savior's forearm, but Nimod hesitated before they could follow. "What of the rest of your crew?" Sectoraus asked as he remembered hearing others chase the creatures into the forest.

"My brethren are strong, they enjoy chasing the canis. It teaches those pack hunters to stay away from our land. Besides, they know the way back."

With that, Draquan turned around and began leading them down what looked like a path worn down by heavy foot traffic. The path was lined with green frilly things that came up to waist level from out of the ground. The ground was soft, and their feet sunk into a thin layer of water. A short way ahead Sectoraus could see two more posts with the fire-that-stayed on each side of the path. There were small trees about, very few and far between, but the small green frilly things covered most of the land. The Cobra stuck his hand out, brushing it against the green things as they walked by.

"Don't ya love the feel of the grass against your palm?" Draquan asked when he glanced over his shoulder, catching Sectoraus. He then stuck out his own hand and did the same.

"Grass?" A small smile came across Sectoraus' face as his palm felt the soft and moist texture.

"Yeah, grass! You never seen grass?" Draquan didn't know what to make of that.

"No, never. Our land is all sand, rock, and magma." Sectoraus explained.

"Oh wow! You've come long and far." Draquan chuckled a little.

"You've been to our land?" Sectoraus was genuinely curious. He had never seen his guide's like in the desert before.

"No, no, not me. The Priestess has told us about the Desertland. We don't go much further than the Dark Forest." Draquan gestured with his bone tool at the forest they were gradually leaving behind.

"Priestess?"

"She's the oldest of our kind. Connected to something we cannot see nor touch by hand and teaches the mystics of the swamp," Draquan explained. The awe when he spoke of her made it clear that Draquan had a deep respect for this Priestess.

Sectoraus thought of Vander. Connected to something from beyond their understanding, attempting to teach his insights, "We have one similar we refer to as the Oracle."

"Ah yes, this word I understand."

As they passed by the two flames Sectoraus could see two more further ahead, "What are these fires-that-stay?"

"Huh? Oh, the torches!? You are a strange one. You don't have anything like that?"

"Our fires stay within the pits of magma. They burn what they touch."

"Yes, that they do, but we here make our own fire, and we use it for food in a fire pit or to guide the way with the torches.

Sectoraus had no idea what Draquan meant by using it for food, *what is food*? But one question at a time; he wanted to know about the torches first. "So, you use these "torches" to see where you are going?"

"Yeah, well, it is dark without 'em." Draquan said, a hint of sarcasm in his voice.

"Fire, I always thought, was too bright for me. Our sight is keen, and we do not have the need for anything other than our own eyes to see in the darkness." Sectoraus explained.

"Must be nice." Draquan snorted.

Sectoraus thought of the slaves and how they often had trouble in the darkness that the Serpenoids found comforting. Even those that had been with them the longest, whose eyes had become altered from when they first arrived, still struggled with their sight from time to time. Perhaps the Krocdylius less similar to the Serpenoids than Sectoraus had first thought.

The Cobra was curious about what Draquan meant by saying they make their own fire. It was a strange thing to say. How does one make fire? Before he could ask, his thoughts were interrupted. A chorus of bellowing roars came from the distance behind and Sectoraus and Nimod jumped at the sound.

Draquan simply laughed at their start, "Calm, desert dwellers. That was just my group, they must've killed something good. There will be a nice feast tonight. After all, this calls for a celebration! We never get visitors. Or at least, not the kind we want to stay." The head warrior's voice faltered, and he remained quiet for a time, "We're nearly there."

The grass had steadily become shorter as they approached a thick clump of twisting tree branches. Sectoraus could see many more torches just beyond the bramble. *Not the kind we want to stay,* Draquan had said. Sectoraus couldn't imagine wanting any visitors to stay, thinking of the slaves back home. Perhaps the plague was here too.

“Say, leader of Serpenoids, I like your necklace there or whatever you call it, especially that dangling one, and those bracelets too.” Draquan glanced over his shoulder at Sectoraus' many chains, his broad collar and cuffs, “Very shiny.”

“That is why I like them myself.” Sectoraus smiled a little, “Gold is one of my favorites. Your necklace is… a bit grim.”

"Gold, huh?" Draquan touched his necklace of teeth, "Well these teeth are trophies. Where ya get this gold? What kind of game you cut that from?"

"It is no game to mine for metals," Sectoraus corrected. "We have laborers that do strenuous, dangerous work to mine for material such as this. It is equally difficult to forge them as well."

"I think there may be quite a lot we can learn from each other, because I have no idea what any of that means." Draquan laughed.

"At least Nimod and I aren't the only ones at a loss." Sectoraus nudged his Serpenoid companion and then all three laughed together. They continued their path as it led to an obstruction ahead.

Draquan squatted down as he slipped through a space between a couple of trees that laid horizontally. As the two travelers squeezed past, the Krocdylius grabbed a hold of a set of branches with both hands and warned: "Now mind your head and arms, there be thorns. We barricade with these to keep the Scrofaciens from coming in. They make great leather, but their hides are too soft for this stuff."

The further they continued, the more questions seemed to rise to Sectoraus' mind. Just about every time Draquan spoke, there was a word that Sectoraus wasn't familiar with. Since he felt he had asked enough questions, he kept them to himself for now. The Cobra figured in time the mysterious lives of these Krocdylius would reveal themselves.

Their guide pulled away the cover of bramble, it opened to a flat land that proved to have a large body of water near the horizon. Out here the scent of brimstone was much fainter, nearly overpowered by a pungent, musky odor. The land was heavily lit with torches. Sectoraus was surprised to see an entire settlement not unlike their own. The Krocdylius roaming and mingling about stopped and turned to look at the newcomers entering their camp. They all wore variations arrangements of the same skin-like material, as well as different types of bone-made jewelry.

The Krocdylius whispered amongst themselves as they saw the tall Cobra and his slightly shorter Serpenoid companion enter from the barricade. There were many Krocdylius of various sizes, some so small they were held in a bundle within another's grasp. Most, however, were taller like Draq and of these larger Krocdylius there seemed to be two distinct types; some with a darker hide and bulky stature like their guide and those with a lighter tone who were more slender.

Spaced apart were mud-made huts that spiraled out from a large roaring fire. Close to that central fire was a hut decorated with various bones and what seemed like skins of different creatures. *That must be the home of this Priestess Draquan mentioned.* Sectoraus was sure of it.

They slowly stepped forward as their guide moved past them, greeting the few who approached curiously. Sectoraus noticed the ground here was firmer than the path they had been walking on but still retained some moisture. It was a darker brown than the ground of the forest. Off to his right he saw a wide, open area away from the huts where a few broadly built Krocdylius stood in a circle watching two others use the sharp bone tools against each other. Even though the Cobra had seen how dangerous those tools could be, he could tell the Krocdylius that used them did not intend harm against each other.

"Come on, Leader of Serpenoids and Serpenoid follower," Draquan waved them forward, "you must meet the priestess."

The Krocdylius warrior led them toward the decorated hut by the burning fire. Over the entryway hung a covering that resembled the material he wore around his waist.

“Wait right here,” he told them as they approached. Draquan pushed back the material over the entryway and stepped inside.

"Mistress, I have brought--" He could be heard from the outside but was quickly cut off.

"You have brought some visitors," her voice rasped. "Let's see ‘em."

Draquan poked his head back out and gestured to approach, "Come in. Be seated."

Sectoraus finally relaxed his tension and collapsed his hood. He went in first, before Nimod followed closely. The slivers of the fire’s orange light that slipped around the edges of the material covering the entryway softly illuminated the Priestess who sat cross-legged on the ground across from where they stood. She seemed small and slender compared to the towering warrior on her right. She wore multiple necklaces made of small bits of bone, and a crown of tusks adorned her brow. The center of one necklace held what resembled a nose that seemed strangely pressed in. She gestured at the ground in front of her, the bones and teeth that dangled from her wrists clattering slightly with her movement.

Sectoraus sat and immediately noticed how soft and comfortable the ground was. His hands felt the fuzzy material that was a collection of hides. It made him think of how the bear and wolf creatures would feel. Draquan smiled when he saw both the visitors enjoying their seats. They all looked at each other, waiting for someone to break the silence.

"They were being chased by a pack of canis," Draquan explained. "They stumbled into the marsh and Sectoraus, the taller one, was knocked down by one of the beasts. That was when I intervened."

"I credit my life to Draquan." Sectoraus said. The Priestess remained silent, expressionless.

"They have traveled far. From the desert they come." Draq said.

"Yes, yes." The Priestess spoke knowingly, "When the serpents flee from the sand, grave times form unusual bonds."

"What is that you say?" asked Sectoraus.

"Something I heard once when I was in deep thought. Prophecy, I believe. Geom speaks to me in subtle ways," the Priestess explained.

"What is Gee-umm?" Sectoraus asked, struggling to repeat the unfamiliar word.

"Geom is the name of the land connecting lands." The Priestess spread her arms open wide. "The world around us."

"*Geom…* I like that," Sectoraus nodded his head thoughtfully in approval. "We have not named our land; we only refer to it as the desert. To be honest, we had not realized there was more than desert here. But about what you said. I meditate as well, only between my brothers, we are of the Cobra Clan. Nimod does not have the connection."

"I have meditated once, but it is unlike what the Cobra Clan can do." Nimod said.

"You meditate with others? You share visions?" The Priestess was now very intrigued.

"We do not have visions. The Oracle does." Sectoraus said. "We Cobras share feeling. I grow wary, I do not feel them like I used to; I fear something is amiss. Possibly the distance has strained us."

"No, not the distance," the Priestess responded quickly. "Space has no meaning to gifts of the mind. I have something for that, something to boost your feelings for thought."

"Please, I must settle my worry for my brothers." Sectoraus extended his hand.

"You are not ready yet." She reached out and closed his hand. "Understand our ways first. Give me time to see if you are worthy of such an experience. Besides, you are tired. Long journey and little rest."

Sectoraus thought for a moment. He was intrigued to know what she could do to help him. He needed to connect with his brothers. The meditative ritual they performed did not strengthen the bond as he hoped it would. It had held on for quite some time and they had put a great deal of distance between themselves, but now it was only faint. He had exhausted himself though, in that the Priestess was right. Perhaps taking recreation was not such a bad idea after all.

Outside of the hut, voices rose in a joyful manner. Sectoraus could tell it was the kind of commotion only congratulations could conjure. The two visitors looked behind them to the entrance; the Priestess remained placid, while Draquan clapped his hands together and spoke, "Sounds like my group has returned! And I'm sure there'll be a feast!"

Sectoraus remained silent until he had noticed Nimod staring at him, waiting for his leader's next move, "We shall rest here and participate in this feast you speak of."

"You have no feasts either!?" The head warrior was shocked. He then stepped behind them and pushed the hanging material forward. "Come on out, let's greet the warriors. I'm sure you have feasts, probably call it different," he said, the last part muttered mostly to himself.

"I will join you all soon," the Priestess closed her eyes, "I need to think for a time."

Sectoraus and Nimod stepped out and met the four Krocdylius that had chased away their pursuers earlier. They had laid out a dead wolf by the fire pit along with a different creature, one of six hooved legs and a lean body, and a couple of slender Krocdylius began to use small, serrated bone tools to peel off the creatures' hides. When Sectoraus wondered aloud at what they were doing, Draquan finally began to comprehend how foreign hunting and eating meat was to the visitors.

“So, you really don’t know what we’re doing here? I don’t understand, what do you eat?” The shocked Krocdylius asked.

“We are not certain what you mean by ‘eat.’” Sectoraus said, “I assume it is the desecration of these creatures. Their burning flesh seems to bring joy to your kind.”

“Of course it brings joy! It keeps us alive!” Draquan laughed.

“It is like the water for you, then?” Sectoraus asked.

“Ah! So you do drink water?” Draquan responded

“Water seems to be essential for life.” Sectoraus said in a matter-of-fact tone.

“That it is, but for us so is eating.” Draquan explained. “All life in the swamps and the Dark Forest must eat and drink to survive. Meat gives us energy, *strength.* Our warriors wouldn’t become so tough without it. The canis provides us with prowess, the cervintils with agility, and the ursarctos with the power to destroy our enemies.”

The guests stared with wide yellow eyes full of awe. They had never forcibly taken the life of another in their past, let alone thought to consume its flesh. The idea was simultaneously appalling and compelling. *It makes sense,* Sectoraus thought, *put the creature inside oneself and then the two become one.* He then thought about how each member of the Cobra Clan had a different special ability about them. *If one were to...* Sectoraus forcibly halted that thought with a shake of his head. The idea made a knot in his gut.

"You... Your kind do not consume one another?" Sectoraus asked hesitantly.

"Oh no, no!" Draquan was genuinely disturbed. "We eat *other* creatures to benefit our society. If we were to eat each other... no, I don't want to think of it."

Nimod and Sectoraus looked at one another and nodded with understanding to each other before Sectoraus spoke again, "That makes perfect sense." The Cobra then grew deeply silent, "Nimod and I are not of your kin..."

"Hahaha!" Draquan hollered so loudly that it caused many in the camp to turn their attention on him. "Wouldn't think of it! If we were gonna eat you, then you'd be roasting on that spit right now."

The other warriors gathered around the fire, settling on the ground completing the circle Draquan and the visitors started. Sectoraus watched the two Krocdylius that attended to the carcasses. The animals were now completely skinned and the Krocdylius had removed the glistening entrails from each. One Krocdylius sliced the flesh from the bone of the hooved creature while the other impaled the wolf on a spike and secured it over the fire. The sliced raw flesh was passed around.

"Why does he mean to burn the wolf but not this flesh?" Sectoraus asked eyeing the heap of meat that lay before him."

"Haha, well first that's a *she*!" Draquan laughed as the cook glared at Sectoraus. "Don't mind him, Tarrine! They have never seen any of us before."

Sectoraus tried to think back to what the Oracle had said about the humans with the curved figures, *female,* he believed the Serpenoid had called them. "You are female then, like that of the Priestess?" He boldly asked the two standing before him.

"Of course!" The two females spat, continuing to glare.

"I apologize. I am unfamiliar with the idea of male and females. The Humans are like that, but for us there are only Serpenoids and my Cobra Clan. Lord Thandrua had always said *him* and *he* about one another, as well as us to *him*, although we lack the components the humans have that are called *males.* Lucifer doesn't have the lower appendage either…" Sectoraus thought about this for a moment. His hosts watched uncertain if they should speak, but the Cobra spoke up once again before they could. "I never thought of these words to have more meaning than what we have used them for, but to be fair, we believed our world was much smaller than it appears to be, and I am learning many more words than I ever thought there to be. Thandrua will be very intrigued.

"Hm, yes, very interesting." Draquan obviously seemed confused and was all the more eager to get back into conversation, "So, *wolf*? Is that what you call the canis in the desert?" Draquan asked.

"Is that not what those vicious furry creatures are called?" The Cobra glanced at the one slowly rotating over the fire that the female Krocdylius cranked with a handle. "It is what my last human referred to them as. Wolves."

"Never heard of such a word. I've only known canis, but how about we agree on *howlers?* For the sake of differences."

"Simple enough. Howler bodes well with me."

"Alright it's settled. Anyhow, you've said *human* more than once. What's that?"

"It is a plague in the desert. I will elaborate further, but I still have questions about what is happening now." Sectoraus and Nimod poked their meat.

"Oh yes, you asked about the meat. That is how this conversation started!" Draquan laughed before he tore a bite from the hunk he held in his grasp. "We eat a lot of our meat fresh and raw. It's more potent like this," he spoke through a full mouth, clamping his huge jaws up and down.

"And the howlers?" Sectoraus asked.

The head warrior took a moment and tilted his head up to gulp down the flesh, swallowing his bite before responding, "We roast any of our kill that stands on two legs. Old tradition of ours, if it walks like us, then we must cleanse its flesh… 'specially the *Scrofaciens.*"

Sectoraus recalled the sight of the lead howler standing on its back legs and how its silhouette almost resembled the humans. He finally took a bite of his meat, watching how the warriors devoured theirs, and chewed slowly. It was tough and very chewy, and something in its flavor reminded him of metal. Sectoraus glanced at his Serpenoid companion and saw that Nimod too wore a displeased expression. Sectoraus continued to chew, attempting to swallow but having no luck. Finally, he grabbed a cup of water before him and washed the flesh down his gullet.

"What does your group do with the rest of the creature?" Sectoraus pointed to the skin placed aside. He smacked his lips, unsure of how he felt about his new experience.

"Ah, let me explain." Draquan closed in. "The leftover pelts are turned into clothing to wear. I see you two don't wear any clothing. The skin is dried, made into leather. We also use this leather as straps, belts, and to make a little cover to the entrance of the huts."

"So, if I understand this correctly, you are wearing another creature's skin around your waist?" Sectoraus pointed.

"Yes, we all are!" The warrior gestured with his arms spread wide, and Sectoraus looked all around him.

"I see..." Sectoraus kept surveying the leather all the Krodylius wore around their waists before returning his attention to Draquan. "And what do you do with the rest of it?"

"Some of the insides are useful as well…" Draquan paused for a moment and took notice to his guests' squeamish faces while they attempted to eat the flesh and kindly told them, "Ya don't gotta eat the raw meat if ya don't like it."

The two gladly handed their share over to their host who put the portions in a pile of leftover meat for the rest of the tribe. Sectoraus and Nimod took in all this new information as the carcass roasted over the firepit. The aroma was unsettling for them at first, but after seeing the salivating reactions of their hosts, they understood the scent was meant to stimulate their appetite. They then took deep breaths, enjoying the taste it would leave in their mouths.

"Anyway, what was I yammering about?" Draquan asked, scratching the top of his head.

"You were explaining to Nimod and myself the usefulness of the creatures' parts." Sectoraus said.

"That's right, now I remember. So, we clean out the bladder and stomach of our game, then let 'em dry out. Once they are good to go, we repurpose them as sacks. Sacks for holding water, that way when we go out for a hunt we can carry some water with us."

Sectoraus thought about that idea. He and Nimod turned to each other and shared an expression of how impressed they were.

"May you show us one of these sacks?" Sectoraus asked.

"Oh of course! I got one right here on my belt." Draquan unhooked a floppy sack from his hip and handed it over.

Sectoraus observed the light brown receptacle, turning it side to side, feeling the water within slosh from one side to the other. It had a stopper on the slimmer end made of leather as well, wound into a ball to keep the water from spilling out. A string of leather was wrapped around that end too, dangling off the side to attach back onto the belt. It was undoubtedly a more practical way to travel with water than the water-stones the Serpenoids had fashioned in the desert.

"Very impressive." Sectoraus handed back the sack.

"The bone-tools, sire." Nimod whispered to Sectoraus.

"Ah yes, and those bone-tools used to peel the flesh. What do you call them?" Sectoraus asked the warrior.

"Those are knives!" Draquan stared in bewilderment. "You don't have any blades in your community? What kind of weapons *do* you have?"

"Weapons?"

"For the love of the hunt! You know, a tool to defend yourself with?"

Sectoraus thought hard as the warriors around laughed. He looked over to Nimod before answering, "We have tools for mining, shovels, pickaxes, to dig in the ground and help us search for metal. We have tools to transport the various stones to the Kiln, carts, and tools to forge more tools with, hammers and tongs. We have tools to restrain our slaves, I suppose that would be for defense. Those are called chains and they attach to cuffs similar to the ones I wear on my wrists" He looked over at the Serpenoid again, "We used our pickaxe to fight off the rock creatures and left it behind. I used my staff to fight off the enemies in the valley myself, but I seem to have lost it in the forest as well."

"Ah, alright. I wouldn't call them weapons, but you sure used them like they were! A weapon is a tool used to hunt; a spear, a blade or knife, to kill your prey before it preys on you." Draquan explained. "The weapons weren't only used to secure our meals, but to defend ourselves too. And not just from the more dangerous quarries out there." There is another race that lives in the dark forest..."

"Another race not like you here?" Sectoraus asked.

"No, not like us at all." The head warrior's answer was grim. "They are our enemy, have been since before my time. They are called the Scrofacien. They are a glutenous species, foul and disgusting with their chunky bloated bodies, their nasty little snouts! They have hands like me and you two do, but their feet are different. Rounded in hooves."

"They sound strange. I cannot bring myself to imagine what they look like." Sectoraus said.

"Well, I hope you never have to see them." Draquan said. "Like I said, our two clans have been fighting and killing each other for as long as I could remember. It had always been an honorable prize to claim the snouted noses and tusks of the Scrofaciens." He showed them the thick tusks hanging on his necklace.

The two Serpenoids nodded their heads, eyes wide. It was such a foreign idea to them, to wear the parts of others. This was a different world than they were accustomed to, nothing like life in the desert.

"You see this scar here?" Draquan pointed out a healed-over gash on his chest. "One of them nasty Scrofacs stabbed me there. Lucky for me the idiot used a small knife. I don't know if he had ever fought one of us Krocs before, but a tiny knife isn't going too deep into our hide."

"Must have hurt." Sectoraus said.

"Eh, not as much as it hurt him when I stuck my blade in his fat throat," Draquan dismissed. "He cut me good though. Well, good enough to leave a mark. You see these?" He pointed out scars he bore on the right side over his ribs. "I was having a good battle with one of them fatties. He slashed at me once with his axe, I parried his axe with my blade, and we locked for a moment. I stared him down in his beady black eyes. Then he caught me off balance and lunged at me. Started goring me with his tusks."

"What happened then?" Nimod spoke up before Sectoraus could. They were equally eager.

"Well, I have those tusks on my necklace now." Draquan smiled.

"I wanna tell them a story next!" One of the other warriors shouted.

"No, I want to tell 'em about the battle with the Scrofacs when an ursac came at us out of nowhere," said another.

"Oh yes, that was great. Those Scrofacs ran away squealing all the way home! Haha!" laughed another warrior, and they all laughed with him.

"Hold on, hold on! I got one more," Draquan stood up and all of his warriors quieted down as they waited eagerly to share their battle scars. "This is my favorite. Check it out." The head warrior pointed at teeth marks above his right knee.

"What happened to your knee, Draquan?" Sectoraus asked.

"We were out on a hunt," he began his tale. "I made a mistake and went further ahead of my crew than I should have. The forest got quiet. I mean real quiet, which only means one thing. Danger! A howler leapt on me. The sucker caught me by surprise and bit deep into my leg, but before the beast could tear the flesh apart--"

"Draq blinded it by pushing in its eyes with his thumbs!" The warrior to Draquan's other side excitedly finished the story.

"Wow, that is barbaric." Sectoraus gasped.

"Then he strangled it with his bare hands!" another warrior exclaimed. "I rushed to help, but by the time I got there the beast was dead. A true warrior Draq is!"

"Hey, a Kroc's gotta survive!" Draquan chuckled, "How about you two? I understand you don't hunt, but what is that scar on your left arm? You both bear the same marking just like that necklace. Is that the emblem of your creed?"

"Oh, this is the Eye of Thandrua." Sectoraus proudly flexed his bicep to show the emblem. Nimod followed his leader and did the same, "It is the symbol of our colony, our fate. It represents all the trials we have overcome and reminds us that our lifegiver, Lord Thandrua, is always watching over us."

"And may we be protected by his presence." Nimod added.

"That's very beautiful. I like that. Lots of meaning, love, and most importantly *honor*." Draq and the warriors nodded their heads.

The two species spoke long, the warriors telling tales of great hunts and battle. The Serpenoids listened and exchanged the differences within their lives. The Priestess finally joined the group while one of the female Krocdylius, Tarrine the warriors called her, served the roast. The Priestess was especially interested in the things Sectoraus had to say about their culture. She listened but did not speak.

The entire tribe of the Krocdylius had crowded together as cuts of the howler were distributed. The Priestess, the visitors, and then the lead warrior were served first. Sectoraus thought it strange as he took bites off the meat. The way it made his mouth work took some time getting used to, but it was not nearly as tough as the raw meat. He began to find the jaw movement was enjoyable and the smoky flavors pleasant. He helped himself to another serving.

As the feast went on and time passed, a fog arose from the swamp. It gradually invaded the village, growing thicker as time progressed. Sectoraus observed the Krocdylius around him yawning with long toothy jaws, revealing their tiredness. One by one, the villagers made their way to their homes. The Priestess had long left the group herself.

"Ah yes…" Draquan stretched out his arms before standing from the group. "Most everyone will be going to sleep here soon, I bet you two are mighty tired yourselves."

Sectoraus' exhaustion was betrayed by a long yawn of his own. Nimod expressed his tiredness shortly after. "Yes, it has been quite the adventure for us both."

"Yup, the fog is when we usually turn in anyway. Gets so darn hard to see, so might as well. Come on." Draquan gestured for his guests to follow.

They didn't need to go far from the fire pit. Their host led them to the hut closest to the Priestess'. The head warrior told them to wait for a moment while he entered the hut himself. Once he returned, he held a long stick in his hand.

"Alright, this is my hut, you two rest up here," Draquan offered.

"Oh, we do not wish to take your chamber from you," Sectoraus countered.

"Oh, no trouble at all!" Draquan dismissed their concern with a chuckle, "While everyone sleeps most of the warriors stand guard. Figured I'd join them and we take turns on who rests. We have a communal hut on the outside of the circle for that."

"As long as we are not intruding," Sectoraus said, "you have given us much already."

"Ah, it's no trouble. I'm sure you would do the same for me had I lost my way in your desert!" the leader of the Krocdylius said genially.

Sectoraus remained silent and just stared into his host's orange eyes. He gave Draquan a reassuring pat on the shoulder, but deep inside he wasn't very sure of that himself. Would they have been so kind to this stranger on their land? The fate of Lucifer and the humans indicated otherwise.

The momentary lapse of silence gave way to a strange croaking sound off in the distance. It interrupted Sectoraus' thought from the subject.

"What is that?" The Cobra asked, looking off to the swamp.

"What is what? The swamp?" Draquan looked out to the water with him.

"No, that sound." Sectoraus clarified.

"Ah, yes that's right! Everything little thing is new to you here." Draquan laughed. "According to the Priestess, they were once another race that shared this land with us Krocs. She referred to them as, *Anura*. Interesting creatures, the way they jump and how their throats supposedly bulge while they make their calls."

"What happened to them?"

"Well, with the invasion of the Scrofacs, the Anura fled into the safety within the swamp, while we remained on the land. Nowadays we just called them the Croaks, on account of their sound is all we have to know of their existence. They swim and live in the depths of the swamp. Pay them no mind, they will not harm us. You would probably never see one, I sure haven't. Besides, I always found their songs to be soothing."

Sectoraus listened for a moment to the rhythmic tone, "Yes, I suppose it could be relaxing. There are no sounds out in the desert. Save for the wind."

"Hmm I don't think I could do it with no sounds. Anyhow, I'll leave you two be. The fog will die down after a spell and I will be back then. If you don't wake and come looking for me first, that is! Rest well, my new friends."

The Cobra and Serpenoid nodded their heads in response. With that, Draquan left them behind and cut his way around the other huts. Nimod went into the hut first and made himself comfortable. Sectoraus lingered outside, gazing out to the swamp as he listened to the deep soft sounds of the Croaks.

Taking in a deep breath of the musty humid swamp air, Sectoraus looked about. The fog was thick indeed, but the Cobra could still see the faint outlines of the huts and the glow of the torches that were posted all around. *These Krocdylius are good folk.* Sectoraus thought. *Kind and open to us strangers... better folk than I.* With that thought, Sectoraus entered the hut and found Nimod already slumbering on a pile of hides. Joining his Serpenoid companion, he too fell quickly into a restful sleep.

Chapter 18
A New Regime

Chunks of gold and bronze debris lay scattered around the charred homes where the Serpenoids once slept during their cycle's end. A hunk of gold bore the countenance of Thandrua; its hollow eyes gazed up to the rusted sky in an expression which seemed sorrowful. The two emeralds that once filled those eyes had been stolen not long after the figure collapsed. The now-abandoned slumber chambers had become blackened from the smoldering heat of the magma, some were melted through and had begun crumbling, some had even been pulverized under the weight of the fallen idols. It was a sight of desolation.

Down by the lake, Vander attempted to continue his routine of meditation with the serene sounds of the water gently washing up on the shore and ebbing into the lake. Unfortunately, he no longer found peace there. He never paid much mind when the Serpenoids had played games and made songs there, that was tolerable to the Oracle.

Now, the daemons celebrated wildly, laughing and joking crudely with one another. Perhaps it was that Vander, being a Serpenoid, didn't understand their context and thus found the daemons' form of games irritating. At times he even felt offended. Many of their songs had been about the massacre of the Serpenoids. Furthering his offense was what they had done with the dead Serpenoids. Stripping the fallen of their scaley hide, the daemons wore the skins on their backs and covering their waists. Lucifer, too, wore the skins, covering his body with a Cobra-inspired cowl at the top and flowing elegantly down to the ground. He called this a cloak.

What the daemons had done with the flesh, however, had caused Vander to feel repulsed and, though he had never experienced the feeling before, he had the urge to vomit. It was a ritual Lucifer had told the Oracle was called "eating." The daemons tore chunks of flesh from the skinless bodies and consumed them.

“It is savage and troubling, this *eating* of theirs,” Vander said, not hiding his disgust.

“Eating was something the humans had done in their past lives.” Lucifer had explained, “It is a great treat for them to finally have meat to eat again. In their former lives, eating food was a necessity to stay alive, just as drinking water is now. Although during their time of enslavement it has become apparent that eating is no longer a necessity in this world.”

“Then why allow them, Lucifer?” Vander begged. “Why allow them to desecrate my kin!? Watching our mass genocide was terrible enough. Must I also smell the roasting flesh of my colony and watch these daemons consume them?”

“Would you prefer that we burned the bodies? Letting all that go to waste?” Lucifer pulled his leathery hood over his head. “I, of course, have no desire to eat them myself, but the Serpenoid hide makes fantastic clothing. We killed so many, Oracle. It would be a shame to let them go to waste. So why not harvest them for this beautiful skin or their lean flesh? Now that the daemons are free, I can’t help but let them enjoy the simple pleasure of the act.”

There were many other acts of pleasure they rekindled from their past lives. "Orgies" was what Lucifer called them, laughing at Vander's concern when he had come to the Dark Lord, saying how the male daemons were shoving their pelvic appendages into where females lacked their extra appendage.

"I thought they were dancing at first." The Oracle had said, "They do things so differently from the Serpenoids, I thought their dancing was very close together and rough compared to the dancing of my kind. Then they were sharing air between their mouths. I thought maybe they couldn't breathe on their own, so I rushed over and saw they were sharing bodies as well. I did not know why at first, but it made me uncomfortable. I had to come to you."

“Oh, Oracle! The naivety of you Serpenoids. Hahaha!” The Lord of the daemons could not keep himself from laughing. “It is an orgy.” Lucifer then explained, “Fornication, not unlike eating, was also a necessity of their past lives. A necessity of reproducing.”

"What do you mean by reproducing?" Vander asked.

"The orgies are different, grouped together and having communal fun. But just simple reproduction required a pair of a male and a female. They would perform this act to produce offspring -- um, smaller humans -- and continue to grow their mortal numbers." Lucifer said.

"I see…" Vander thought for a moment, not hiding the disgust in his face, "and why must they create these smaller humans?"

"Because of humans' mortality," Lucifer explained, "they needed to reproduce in their short pathetic lives, otherwise their egos would die with them. Fornication didn't stop at reproduction though. It was also an activity that the humans found great pleasure in and so they would perform this act aside from reproductive purposes. In any case, I am confident that in this life their fornicating would not create any offspring. Merely a simple pleasure of a past life, just like their craving for food."

The orgies seemed to be one of their favorite activities. Vander could not understand it. He thought it tiresome and confusing; there were always so many grouped up together, moving this way and that. It was constant, the orgies and celebration, sleep didn't seem to hold any back. With the Serpenoids, the Oracle at times found solace during the end of a cycle to meditate by the lake while the others slept. Lucifer had yet to organize a cycle system like that of Thandrua's. Under the Dark Lord's rule, he allowed the daemons to have liberty to choose their own slumber times.

The daemons goofed around, made songs, broke into fights, had orgies, then passed out into slumber. But while some slept, others were just waking or still engaged in activities. There was no moment of collective rest, thus after a great deal of time waiting for when the daemons would tire and go find rest elsewhere, Vander finally gave up his favorite spot and went to accompany his new master who waited at the Kiln.

"No, you imbecilic, disgusting fool!" Lucifer's voice boomed through the tunnels of the Kiln, "Follow my design, they are bricks, just simple bricks! You had made thrones and statues, and various forms of jewelry but you cannot make evenly shaped bricks!? They will not hold if they are not shaped correctly! Has all this time enjoying our slavery caused you to lose your forging skill?"

Vander entered the Kiln and stood back, hesitant to advance. He watched Lucifer standing above a Serpenoid who crumbled to the ground. Lucifer wore his cloak despite the excess heat of the Kiln. He kept the cowl down.

"Please, Master, forgive me!" The beaten Serpenoid groveled at the Dark Lord's feet, "I will make them again, I will make them better and faster. Just don't punish me!"

"Mercy? You want mercy!? Pathetic!" Lucifer shoved the Serpenoid away with his foot, then motioned to a heavy-set daemon whose face peeked through the jaws of a Serpenoid's skull that he wore over his head, "Give him the chain. Five lashes."

"Very well, my Lord." A sickening grin spread across his heat-blistered face and his eyes were malicious, glaring through the jaws of the Serpenoid skull.

"As for you," Lucifer strode to another side of the cave where a Serpenoid who stood by a slab of metal perked up, stricken with fear, "the table is turning out nicely."

"T-thank you, your Worship." He quivered in fright, then gestured to the design that had been carved into the wall beside him, "Just following your design, your *masterful* design. Over here I will place the restraints. Four of them, one in each corner."

"Good. Keep at it and perhaps you will get the chance to slumber for a while." Lucifer slid his hands over the sleek metal, "And you, how is that... ah, Oracle, please come in!"

Vander stood in the tunnel, looking into the wide room of the Kiln. He hesitated for a bit before stepping further. Since the rebellion, he had felt uncomfortable being near his enslaved kin. Uncomfortable and shameful. The fact that he was the only one left with freedom made him feel like a traitor to his race. If the Serpenoids themselves felt this way, they did not show it. In fact, they seemed to respect him even more, always bowing to his presence and groveling at his feet.

"What brings you here, my Oracle?" Lucifer clapped his hands joyfully.

"I grow tired of the daemons' festivities." the Oracle signed, "I cannot successfully meditate with all the distractions."

"Oh, no no no, that will not do. You know how I urge you to commune with... *It*."

"Perhaps if you call to end the cycle, order the daemons to slumber."

"Do not mistake me for your former master. There is no need for that with me. Everyone shall sleep when they need to and rise when they are rested. Doesn't that sound nice?"

"But how will we differentiate one cycle from the next? I myself grow weary, never knowing when to slumber. Since you have taken over, I have only slept about four times and I am sure there would have been more than seven cycles past."

"No, unacceptable. You were dependent on another to determine when to rest and dependency is a grave weakness. That is not the Luciferian way. When you tire, just sleep. Simply done! Besides, what need do you have for counting cycles? As long as you breathe there is but one cycle that matters. From when you first open your eyes until your body dies."

"I will try, my Lord, but can there not be a moment when you tell the daemons to vacate the lake? I enjoy meditating there most."

"I am sorry, Oracle, but I cannot ban my followers from the water. It is the most joyful place in this terrible land. I take away the liberty of the lake, then there will be chaos! It's meditation anyway, you can choose to do that elsewhere. Anywhere!"

"It is just my favorite place... and did you not make it a point of how important it is for me to speak with the Cre-- excuse me, my Lord, with *It*?"

"I see what you are trying to do. I'm impressed, very devious of you. You will have your solitude in time, I assure you. Once my kingdom is built you will have your own quarters within the citadel. Now, come with me. I need to pay a visit at the quarry."

The Oracle waited for Lucifer to lead the way, allowing room for the dark lord's cloak to trail behind. Before he followed, Vander was stopped by a tap on his shoulder.

"Excuse me, Oracle." A blacksmith quickly knelt, head bowed, and hands outstretched, presenting him with a bracelet, silver and decorated with gems.

"More jewelry?" Vander sighed. He already had plenty to show around his neck and around his wrists. He supposed they would give these to him often, though the jewelry he had never cared much for.

"Gorgeous!" Lucifer said. He had turned back to see why his Oracle hadn't been following him. The Dark Lord just stood there smiling at Vander with the same expectant expression he had each time Vander was presented with these gifts, encouraging the behavior. Vander felt as if he couldn't refuse.

"The offering is appreciated." Vander thanked the enslaved Serpenoids, bowing his head in gratitude.

"Pathetic." One of the daemon guards snorted at his compassion.

The fallen archangel and the Serpenoid exited the Kiln and trekked across the soft warm sand. Vander didn't want to go to the quarry, but he couldn't refuse Lucifer. As much as the Oracle hated the Kiln, he loathed being at the quarry even more. The sight of the remaining Serpenoids breaking their backs mining wasn't all that troubled him. It was Lucifer's trophy, tethered to a tall metal pole that one had to pass to get to the mines.

"Why, hello up there, Thandrua!" Lucifer waved happily at the broken beast whose arms and legs were chained behind him and around the pole.

Thandrua lifted his hanging head slowly to watch his mocking captor stroll by. He let out a deep sigh and nothing else. He was weak. Not a drop of water since he was overthrown from his reign. Thandrua shifted his sight to Vander; Thandrua's right eye was closed shut and swollen over, the other was bloodshot and had a glazed-over look. Blood dripped from a split on his lower lip. The two made eye contact for only a moment before the Oracle had to turn away in shame.

They arrived at the fence bordering the deep quarry. It was a particular spot where Lucifer had Thandrua's former throne placed. The new king plopped down and placed his legs on a rock positioned in front of the elegant seat. Lucifer flicked his cowl over. He favored this spot, at the angle he sat he could still watch Thandrua dangle from the pole while enjoying the view of the Serpenoids' heavy labor.

"Ahhh! Beautiful!" Lucifer took in a deep breath of the dry sulfuric air, "Listen to that, isn't it lovely? The clanging of tools upon the coarse stone, echoing throughout the wide space they have to scavenge through. Reminds me of the past. Oh, the good ol' days, forming new alliances, plotting my rebellion to overthrow the false god. Nostalgia is such a trickster. Everything always seems better after it happened, making one forget the traumas they endured."

The Oracle remained silent; he understood that Lucifer mostly talked just to hear himself speak. Besides, they both knew how much Vander loathed the sites. It did not stop the Dark Lord from leaning forward and pointing into the abyss, directing Vander's attention to the occasional Serpenoid that fell from exhaustion only to be beaten back into labor.

"Nothing but Serpenoids working hard, and the only daemons down there stand guard, whipping those snakes into shape. Now, I know what you're thinking, 'Master, wouldn't it be more productive if daemons and Serpenoids alike mined for material?' Well yes, it would definitely be more efficient, but how many Serpenoids aided us when we built Thandrua's statue? How many assisted us when we scavenged for gold with no sleep and no water? You give and you receive, Oracle. Your kin receive only what was given to us and what is due in return, *ten*fold."

"I understand, Lord Lucifer." Vander scanned throughout the quarry, his eyes saddened.

"Soon my devices will be complete, then Orpheus and Phineus will get the special treatment that your brotherhood most especially deserved. If only that strong-headed Sectoraus were here. I would love to experiment on him first."

"He will return, you know, most likely Solarious as well." Vander wasn't sure if he should have voiced that glimmer of hope at all.

"Solarious? We shall see, but Sectoraus? There are many dangers out there, Vander, and if the Cobra is strong enough to survive, then I am sure his ego will only have grown by the time of his return. That I am counting on, for the more prideful, the more succulent it is when they break."

"Whatever pleases you, my Lord. They are both alive, I can assure you. I can feel them still."

"Ah, so your powers hold? Good! Now center yourself, Oracle, and meditate. Distraction will not find you here from any *celebrations.*"

Chapter 19
Expansion of the Body and Mind

Twigs snapped and bushes rustled as ten bodies cut through the thick of the forest. The dark green blurs showed that eight of them were the Krocdylius, but between the lead and the other seven was a taller beige figure and a yellowish green one behind him. Sectoraus and Nimod tagged close to their mentor as the group pursued a large six-hooved creature. It bellowed in fear as it attempted to lose its pursuers.

The Cobra and Serpenoid huffed for they had been running a long distance. The Krocdylius kept their exhaust well-hidden, breathing rapidly but quietly as well. Draquan, on the other hand, expressed how much joy he gained through the hunt, laughing to himself as they closed in on their prey.

The land up ahead was separated by a slope on the left side while the right climbed up into a hill. The game veered left and galloped down.

"Keep on it!" Draq ordered as he broke away to the right, "I'm gonna take the high ground and cut it off." The lead Krocdylius sprinted upward, reaching behind himself to pull out two short daggers from his belt. Sectoraus didn't say a word, simply nodded, and when he saw that the other warriors had pulled out their long bone blades, Sectoraus and Nimod each raised the wooden spears they held as well.

The creature was close; Sectoraus could hear its breath, then he heard the pleasure in Draq's battle cry as he leapt from the short cliff that was off to the right and landed onto the game's back. He sunk his two small blades into the thick hide of the creature as he landed. It yelped but did not fall. The frightened creature thrashed this way and that until it successfully hurled Draquan to the ground. Just before the spiral-horned beast stomped down, rearing up on its back four legs, it was struck with a spear to the side of its neck.

"Aha yes, yes!" Draq cheered as he rolled away from where the beast fell and jumped back to his feet. The creature whimpered as it spasmed on its side, thrusting its horned head around. The spear still stuck out from its neck. "Which of-- oh, grab your spear and thrust it into the chest." The leader ordered Sectoraus as he saw that the Cobra stood empty handedly.

Sectoraus approached cautiously, and as he dislodged the spear from the beast blood gushed out of the wound. The creature tried to rise from its side, but the wound or loss of blood had hindered its motor skills. With his two clawed hands holding firmly onto the shaft of the spear, Sectoraus put all his weight behind it as he drove it up between the prey's two front legs.

The warriors collectively roared, pumping their weapons into the air. There was a savage glee within their roaring and in their orange eyes as they encouraged their trainees to cheer with them. Nimod and Sectoraus joined in, even if their roar wasn't as primal.

"Now, Sectoraus," Draq crouched down to the beast and began to cut where he had removed the spear, "Since this is your first kill, it is a tradition for you to take a bite of its life." After fishing his hand around inside the chest cavity, the Krocdylius pulled out the creature's thick heart and presented it to Sectoraus.

The Cobra inclined his head and held the still-warm organ in his right hand. He looked to everyone who stood waiting, eager for Sectoraus to claim his first. He could tell the Krocdylius were starting to salivate from the sight of the dripping blood. Nimod held a hardened face as he gazed upon the raw flesh but kept any objections to himself. Finally, Sectoraus lifted the heart to his fanged mouth and tore off a large chunk. The warm, dark red fluid spilled over his mouth and trickled onto his chest as he chewed the rough muscle. After Sectoraus swallowed, he raised the bitten heart in the air and gave one more loud roar of victory.

"Excellent job on that kill." Draq congratulated Sectoraus as the group trekked through the forest heading home. After gutting it clean, they had divided the carcass up to distribute the weight, each hunter carrying a different part of the animal over their shoulders. Being Sectoraus' first kill, he carried the head.

"I hesitated," the Cobra dismissed the compliment, "and at first I merely wounded it. It could have killed you."

"But it didn't. You aren't guaranteed to kill your prey with the first strike and especially not on your first hunt!" The Krocdylius turned his head and chuckled with the rest of his team. "You did far better than any of us during our first hunt. None of us got a kill in, I know it took me at least three hunts before I tagged my first… and that is not including the demonstrative hunt."

“But that first kill was when Draq became head warrior too," one of the two Krocdylius that shared the weight of the game's torso chimed in.

"You were promoted even though it took you three hunts to get one yourself?" Nimod asked with a hefty leg slung over his right shoulder.

"Tell them, Draq!" Another warrior said, "Draq's story is legend.”

"Oh, I haven't told this one in a long time." Draquan cleared his throat, "I was a young Kroc, still developing my armored scales so I was clad in bone armor. My father, who had been the head warrior, was my biggest mentor. Taught me alongside his students. He had started my training when I was much younger than the average. I was the shortest during my first hunts. On the third, Hulorr - that’s my father - had decided to take me into the Dark Forest. Just the two of us. He thought a more intimate experience would give me a better chance at killing something. He was a wonderful mentor. All the other young warriors were too skilled for my level."

They all paused when a lonesome howl called through the air. After checking their surroundings, they figured the wolf had been a safe distance away and they continued on. They were deep within the wood, and it was a maze of a path they were taking back.

"We had left the camp for a long time and took rest by a nice pond we found," Draq continued.

"I thought you said never to rest by watering holes?" Sectoraus inquired.

"Yes, and this story will explain the reason why you shouldn't. See, everything I have taught you so far has been passed down by my father and to him by the head warrior before him. The watering hole tip is my own addition. We drank from the pond, and I was still young so I wanted to swim in it. My father allowed me. I splashed around, made a great deal of noise and had lots of fun. I convinced Hulorr to join in on the fun, he placed his weapon by mine on the ground and he splashed around with me."

Draq became silent then, and the group continued matching between the many trees. The rest of the Krocdylius' faces grew grave. Sectoraus knew the next part of the story wouldn't be as joyous as it started.

"I chased Hulorr out of the water and dived back in myself. As he ran about pretending to be terrified of me, an Ursarctos -- I believe you called it a bear -- rampaged into the clearing. Being unarmed, my father darted for his blade, but the beast attacked him, slashing his leg with its clawed paw. Once he was down, the colossus gripped him by the neck with its mandibles and rammed him into a tree. I ran out of the water and reclaimed my spear, which I threw at the beast. The spear stuck into its back, but the Ursarctos' hide was so thick and it was so preoccupied mauling my father that it didn't seem phased. I grabbed my father's blade then and ran to the beast. I sliced into the back of one of its hind legs that it stood on as its two front paws tore at Hulorr, then grabbed onto the spear that still stuck out from the creature's back to pull myself up. I secured myself on the beast's shoulders, reached around from the back and slit its throat."

"It takes about four of us to successfully bring down an Ursarctos. He was just a pint!" a Kroc holding a leg said.

"I was lucky it didn't fall back and crush me." Draq now held out his sword, "My father bled everywhere and would have died in seconds. Before I could let him go, I managed to cut out that creature's heart and bite the life of my first kill in front of him. I gave him that honor just before he stopped struggling... When I returned, pulling Hulorr's body with one hand and the Ursarctos' head in the other, the Priestess declared me the new head warrior. You see, to become head warrior it is customary for the elder to choose his top students to fight against one another. The winner later would fight against the elder and if he won, he claimed the rank. Since Hulorr did not get that privilege, me being next of kin and avenging his death automatically made me the rightful heir."

There was a long silence as they listened to the wind pass through the trees. The sounds of different critters could be heard scurrying across the ground, chirping and squeaking in the distance. Finally, Sectoraus spoke up, "You rightfully deserved to become head warrior. As I had told you, we encountered a bear, an *Ursarctos,* upon entering the forest. I can only imagine the fear you were stricken with."

Draquan stopped dead in his tracks and the rest did as well. His head perked up and his orange eyes glared around, trying to see through the dark beyond the trees. Having better eyesight, Sectoraus and Nimod joined in seeking for any sudden movements. The head warrior opened and closed his elongated jaws as if tasting the air.

"What is wrong?" Sectoraus' voice was quiet, "There is nothing. I cannot see anything nor hear anything at all."

"Exactly." Draq whispered, "It's too quiet."

All at once, falling from the sky was a barrage of stones followed by a series of high-pitched squeals and snorting. Seeming to come out of nowhere was a large group of bipedal beings. They wore the parts of armor that resembled Krocdylius hide, covering their soft bulbous bodies. The Krocdylius instantly engaged in battle against the attackers that wielded weapons made of stone and wood.

Sectoraus noticed they smelled awful and looked even more disgusting as one pushed him up against a tree. Snot dribbled down from its snout and the tusks in its mouth seemed to jut out at odd angles. He guessed these must be the notorious Scrofaciens that the Krocdylius quarreled with. Sectoraus conjured up all his strength and pushed back at the creature, knocking it down. When he looked down at it, at first he thought its feet were nubbed, but then realized they were hooves not unlike the creature they had just hunted.

Sectoraus was able to procure his spear and drive it between the layers of armor that covered the being's chest. The creature gurgled on its own blood and spasmed for a moment before it stopped moving altogether. Another ran at him before Sectoraus could gloat about his kill. The Cobra kept his spear raised and held it horizontally as the new enemy slashed with its stone-made axe. It was much stronger than the wooden spear and snapped Sectoraus' weapon in half with a sharp crack.

Before the snorting slob could cut him down as well, Draq drove his blade into its thick shoulder. The yelling and taunts morphed into a single muffled sound. All the movement was dizzying and Sectoraus felt completely helpless. Before he knew it, the Scrofaciens were squealing away, though not before snatching up of the meat as they retreated, and the Krocdylius roared behind them, raising their blades in victory.

Sectoraus looked around, then realized three of the Krocdylius weren't cheering with the others. Their lives had been claimed by the enemies. That was also when he noticed Nimod, who lay sprawled out, tongue lolled to the side, the top of his head caved in.

***

What was left of the meat roasted on a spire; the fat dripping from the flesh sizzled in the searing flames. The Krocdylius from the hunting party recounted the ambush to some of the villagers. Away from the camp in a marsh field, Sectoraus and Draq circled around each other, each holding a single blade.

"I shoulda taught ya how to fight with a blade long ago." Draq's voice was subtle, composed, his eyes locked onto Sectoraus' as he clutched the hilt in his hand, "I was caught up with our traditions."

"Tradition is necessary. I understand." Sectoraus backed away as Draq stepped forward, "I felt strong using the spear in hunting, but in close combat I was at a loss. And poor Nimod."

"Good, mind your distance... Nimod might have survived if I had given you two blades." Draq slashed down and Sectoraus blocked, “It wasn't the rocks they threw that got him but a hammer to the head.

"He will be remembered." The two locked blades, Draq gained the upper hand as he pushed his weight into Sectoraus.

"Remember, don't think of just holding the weapon in your hand, it must become an extension of your arm."

Sectoraus stepped aside and nudged the Krocdylius away. He shifted his grip and advanced forward. The Cobra took two steps forward and swung the bone-blade in an upward arc. Draq countered with an overhead attack. Parrying, Sectoraus spun to the right, swinging his weapon behind him and connecting with Draq's blade.

"Very nice!" Draquan straightened up and sniffed the air, "Your kill smells about ready, but I still think your first should be eaten raw!"

“Speaking of tradition, I am grateful that you ordered the meat to be roasted on my behalf. I do not wish to impose.”

“Forget it! Let's get back to camp. After, the Priestess wants to speak with you."

***

Despite the few chunks of the cervintil the Scrofaciens stole, the village still had a grand feast. Sectoraus had come to fancy the idea of eating and the gathering of feasts; this was the fourth one since his arrival. The Krocdylius didn't keep track of their time under sleep cycles like the Serpenoids had, but for them that was more frequent than usual.

"We live in a continuous timeline," the Priestess had said once, "sleep neither ends nor begins anything. Therefore, there is no need to differentiate the time passed from the time ahead, for it is all the time now."

Many took slumber during the same time as others. Sectoraus noted that their collective time for slumber coincided with a thick fog that would arise from the swamp. By then most of the villagers were already yawning and eager to lay to rest. Unlike the Serpenoids, not all unanimously slept at once. While the villagers drifted in their sleep, a number of warriors remained alert, patrolling the grounds.

Sectoraus, ever so set in his ways, needed to track what he still referred to as cycles. So, he had slept and risen with the rest of the village for what came to be a total of sixteen cycles. The Krocdylius didn’t usually hunt as frequently as they had during the Serpenoids’ visit. The swamp dwellers dried and stored meat to eat when necessary and only feasted when they would set out on a hunt. Something about maintaining the balance of the forest, Draquan had mentioned, otherwise they would go out and claim a meal every chance they had. When Sectoraus and his party came, the warriors had just set out for a hunt. The second had been to continue treating the new guests. The third was what the head warrior called a "demonstrative hunt," a tradition for new warriors to join a hunt unarmed just to watch and experience it for themselves.

Sectoraus laughed and awed at the different stories the warriors told of their first kills. Even though the Cobra loved the company and enjoyed his meal, he was very solemn inside. The thought of Nimod pained him. The brave Serpenoid was the last one left from his expedition team. They had traveled so far together and discovered many things. Sectoraus had witnessed the deaths of many Serpenoids, but it was different with Nimod. They bonded in a way he had never experienced before. Nimod and Sectoraus, together, learned what it meant to be a warrior and a hunter. Draq had stressed that the bond between warriors was tethered tighter than anything else and no two warriors were connected better than the ones that trained together.

In his long life, Sectoraus had been lucky to never lose anyone that he strongly connected with before. Lord Thandrua and the Cobra Clan had always made it through despite the obstacles that faced them. The warrior's bond he made with Nimod connected the Cobra to the Serpenoid in a way that could match the one he shared with his clan brothers. His mind raced with concern for them.

Sectoraus doubted his sleep cycles synchronized with Thandrua's cycles. Coinciding with the fog made it more rhythmic, like it had for them to sleep during the light in their old world, but he noticed after a feast the Krocdylius would hurry off to their quarters. Whenever his stomach would grow full, he understood their eagerness for slumber. But how long had he actually been away now? This question rolled around in his head. During the journey that led him to the swamp, they had stopped and rested twice, but how many cycles passed during that time? Sectoraus guessed Lord Thandrua would have announced at least three since his departure. Was it three cycles he wandered? They had only slept once, but he thought they could have rested again. Perhaps four, or maybe even five, but he didn't think it could have been much longer than that.

As much love and concern as he had for Thandrua, he knew they were just fine, despite his severed connection to his clan. There was truly nothing to worry about in their home. The desert was a sanctuary from storms, and they had a water source that never depleted. What was there to worry over? The slaves? Sectoraus knew the slaves were well managed and locked away with their fence and chains. What troubled him most was Solarious' whereabouts.

His faithful companion had left the colony as well. Sectoraus had not only discovered different regions of land, but various lifeforms and, unfortunately, enemies as well. What could have Solarious discovered in the Solariside of Geom? Were there forests filled with beasts or swamps occupied by barbarians? Did he encounter different beings that quarreled with each other? Or were there even more different regions beyond the other horizon, something more unknown than the new world Sectoraus had discovered?

Too many questions swirled, and not enough answers were available. Sectoraus pushed down his anxieties while swallowing the roasted meat. After one warrior told his tale, another would step up and tell theirs. The meat had diminished and now all servings had found their place within someone's hands. Those that had already finished went into their huts. Draquan laid on the ground, head propped on a rock and picked at his various teeth with a splinter of fractured bone. Sectoraus was also done with his meal, and the young Krocdylius and the warriors that weren't on the hunt urged the Cobra to tell of his hunt. Draq stood up before Sectoraus could accept the offer.

"His tale will have to wait for another time." Draq waved his hands dismissively, "The Priestess has been waiting for the meal to end to speak with our new warrior."

"Ah, yes." Sectoraus stood up and wiped the grease from his hands on a fur that was handed to him, "Lead the way, head warrior."

"No." Draq extended his hand toward the Priestess' hut, "Just you."

Sectoraus inclined his head to excuse himself, the villagers nodded silently in return. A light fog had already started to flow over the swamp and off to his sides he could see some villagers extinguishing the torches by their homes. As he approached the hut decorated with the hides and trophies of other creatures, Sectoraus straightened, inhaling the cool air. He thought of Nimod one last time before bending down and pushing open the door to the Priestess' chamber.

"Sectoraus." The Priestess greeted him, sitting across from the entrance.

"Draquan informed me that you wished to see me." Sectoraus didn't take a seat until the aged Krocdylius waved to the spot where the Cobra stood, a brown fur rug between them.

"Enjoyed your meal?"

"Very much so, yes." He smiled and relaxed a bit, "Why had you not joined us with the feast? This was my first kill."

"Yes, Draq told me of how you saved him. I'm sorry I didn't attend, no disrespect to your kill. I have been preoccupied. Besides, I am not used to eating so often."

Sectoraus hadn't taken notice of the small clay bowl that sat between him and the Priestess. It wasn't until she dropped a small object into it that he glanced down. Before he could ask anything, she spoke again, "Have you enjoyed your stay with us? The knowledge you absorb from the warriors?"

"Yes, and I am grateful."

She took up the bowl into her hands and began to grind its contents with a pestle. It crunched, whatever was placed in there, and as the crunch became grittier a strong earthy smell wafted its way toward Sectoraus.

"This is called wak-katta. It is a strong and powerful root that is found only in the marsh." She poured a small amount of water from a cup she kept by her side. “It is to be ground to fine powder, then made into a paste with water... You still do not sense those you meditate with." This last was a statement, not a question.

"I do not."

The Priestess continued to work the mixture, "When I say the wak-katta is strong, I mean it contains power. This power has only been consumed by the priestess before me, myself, and the priestess that will succeed. I have yet to meet another who meditates before you arrived, so I now make this in your honor."

"You have allowed me much. I cannot express the depth of my gratitude."

"You will take a handful of the paste, and only one handful, and place it into your mouth. Let it slowly run down your throat as you sink into the depths of your meditation."

Sectoraus reached out to accept, but lowered his hand after the Priestess continued to grind with the pestle.

"There is but one more ingredient." She held onto the bowl with one hand and handed a small blade to Sectoraus with the other, "Slice into one of your palms. The blood will complete the mixture, better connecting you to Geom, and marking the wak-katta for you and you alone."

The Priestess leaned forward, holding the bowl between the two of them. Sectoraus looked down at the brown paste, then into the Priestess' orange eyes. He fixed his eyes onto the jagged blade carved from some animal bone that he held in his right hand, then to the open palm of his left. Placing the blade onto his flesh, he hesitated, took in a deep breath, and made the cut. He grunted slightly but was too intrigued to truly feel the pain.

"Good." The Priestess said and squeezed his palm over the bowl. The red blood ran between their fingers and dripped into the brown paste. It seemed to twinkle for a moment, Sectoraus blinked his eyes, not believing the mixture had produced a light. If it had, it was gone now. The Priestess sat back and turned the pestle more.

Sectoraus steadied his breathing, preparing himself for a deep meditation while he waited for the concoction to be ready. The Priestess nodded her head in approval while staring into the bowl in her hands. Finally, she handed it over, "Now, just enough to fit in the cup of your palm. Do not swallow. Let it linger in your mouth."

Sectoraus winced slightly as the goop sat on his tongue. Its flavor was pungent and tart, he felt his full stomach tighten. His instinct was to spit it out, but instead he closed his eyes and breathed through his nostrils. He tried to clear his mind as he felt the slime ooze throughout his mouth.

Inhale. Exhale. Inhale. Exhale.

The wak-katta began to settle down his throat. He kept his eyes closed, but remained keenly aware that the Priestess watched him, studying his composure. He tried to let go of that awareness and dive into his mind.

Inhale. Exhale. Inhale. Exhale.

When he first entered the Priestess' shelter, he could barely hear the indistinct babble from those that still gathered at the feast. Her hut was quiet, peaceful. Now, he might as well have still been sitting beside Draquan. The head warrior's voice was distinct as he spoke of his feelings on Nimod's fate.

"Both students showed promising skill and a thirst to learn. It is unfortunate that Nimod was taken before he completed his training. And even though it is the way of the warrior, to live a short life, I can't help but feel responsible. I lowered my guard completely and who knows how long those two have been wandering only to die in my care. Now Sectoraus is alone. Lost all his tribe that journeyed with him and far away from home."

Sectoraus wanted to tell him that the guilt wasn't his to hold. Besides, Draq had lost only the one under his care, but Sectoraus lost the whole team that was to accompany him during his travels. Before he said any of these things though, he remembered he was in the Priestess' hut. Or was he still? He was well aware of all the warriors that sat around the firepit with Draq. He could even feel the comforting heat of the fire itself as it warmed his chest and throat.

The fire. That wasn't what warmed him at all, now realizing the wak-katta no longer sat in his mouth, but the remnants trailed down, coating his throat. It was warm -- no, it was hot, and his body began to squirm uncomfortably. *Do not swallow*, he reminded himself, or did the Priestess say it to him again? He couldn't tell and didn't dare open his eyes. Concentration was what he needed.

Inhale, exhale, inhale, exhale.

Sectoraus squeezed his fists tight. He wanted to clear his mind, but it was difficult to concentrate over how loudly the warriors spoke. He could hear the howlers, howling in the forest. He could even hear the victorious sounds of the Scrofaciens as they gorged themselves on the meat stolen from the hunt earlier.

No, he wasn't hearing those things. Sectoraus had to remind himself again that he sat in the confines of the Priestess' hut. He reminded himself of the importance of clearing his mind to meditate; he had to stop thinking and yet he could not. It seemed he thought of everything at once and the more he tried not to think, the more he could hear. The critters that ran throughout the Dark Forest, twigs snapping, the trickle of a shallow stream, the restful slumber of the stone monsters in the valley, the rushing of the vast river of lava, the dense silence of the desert.

It was as if his mind traveled to these places, or perhaps it was his memory being recalled from the journey. He no longer fought against it as he could hear the sounds of the slaves' labor in the quarry, the chiseling of stone, the shouting. There was a heavy pain within the quarry however, pain inflicted upon the slaves.

His own pain had transferred, no longer burning in his throat but ripping across his back. Sectoraus clenched his fists even tighter as the skin across his back seemed to rip with a striking force. Then it was gone as his awareness continued to stretch. He could hear the wind rustling through tall grass, the thunderous sound of many hooves galloping through a wide clearing. Finally, he could feel the distinctive connection to Solarious. Something was wrong. Solarious was frightened and in a darkness furthest from the Cobra's keen eyes.

Inhaleexhaleinhaleexhaleinhale

Sectoraus opened his mouth and gasped for air. His body felt as if it were falling. Falling fast, hard, and from an enormous height. Everything he had heard before exploded in his ears. He clenched his teeth as he was filled with unbearable pain; Solarious was terrified,

Orpheus and Phineus shrieked in agony, Vander cried in shame, and Thandrua was filled with a deep sorrow and guilt.

Sectoraus' eyes shot open, “By Thandrua!" he gasped and rose to his feet immediately, taking in his surroundings. He was in the confines of the hut with the Priestess sitting across him, expressionless. He closed his eyes tight, then reopened them, not believing what he was seeing. Sectoraus looked down at the wise Krocdylius that now looked up at him and could only bring himself to say, "I must leave."

Section V
To Become a Hero

Chapter 20
The Way Back

Sectoraus had been frightened by the visions he experienced. He was certain Solarious had found trouble on his journey. Sectoraus was even more certain that the colony was in danger or soon to be. The celebrations of the night's feast seemed to have continued on. The thin doorway covering allowed the joyful voices of the warriors to seep in, along with the faint flicker from the fire pit. The light orange glow cast shadows throughout the hut and made the Priestess' eyes more luminescent as she stared up at Sectoraus. She made no protests at his decision to leave; perhaps she understood what the vision had told Sectoraus. After they stared at each other for a while she gestured to the doorway behind him.

Sectoraus had stormed out of the Priestess' hut, and whatever conversation held by the warriors that sat around the firepit ended. Draquan stood to approach the Cobra, "Hey there, turning in or care to join us?" Sectoraus just walked right past and aimed straight for the barricade. Draq looked back at his clan, perplexed. They returned the look before the whole group shifted their sights to the Priestess' hut. Sectoraus was already halfway through the bramble and deadfall when Draq caught up to him.

"Sectoraus, wait! Be easy, my friend." Draq urged the Cobra to calm down.

"My colony is in danger!" Sectoraus yelled when the Kroc held him in place, "My master is in trouble! I have to go, I have to go back!"

"You haven't finished your training," the head warrior said, "I won't force you to complete it fully, but you must continue further than where we left off."

"I cannot stay. I am deeply grateful for all the care you have given me, all the knowledge you have shared. However, I must leave."

"You say there is danger, but you do not know what danger there is. You might need to fight, and it won't do you any good if you don't develop your combat skills some more. Please, for your safety, let us train longer."

Sectoraus stared out into the barricade in silence, thinking, before he responded, “You make a compelling argument, Draquan.”

“You have been calling me Draquan this whole time.” He laughed beneath his breath. “You have feasted with me, you have fought with me, you have studied beneath me, and most importantly you have saved my life… Please, you are one of my warriors, just call me Draq.” The head warrior placed an arm around Sectoraus' shoulders and guided him back to the camp.

Sectoraus was set on leaving then and there, but the warrior made his point clear. If Thandrua and the Cobra Clan were in danger, there must be a threat Sectoraus wasn't prepared for. Despite the urgency he felt to hurry back to his far away home, he remained in the swamp for a few cycles more.

***

Sectoraus stood in the center of a ring surrounded by Krocdylius warriors bordered with flaming torches. The Krocs snarled, gripping tightly onto wooden batons while Sectoraus paced in a circle to keep everyone in sight. In his grasp he held a long combat stick, with his two hands he kept it close to his chest. From outside of the ring stood Draquan, staring with his arms folded.

“Remember to block only,” the teacher directed.

“Understood.” Sectoraus continued his pace.

“Ok, now!” Draq commanded.

A warrior behind Sectoraus lunged, swinging his baton high. Hearing the stomping approaching, Sectoraus spun quickly and raised his staff, stopping the baton from smashing his face. Then at a battle cry from his right, he twisted his weapon and blocked another warrior's attack to his ribs. The third Kroc came charging and Sectoraus slid to the side allowing the charging brute to crash into the other.

“Hahaha! Very nice!” Draq clapped in approval. “You may begin attacking!”

Sectoraus twirled the staff between both hands as his adversaries regrouped. They all stared intently at each other before the three warriors lunged at him. Sectoraus immediately parried and redirected their attacks to become his own. Using one end of the staff to block high while the other end could strike someone from behind his vision.

The duel was a blur and the head warrior grinned, displaying a long row of thick teeth. Sectoraus swept the ground with the stick, tripping one opponent while another skipped over it. The third came from behind and landed a heavy blow to the back of Sectoraus' head. He recovered slowly as the warriors enclosed on him. Sectoraus continued to defend against their barrage of attacks until Draquan gave the order to stand down.

"That's enough for today!" He roared. "Sectoraus, you are such a promising student. It's a shame you must leave."

When the Cobra was eager to flee, he had not considered what supplies he would need in the journey back to the desert. In his impulse, Sectoraus would have left completely unprepared; he was grateful Draq had made him stay. It gave him the time to think about what he might need. Water was of the utmost importance. Realizing that the cups and bowls the Krocs used for water wouldn't travel well, Sectoraus asked Draq if they could gather big enough stones to hollow out and use as containers just as the Serpenoids had done, but Draq had a better idea.

Draquan took Sectoraus to a place just outside of the camp where a strange pile of wood laid on the ground. It wasn't until Draq grabbed ahold of one side and pulled it over that Sectoraus realized all the sticks were tied together creating an inconspicuous door. Underneath was a hole that seemed to hold extra supplies of a variety. There were stones placed along the sides of the walls to keep the moisture out. Draq had reached in to grab something.

"We clean out and preserve the bladders from our prey and they become useful sacks," he handed Sectoraus one of the floppy bladders, browned with age. "We only use them if we go out for a long hunting trip. These should help you out much better than some rocks. They will only weigh you down as much as the water they hold."

The concept was ingenious to Sectoraus. Not only would they be lighter to carry, but the bladders could hold more water and they would be easier to store since they had no solid shape, unlike the stones. He knew he wouldn't need too many for his trip, he thought two would be enough. Each sack had a string attached for slinging over a shoulder.

Draq refused to allow Sectoraus to go on his own, recommending that some warriors accompany the Cobra and even urged him to go to the desert with them. Sectoraus was stubborn though, and said how this was his own duty. It was personal and he wanted to keep it that way. When it became time for Sectoraus to leave, still unsettled with the idea of him venturing alone, Draq managed to get Sectoraus to agree to at least have a few warriors escort him through the Dark Forest.

"Please take care," the Krocdylius warrior pleaded, "the Dark Forest can be tricky and I don't want your hero's journey to end so abruptly."

"Again, I'm much obliged for, well, everything." Sectoraus shook Draq's arm, "This has been quite the experience."

"Before you go," Draq turned to a female Krocdylius behind him that passed a bundle into his thick arms, "here, this blade is for you. You can hang the sling over your shoulder to carry it for you."

Sectoraus held the gift in his clawed hands and pulled the blade out of its pouch. He scanned his eyes across the yellowish-white bone and very gently ran a finger across the jagged blade,

"Thank you so much, my friend." He placed the sling over his head and onto his left shoulder, letting it hang across his chest. Sectoraus felt the cool emerald from his Eye of Thandrua amulet before he removed the necklace and held it outward to his host, "Draq, please take this. It is made of my favorite metal, gold. Now a piece of me will be with you always."

"I am honored." Draq accepted the token and placed it around his neck before putting a hand on Sectoraus' right shoulder, "You and any you vouch for are welcomed here always."

Just as Sectoraus approached the barricade that exited into the marsh, he looked back at the crowd of villagers that gathered to see him off. He noticed the back of the mass began to part and it wasn't until the front of the group stepped aside that he saw the Priestess was slowly walking towards him.

"You have come to see me off as well?" Sectoraus smiled.

"Of course. It isn't often that an outsider joins us, much less becomes one of us as you have." Her voice was leveled, her expression was emotionless, but Sectoraus could feel the unspoken affection, "I have also shared with you something I have never shared with any of my clan."

"Very much obliged." Sectoraus inclined his head.

"The priestesses before me would have done the same, I'm sure." She stood before Sectoraus, her orange eyes staring directly into his yellow ones, into his very soul, "Beware, Sectoraus. A great change has come, but an even greater change is still in motion. Farewell, leader of Serpenoids," and with that she turned around and walked back through the crowd.

Sectoraus and the four Krocdylius warriors trekked through the forest undisturbed. Sectoraus didn't think it was possible. It seemed that the forest was overrun with all kinds of adversaries, but none showed their faces while the group cut through the wood. They avoided watering holes, kept their distance from any possible howler dens, and not once did they stop their feet. At one point, they heard the distant roar of an Ursarctos, but if anything, it caused them to move forward even faster.

What a sight for sore eyes it was for Sectoraus to break out of the forest's darkness and see the oozing river of lava as he stood on top of the overlooking hill. Just down into the valley, it was close enough for Sectoraus to hear the rushing and bubbling sounds. It was like music to the Cobra. Before he decided to continue his quest alone, he asked the warriors to wait and watch him cross the river first.

He had one more danger to surpass before reaching the desert as he descended the hill into the valley of stone. He did his best to remain silent as he eyed the piles of rock that laid about, seemingly innocent. Remembering when he first went through the valley, how the stone monsters hadn't stirred until Playtoug fell into the lava. It was his screams that awoke the abominations. The Cobra kept his breath short and soft, doing his best not to make a single disturbance. Sectoraus inched his way closer and closer to the lava, then he stopped. Abandoned off to the side, Sectoraus could see the cart the slaves had carried with their water supply. The water filled rocks were scattered on the pebbly ground. A large pile of stone laid nearby. *Do not risk your life,* Sectoraus warned himself, *you will do just fine with these two sacks.* He continued onward. This time, creeping as silently as possible, Sectoraus made it safely to the shore of the lava.

The Cobra turned, just before stepping onto the first stones he spotted that jutted out from the thick liquid, and gazed back at his protectors watching on the hill in the distance. Sectoraus raised his bone blade into the air as a gesture of thanks and farewell. The warriors responded the same, refraining from hollering their victorious roars.

Sectoraus crossed over six stones before getting about halfway across the river. His feet shifted as he remembered how warm to the touch the stones were. They seemed to be even hotter now that Sectoraus had become accustomed to the cool moisture of the swamplands.

Once Sectoraus had carefully crossed over the rushing lava, he took a well-deserved break. It felt like a lifetime ago to him that the expedition leader and his team took a break at the very same spot. How ignorant they were then, of the dangers that lay ahead and of their world as a whole. Sectoraus thought himself to be the most ignorant, leaving everything behind the way he did. *I should have never left. I should have never suggested the journey.*

He remained seated on the soft orange sand well after he drained some water. With his foot he toyed with something hard just barely underneath the sand. His claws clicked on it before he realized it was the remains of his slaves' shackles. *I shall hold them in my memory.* He thought of how obedient they were, then found himself shocked when he was overcome with regret. He had never even asked for their names.

This is no time to sulk, was the thought that gave him the power to rise to his feet once again. With his back to the river, he gazed towards his right and watched how the lava curved further down, running adjacent to his position, snaking its way beyond the horizon. He knew he could follow the flow of the lava and take it directly to the back of the Kiln. However, he could see the faint markings of the footprints he and his company created. Sectoraus traveled forward, keeping the curve of the river parallel to his right and following the path before him. This was the path Sectoraus took when he first came out this way and this would be the same he would take back, leading him to the lake.

In time, the World's Mountain came back into view over the horizon. The Cobra took hold of a bladder that hung just under his left elbow and popped out the stopper. He drained its fluids quickly and tossed the container to the side. The Cobra centered himself for a moment as he gazed to the peaking colossus. *Thandrua*, was all he could think of, staring at the rockface. Taking one more deep breath, Sectoraus broke into a jog which soon became a full-on run.

The water in the remaining sack slushed rhythmically with each stride. Sectoraus' bone blade, secured in the sling at his right side, bounced along with him as well. He panted heavily as he covered the great distance in a short time. Before long, Sectoraus could vaguely see the peak of the World's Mountain touching the red-orange sky; he was getting nearer.

As the mountain's peak rose further above the horizon, Sectoraus stopped his run. Something felt off to him, but he couldn't figure out what it was. He no longer held the mountain in direct view, but aimed just to the right of it. He knew if he continued on the path he was taking he would eventually reach the quarry and then the valley where the colony rested. Some part of his intuition told him not to return directly there. Not just yet.

As he approached the mountain, he began to find it odd he couldn't see Thandrua's shrine from the horizon. And surely they should have completed his own statue by now? Sectoraus had been looking forward to seeing the large welcoming figure of Thandrua upon his return. *Why can I not see it?*

The need to be with his brethren and see Lord Thandrua was dire, but with the monuments not ever coming into his view, Sectoraus knew something was wrong. Something terrible. He didn't know what it could be though. All he did know was a thought that he couldn't ignore, *Do not return just yet.*

Chapter 21
A Crude Homecoming

Sectoraus altered his course and now aimed for the World's Mountain as his destination. In this route he would completely bypass the quarry and approach the far side of the lake. That was where he felt he needed to be. He needed to keep a distance and observe his colony before returning.

Sectoraus had done his best to keep track of his cycles in the swamplands, but since he left, he had lost complete sense of his time. Arriving at the foot of the colossal peak, he began to climb, and found refuge in a cave within the World's Mountain. From a safe distance, he gazed over the lake to the far side where his colony would have rested.

The beings that gathered by the lake weren't his Serpenoid followers, but the slaves that now seemed to run rampant. The soft-skinned beings danced and sang in wild ways, and they never seemed to stop whatever celebration they honored. Because of this Sectoraus couldn't tell how many cycles had passed. He watched and waited until he tired and then he would refrain from sleeping as long as he could. There were two separate times when he went into a soft meditation to replenish his energy. Eventually he had to sleep, even just for a short while. When he woke, the humans were still awake, mostly.

Sectoraus kept his sights fixed on what used to be the Serpenoid colony. A few of the chambers remained, very few, the others had been demolished to rubble. There was a structure surrounding the valley and seeming to stretch beyond that. There were two large walls still under construction going towards the lake from the valley behind. From Sectoraus' distance he could barely see that the walls were composed of blocks. The blocks and walls were a brownish-orange color and he thought of how the Serpenoids had made the clay from the sand to build their slumber chambers.

It was not the slaves that worked on the new construct, however. Sectoraus was disturbed to catch sight of the Serpenoids, and too few of them at that, running up and down scaffolds and placing blocks together, slowly creating wider and taller walls.

The sounds of the humans' celebration filled the land. It wasn't until after he finally took rest that his refreshed mind noticed a very different sound, something very disturbing. Screams of agony hovered in the air. The screams increased more and more as time went on. Even though the sounds were faint with distance, one roar of pain outweighed the rest.

Thandrua, Sectoraus gasped, standing at the mouth of his cave. He had yet to catch sight of Thandrua, nor Orpheus and Phineus for that matter. Only the Serpenoids seemed to be working on the walls. He could see the humans forced them to, threatening them by slashing the Serpenoids' backs with long chains and using what seemed to be very shiny blades pointing at them. Just over the valley, Sectoraus could see the top of what might have been a large chamber, but constructed completely of metal. It was strangely shaped as well, not rounded like they had made theirs or even the huts in the swamp, but flat on all sides. Sectoraus thought perhaps his kin were kept within the construct. He would have to make it over and see for himself.

There was one, however, Sectoraus hadn't had any trouble of finding. It was the Oracle. Off on the side of the lake, a good distance from the celebrations, there sat the Serpenoid. Unlike all the others, Vander didn't assist in the construction at all. In fact, it seemed that Vander was at liberty to go about and do as he pleased. Sectoraus often saw the Oracle returned to the spot away from the lake to sit on the ground for great amounts of time. There were a few boulders and dunes that rested in the area. Sectoraus assumed he was meditating, but at times he couldn't shake the strange sensation that the Oracle was staring directly at him.

Vander could not possibly see me from this distance, but if I could see him... His mind remained troubled over why the Oracle was separate from the rest of the Serpenoids, it even seemed that the humans were respectful towards him. Sectoraus did not understand what was happening, but figured this much was evident; the slaves were now in power and had enslaved the Serpenoids in return.

Sectoraus had to make his way across the river and speak with the Oracle. Eventually, he got his chance, but not after another great amount of time during which sleep eventually crept up on him as he prolonged the inevitable. From what Sectoraus could see, most of the humans were finally slumbering and a few others had left the lake shore. Vander was in his usual place, meditating, and Sectoraus knew this was his opportunity.

He covered his body with wet sand from the shoreline, the orange was darkened with moisture, and went for Vander's location. Sectoraus made sure to keep low to the ground and used a few sand dunes that he passed as coverage while scanning the area for wanderers. His sneaky slithering took him a longer way around, but he finally found himself creeping up to the Oracle from behind. At last, Sectoraus stood directly behind him, now seeing how the Oracle wore layers of jewelry not unlike how Thandrua had. Vander stirred, sensing his presence.

"You know Lord Lucifer does not tolerate anyone to disrupt my meditation." Vander spoke without opening his eyes to see who approached.

"*Lord* Lucifer!? Have you already forgotten your masters?"

In a quick motion, Vander stood and spun around to face the Cobra. Vander's eyes widened as he watched Sectoraus' hood expand. Even his slitted pupils formed ovals.

"Sectoraus, y-you have returned!" Vander was clearly startled. "Thank goodness you are still alive."

"*Are* you thankful? Seems like your new allegiance bodes well for you." Sectoraus eyed the Oracle's attire, "Lots of jewelry, is that what your treachery comes down to?"

"Forgive me, Sectoraus, but I believe it was jewelry that blinded Thandrua and you from seeing your wrong doings. The daemons simply wanted equality; Lucifer on the other hand... he has an unquenchable thirst for power. For vengeance."

"Daemons?" Sectoraus was perplexed.

"Oh yes, my apologies. It is what the humans now call themselves."

"And now you dress yourself as royalty. Now that these *daemons* take power?"

"I assure you, Sectoraus, I had no hand in the slaves' uprising. Lucifer had been plotting against us for a long time, under our supervision. He only spared my life for the gifts I have as the Oracle. I feel as if I cannot refuse to wear these."

"How convenient that it all works out for you."

"Again, had it not been for my gift, I would be enslaved with the rest of them... or slaughtered like how most were. Trust me, I see these jewels as my own form of shackles."

"Wait, did you say slaughtered? The Serpenoids are..."

"Dead, yes. Most of them anyhow. Very few remain, their lives spared."

"Spared, but as slaves?"

"In all fairness, did we not force the daemons into the same fate?"

"What of my Clan? Thandrua? I have not seen them."

"Have you been watching us?"

"For some time, yes. I hoped to have found Thandrua, but nothing."

"I thought I had felt your presence. Thandrua, Orpheus, and Phineus are often kept in a separate section of the quarry. Their fate is worse than the Serpenoids. As for Solarious, he has yet to return."

"I must get to the quarry then."

"No, spare yourself. What Lucifer has done to them is... unfathomable."

Vander let his head hang, eyes fixed upon his feet on the ground. Sectoraus grabbed the Oracle by the necklaces. He pulled tightly, Vander's feet were lifted off the ground. They faced each other, snout to snout, and Sectoraus' frustrations broke out in a hiss. His fangs were bared, saliva dripping, "Tell me, what has become of them!?"

"They are being tortured." The Oracle squirmed in the air, and finally Sectoraus slackened and lowered him back to his feet.

"They remain in the quarry, having pain inflicted upon them. Lucifer had the Serpenoids make special devices for the horrendous acts. There seem to be no limits, no end."

“You speak of loyalty to our kind. What would your new master think of this?"

"I will always be a Serpenoid."

Sectoraus stepped away and looked in the direction where the quarry rested, "I will save them."

"Yes, you will, but now is not the time. Spare yourself for now, do not gaze your eyes within that madness. Besides, there are too many guards, you cannot breach their security alone." The Oracle began to walk away slowly, "Come, follow me."

The Oracle walked casually as Sectoraus followed close behind, constantly looking for any of the daemons that may be about. They walked closely by one of the walls, keeping it on their left. They had come up to the large chamber Sectoraus had seen earlier. He ran his eyes up and down the metallic structure, noting how rigid it was. Four straight, smooth walls and a perfectly flat roof. Sectoraus continued to follow his guide and moved past the chamber to a small attachment around the back. This was a much smaller chamber, something Sectoraus thought more suitable for resting.

"They call this the armory." Vander said.

"Armory?"

"It is where they keep their swords, the tools they forged for their rebellion. It is not unlike that thing you have hanging on your hip. Is that made from *bones?* How did you manage to get that anyhow?"

"That is a story for when there is more time. What of the larger chamber? I thought Thandrua would be in there when I was scouting."

"That is only one section of what will become of Lucifer's citadel. The Dark Lord rests there now. He has plans to develop an enormous kingdom. Never mind that now, help me open this door, the metal is heavy to move. Grab onto the handle there."

The two tugged at the lever of the heavy metal door that dwarfed them in size. Ever so slowly, the door creaked open, polluting the air around them with a cloud of sand as the door dragged across the ground. Sectoraus was caught in awe as the shimmering glow shone through the clouded air. The room was not very deep but was completely stocked from wall to wall. Shiny metal swords and broad axes hung on the walls, and in the center there was a pile of weapons in disarray, along with many blades of various shapes and sizes.

The obscene amount of bronze and iron captivated Sectoraus' eyes. It felt like an eternity since he had gazed upon the precious metals that he once fiended for. Time seemed to stop until Sectoraus heard what seemed like a distant sound, which turned out to be Vander's voice.

"You should take a sword." The Oracle advised, "There are plenty here and they will not notice one missing. They do not keep an inventory anyway. The metallic sword may prove more efficient than your bone one."

Sectoraus stepped slightly into the armory, as far as he could anyway, and looked at all the options. Once again he felt himself become mesmerized, but regained focus as he reminded himself that time was of the essence. Finally, he chose a sword that laid in the pile. When he first lifted the weapon, he had to place it directly back down for he hadn't anticipated the weight within the blade. He lifted it with greater strength the second time and slowly backed out of the armory, staring at the bronze, cross-shaped hilt.

His eyes ran up and down the arm-length blade as he twisted the sword in his hand. The blade was broad, but had been pressed very flat. Staring at the thin edge, Sectoraus could imagine how the weapon should easily cut through any hide and possibly any bone without trouble.

Vander gazed at the Cobra leader with wonderment. It was a beautiful sight to behold the weapon in the hands of the Serpenoid hero. The silence seemed long before the Oracle remembered something and took a step into the armory himself. After rummaging around he found what he was looking for and pulled out something silver that was formed in the shape of a blade, "Here, take this as well. It is a holder for the sword. Lucifer called them 'sheaths'. You can carry it on your hip, securing it with the belt."

Sectoraus took the sheath from Vander's claws, looking at the patterns and designs etched into the casing. Then he pulled the belt attached to it, feeling its eerily familiar texture. His eyes went wide when he recognized the pattern on the belt. Even though he knew the answer to the question he was about to ask, he asked anyway, hoping he was wrong, "What... is this leather? Where is the leather from?"

The Oracle not only stepped away from Sectoraus but dropped his head in shame. He couldn't look him in the eyes. "They took the skins of the fallen Serpenoids, made lots of garments and belts with them..."

Sectoraus dropped the sheath as if it was scorching hot and stepped away. His grip on the sword's hilt tightened; he seemed as if he were about to shout but instead he dropped to his knees, "That is what they wear. I cannot believe it. That is what I have seen them wear on their torsos and around their waist."

"It... it is appalling, yes." Vander stepped closer, placing a single hand onto Sectoraus' shoulder.

"I cannot wear that – that thing!"

"Sectoraus, you cannot carry the sword the whole time alone. It is heavy and will become heavier as you walk with it."

"I will not wear the skin of my kind."

Sectoraus remained there on the sand, trying to come to terms with the revelation. Vander didn't know what to say; he didn't want to pressure Sectoraus. He understood the Cobra's protest, his sorrow. A thought came to him, and he picked up the discarded sheath, then fiddled around with the knot before removing the belt.

"Sectoraus," he approached cautiously, "perhaps you can fix the sheath to the belt you already have, no point in using two anyway."

Sectoraus took the holder once again and stood up. He stuck the sword into the sand and with that free hand he undid his own belt, threaded an end into the loops in the back of the sheath and let it hang from his left hip. Sectoraus took the sword up once again and slowly inserted the blade into the casing, the metal of the sword scrapping against the metal of the sheath.

"Yes, that looks very nice." Vander kicked the Serpenoid skin belt back into the armory, "Now you have to leave. Help me close this door and go to the land at the other side of the lake. You must travel Solariside and find your brother. Perhaps any others out there that might be able to aid you. You cannot save us alone, but I know you can lead heroes to help you do so."

Sectoraus did not know whether to respect the Oracle or spite him. The Cobra had never cared for Vander in the first place. Things were different now. There was but a finite amount of Serpenoids left, and Vander was the only one still free. Sectoraus was grateful for the weapon and inclined his head in gratitude before turning away.

“Wait, Sectoraus,” the Oracle reached out to the Cobra’s shoulder, “there is something else I must tell you.”

“What more horrors are there to tell?” The defeat was heavy in Sectoraus’ voice.

Vander grabbed the Cobra by both shoulders and peered deep into his eyes. Their gaze lingered before the Oracle spoke, “Lord Thandrua is not the lifegiver we have believed him to be, but there is another.”

“...The Creator?”

“You know of this being?”

“Thandrua once spoke to me about a light that spoke to him, that showed him how to travel to the sanctuary of this world. Then he mentioned the same name when his face was scarred.”

“You never told us.”

“I had to protect our lord’s reputation… perhaps I was fooling myself as well.”

“Well, Sectoraus, we all know now. I have known since this Creator visited me all those cycles ago. Before I became the Oracle. I was urged to keep it to myself.”

“That is why Thandrua kept that premonition of yours a secret, but why from me?” Sectoraus stepped back and shook his head, “Your story of Lucifer, the world he was from? What does he have to do with the Creator?”

"The Creator created all."

"So then, my thoughts were correct. Lucifer is one of the Creator's minions, brought here to corrupt our way of life."

"Lucifer *was* a servant of the Creator, but he betrayed his place there. That is why he was banished. He lived in the same world as the Creator, leading their race, building an army. His instincts seem to have remained with him here."

The two fell silent for a while. Sectoraus unsheathed the shiny sword and swung it side to side before he spoke again, "Thandrua is still my master."

"The Creator is my teacher, but Thandrua will always be my leader, yes." The Oracle agreed. "Even while I serve Lucifer. It is survival, not out of want. Thandrua does not have to be the lifegiver to be our king, the hope for our kind."

"I must kill Lucifer."

"I do not believe he can be killed, but stopped? Definitely."

The joyful sounds of some daemons laughing grew near. Sectoraus returned the sword to his side and Vander urged him to leave. As Sectoraus slunk past the way he came, blocking himself from view behind the dunes and boulders in the area, his thoughts remained on Vander. For the first time since the Serpenoid's anointment to Oracle, Sectoraus finally felt the respect for him that he had denied him all this time. Sectoraus reflected on how easily the Serpenoid could have yelled and alerted everyone of Sectoraus' presence. However, that was not what he did. Instead, Vander opened up to Sectoraus and gave him a new weapon. *For the few of us left,* Sectoraus thought, *we must all stick together.*

Chapter 22
The Search for Solarious

Sectoraus returned to the cave he was taking refuge in and glared out over the lake. He could see figures moving about and knew the daemons were active once again. Sectoraus' head throbbed with all the painful information he had received, most especially the revelation of the Creator. After all the questions, after all the convincing and half-truths, it was revealed. Thandrua was no almighty lifegiver.

I fooled myself this entire time! Even when Thandrua himself had questions, had doubts, it was I who continued to feed him this notion of being the lifegiver. He even tried to tell me about the Creator, but I had to continue the lies! Vander knew this the whole time and only kept it to himself because Thandrua forced him to! And Thandrua could have only wanted to keep such revelations quiet because of how much secrecy I trained him in. I am not upset with Vander, nor am I upset with Thandrua. This truth is shocking, but it does not change the fact that Thandrua has been here with us this whole time. He has been the strength that keeps us together and that is far beyond the fantasy of being the lifegiver. He will always be the king. I must save him, save my brothers, and liberate my Serpenoids!

Before Sectoraus could venture away he needed to replenish his water supply. He felt the cottony stickiness inside his mouth with his tongue. He crouched low and made his way to the shoreline. Sectoraus hoped he wouldn't be spotted as he sipped water from his cupped hands. Sectoraus than refilled the one water pouch that he'd kept. He splashed the cool liquid in his face, but his head continued to throb as he heard the screams of pain in the air. *I must save them*, he thought to himself and gazed off to his left, in the direction his lost brother had journeyed. The Solariside of Geom.

Solarious, he felt a familiar presence, *why have you yet to return?* Confident in the metal and bone blades he was armed with, he started off in a run. He knew running without an idea of destination would only drain his energy, but he had to act quickly. His kin had already suffered enough. How much more could they withstand?

Sectoraus cursed himself and regretted ever leaving for his journey. He felt lost and powerless; he was warned something would be different on his return, but he hadn't imagined anything such as this. The slaves in power, the Serpenoids slaughtered to the minority, and the torturing of his master and kin. All this must have been the pain Sectoraus felt in his vision. His whole world had changed, as if stuck in a bad dream.

As Sectoraus ran, he thought of what he had sensed from Solarious in his vision, the fear and darkness, then thought about what could happen to himself. *What obstacles await me?* He wondered as the warm air whizzed past his face. Now well aware that Geom was home to many different beings, what other kinds would he run into? And would they be friend or foe?

Sectoraus thought back to the swamplands, the various tales the warriors told. Tales of tracking the monstrous ursarctos and how its hulking force took the combined efforts of multiple warriors to wound. Stories of avoiding the territories of the savage pack-hunting howlers, and the times both hunters' paths would intersect. These creatures were vicious; Sectoraus felt lucky to have survived the forest, but what troubled him more were thoughts of the nefarious Scrofacien.

The Scrofacien weren't animals living off instinct just trying to survive, but beings with their own intellect. Draq told him that the Scrofacien, or "Scrofacs," had their own society within the Dark Forest. They were menacing, trying to find their way into the swamp camps of the Krocs. Preying on the hunters to steal their game, weapons or even the Krocs' very lives. They mutilated the Krocdylius just as the Krocs did to their food, using the hides as garments. The Scrofacs' skin was soft and fleshy, easy to wound, so they created armor from the thickly scaled hide of the Krocs. As vengeance for these assaults, the Krocdylius tribe found honor in collecting the vile enemy's snouts and tusks. Very rarely did they ever eat the meat of their ancestral adversary. It was said that the meat of the Scrofacien would drive a Kroc mad, which was why they developed the philosophy of cooking any meat that walked on two legs. However, even as tempting as the succulent meat seemed, roasting with its dripping juices sizzling over the fire, to eat a Scrofac was done only under desperate circumstances.

Perhaps it was beings such as these that have taken Solarious. Beings with nothing but malicious intent to those around them. Sectoraus dismissed the thoughts that began to creep up of how he and Thandrua had treated the daemons as their slaves. He wondered if that was how rivalries like that of the Krocdylius and Scrofacien began. If there was a misconnection from one group to the other and the rest unfolded into ignorant prejudice. *Perhaps there will be benevolent beings in Solariside as well.*

Off to his left stretched a row of mountains all connecting into a massive chain. He assumed these started by the World's Mountain and ran through the region. They were a great distance away, but Sectoraus felt a comfort with some kind of landmark to guide him.

He thought back again to Draq; he was grateful the head warrior had instructed him in the art of defense, now knowing of the fate of his kin. During his entire life, surviving severe natural disasters, the dangers of the burning Sun, traveling great distances to different lands, the Serpenoids had never known of fighting. This was a weakness Sectoraus now knew no way of preventing. Lucifer had known this and used it to his advantage. He organized and trained the slaves well.

They created tools of death, weapons, things the Serpenoids never had any use for, and it had taken them by storm. Sectoraus tried not to bestow anymore guilt upon himself for leaving on the journey; it wasn't his absence that led to the rebellion, it had been inevitable. *How could they have defended against that?* Besides, had Sectoraus stayed, he would have met the same fate as his brothers, as his master. No, he had to go on the expedition, he had to ally with the Krocdylius and learn to fight, for now there could be hope with Sectoraus. If he could find Solarious, together they could get the help they would need to free the surviving Serpenoids and Thandrua.

The lands were vast. The air was thin and silent, save for the thud of Sectoraus' running steps against the hardening ground. His rhythmic pace decreased as exhaustion and fatigue began to seep in. Sectoraus stopped running and panted, trying to catch his breath. He closed his eyes and focused on recharging his energy.

His mind drifted to the swamp as he thought of the friends he made there. The memories of the wonderful feasts played in his mind, he could still hear the joy and laughter of the villagers. Those sounds were drowned out, however, when he thought of the agonizing screams of his brothers and master. His emotions were out of control as he felt the anger building up. The next thing to come to his mind was the Krocdylius priestess as she stared deep into his eyes. Sectoraus couldn't shake the feeling that this wasn't a simple memory he was recalling.

"You have too much on your mind," she said. "Do not let your emotions make you forget how to meditate. Clear your mind."

Sectoraus pushed the thought away and took in one long breath. Then he let go of all other thoughts. He opened his eyes and gazed at the desolate terrain, as his energy recharged. With his second wind, Sectoraus drained about half of his water, and he returned to his run again. Sectoraus had left the desert behind as he entered an open plain.

He stopped for a moment to observe the new surroundings. The ground was prickly to the touch, covered in yellowish grass. Sectoraus always thought he could see far, but from here far held a new meaning to him. Aside from the mountains, he could see beyond to the blurred view of the distant horizon. The ground seemed raised some distance further ahead; all he could do was keep moving.

Sectoraus began to run again. He panted, his muscles tightened. Each step he took he also huffed out a long breath. Sectoraus once again closed his eyes to regain energy. His concentration was cut short when he felt something brush against his knees, his waist, and then his chest. He startled as he opened his eyes to reveal the grass obscuring his vision. Where he had stood before, the grass was shallow, only to his ankles, but here he was engulfed by yellow grass that grew over his head

He no longer felt safe, an eerie sensation he recognized all too well from hunting in the Dark Forest. He couldn't help but feel as if he were being watched. Sectoraus inched his way through the thick grass before readying his metal sword, a metallic scraping sound ringing out as he drew it from its sheath. With sword in hand, Sectoraus began to hack through the grassy wall before him.

The tall grass fell effortlessly with each slice. The blade was truly sharper than any knife made from the bones in the swamp. The grass was bunched together thickly. Each time Sectoraus made one slash he gained one step forward into more grass. He made good progress until his arms began to tire. It was a tedious task. Luckily, a short while later he found a clearing with a small pond.

Without a second thought, Sectoraus hopped down to his knees and splashed water into his mouth and onto his face. He gulped the water down his throat, scooping with both hands. He let go of his awareness almost completely, until the sound of footsteps softly approaching startled him.

He heard the close movement rustling the grass as he saw a blue, feathery hand emerge through. Remaining on his knees, Sectoraus stared, frozen, as a small feathery face peered through the grass. It seemed to be very short in height, like the Krocdylius younglings, and it stood on two brown legs that looked almost reptilian. Its pelvic area was covered by a pale animal hide and the rest of its body was covered in soft blue feathers. Its head cocked from side to side as it stared at Sectoraus. The being's face was almost like man, aside from the feathers.

Off in the not-so-far distance came the sound of a long, bellowing horn. The blue creature ran off. A heavy silence lingered. Sectoraus felt uneasy. His first thoughts were how the Dark Forest would become silent as a predator approached. *Is something hunting that small creature? Is there something stalking me?* From the ground he felt a rumbling thunder. *No, not thunder, hooves.*

The horn's bellowing tone sounded again, this time much closer. Sectoraus sprang to his feet, his hood flaring out and his sword held tightly in his right hand. He heard the panting sound of many breaths and hooting calls. Sectoraus knew a large group was coming right for him. He waited a few more seconds, then ran off. Splashing through the shallow pond to the other side where he'd seen the feathered creature disappear, and ducked into the grass. Looking over his shoulder, he caught a glimpse of his pursuers as they entered the clearing, but he kept running. He saw at least three and they were mounted on large hooved animals.

Sectoraus didn't know where to go, he just knew he couldn't turn back. The galloping thunder rolled behind. Through the grass off to his right he saw a black figure dart past, then on the other side he saw another neigh as it effortlessly ran past him to the front. His route cut off, he gripped his sword tightly as the realization they had surrounded him sunk in. Five huntsmen covered in extremely bushy grey fur circled him, all riding on large, black-skinned animals. The mounts all made whinnying, neighing sounds and snorted intimidatingly as the hunters shouted and yelled, ensuring their prey had nowhere to run.

Sectoraus moved within the circle, attempting to keep the five in sight. Their faces and hands were free of the coarse fluffy fur that covered the rest of their body, revealing their dark blue eyes and rounded muzzles. Crowning their heads were two thick horns that spiraled upward. Three of them held mallets made of stone and the other two carried spears. Slung around the arm of one was a hollow horn, the smaller end of which the woolly beast pressed its lips against and blew into it, creating the bellowing sound Sectoraus had heard when they approached. The other four cheered before throwing a net over Sectoraus.

"We found another!" One shouted, "They will be pleased!"

Frantic, he attempted to fight his way through, but this was something Sectoraus had no clue how to defend against. As he struggled, he became more entangled and dropped to the ground. Suddenly, a thought came to him; he stuck the sword through and ripped open a hole at his legs. Sectoraus tried to stand but fell to his knees as the hunters whacked him with their weapons. Sectoraus hissed and tried to fight, but there was little he could do, being so outnumbered.

On the verge of defeat, Sectoraus heard a yelp from one of the attackers, then saw it fall to the ground. A thin wooden stick stuck out of its neck as a crimson spray of blood spurted out from it. The others all turned towards the sound of more thunderous galloping.

The net obscured Sectoraus' vision, he could only see more of the hooved mounts close in, then the sounds of a struggle. He caught glimpses of red and blue and heard a few moans of pain before two of the horned creatures bolted off on their mounts. Sectoraus still struggled within the net when the four remaining hooved creatures approached him, and the riders dismounted. He stopped, listening to them murmur amongst themselves. The brightly colored figures soon approached him and lifted the net from the captive.

Sectoraus rolled back at once, drawing a sword in each hand as he hissed. Before him were four beings, like the short blue feathered creature he saw earlier only bigger. There were two with red feathers, one with blue, and one green. They wore waist coverings made of seemed to be leathery hides, and their faces were painted black and white with lines and patterns. They also had beads braided into the frill under their arms. They cocked their heads from side to side, watching Sectoraus, then turned to speak amongst themselves.

Seeming to reach a decision, the blue one stepped forward. This creature had a row of feathers that were clearly not its own, going from the top of its brow down to the back of its neck. The first feather was a dark red and each that followed was a different color from the last, gradually becoming lighter to the last that was a brilliant yellow.

“Greetings.” The blue one approached, palms held outward showing peaceful intentions. “You are safe with us, isn’t that right fellas?”

The others lowered their bows and secured the arrows. Sectoraus’ hissing subsided as he scanned the newcomers before putting his blades in their sheaths. He held out his right hand, looking into the black round eyes of the blue one. The blue one stepped forward and gripped Sectoraus’ arm. They both gave one solid pump. Sectoraus relaxed his hood before speaking.

"I am Sectoraus, king of the Cobras, leader of the Serpenoids."

"I am Leukai," the blue one said, nodding, then gestured behind, "war party leader of the Aviaan tribe. Please come with us. We must tell you of your brother, Solarious."

Chapter 23
A World of Torment

Lucifer was ecstatic as he felt his two large feathery wings stretching behind him. He stood thigh-deep in the lake with his serpent-leather cloak discarded on the shore. Lucifer thought about how long it had been, possibly eons, since he felt the grace of his wings. He never realized until now how unappreciative he had been of the sensation of simply feeling the wings on his body. The slight weight behind his shoulders. The motion of the wings flexing. The air that breezed through the feathers.

Lucifer began to flap his wings ever so slowly. The water rippled as the tips of his wings grazed the surface. Looking into the blood-orange sky, Lucifer thought he saw a twinkle of light. *The Creator*, he wondered. He flapped his wings harder and jumped into the air, mouth wide with happiness, arms held open to embrace the glimmer of light. However, Lucifer did not ascend. He felt a strange force, the air was heavy on his shoulders and so he flapped his wings harder still.

Surely Lucifer's wings should have lifted him into the sky, but looking down, the Dark Lord was still just above the water. He hadn't even completely jumped out of the lake, for his left foot was still submerged. Then it was no longer the force of gravity that kept him from his ascension but, looking down again, he saw a frost had crept over the water's surface that surrounded him.

With a start, his elegant wings stopped fluttering and he dropped back into the water. Lucifer's pale hand gently touched the surface, rippling the water in effect. It wasn't frosted over at all. Lucifer looked skyward and leapt up once again, this time flapping furiously and the water froze again, hardening instantly. Lucifer had nearly made it out of the water, but once again his left leg was held back, caught in the thickening ice.

Lucifer screamed in anger and pushed his wings harder and harder. The air around him was chilled to his skin. The hairs on his arm rose as he saw more and more of the ice spread across the lake.

His wings were a blur as the white feathers began to flutter off, one by one. Lucifer yelled even more with his frustration, while feathers fluttered all around him in a white storm. Finally, he stopped flapping and fell to the water, now unfrozen again.

Lucifer glanced over to his left wing, then his right wing; they were black. The skin on them appeared to be leathery and scaled. They arched, rigid and pointed, completely unlike their softly rounded, feathery appearance before. It reminded him of the wings for an animal he once had designed that dwelt in caves. They were rodents with wings, the only creature in the mammalian family to bear wings. He had called them bats. He screamed with fury and pounded on the lake with one hand. The water made a loud splash and hit his face.

Once more, he jumped and began to flap his wings. This time he found himself sitting upward, realizing he had just awakened from a dream. *A nightmare*, Lucifer thought to himself. It had been the same one he'd been having for some time now. It fueled the anger which he used to center himself. He was sleeping on the floor of a vast room, almost completely empty save for Lilith who continued to sleep on the hard floor next to the fallen archangel.

Lucifer got to his feet and walked over to the cut-out in the wall across from him. He picked up his Serpenoid-skin cloak from the ground and looked out of the window that viewed the desert in the direction of the quarry. He threw the cloak over his wingless back and held it at the neck with his right hand.

"Lu-Lucifer?" Lilith stirred awake, moving her head side to side as she scanned the room for the Dark Lord, "Bad dream?"

"Yes, Lilith," he didn't turn to look at her but continued to gaze out the window, "same as before and same as before that one."

Lilith stood, her lower body covered in a small leather skirt. She stepped across the stone floor toward Lucifer, the skin of her feet blackened and cracked from the heat. She collected the crown Lucifer had left on the floor and stood at his right. Lilith placed the crown upon Lucifer's white hair. Reaching across his back, she grasped his left shoulder, as the fingers on her right hand brushed against the smooth scales of her skirt. The two watched the dry horizon in the distance.

"I'm sure your wings were a marvelous sight to behold." Lilith said lightly, almost as a whisper, as if to not disrupt the silence.

"That they were," the Dark Lord sighed. "What they turn into in the dream, those dreadful things, I cannot even find the words to describe how it makes me feel."

"Do not trouble yourself, my Lord. I would long for my wings if I ever had the ability of flight."

"And yet, it isn't the wings that troubles me alone. The dream is so much more. Do not misunderstand, I am terribly grateful for claiming this land, for you and all my followers. Yet, deep down inside, I truly wish to leave this place and return to the world of Heaven."

"Have you not told the daemons time and again how we must surpass our former lives?"

"It is why this isn't something I go announcing." Lucifer snapped. "Probably why it haunts my sleep. Keeping it all in. It is different for me, however. As humans you were all mortal, *ordinary*, then stripped of your memories, and now given a new life. I am eternal, my life has yet to end but merely continues on its linear path. My existence there meant something, something grander than anything you humans could possibly understand!"

Lilith stood there silent for a while, "Do you miss the Crea--"

"Do not say that name!" Lucifer spat, then turned away.

"My deepest apologies." Lilith stared out in silence again. After a few moments she returned to Lucifer's side. "Well, all I can say, my Lord, is that here you mean something. Something grander that any of us as humans could understand, but as daemons you are *the Great One*. Our Lord and Savior. You are what gives us meaning, passion. Here, you are God!"

Lucifer moved away from her, breaking her closeness. He flicked his cowl up, covering his crown, before speaking again, "I am many wondrous things, my dear, but the Almighty itself is not one of them."

"You think that matters to any of them?" Lilith moved closer to Lucifer, "You rule all, you know all! You are *our* God, the one we will worship for strength in times of weakness." She pulled him toward the door, "Come now, let me grab my dress and let us go see your toys."

Two double doors opened outward from the metallic building. Lucifer strode out with his cowl still pulled over and Lilith was attached to his side. She wore a long Serpenoid-skin dress that trailed behind her just as the Dark Lord's cloak did. Lucifer paused for a moment and scanned the area before him. There were several daemons about, and they acknowledged their lord by bowing their heads. Lucifer stared at them then gestured downward with his right hand. The daemons lowered to the ground in a formal bow.

"Ah, yes, that's more like it." The fallen archangel smiled and looked towards the World's Mountain in the distance before turning his back to it and began to walk towards the quarry. They passed some of the leftover debris from the shrines and other former Serpenoid possessions. Lucifer stopped when something caught his eye. It was the large golden circle containing the still intact Eye of Thandrua.

"Lilith," he looked to his companion, "what do beings use to worship more than a deity alone?"

"I am not sure... what do they, my Lord?" She looked puzzled.

"A symbol, something to wear, to hold, to flash in times of war." Lucifer explained.

"War, Lucifer? What war?" Lilith was more confused.

"Peace is but a dream. War inevitably finds its way," Lucifer searched around for any of his followers close by and to his luck he saw two daemon guards wearing Serpenoids skulls, escorting several chained Serpenoids toward the Kiln. "You there, guards!" Lucifer flagged them down and waited for the one that ran the short distance to his location.

"What can we do for you, Master?" The daemon rasped through the fangs of the skull. The skin all across his body was scaled from dehydration.

"That thing," Lucifer pointed to the Eye of Thandrua, "have your slaves take it to the Kiln with you. I will be there later to instruct some alterations to it."

"As you wish, my Lord," the daemon turned to his group and shouted, "Pharmca, bring the slaves over! We are to take this symbol with us!"

The slaves were kicked into gear as they approached the large emblem. The daemon referred to as "Pharmca" ordered the slaves to carry their cherished symbol, then looked over to his master.

"My Lord, we will be awaiting your instruction. And dear Lilith, when will you come down to the lake and join us in the festivities?"

Lilith glared at the daemon who stood smirking at her with cracked blistering lips from beneath the mask. Lucifer straightened up and lowered his hood, "It would be wise if you run along on your way and nothing more."

"Right away, sir!" Pharmca cowered away.

Lucifer and Lilith began walking away as four Serpenoids lifted the metal scrap between themselves. Their pace was slow and Lucifer kept looking behind him to the group that moved closer and closer to the Kiln. He would sigh each time he turned his head back in the direction they walked.

"Insatiable, wasn't he?" Lilith huffed.

"No, not that," Lucifer waved the comment away with his hand, "You don't enjoy the attention? I think I would, if I were human."

"Not the type of attention *they* give. I just want to be left alone, and yet they holler at me and think they're being cute. In this life I don't think that is something I yearn for anymore. The attention does get tiresome, don't they have enough women to lust over?"

"Ah, but you are the most beautiful. I protect you when I can, but honestly, I would exploit that power. Perhaps it isn't necessary now, but there will come a time. You will know when it is needed. Or perhaps I just enjoy all too much when my beauty is recognized."

They remained silent for a time. Lilith felt uneasy at her savior's suggestion to exploit her body. She would not think to voice such discomfort, however. Lucifer again looked behind him and let out yet another sigh.

Lilith broke the silence again, “So what does trouble you?”

“Impatience. I want my new symbol, I can't stop thinking about it.”

“If we could only travel faster than our own two feet! The quarry is still quite the hike ahead.”

“Not to worry Lilith my dear. Very soon I will cut the festivities short to further train my army. The Serpenoids were bright in searching the land. There are many resources out there and there are different breeds of creatures that will do wonders in our servitude. Such as horses we could travel upon.” Lucifer stopped abruptly and Lilith continued a few steps forward before she responded.

“Lucifer?”

“Change of plans. I am going to the Kiln now because I truly cannot stop thinking about this. I bother Thandrua all the time anyhow. I shall visit him later on.”

“As long as you’re in a better mood, that was the point.”

“I will be very soon.”

The two turned in the opposite direction and picked up their stride. Lucifer had a gleeful expression as he eagerly approached the Kiln. He felt that he hadn’t had anything exciting to look forward to, other than the very slow progression of his kingdom, that is. The slaves were just setting the golden emblem of the Eye of Thandrua down when their ruler stormed in. They listened intently as Lucifer gave them his instruction: remove the centerpiece, add a couple extra beams for connecting lines.

Lucifer sat on a rock and watched the alterations, waiting for the metal to cool and harden. Lilith had left Lucifer to himself when she grew bored and returned to their shared place of solitude. The sweltering heat of the Kiln forced the Dark Lord to drape his cloak draped off his shoulders, but he was determined to see the emblem to completion. Great lengths of time passed; Lucifer watched as new guards came in to rotate shifts. Finally, Lucifer stood up and clapped his hands when the slaves poured water over the red-hot metal and steam arose as it sizzled.

"Alright, I will need a group to follow me to the quarry," Lucifer commanded. "There we will display the emblem within the torture pit."

Lucifer stood on a thin metal platform, holding his hands together as he descended into the quarry. At each end of the platform were chains fixed with pulleys and two enslaved Serpenoids tugged on the left chain, lowering the Dark Lord to where there was a walkway halfway down the quarry wall. A single daemon wearing a Serpenoid skull-mask stared down at the Serpenoids that worked the pulley; he kept a single hand on the hilt of the sword fixed to his left hip, ready to draw. The guard relaxed as Lucifer stepped onto the hard ground.

"Raise the elevator and order the boy up top to latch it until I am ready to leave." The fallen archangel ordered, barely looking at the guard.

"As you wish, my Lord. Alright, let's lift this thing up!" The guard barked at the slaves who quickly moved to the right chain and pulled. The platform gradually raised back to the surface.

Lucifer glanced to the right where the walkway met another elevator that would lower into the main mine. It was tightly latched with a lock and a daemon guard stood beside it wearing a key on a chain around his neck. The guard gave a curt nod to his leader but got nothing in response. Instead, Lucifer moved to the left where the path was long and curved downward. He didn't pass a single body as the path led into a tunnel that went further down into the quarry. The groans of one that was in great pain but too exhausted to scream echoed throughout the tunnel. Following the groans came the sound of a heavy hammer bashing onto something metallic.

The tunnel opened into a wide room with several armed guards. Within the center of the room was a large circular pit. The pained sounds rose from deep within. Just outside the pit stood the two guards Lucifer had spoken to earlier. They rushed slaves that crouched on the ground, securing a chain with a large nail into the hard ground.

“They are almost done, my Lord,” one guard said as Lucifer approached, “They are securing the last nail now.”

“Very good. When they are done, secure the slaves in the lower level and then you two may enjoy your festivities for now.”

“Thank you very much, Dark Lord.”

Lucifer stood at the edge, looking down into the pit. Against the side of the pit was a large mass of crimson muscle, Thandrua. Bolted to the wall behind the former ruler was a chain that split in two, connecting onto each of Thandrua’s horns. A collar was strapped around his thick neck, affixed with a double-sided, two-pronged fork which served to keep his head in the perfect position to look directly forward and nowhere else. Where the prisoner was forced to look stood a daemon guard wearing a blackened Serpenoid skull. The daemon turned a crank which tightened four chains with each turn. Those four chains were connected to cuffs tightly secured at the ends of Orpheus’ thickly muscled arms and legs, overextending his limbs across the metallic table he laid on.

Thandrua wanted to look away, but he could not move his head. There were streaks of drying blood that ran down from the bottom of his chin to his chest, from a much earlier attempt to lower his head. All he could do to avoid Orpheus’ torture was shift his eyes to the left, falling onto Phineus.

Phineus jogged in place, tugging a chain that was attached to his collar. The chain extended behind him, going through a narrow hole in a metal slab as tall as the Cobra, and wrapped around a large gear with a weight dangling at the end. Standing behind the slab was another guard with a black mask, both hands gripping a clamp which held a red-hot coal. The guard pressed the coal onto the slab, moving it side to side to heat the metal. Occasionally, the guard would dip the coal into a container that held a small amount of magma. Each time Phineus would tire and slacken the chain, the weight at the other end would slowly drop causing the chain to retract. Phineus’ scaled back was seared in large patches, blistered burns covering large swathes of his skin which bubbled up to reveal tender red flesh.

"Oh guards, you may pause in your work for now," Lucifer called to them brightly as he sat on the edge of the pit.

Phineus' torturer dropped his clamp and detached the weight, letting the agile Cobra fall to his knees. The one beside Orpheus turned the crank three times in the opposite direction allowing the chains to slacken. They stood side by side, gazing up at their leader.

"Remove the fork from Thandrua's collar, I want him to look up at me."

Both guards moved toward Thandrua, one grabbed the fork as the other stood on a stepstool to hold Thandrua's head back. As soon as his chin no longer held the fork in place against his neck, the torturer turned it sideways and immediately the former deity dropped his head. He groaned slightly, but as the daemon stepped down from the stool his groan turned into a growl. Thandrua's head shot up and simultaneously he bent his leg forward to deliver a swift kick to the torturer's back. Quickly the other torturer turned to grab his chain whip and in a flash gave Thandrua two lashes that split the skin on his chest. Thandrua slumped back against the wall with a grimace, one hand over his new wounds.

"Very good, very good indeed!" Lucifer laughed as he clapped his hands. He sat at the edge of the pit, his feet dangling above the emblem that now hung in the pit, "Still have some spirit in you now, huh?"

"Is that… a new… device?" Thandrua tried to speak between large huffs of air.

"You like what I have done?" Lucifer smiled down, "Recognize it at all? The symbol of your fate? I improved it though, made it my own. It's a five-pointed star. I had them remove that tacky representation of your "all-seeing eye" and connected these ends here. Why a star? Well, that thing you all learned to cower from and fear in your old world, the Sun? It may not look like it to any on Earth, but that is a star just like all the others. I figured what better way to represent my triumph over the Serpenoids, over *you,* Thandrua, than to symbolize my reign with a star of my own. I call it a Pentagram."

"You have defiled every aspect of the culture I tried to establish," Thandrua sighed, eyes locked onto the upside-down star that hung before him.

Thandrua could faintly see the welding in certain spots that transformed the Eye of Thandrua into this Pentagram. He looked passed the additional metal and sought to only see the intersecting diagonal lines that represented refuge to him and his colony all those cycles ago. A shine seemed to illuminate from those original metal parts, a shine only seen to Thandrua.

The muscles around his scarred left eye began to quiver and twitch. He wanted to rub the irritation in his eye, but the pain in his chest was greater, he did not want to move his hands. It seemed only now that he remembered the constant burning from the scar, for it had never stopped, his mind only had become preoccupied with the pain of his torture. The thought then occurred to him, it seemed only fitting that the symbol that once led Thandrua and his people to salvation was also the same symbol to warn him of his damnation.

Lucifer could not read minds, but the anguish in Thandrua's face told him everything he wanted to know. "Yes, that's it Thandrua," a devilish grin spread across his face, "everything that was once yours is now mine, being used against you. I will make better use of it all. I have built civilization once, this one will be easy and grander than anything I have sought out before.

"In time, this entire world will be mine and all its inhabitants will be under my rule. Oh yes, that's right, you and the Serpenoids are most certainly not the only beings that dwell in this domain. There are so many that have never heard of Lord Thandrua and in time they will all live side by side with the rest of my prisoners, belittling your former godly status so much more!"

Lucifer stood up joyfully, the torturers chuckled underneath their masks. Orpheus screamed in frustration and tugged at his restraints. Lifting his head as much as he could, the brutish Cobra peered over to his former god.

"Do not listen to him, Lord Thandrua," Orpheus said. "You may not be the lifegiver we thought you to be, but you will always be our leader. If there are any others that join us in this doom, they will not hear of the tales we thought to come from your almighty power, but of all the true memories from your strong leadership that we still hold."

"I don't know how you have entranced them all, but their allegiance to you is impressive," Lucifer awed.

"Lucifer," Thandrua straightened and looked up at his oppressor, "free the Cobras, free all the Serpenoids that remain. I will stay here, you can continue this punishment I certainly deserve, but they are innocent. All of them, please."

"Oh Thandrua, that's no fun, do not break just yet," Lucifer tsked. "Besides, I will have to decline your noble offer. You see, your penance isn't the physical torture I put you through, but the mental torment you gain from your followers' pain and knowing that you, Thandrua, put them there. Guards, let these two rest for now, their pain is greater when they have more energy. As for Thandrua, chain him back up onto his post."

Chapter 24
Lilith

Lilith left the Kiln behind and her companion, Lucifer, with it. He was preoccupied, waiting on the creation of his new symbol. She was glad that he had something new to look forward to; the fire that fueled Lucifer seemed to simmer down after the rebellion. In these new cycles, he seemed uncertain of what to do next. She was happy to see the spark in her leader as he went to the Kiln. However, Lilith did not see any reason for her to linger in the smoldering dark cave if she didn't have to. The few times Lilith spent in the Kiln as a slave was more than enough.

The place smelled foul. Well, to be honest the entire desert did. However, there was something about the tight quarters of the Kiln that made the sulfuric scent all the more acrid. It was not only unpleasant to smell but irritated her eyes as well.

As Lilith left the Kiln, she rubbed her right eye gently. The itch did not cease, if anything it seemed to only itch more. In another moment the irritation spread to her other eye.

"Damn!" She cursed as she now rubbed both burning eyes. "Feels like there's sand in my eyes now. Great!"

Lilith gave up on rubbing the sensation out of her eyes. She slowly opened them both up. She was headed to the large metal structure that she and Lucifer slept in, but now she looked to the side. There was a hill, and that hill led right down to the lake.

I should go there and wash my eyes out, Lilith thought to herself before walking in that direction. The sand beneath her feet was hot, very hot. After all this time, she thought she would get used to it, but not nearly enough. Her feet were blackened, cracked, and calloused over and yet the sand still seemed to burn.

That sensation was relieved as she descended down the hill and felt the moist sand cooling into the cracked soles of her feet. The best part of this entire dreadful desert was right here, at the shore of the everlasting lake. The sand was cooler and wet. The moisture that seeped in from the subtle waves washing onto the shore made the sand feel softer yet also more firm.

Of course, the lake wasn't the most peaceful of places to be. It was loud with the rowdy activities of the freed men and women. She sneered at two guys she saw that were fighting one another, just for fun. *Barbaric!* Is all Lilith could think as she made sure to avoid them or any of the others while stepping into the water.

Ah, yes! Lilith stood still, letting the water wash onto her feet. The water was lukewarm, but still refreshing to the touch. This had to have been the only "cold" place to exist in this world. Lilith took a couple more steps forward. The water covered her ankles. She then slipped out of her dress, balled it up, and threw it back onto the sand.

Now bare of her clothes, Lilith plunged into the water. Submerging her head, she felt the sand beneath with her hands. She quickly stood back up and flicked back her long, wet hair. Where she stood now, the water reached just below her waist. Cupping her hands, Lilith gathered water and splashed it onto her face. She blew the water from her mouth, what a sweet release it was, and rinsed a second time.

Lilith let out a long delighted sigh of relaxation. Slowly rubbing her eyes, she opened them and felt refreshed. Her eyes, body, and mind. This was what she needed, and she understood why so many were called to the lake.

She stood there looking out over the lake, feeling the top of the water with her palms. The water splashed against her buttocks. Lilith wished she could remember her past life to reflect on at this serene moment. All she had were fleeting images and emotions.

Instead, Lilith reflected on the past of her current life. Her life in this hell. How agonizing it was living in the dark and dirty quarry, chipping away, hoping to find something useful to the Serpenoids. Those tools required so much energy, which she did not have because of thirst and exhaustion. It was like that for everyone, but Lilith was lucky.

Being in Lucifer's favor, he had made sure she didn't have to labor nearly as much as the rest of the slaves did. She rarely had to work in the Kiln as well. Lucifer knew all the tricks to keep her from the Serpenoids and keep her in the quarry. It was much easier to hide out of sight and slack off in the mines than in the forge.

Lucifer was very kind to her. Lilith didn't exactly know why. Perhaps it was because she was the first to be "awakened." She knew many of the men, as well as some women, were very infatuated with her and admired her because of her beauty. Lucifer did recognize her beauty of course. He was very vain himself and seemed to feel the need to remind Lilith of her looks very often.

Whatever his inscrutable reasonings were, Lilith knew Lucifer wasn't after her in a sexual way. No, not in the least. He didn't even seem to have the necessary part required for such a thing. That made Lilith care for him all the more. He was true to her, and so she did not care why he favored her.

She was grateful for Lucifer's close care. Had it not been that way, her skin would have been more damaged, just as the other daemons were becoming. Their appearance was still continuing to alter and change even now that they were no longer enslaved. She was sure living in the quarters with her Lord slowed her body's deterioration. Wearing clothing probably helped with that as well. Lucifer had told her that soon she would have a cloak of her own to better protect her from the heat.

Lilith shut her eyes tightly and tried to think of her previous life once more. Again all she could muster up were images and feelings. She could remember the images of a man in her life, but were there any feelings towards him? Nothing very strong, if at all. Not like the partnership she has with Lucifer. Not in the same way Lucifer makes her feel. She wondered, just for a moment, if possibly what she was feeling for Lucifer might be l--

An abrupt peal of laughter broke out on the shore near her, taking Lilith out of her thoughts. Lilith closed her eyes briefly, tuning out the noise around her from her fellow daemons. Looking up, she gazed at the incredible mountain all the way across the lake; from this close up it seemed to brush the rust-orange sky. The mountain view, the lake, the beautiful soothing sound of the gentle water. She took in slow deep breaths and exhaled them just the same. She felt serene and at peace.

Lilith heard the sound of splashing water coming up to her. She closed her eyes, pretending not to notice. The movement approached closer still, cutting her away from her Zen.

"Oooh, baby!" A man whistled behind her. "So, you came to join the festivities for once?"

Lilith released a long, exasperated sigh, "Why are *you* talking to *me*?"

"Come on, girl." The man grabbed Lilith's shoulder and turned her around. "We both know why you're here."

Lilith stared at the man. He stood a head taller than her. She kept her eyes fixed on his, determined not to look down at what he might possibly be trying to offer, doing nothing to hide the disdain in her stare.

"A beautiful woman like you, flaunting your stuff around. Come on, you know what goes on here." A sickening grin spread across his face. "Can't help myself."

"Well, you'll have to," Lilith pushed past him. "Bye!" She began to head to the shore.

"Hey now, don't be like that!" He called out to her.

The daemon followed after her. Lilith picked up her pace. The water was shallow, but there was still just enough to slow her down. She had just made it to the shoreline. She saw her dress close by on the dry part of the sand, but the daemon had caught up to her.

"Hey, I said don't be like that!" He shouted at her before knocking her down into the wet sand.

Lilith fell onto her knees, hard. She gasped from the shock of the impact vibrating up through her bones. Some of the people nearby heard and saw the commotion. They looked over to what was happening, but nobody acted.

"Leave me alone!" Lilith yelled as she tried to get up before she was pushed back down.

"You left Lucifer behind for a reason. No one here to get in our way," the daemon said, standing above her.

The others came up to them, but they didn't help. They just stood there watching. The man, the *daemon* turned her over, whispering, "Just you and me."

Lilith gave him a piercing stare and screamed at him. She did not scream out of fear, but out of anger. Lilith quickly pulled back both her legs and kicked out hard, knocking the wind out of her attacker. He gasped for air as she pulled back her right leg again and struck it out, cracking his jaw.

The onlookers all cheered her on as they saw blood spurt from the daemon's face. He fell back into the water. Lilith stood up, hovering above him. The daemon slowly looked up at her, right before she spat in his face.

"Just you and me," Lilith said coldly, then punched him dead center on the nose, relishing the crack she felt in her knuckles.

The daemon yelled and reached up to his nose as it gushed out blood. However, Lilith wasn't done with him. She continued raining down blows on his face. After his blood covered her fist and arm, and his nose became concave, she shoved him over and kept his head in the water with her foot on the back of his head. The daemon struggled for a short while, but he'd had little enough fight in him before Lilith decided to drown him anyway. Finally, the body stopped quivering in the water and Lilith removed her foot from his head, which now bobbed up and down on the water.

"Someone discard his body!" Lilith demanded, turning to her audience.

The group of daemons shied away and said nothing. They seemed to be looking anywhere else but at Lilith herself.

Someone from the back finally broke the silence, "You killed him, you take care of him."

"Who said that? Who!?" There was a crazed look upon Lilith's face. "You watched! You all watched and did nothing! I know all of your faces. Think what the Dark Lord will do if he finds out one of you pathetic, miserable, meatbags attacked me while every single one of you watched?"

The daemons continued to remain silent as they looked at one another.

"Lord Lucifer needs his servants for their craft. But he will need someone he can test his new devices on. There are always plenty more daemons." Lilith glared at them. "You are all expendable! So, somebody bury this crap in a ditch or dump him into the lava, or our Lord will know just how loyal you all truly are."

The daemons shifted uncomfortably. No one wanted to be on the receiving end of the Dark Lord's wrath, especially not after standing by and watching his companion in the struggle that she was in. Two men came forward. Their steps splashed as they entered the water. Each one grabbed the dead body by his arms and pulled the corpse out.

“Thank you.” Lilith said, more composed. “The rest of you, leave me. I just want to relax, *alone*.” Lilith turned her back to them and brushed off the sand that stuck to her skin. She waded further into the blood-filled water and sighed peacefully.

Chapter 25
The Aviaans and the Prairie

Sectoraus sat behind his new blue-feathered friend, Leukai, straddling the large creature that galloped upon four legs. They ran through the grassland at a speed Sectoraus had never fathomed of traveling. He could feel the air cutting past them as the breeze slicked over his scales. The feathery frill under Leukai's arms flapped back in the wind, brushing against Sectoraus' face, as did his braided feathers.

The ride was not only uncomfortably fast, but bumpy as well. The wise Cobra who continuously showed bravery in the face of death-defying danger now kept both arms wrapped tightly around the waist of his guide, eyes closed shut.

Out of the tall grass, they reached a wide prairie with small rolling hills. The ride itself did not feel terribly long to Sectoraus, but he was sure they covered much ground at the speed they had traveled. The Aviaan kicked his heels into the side of his mount at the same time he shouted a command. The high-speed creature stopped almost immediately.

The Aviaan camp was spread wide with various shelters built in a spiraling form surrounding a large fire pit. The domed homes were made of animal skins and propped up with long sticks. The others from the war party rode on past the shelters to a wooden fence containing more of the hooved animals. Leukai led Sectoraus toward the center of the homes, where others seemed to have gathered. The Aviaans bore feathers in several colors, but mainly red, blue, or brown feathers

"That is a very interesting way of travel." Sectoraus sighed in relief, still feeling a bit woozy from the ride.

"Ah yes, I was told that equis are foreign to your region." Leukai chuckled in response, "As most things are in this part of the world, I'm sure."

"Yes, that they are," Sectoraus looked over to where the equis were kept and studied them for a moment. From a distance, he thought they were elegant with their long smooth hair flowing, the way they flicked their tails side to side, and the soft neighing and snorting sounds they made. He thought of the onyx stones when observing how the animals' black hair and skin stood out against the yellow grass. Although many of them were dark in color, there were also a few that were brown, beige, spotted, and even black-and-white-striped.

Finally, Sectoraus looked over to Leukai again. "How do you know of Solarious?"

"We will speak of him shortly. First, I must introduce you to Chief Ocia."

They squeezed between two shelters and crossed the open circle. Young Aviaans ran about playfully, chasing one another and pretending to shoot each other with their child-sized bows. The younglings stopped to gawk at the Cobra as he passed by. In one area were what Sectoraus could now recognize as the females of the race. These Aviaans were covered in brown feathers, and they sat on the ground in a circle with a pile of animal hides. A couple scraped fur off of a large hide while three others mended and cut parts off.

Crossing the circle, they came to a shelter painted in symbols and patterns, with the doorway well-decorated in assorted feathers dangling like frills. It reminded Sectoraus of the hut the Priestess of the Krocdylius lived in. Center of the colony and well-decorated, Sectoraus understood this was a sign of great importance. He recalled how his royal chamber in the desert was built significantly larger than the rest and Vander's own shelter had a large Eye of Thandrua propped by the entrance, and smiled to himself, thinking of the similarities that instinctually had developed even amongst such different peoples.

"One moment," Leukai placed his hand in front of Sectoraus before poking his head into the home.

Sectoraus looked around uneasily, catching just about all the villagers staring right at him, muttering amongst themselves. It was different, however, than how the Krocdylius had looked at him when they first saw the Cobra enter their village. Leukai knew of Solarious, so obviously they had seen the other Cobra. They didn't look at Sectoraus as one did at something never seen before, but they seemed apprehensive about something, uncertain whether to go up to the other Cobra and speak with him or not. Finally, his guide turned back to him.

"We may enter now," Leukai said, beckoning.

Following Leukai's lead, Sectoraus ducked his head as they entered the hut. The frilled doorway allowed light from the fire outside to illuminate the interior, which was completely covered in feathers. In the back sat a yellow Aviaan, his face lined with wrinkles. The two stood, their heads still bent, until the chief gestured for them to sit. They did so.

From the top of the chief's head, falling down along his face and past his chest, he wore two braids of feathers. The feathers were red on his right and blue on the left. With his small finger he flicked the blue braid behind his shoulder.

"You are the other Serpenoid." The way the chief said it was more matter-of-fact than a question.

"I am Sectoraus. You know of my brother?" Sectoraus, eager for answers, dropped his formality.

Ocia stared at him blankly, then shifted his gaze over to Leukai, "Where did you find this one?"

Sectoraus exhaled in frustration but held his tongue. It seemed not long ago that he was the one who was rude to a stranger that didn't know of the Serpenoids' customs. He was unaware of the Aviaan culture and didn't know the situation. Now was not the time to argue.

"He was by the pond," Leukai replied. "Saundre alerted me of his presence and we rescued him just before the Aegagruians could haul him away."

"Ah, is that so?" The chief stroked the long feathers on his chin quizzically and ran his black eyes up and down Sectoraus, "What brings you here, Sectoraus?"

"My brother, Solarious, journeyed toward this region many cycles ago. He has yet to return and it is of the utmost importance that I speak with him," Sectoraus stopped and looked to Leukai, then back at the chief. "Leukai had mentioned my brother. I must see him, would you inform him of my presence?"

Leukai studiously kept his gaze on the wizened Aviaan, avoiding Sectoraus' eyes. Chief Ocia continued to stroke the feathers on his chin but hadn't said a word. It was actually quite silent in the hut as both Aviaans sat solemnly. There was something unspoken between them. Sectoraus could hear the crackle of the fire outside, the giggling young ones that ran around, and indistinct conversations, but he continued to stare at the chief expectantly.

The chief seemed to be choosing what he wanted to say before deciding on the right words, mulling them over in his mind. Finally, he nodded his head, "Solarious was a pleasant one, yes indeed. Much heart and loyalty to you and the one called 'Lord Thandrua.' After his team's journey turned for the worst, Leukai as well as a few others escorted him out of the prairie where the grasslands meet the sand. However, after Solarious had seen that your tribe was held captive he returned immediately, regrouping with Leukai. We took him in as our own." Chief Ocia studied Sectoraus for a moment, "How is it you managed to escape your captors?"

"Like my brother, I, too, was away. He had not requested for your aid to help Thandrua and the others?"

"We do not typically leave the safety of the prairie. I had already allowed them to take him home. Anyway, we couldn't risk the possible loss for any of our tribe."

"I see," Sectoraus dropped his head, then looked up again into the chief's eyes, "It is much appreciated for assuring his personal safety."

"That I cannot accept."

"Humble, I admire that. Now, Solarious. Take me to him."

"Unfortunately, I cannot do that either." The chief gestured over to Leukai.

The blue warrior cleared his throat after noticing the attention was brought onto him, "Just recently the Aegagruians invaded our camp. Took two of ours and... your brother."

The news of his brother stunned Sectoraus, but only for a moment.

"You sit here and do nothing!?" Sectoraus stood abruptly, fists clenched in anger.

"The Aegagruians live in a dangerous place, and they keep their prisoners in an even more dangerous tomb. We do not go there," Chief Ocia said matter-of-factly.

Sectoraus screamed in frustration before he fell to his knees. "I will become the last, then." He said to himself as he stared at the ground.

Sectoraus had come so far, only to feel that his hopes were further away than ever from being fulfilled. He closed his eyes and took in two deep breaths; he could feel the pain from Phineus and Orpheus. Sectoraus wondered how much more could they endure before their will to live met its limitations.

What was he to do now? Sectoraus couldn't possibly find Solarious on his own. When he tried to feel for him, Sectoraus could only sense a suffocating darkness. Was he to search all the lands before finding out that Solarious had been killed? Surely the prisoners in the quarry couldn't wait that long, but was Sectoraus to go and free them himself? How long would his fight last before he himself is struck down?

"Solarious may still be alive," Ocia turned a sympathetic gaze towards his visitor. "The Aegagruians use their prisoners for an evil ritual of theirs. I understand that the victims do not lose life for quite some time."

"Tell me," Sectoraus demanded, "tell me where they reside and I will go there myself. I will save him!"

"That I can allow. We can give you supplies as well as the information you need. I only ask of you for one thing. Do not bring that evil back with you."

"The only thing I will bring back will be Solarious and your lost ones." Sectoraus said with great confidence.

Chief Ocia slowly stood up on his two feet. A small smile formed on his wrinkled face, but his eyes seemed sad as he offered out his right arm and said, "I hope you find them. I truly do."

"Thank you." Sectoraus said, grasping the chief's forearm.

Leukai came over and ever so gently placed a hand onto Sectoraus' shoulder, "Come, let's get you set up," he spoke softly.

"Yes, time is pressing," Chief Ocia added, "every moment that passes takes away a moment of opportunity for you to save them."

Leukai led Sectoraus out of the hut as Chief Ocia sat himself down, slowly crossing his legs again. Curious folk from the tribe seemed to have gathered just outside of their chief's hut. Maybe it was the curiosity of another Cobra to visit them from the far lands of the desert. Or perhaps they heard Sectoraus' shouting. Judging by the soft, composed manor that Chief Ocia had about him, Sectoraus figured that shouting within his hut was not a common thing to hear. If it ever happened at all, that is.

Everyone stepped aside to allow the two passage through the crowd that had formed. Everyone was silent. Leukai paid no mind to them and continued to move forward, eyes straight ahead. Sectoraus on the other hand could not help but look around at all of their black eyes staring at him. It wasn't fear, nor curiosity that Sectoraus saw in those eyes, but an understanding. Sympathy.

They all might have lost someone they cared for to these Aegagruians at some point in their lives. These abductors. Sectoraus looked over his shoulder to see the Aviaans continuing to watch him as Leukai pulled him past a hut. They passed by a few more huts, moving to another layer outside the inner circle. Sectoraus continued to follow his guide through one layer after another, moving this way and that around the huts. The blue warrior brought Sectoraus to a large shelter outside of the village.

"You have weapons, I see." Leukai looked Sectoraus over, eyeing the blades that dangled at his side. The metal sheath caught his eye the most, "I have never seen anything to shine like that before."

Sectoraus pulled the sword out of its sheath, "They call it a sword. The daemons." Sectoraus explained. "In the desert we create metal. That is why it shines so. Metal is precious to us."

"It looks very nice. Very sharp."

"This is the tool that the daemons used to overthrow my lord."

"I know about your tribe. I'm sorry that happened." Leukai fixed his sight on the bladder-made sack fixed to the Cobra's belt, "That pouch holds water?"

"Yes, I acquired it from the swamp," Sectoraus put the sword away and unhooked the deflated sack, "but there is almost nothing left inside."

"We have water in here. We can refill it." Leukai gestured to the entrance from where they stood. As they entered, he turned back to Sectoraus, "You said you were in the swamplands?"

"Yes, I spent many cycles there." Sectoraus answered as he crossed the threshold into the large hut.

The place had a few barrels around the room, piles of animal pelts and furs, and a few bows hung along the walls. There was a table with some wood and stones and beside that were finished arrows and spears to choose from.

Leukai took the pouch from Sectoraus and went to the nearest barrel. He crouched down to a little spout turned to the side, placed the opening of the pouch to the spout and turned it vertically. Sectoraus now saw that the other barrels also had a single horizontal spout each. He could hear the sound of water pouring into his empty sack.

"You keep water in there?" Sectoraus asked.

"That way we do not have to travel to the pond every time someone gets thirsty." Leukai answered. "That way we don't have to leave our sanctuary." As the sack inflated, some water began to drip along the sides. Leukai removed it from the pouch, letting some of the water pour onto the ground, then turned the spout, stopping the spillage.

"The swampland, what was it like?" Leukai asked while handing the full sack of water to Sectoraus.

"I am assuming that since you are not permitted to leave the prairie, you have never been there yourself?"

"You assume correctly, but I have heard of it." Leukai led Sectoraus outside again. "Chief Ocia has told of a time, before he was young, when the tribes of the prairie had a union with the dwellers of the swamplands. A time before a mountain erupted and a red river of fire altered the landscape."

Sectoraus paused, considering this story. "It seems what I consider to be my sanctuary has been quite the opposite for others."

"Come, follow me." Leukai led Sectoraus away from the hut of supplies in the direction of the fenced-in animals. "So then, you met others there in the swamplands?"

"Yes, a tribe called the Krocdylius. They seem brutal, but were very kind, very generous." Sectoraus explained, "They took me in, as well as a Serpenoid who was named Nimod. We were the sole survivors of my expedition and the Krocs fed us, took care of us, and taught us how to fight."

"That was very noble of them."

"It seems to me, you and your tribe did the same for Solarious. At least, that is what I have understood."

"We did. We taught him our ways. We invited him into our tribe. He was, to me, just another Aviaan who had lost his feathers."

They stopped right outside of the gate to the fence. The equis trotted around, a couple walked up to the two that stood by the fence. Sectoraus was clearly hesitant.

"Please, do not worry," Leukai encouraged. "They are kind and will not harm you." The blue warrior opened the gate, "Come in and I will show you yours."

As they stepped in, Leukai held out one hand to the curious animals behind him. They stepped away as he closed the gate with his other hand. The black and white striped one that Leukai had ridden upon earlier came up to them. Leukai gave it a gentle pat and cooed softly to it before moving along. Finally, they found what Leukai was looking for.

"This equus will become your companion, he is the best of the herd and quite unique. Only one other similar to this one, but the mare was taken long ago." Leukai pulled the Cobra to a jet-black stallion whose forehead was crowned with a single pale, spiraled horn, "Just feed him this and then he will be yours." He handed Sectoraus a handful of grass.

"Equus?" Sectoraus grabbed the grass, "You had referred to them as equis earlier."

"Equus is the lone animal, it is the group we call *equis*."

Leukai clicked his tongue and beckoned for the black stallion to follow them. It did so without hesitation. Sectoraus opened the gate as Leukai led the equus outside the fence. The elegant creature flicked its tail side to side. Sectoraus stared into his red eyes and presented the offering. The equus and Sectoraus maintained eye contact while he ate from his hand, building a connection.

"This is such a wonderful specimen, but he has never been claimed by any." Leukai stroked the long black mane as the equus nudged Sectoraus' hand with his snout, "He seems to have taken a great liking to you. He wants you to pet him."

Sectoraus stroked its long muzzle.

"He's yours now." Leukai said. "You should name him."

Sectoraus took his hand off his new ride and looked him over. He stared at the single horn in the center of his head.

"Unicornis." Sectoraus said.

"Unicornis," Leukai repeated, nodding his head, "Uni for short?"

"Uni is endearing, I might just call him that from time to time." Sectoraus thought about it for a moment. "Unicornis, however, is strong, has a great ring to it. Just feels right, Unicornis." Sectoraus repeated it proudly.

"I wonder what it could be, Sectoraus?" Leukai smiled at him. "So, anyway, there are a few things I must tell you before you go."

"Of course! After all, I do not know *where* it is that I must go."

Leukai pointed past the settlement, out into the prairie, "You must travel in that direction. Over the horizon you will be greeted by mountains. Head straight for the mountains. You should come to an area of large boulders at the foot of the mountains. The Aegagruians live in the mountains, but by the stones you will find the camp of their scouts."

Sectoraus looked to the horizon. He thought about the directions and hoped he went to the right part of the mountains.

"These Aegagruians, have they been your enemies for long?" Sectoraus asked.

"I have known for Aegagruians to be the mortal enemies of the Aviaans, since before the time of our chief; stealing food, water, and our people. They took prisoners not for themselves, but for the ones they worshipped. The true ones to fear."

"There is a more dangerous threat? Do the stones come to life?"

"The stones? No, no. The scouts have settled camp outside of a deep cavern. Inside the caverns reside terrifying creatures, the *Arania*."

"What are these Arania?"

"I am sorry, Sectoraus, but there isn't much that my tribe knows about the Arania. All I can say is that they produce a thin, but strong substance called 'silk.' The only place we travel to, outside of our territory, is there. In times of desperation, we go there at our own risk to steal the silk the Aegagruians gather from the Arania. We use it for various purposes."

"I will handle them." Sectoraus was confident about this.

"You might not have any difficulty fighting off the scouts. There are only ever a few of them at a time in the camp. They might try to lure you into the caverns. Get rid of them before they do."

"I am much obliged for the knowledge and assistance that you have been able to give me." Sectoraus took in Leukai's arm.

Sectoraus took a moment to himself, absorbing all the information, then lifted himself up and onto Unicornis, swinging his right leg over the back. The steed shifted slightly at the weight change, which caused Sectoraus to grip tightly, steadying himself.

"It will take me awhile to get used to this thing," Sectoraus laughed nervously.

"Once you really get going you should be fine." Leukai smiled at him. "Remember what I told you."

"Yes, I will be careful. Thank you for everything, Leukai."

"It is my pleasure, Sectoraus." The blue feathered warrior's face grew grave, "No one has ever returned from the domain of the

Arania... May you find your brother." Then Leukai slapped the haunch of the equus and with a startled whinny it took off.

Sectoraus hugged tightly onto Unicornis' neck as the wind passed his face. Even though he had just ridden on one of these with Leukai, he couldn't get over how fast they ran. The rapid thumping of the animal's hooves matched the anxious heartbeat within the Cobra's chest. He felt the sickness in his gut subside as he grew used to the rapid up and down movements of the mount. Finally, he felt comfortable enough to loosen his grip and straighten up.

Squinting through the whizzing, stinging air, Sectoraus gradually began to find himself enjoying the ride. Before long, he saw the mountains peek over the horizon, where his destination lay. Sectoraus hoped to avoid being captured. He thought of all he learned. It would be surviving the Arania threshold where the true challenge resided.

The black stallion maintained a consistent speed as it cut through the tall grass to the fast-approaching mountains. Off to his far right, Sectoraus heard the thunder of hooves. He glanced to the side, anticipating incoming Aegagruian scouts. Sectoraus was surprised by what he saw. A herd of large wooly beasts with short horns stampeded through the plains. Sectoraus recalled seeing their thick fuzzy hide used as blankets by some of the Aviaans.

The beasts, paying no mind to the equus-mounted Cobra, rumbled past and around Sectoraus. His companion froze on the spot and neighed nervously as they moved past, seemingly toward a specific destination they could not stray from.

"Easy, Unicornis." Sectoraus stroked the mane of his mount to calm the creature, assuring that there was no real danger. Sectoraus held his breath as he watched the stampede; it was a majestic scene.

Once the hulking beasts were far off in their own adventure, the lone Cobra kicked his steed with the back of his heels and they were off once again. Sectoraus continued to think of Leukai's warnings of the upcoming enemy. Legend was that the Arania preferred the flesh of a conscious being over any non-sentient creature. With beasts as hearty as those that had just passed, Sectoraus couldn't imagine why. Sectoraus guessed that was why the

Aegagruians had taken the Aviaans and his brother. Contribution for the silk.

Sectoraus was confident he would rescue his brother. Leukai said that there was no guarantee the prisoners would still be alive, but Sectoraus could feel his brother and that was all the reassurance he needed as he reached the mountains looming ever closer.

Chapter 26
Into the Domain of the Arania

The jagged mountains were near enough now that Sectoraus could clearly see the foreboding cliff faces made up of layers of gray and brown rock. Sectoraus brought his mount to a halt as the grassy terrain he had traveled through ended in a blockade of boulders, just as Leukai had described.

Over the boulders, Sectoraus could see the signs of smoke. A campfire from the Aegagruian camp. Ever so slowly dismounting the equus, Sectoraus gave him a pat on his nose and Unicornis sighed with affection.

"You wait here," he told Unicornis before deftly climbing the rocks, his black claws searching for any spot to grab ahold of. Sectoraus scaled his way up and over, leaping down to a dirt path with a soft thud. The area wasn't clear; rocks jutted about here at the foot of the mountains, their roots growing out of the pebbly ground.

After hiking through a bit of a maze, Sectoraus peeked around the stone and saw the flicker of fire. He was in the camp. More huge lumps of stone seemed to be placed perfectly near the fire. It took Sectoraus a moment to realize these weren't boulders of the mountain, but stone-built shelters. He threw himself behind a boulder as he glimpsed a shadow coming out of one of the shelters. It was an Aegagruian.

Standing tall on its two hooved feet, the wooled creature stretched its arms and bleated a wide yawn. *Perhaps this is their time of slumber*, Sectoraus thought hopefully to himself as he crouched low to the ground, watching from behind his cover. *What better time to invade enemy territory than whilst they slept?* The Aegagruian moved to the low fire and stoked it with a spear before tossing a piece of wood into it. Sectoraus approached closer, bracing his right hand on the stone that covered him. His fingers passed over a few loose pebbles that lightly clattered as they rolled off. The horned enemy glanced back, right in Sectoraus' direction.

Quickly, Sectoraus pulled behind the boulder. He held his breath, waiting. Then he heard it, hooves crunching on the pebbly ground, getting nearer. He had been spotted!

Very quietly, Sectoraus withdrew his sword and shifted to the other side of the boulder, hoping to catch his seeker from behind.

The steps were even closer now and he could hear its heavy breathing. Suddenly its advance stopped. Sectoraus rolled around the other side. Now the Aegagruian stood where he had been. Sectoraus crept around, positioning himself behind the enemy. It snorted in frustration and stroked the tuft on its chin.

Sectoraus had been holding his breath as he now stood directly behind. He pulled back his arm and drove the sword through the middle of his foe's back. He thought it attempted to scream, but the Aegagruian just let out a quiet wheezing expulsion of air as blood spurted out of its mouth instead of the scream. Dropping the spear with its quivering hands, it rolled its head around to stare directly into Sectoraus' golden eyes as the Cobra's hood unfurled. Sectoraus sliced the sword upward, stopping at the chest and retracted his weapon. The body collapsed with a lifeless thud.

Scanning the other stone shelters, Sectoraus proceeded through the camp, but not before wiping the dripping red blood off his blade with his knee. He minded his footing as he crept by the entrances of the shelters. His presence was still covered, he hoped he could get Solarious and return to the equus before any others would wake.

Now with the fire and the camp at his back, Sectoraus glanced up the mountain in front of him, then back down to the gaping opening of the caverns. With the fire lit behind, the inside seemed black as the starless skies of the earliest days in his first world. He exhaled and whispered, "In the name of Thandrua," before stepping into the void. He followed the long dark tunnel, both hands wrapped around the hilt of his metallic sword, ready to strike.

Wind howled past him, and before long he found himself at a fork. He glanced down the right tunnel, then down the left. Sectoraus extended his arm and held his palm out to one and then the other. He felt a breeze coming from the left, so that's where he continued. As he progressed the tunnel became wider, producing more stalagmites and stalactites. Finally, the tunnel opened to a vast cavern.

"By Thandrua!" the king of Cobras gasped. His voice echoed, for it was huge and many more tunnels seemed to connect in the dark and wet cavern. Sectoraus' nostrils flared as he sniffed the strong, musky odor within. Glancing up at the ceiling, he was perplexed to find it covered in a white, silky material. Leukai had warned him that the Arania produced a sticky webbing that they used as a net or restraint for their prey. Very cautiously, Sectoraus advanced further in the cavern. He noticed the webbing seemed to be formed into vine-like structures that branched from the ceiling to many different points in the cavern. Sectoraus looked down some of the tunnels, only to see they were obscured with the web.

Echoing drips of water and Sectoraus' breathing was all that could be heard, until he crept by a tunnel where he stopped in his tracks. Very faintly, he heard a moaning.

Solarious, Sectoraus thought to himself. A sheet of webbing hung over this tunnel; perhaps that was where the victims were kept. He stared at the web as it swayed very gently in the air currents. Sectoraus lifted his sword and hacked through it. He turned when he heard something shifting behind. There was not a thing to be seen. Sectoraus shook his sword hard a few times before finally getting the web off.

Venturing down the tunnel, he could hear more moans reverberating through the empty spaces. He found himself in another cavern, one much smaller than the previous. Here, the walls were completely white with web and that musky aroma was more pungent. Scanning the cavern, he found bundles of webbing along the walls. The bodies of the victims, he presumed.

Something felt strange as he made his way to the center, something was off. Swinging around he heard movement but found nothing still. Sectoraus heard a rapid clicking sound echoing down from another tunnel, it sounded distant, but obscured by the echoes. He couldn't determine its origin.

Once the clicking stopped, he began to observe the bundles nearby. The webbing was almost translucent, and he could see a figure on the inside. Hastily he scraped off the webbing with his claws to reveal the petrified face of a pale and featherless Aviaan.

The moaning returned.

Sectoraus glanced down, noticing the sound coming from the bodies deeper into the tunnel. At the furthest end of this room he found three bodies; he could see them move as they breathed. He began to tear the sticky, fibrous bonds and with a gasp, a red Aviaan stared back with fright.

"Solarious, how did you get free?" His voice was small from fatigue.

"I am *Sectoraus*, I'm here to rescue you."

Before completely freeing the helpless tribesman, Sectoraus ripped through the next bundle of web to find the face he was looking for. Eyes half closed and expression weak, the limp head of Solarious shifted to look at his rescuer in the face.

"You came." Solarious wheezed.

"It is wonderful to see you alive." Sectoraus already began to feel relief.

"Rejoice later." Solarious said, but the joy in his eyes was unmistakable.

With three slashes at the webbing, the three cocooned bodies tumbled to the ground. Solarious and the red Aviaan started ripping through their webbing while Sectoraus uncovered a young brown Aviaan. The eerie clicking sound returned. Sectoraus looked around, the sound seeming to come from many directions.

"We must go... they know you are here," the other Aviaan urged.

Sectoraus freed Solarious completely and handed him the bone blade hanging from his belt. Both released the two still-living Aviaans. The clicking grew to a cacophony.

"What is that sound?" asked Sectoraus.

"*Them*," Solarious responded. "Now, we go."

The four ran out of the storage cave with Sectoraus at the lead, going back through the tunnel he came from. Sectoraus could hear something, several somethings, approaching quickly behind. Once in the big cavern, Sectoraus stopped to look at the cords of webs that quivered with vibration.

"Keep moving!" Solarious shouted and with his blade he severed the cord Sectoraus was staring at. With a screeching sound, a strangely shaped black creature fell from the ceiling, then many more collected behind, swarming towards the escapees.

They continued to run before they were cut off by an Arania that zipped down from above. Sectoraus suddenly found himself face to face with eight red beady eyes. He saw a flash of movement as the creature clawed at his chest with a barbed and pointed limb. Sectoraus instinctively kicked out, and felt his foot connect with its fleshy humanoid torso as the creature stumbled back over its bulbous lower body.

Within seconds the creature scurried upward, standing on its eight insectoid legs, then charged at them. It snarled and slavered as it approached. Sectoraus, in one singular motion, severed the two arms that jutted out from the torso. A pale green fluid gushed out from the wounds and the monster retreated as the swarm closed in.

The four of them continued to run when the brown Aviaan was ripped from the group. A vine of webbing entangled her foot as an Arania reeled her in. Solarious quickly turned and sliced the line, then slashed across the face of the multi-eyed thing.

Another Arania jumped on Sectoraus' back and strangled him from behind as it wrapped its pointed legs around his body and proceeded to bind him in a web from its bulging lower half. Its efforts proved futile, however, when Sectoraus drove his sword through its head.

They continued their escape. Looking over his shoulder, Sectoraus saw the approaching swarm; some stopped to feast on the dead Arania in a frenzy while the rest advanced, their many legs skittering along all walls of the tunnel, clambering over one another in their pursuit.

They were making their way through the long final tunnel when the red-feathered Aviaan fell to the floor. An Arania jumped on top of the tribesman. It spread its mandibles, revealing its small razor-sharp teeth, before tearing into the Aviaan's face. The others didn't stop.

As they reached the mouth of the tunnel, turning back they could see the swarm as it piled over the fallen Aviaan. His arms flailed about, screaming in terror. The Arania held him close to the ground as their growing mass muffled his screams. The others didn't wait to see clouds of red feathers explode as the creatures tore into and consumed his flesh.

The trio fled outside of the cave, greeted by the warm embrace of the dwindling campfire. Quickly, they all turned around to face the mouth of the Arania domain. Sectoraus held out his blade stepping in front of Solarious and the Aviaan and held down a stance that would let any attacker know, this is where it ends. The three glared into the dark of the cave as the approaching clicking sounds grew louder.

Suddenly, the black abyss contained movement and the glowing red eyes appeared. Sectoraus could see the many legs of these beasts, stopped by the mouth of the caves. He gripped his hilt tightly waiting for them to pounce. They didn't. Just as quickly as the Arania gathered at the entrance, they disappeared back into the dark. The trio felt relieved.

"Solarious," Sectoraus grabbed his brother's right arm to shake in triumph, but then pulled him in for a tight embrace. "I thought I might be alone."

"It is good to see you again and here with me," Solarious broke from the hug and dropped his head, "but what of the others? And Lord Thandrua?"

Their attention was ripped from each other as they heard the bellowing horn coming from the Aegagruian camp. Three short notes arose along with the clatter of the warriors banding together. The young Aviaan moved in closer to the Cobra brothers. "They're coming, they're coming for us!" she shouted with hysteria, "They're coming and we'll be forced back in there with those *things*!"

Sectoraus tightened his grip on the sword's handle and pointed it forward. "We aren't going anywhere, young one."

A row of the woolly enemies came into sight from the camps. They pointed their spears in the air as they bleated and made war cries. Sectoraus held his ground, forming a defensive stance with his blade and staring into the army marching their way. The young Aviaan hid behind her rescuer, shivering in fear.

Closing his eyes for a moment, Sectoraus took in a deep breath and Solarious imitated the same defensive stance at his brother's side. The two hissed through their fangs with their hoods spread wide as the Aegagruians approached ever closer.

From behind the front line, two other Aegagruians stepped to the side, preparing a net. Sectoraus' hiss became a snarl as he bared his white fangs and held a gaze of pure anger. The foes were practically a body length away from the trio when Sectoraus charged forward. Solarious followed behind.

The ground was bare between the opening of the caverns from which they had just left and the boulders that stood where the Aegagruians marched from. They ceased their advance when the two tall Cobras came toward them.

Sectoraus launched himself through the space between them with stunning agility, catching them off guard as he leapt in the air, kicking off one of the boulders to the right and spinning completely around. With the momentum of his descending arc, he decapitated the adversary in the lead even before he landed and engaged in combat.

The Aegagruians broke formation and the single-file line became a disorderly cluster, holding their spears out to defend against the Cobras' attack. Their wooden weapons seemed an even match against the bone blade Solarious held, but Sectoraus' weapon was something else entirely. With sheer force, the metallic blade cut a spear in half with a snap and penetrated the opponents' chest with ease.

The Cobras fought quick and hard, dodging their attackers' assault, but they were still only two fighting off a horde of savage brutes. Sectoraus and Solarious pressed their backs against one another and moved in a circle, attempting to better keep the opponents at bay.

They were surrounded, but confidence held tight in their attacks. Their offensive assault had diminished as they now parried blows and kept their feet moving.

Out from the huddle of attackers, Sectoraus could see the young Aviaan taking cover behind a rock, with three warriors headed for her direction.

"Solarious," he whispered, "hold your ground, I must save the young one."

"I will be fine here, brother." Solarious said as he pulled his blade from a dying enemy.

Sectoraus let out a battle roar before jamming his sword into the nearest Aegagruian and hacking his way out of the group. He ran toward the three pursuers closing in on the fearful Aviaan. Sectoraus grabbed one of the Aegagruians' spiraled horns and with brute strength yanked backwards, pulling the creature's back into his blade. The victim released a gurgling yelp and the other two turned in response.

Sectoraus kicked one square in the chest, sending him to the ground. The other grabbed hold of Sectoraus' armed hand. The two danced about in a struggle, one to regain dominance over his weapon and the other to procure it. The young brown Aviaan saw her rescuer's struggle and took a moment to recover one of the fallen enemy's spears. With a shrill war cry, the Aviaan impaled the spear into the left leg of Sectoraus' attacker. The Aegagruian yelled in pain and Sectoraus clasped onto the enemy's throat with his free hand. The Aegagruian gasped for air as its eyes bulged.

The opponent Sectoraus had kicked to the ground found his way back onto his hooves. The Aegagruian tackled Sectoraus to the ground and Sectoraus' weapon glinted as he lost his grip and it clattered to the ground beside him. The two tussled in the dirt. The tables had been turned, now Sectoraus wheezed to breathe as the Aegagruian sat on Sectoraus' chest tightly clutching his throat.

The Aegagruian released his grip to hold up a spear above his head. Sectoraus grabbed his neck, too weak from being strangled to move; instead, he just hissed as the Aegagruian readied himself to jam the spear down into the Serpenoids' skull. Sectoraus closed his eyes, thinking of how he failed Thandrua, before he heard the sound of flesh being pierced.

When he opened his eyes he saw the scout sitting on his chest still clung onto the spear he held over his head. An arrow stuck out through his left eye. The body slumped down, collapsing beside Sectoraus.

Sectoraus heard approaching thunder. Standing up, he witnessed the Aegagruians scatter from Solarious as the Aviaan war party approached. Leukai led the group, cawing his war cries while pumping his left fist in the air. Arrows soared over his head, connecting with various enemies.

The Aegagruians retreated to the camp, the uninjured ones at least, as they hopped onto their equis and sped away, abandoning the mayhem.

Dismounted from his black-and-white stallion, Leukai hovered over Sectoraus, extending a familiar hand. Sectoraus pulled himself up, then grabbed his sword from the ground and returned it to its sheath.

"You came," Sectoraus said with surprise as well as relief.

"Your bravery and dedication to go alone, not only through the Aegagruian camp, but into the lair of the Arania, left an impression on Chief Ocia." Leukai turned to the other Cobra, "Good to see you again, Solarious."

"The feeling is mutual," Solarious inclined his head in return.

"We are both much obliged," Sectoraus turned to look back at the cave. "If he realized this before, we could have had another one for you."

"Well, I could not ignore the call for help from Uni." He smiled.

"What do you mean?" Sectoraus didn't understand.

"Your steed is more loyal than you realize, then." Leukai placed a hand on Sectoraus' shoulder, "He came back to our camp in a frantic state. I knew then that we had to come for you."

"I am indebted to that animal." Sectoraus felt good, "We managed to save the youngling." The young Aviaan stood by Sectoraus. "What is your name?"

"I go by Wakia," she responded before hugging the Cobra tightly. "Thank you so much for saving my life!"

"Yes, we are all thankful," Leukai hopped back onto his equus, which snorted as he sat upon it. "Wakia, you can ride with me," and pulled the young one up. "Looks like with your mission a success, you will need another equus."

Leukai smiled at the Cobras, then glanced at the abandoned camp, "Those cowards left a few equis behind. As long as Solarious has one, we will take the others with us. You should search their camp, they fled in such haste I'm sure you can find a few useful things left behind."

"They're not coming with us?" Wakia was more asking Leukai, but directed her question to the Cobras.

"No, Wakia, I now must save my own tribe." Sectoraus placed a hand on Solarious' shoulder. "That is why I came for Solarious, and that is where we must go."

"Yes, best of luck to you both." Leukai steered his striped mount around, then he circled his pointer finger around his head to get the others attention. "Back to the camp!"

"Wait!" shouted Wakia, causing the riders to jerk before kicking their stallions into gear. "That's it? We are just *leaving* them?"

Leukai let out a sigh, "Yes, they must go back to where they come from. That is a distance too grand for us, Chief Ocia will not allow us to go."

"Then I'm not going back." Wakia jumped down and moved toward Sectoraus, "Chief Ocia would've left me for dead, but Sectoraus saved me. I owe him my life."

"Oh Wakia, there is no debt between us." Sectoraus smiled down from his mount.

"No, it's not about debt. One of the Aviaan principles is to stick by each other, one big family. I have seen two other kidnappings for the Arania sacrifice and we didn't try anything to bring them back. Our tribe does what it can to defend itself and prevent these things from happening, but once someone is taken from our camp, it is like they are already dead. We travel farther to hunt the bovina then we would to save our own!"

"Wakia, come on, this isn't the time for politics." Leukai extended his hand.

"No, you wouldn't understand. What Solarious and I went through, our bond has become greater than that of a hunting partner. I was taught to stick by family and Sectoraus has shown the loyalty of family far beyond what I've observed within our tribe. There are only two of them, I don't know what they are up against or the trials they must face, but I have learned the way of a warrior through you and I am willing to fight for their cause."

Solarious smiled to himself, they had developed a bond of trust even before the kidnapping, learning alongside each other as Leukai taught them the Aviaan techniques of tracking and hunting. That bond had solidified tighter than ever with what he and Wakia experienced in the caverns.

Sectoraus looked to Leukai, who seemed heavy with thought. Even he had told Sectoraus that he was willing to assist any friend of Solarious. Then he looked back at Wakia. Sectoraus admired the young one's protest. Only he knew of the travesties that awaited them and he was certain that he and Solarious couldn't handle them alone.

Sectoraus sized up the aspiring warrior, her brown feathers pale despite how matted they looked from being captive in the caverns. There was very little frill hanging under Wakia's arms; she truly was young, but her spirit was engulfed in flames.

"Wakia," Leukai said after a long silence, "you may not think so, but I do understand. Stay with them." He removed the satchel of arrows from his shoulder and tossed it along with the bow to Wakia, who caught them with both hands. "Do know that if you go, the chief will not accept you back to the tribe. From this point on, you will be shunned."

"I understand. Besides, Chief Ocia would not allow me to fully become the warrior that I want to be. He has been pushing me to study the crafts with the mothers," Wakia slung the satchel over her left shoulder, "but that is not where my heart is. As of now I fight for Thandrua." The two Cobras stood at both sides of the young Aviaan and placed their palms on her shoulders.

"We will keep her as safe as possible." Solarious reassured.

"I'm sure you will. Take care." Leukai kicked his equus and with a great neigh it took off. The others followed behind.

The trio huddled close together, Sectoraus and Solarious closed their eyes and tried to reestablish their mental bond and Wakia imitated them. They stood there, holding onto each other in a meditative trance until they could all feel one another, outside of their physical grasp.

When they were done, they moved into the campgrounds. Wakia collected the equis together, making clicking noises to get the animals to move towards her, while the other two began to search through each shelter.

A small stone pool glistened with water, and Wakia cheered with joy as she splashed her face with the cool crisp liquid. "Let me know if you find any food, I'm starving!"

They continued to look around. The trio found a few spears and several daggers carved from stone, which they put in a pile of things that could be of use. Sectoraus found a long hollowed-out horn, he put the small end to his mouth and blew out, causing it to bellow. Now hearing it outside of the Aegagruian attacking, he decided he liked the idea of the horn and put it to the side to take along.

Inside one of the shelters, Solarious found some meat that had been dried to jerky. He took a bite for himself, chewing the tough, savory snack, then gave the rest to Wakia. The young Aviaan stuffed her face full with the jerky, but kept some aside for the journey to come. After the search, they all decided to rest before traveling to the desert.

When they awoke with the next cycle, they each took turns to refresh themselves in the small pool. Sectoraus was still pensive about what he had learned of Thandrua and the Cobra Clan, most especially Thandrua. Still, he thought it was only right to give Solarious *all* the information he knew. He sat down his brother before opening up.

"There are many things I must tell you about Lord Thandrua and everything happening in our home." Sectoraus spoke carefully.

"I saw that they were all captured." Solarious said.

"Yes, but it goes further than that." Sectoraus took in a deep breath before speaking. He needed to linger on the moment, for once he verbalized the truth aloud, the more the truth would solidify.

"Thandrua is not our lifegiver."

"What do you mean? I do not understand."

"For too long a time, Thandrua and I maintained a fabrication that he was almighty. Perhaps I myself did not want to believe that our lord was not the savior and lifegiver we built him up to be. It seemed to make so much sense, him coming after the first rain. Thandrua, however, always questioned himself. He seemed to have always known he was not what we worshipped him as."

Solarious was shocked, kept shaking his head. Everything he had known was a lie! He was a good audience though and kept his disbelief to himself. He sat there and listened to all of Sectoraus' information. He learned about the dreams Thandrua had of this world and he learned about the entity called the Creator. Sectoraus told his brother that Orpheus and Phineus were being tortured while the last remaining Serpenoids had replaced the humans, which were now called daemons, as slaves. Finally, Sectoraus told him how Vander lived freely amongst the daemons, but had aided Sectoraus in procuring a weapon and had given him information.

While Wakia and Solarious readied their equis, Sectoraus stood outside the camp and gazed in the direction of the desert, his home. He realized now that when the Aegagruians had fled their camp, they went in that direction as well. He knew that hadn't been the last he would see of them.

Their supplies strapped onto each equus, the mounts now stood ready and waiting. Solarious stepped to Sectoraus' right side and looked out to the horizon with his brother in silence for a few moments before speaking.

"So, brother Sectoraus, what now?"

"We rescue Thandrua and the others."

"You think we will succeed?"

"Definitely, but not as three."

"You suppose then we will find someone to aid us?"

"Trust me, brother, I know of a place."

The three companions hopped onto their steeds. Sectoraus looked ahead; it was time to go back from where he came. Unicornis began to walk forward, the other two patted their equis and they followed.

Another long journey stretched out before them. They would have to pass through the desert undetected. They had to cross over the river of magma and creep through the valley, avoiding the stone monstrosities, before they could cut their way through the Dark Forest to where Sectoraus knew he would find the help he needed.

With two kicks of his heels to the horned equus' side, Unicornis neighed before it broke into a steady run, and the other two followed closely behind.

Continued in Tenebris: The Unholy Wars

Special Thanks

Darrell Johnson for guiding me in the right direction, **Jamie J. Apgar** for the amazing cover art and interior art, **Luis Gallardo** for the cover design, business cards and linktree setup, **Julianne Bar** for interior art, **Jaeger Spratt** for interior art, editing, production, and insuring that I didn't delete this document, **Sophia Anon** for art tips and promotional artwork for "The Creature," **Harry Carpenter** for the self-publishing tips, **Julie Yandrofski** for encouraging to live my dreams, my friends in kindergarten for playing along while I drew demonic symbols in the sand as we fought demons in the game I created called "Cobras," and finally but not least the 2014 crew of **Primanti Bros. Market Square** for taking good care of me while I worked on this and conceptualized many more tales to come.

About the Creator

Javier Antonio Barrios is a Northern Virginian native with a love of all the arts. Raised in a family of movie buffs, Javier has had a longstanding love for the art of film and always wanted to make movies. In particular, the genres of horror, sci-fi, and fantasy provided the inspiration to begin delving into realms of his own making. Of course, as a child he did not have the resources to make the types of movies he envisioned, so he turned sharing his stories through word. Being a poet at heart, Javier has also channeled his urge to tell stories into music and has for over a decade been in a creative partnership with a fellow musician. In his debut novel, Javier now sees the culmination of a lifetime of storytelling made manifest in physical form, and looks forward to bringing to life many more stories both fantastical and macabre.

CPSIA information can be obtained
at www.ICGtesting.com
Printed in the USA
BVHW070220170123
656382BV00001B/35